Like a Wildflower

Samm Wilde

Author's Note

This story features two characters who live with anxiety in different ways. The FMC struggles with over-apologizing and self-doubt, while the MMC experiences social anxiety. Their journeys aren't meant to be perfect. Just honest, messy, and hopeful.

As someone who suffers from generalized anxiety disorder, I wanted to explore how love can exist alongside anxiety —not as something that "fixes" it, but something that learns to move with it. Because, at the end of the day, anxiety is a real part of many people's daily lives.

If you see parts of yourself in them, you're not alone. Please take care of yourself and read at your own pace. —SW

Content Warnings:

- Brief mention of parental deaths (not graphically described)
- Mentions of grief in passing
- Profanity

- Explicit sexual content
- FMC and MMC both have different types of anxiety
- Depictions of a toxic work environment
- The animals don't die

For anyone who's ever been told they're "too much."
I hope your enemies step on a thumbtack.

Like a Wildflower

SAMM WILDE

Chapter One

Joey

There's no greater feeling than driving with the windows down, a cool breeze blowing through my hair, and a pit of existential dread sitting in my stomach.

My orange 1967 Volkswagen van, aptly named Poppy, has less than a quarter tank of gas, and I'm still a hundred miles from Hemlock. With the sun setting behind the dense forest surrounding me, I have a sneaking suspicion I'll be in for a long night.

To make matters worse, my phone is dead, along with my external battery. I can guarantee my older brother and sister sent out a twenty-person search party when my location stopped updating a few hours ago.

I'm not the best at calling or keeping them updated on my whereabouts, so we found a common ground with location sharing. If I'm lucky, my last known location registered somewhere after I crossed into Oregon, meaning that if I end up dead on the side of the road, they can easily find my corpse.

Maybe. Maybe not.

The bears may drag me into the forest before they find me. *Does Oregon have a big bear population? How many states do? Should I be carrying bear spray on my travels?*

I feel like I should know these things. The public school system clearly failed me in this respect.

Shaking off that train of unnecessary thought, I thread my hands through my auburn hair. It's seen much better days, that's for sure. I can't remember the last time I ran a brush through it, and I'm about 90 percent convinced I heard a bird chirp in there yesterday.

With an exhausted sigh, I crank the knob on the stereo my brother installed. Then, with hands at ten and two, I drum along to the beat. As the forest flies by on either side of me, I absentmindedly murmur along to the tune that my Lord and Savior Stevie Nicks is singing.

Speaking of my Lord and Savior, I mutter a silent prayer that I come upon a gas station soon.

This road is familiar and unfamiliar at the same time. I'm typically more of a landmark girl, though I wouldn't mind having access to GPS. Except even if my phone weren't dead, I doubt I'd have service out here in the forest. The dense canopy of darkness that shrouds me now has gone on for mile after painfully long mile.

With every road marker I pass, the heavy pit of anxiety in my stomach sinks deeper. I'd love to say I'm usually more prepared than this, but the truth of the matter is *I'm not.*

Though I inherited my love of traveling from both of my free-spirited parents, who died unexpectedly a year and a half ago, my siblings are comfortable homebodies who never venture too far from our hometown. I respect and admire that about them, and maybe there's a small part of me that wishes I felt that way. But right now, at thirty-one, I have no motivation to settle down.

For as long as I can remember, I've felt like I don't belong. I was the kid who was always picked last in gym class. I was never chosen as a partner for the science fair and didn't have a date to prom. Though not being picked in gym class pissed me off the most. I was taller than most boys in my fourth-grade class, and I could serve the shit out of a volleyball. In fact, I almost broke a kid's nose once when I spiked the ball a little too hard.

The teacher wasn't pleased.

I wasn't that sorry about it. The twerp had it coming.

My parents were kind, gentle people who would trap spiders and free them in their garden. The type of people who did all they could to avoid hurting the feelings of any living being. *I can relate to that.* So when I explained what was happening in school, they comforted me and reassured me, but I could see the hurt in their eyes. As an adult, I can look back and see how badly they wished they could take away my pain.

Since then, my life has felt akin to a game of kickball. I'm either getting picked last, using someone as a human shield, or being metaphorically hit in the face with the ball called life.

I've never felt like I belonged.

I'll forever and always be the *too much* girl.

My hair is too wild, my clothes are too bright, my emotions are too strong, and my laugh is too loud. I've even been told that my expressions are too *expressive.*

Whatever the hell that means.

I'm a drifting soul, endlessly searching for the place where I fit in.

My safe spot.

A place where I can unapologetically be myself.

Have I found it yet? Obviously not.

Will I ever find it? God, I hope so.

If not, my siblings are in for a lifetime of torture. They're the one bright spot in my life. They see me down to my very soul and have stuck by me. They support all my rights *and* my wrongs.

Even if that means they have to rescue me sometimes.

Like now. Oh, how I wish my sister Charlie would jump out of the woods like a feral forest creature and save me.

With another look at the fuel gauge, I note that the needle has moved awfully close to the one-eighth mark.

Frustrated tears slip from my eyes. I should've known better. My dad taught me to always keep the tank full in preparation for an unplanned adventure, but time got away from me and I forgot. Now I'll be stuck here on the side of the road, hoping another car appears soon and will stop.

And hopefully I won't end up murdered.

I can just imagine being murdered by a serial killer or eaten alive by a bear and then meeting my parents in the afterlife.

What a fun conversation that would be.

Nothing says "welcome to the afterlife!" like being scolded by one's parents for poor planning.

I wipe the stray tears that have fallen from my eyes and keep my gaze focused on the right side of the road, willing a gas station to appear. The sun has officially dipped below the horizon and the damp roads are dark in the midst of the forest, the only light coming from Poppy's headlights.

When another set of headlights flashes in my rearview mirror, a mixture of hopefulness and panic settles in my stomach. The vehicle approaches quickly, and when it's so close I can barely see their headlights, they honk.

What. The. Actual. Fuck? This isn't a good sign.

Looks like I might actually say hi to Mom and Dad tonight.

Sweat beads on my temple as my heart pounds in my chest.

The vehicle swerves into the opposing lane and zips up beside me.

I keep my eyes fixed on the dark road, careful not to make eye contact with what must certainly be a serial killer.

"*Joey, pull over!*" a deep voice yells.

My stomach lurches. How does the killer know my name? Oh god. How long have they been following me?

"*Josephine Iris Thorne. Pull over now!*" the man bellows.

With my hands white-knuckled and shaking on the steering wheel, I slowly look over at the car alongside me. The anxious breath I was holding expels from my chest when I discover the identity of the driver.

My brother Jack.

Immediately, I slow down. Once I've pulled Poppy to the side of the road, my brother pulls up behind me and climbs out of his car. As he stomps toward me, his movements angry, I wince.

At my window, he knocks.

Rather than roll it down, I keep my focus fixed ahead and shake my head.

He lets out a grunt. "Roll it down, Joey."

Oh, he's *pissed.*

I stay silent and don't move. Like a fawn when it senses danger. It lies down, doesn't make a sound, and refuses to make eye contact.

Jack knocks on the window again. "Roll the window down. Now." He grits the last word out through clenched teeth.

I inhale deeply, then let out a resigned sigh. My hand inches toward the crank and slowly rolls the window down. "Oh my god," I chirp, hoping my cheerful tone will discourage his anger. "What are you doing out here? You're looking so. . .rested!"

His face is blank as he stares back at me. Not even a twitch of the mouth. Bro's got a poker face that would make professionals weep.

Swallowing down the anxious lump in my throat, I blink, breaking the stare down. "How did you. . .uh, find me?"

His eyes are the same color as mine. As Charlie's too. Except his are a little more distressed under the moonlight. "Looked at your location," he huffs. "Saw it wasn't moving. Drove up and down the road knowing you'd eventually pass through this part."

"I'm always flattered when you and Charlie stalk me," I say, beaming. "It's exciting. Like living in a thriller movie. Makes me all warm and fuzzy inside."

He pinches the bridge of his nose, clearly over my behavior already. "Between your poor planning and Charlie's lethal scowl, someone has to be the levelheaded one in this family."

Okay, he makes a fair point. I'm not the best planner, but

that's only because I believe things will work out the way they're supposed to regardless.

You know, fate and all that.

Could a little preparation lead to a more preferable outcome? Yes. Will I do that going forward? Eh. I'll try.

Also, is he calling himself levelheaded?

"You? Levelheaded?" I scoff. "Did you and Charlie vote on this without me?"

He sets his hands on his hips, a small huff of air escaping him. "You really don't think I'm levelheaded?"

I blink slowly. "You organize your socks by color and get weirdly excited when a new vacuum comes on the market. I think that's tipping too far to the other side."

"How do you know about my sock organization?"

One time I babysat Lucy, his daughter, and let her have ice cream for dinner in exchange for embarrassing information on him. She stayed up till midnight screaming and jumping on the furniture like a possessed demon, but it was worth it. I gathered enough intelligence to last me years.

"I plead the fifth." I lift my chin, my expression as blank as I can manage.

"Of course you do." He leans in, assessing Poppy's fuel gauge. "You miscalculated again, didn't you?"

My shoulders sag. "Guilty."

He lets out another disappointed breath, his flannel-clad chest deflating. He should probably go to the doctor to get checked for asthma or COPD. Maybe he's inhaling too much sawdust.

As the baby of the family, I *should* get a pass for my minor lapse in judgment. Usually my miles-per-gallon calculations are pretty spot on. I must have messed up somewhere a couple hundred miles back.

"There's a spare tank of fuel in my truck. I'll be right back," my brother says. The gravel beneath his boots crunches as he walks away, shaking his head and muttering to himself.

Slumping against my seat, I drop my head back. Though I can't help but smile.

Despite my love for traveling, it feels good to be back home.

Chapter Two

BECKETT

I'M STILL NOT sure how I feel about being back home.

At my core, I'm a simple guy. Traveling to new places, helping others, and riding my motorcycle keep me content.

That's why I typically find myself at small hospitals in tiny towns full of unique residents. Near the end of my last travel assignment, my mom not so subtly mentioned that it had been a while since I visited her. I figured I'd kill two birds with one stone and take an assignment at Pacific Care Hospital in my hometown.

On paper, Hemlock, Oregon, seems like the perfect place. In reality, I come home from my shifts in the emergency room questioning my sanity more often than not, wondering if rather than working as a travel nurse, I should switch careers and move to one of those research stations in Antarctica.

I've never had this kind of experience in any of the places

I've worked. Maybe it's in the water here, because this hospital is overflowing with eccentric people.

For the next thirteen weeks, I'll spend all my working hours in the middle of a raging inferno of ridiculous scenarios.

Adults sticking things in inappropriate places.

You didn't just "fall" on it. Do I look that dumb to you?

College kids complaining about headaches.

You're dehydrated from Thirsty Thursday. Chug some water.

People with "mysterious" stomach pains that only happen when they eat.

You have irritable bowel syndrome. Stop eating cheese.

Leaning back, I twirl my pen and remind myself of the reasons I became a nurse. Because this hospital is testing my limits and I haven't even been back in town for a full week.

I close my eyes, inhale, and silently chant the mantra I created for times when my sanity is being pushed to the edge.

I became a nurse because I love helping people and wanted to follow in my mom's footsteps.

To help ease the pain of others, even if temporarily.

To be their support when they're frightened and all alone.

To be an advocate for those who feel voiceless and to fight for the care they rightfully deserve.

As I exhale, I open my eyes. Good. I feel calmer already.

Sort of.

The emergency department is relatively quiet tonight. Not that I'd ever utter those words out loud. Doing so would be an easy way to tempt fate and get a massive influx of patients, and the hospital is already understaffed. Yesterday, the custodian mentioned how empty the ED was, and within an hour, an entire high school soccer team came in with a horrific case of food poisoning. It got so bad that a couple of us had to step outside for fresh air before we ended up sharing a room with one of the scrawny kids.

The mom in charge of the snacks that day better be banned from ever doing it again. *Yikes.*

When I say it's quiet in here, I mean the only sounds are the incessant beeping of monitors, the squeaking of orthotic shoes on tile floors, and rolling of hospital beds to new destinations.

I pinch the bridge of my nose and let out a deep sigh, willing away the headache that's threatening to arrive. I have a long night ahead of me. Raking my fingers through my blond hair, I turn back to charting my last patient.

A twenty-four-year-old man who dislocated his shoulder while putting his jacket on.

Before that, I saw an older woman who cut herself with a plastic spork.

Before her, a child with three Legos stuck up his nose.

I was less annoyed with that one because that kid must have been very determined to get those things wedged into such a tiny nose.

Eyes gritty from staring at this screen for so long, I blink and dig my eyedrops out of my pocket. I slept in my contacts last night because I was too exhausted to bother removing them, and I'm paying for it now.

"Turn that frown upside down. You're too pretty to look so melancholy," Tabitha, who's suddenly appeared behind me, says. "We aren't *that bad* here. Or maybe we are and I've become immune to it," she mutters.

Tabitha is the charge nurse in the ED. She can't be more than five feet tall with salt-and-pepper hair and a sharp tongue. She has the kind of brazen personality that a person wants to hate but can't because she naturally garners so much respect. Plus, the strength she displays despite her short stature is downright admirable. Just yesterday, she took down a two-hundred-and-fifty-pound man who had three too many shots of tequila from a bachelor party gone awry.

I spin in the squeaky chair at the nurses' station and zero in on her.

She does the same to me, surveying my heavily tattooed forearms. Both arms are covered in full sleeves with intricate botanical designs that weave all the way up past my shoulders. A single eyebrow of hers arches up, and a subtle nod of approval sparkles in her green eyes.

I pushed up the sleeves of the black shirt under my scrubs earlier because I was getting warm, but now, stomach sinking, I tug them down. Suddenly feeling too aware of my own skin.

But Tabitha interrupts my motion by touching my shoulder. "Don't roll those down on my account. I enjoy having nice things to look at while I work," she quips. "Keeps the employee morale up, you know?"

I groan. "You're a walking, talking HR violation, you know that?"

She gives me a dismissive wave. "Eh. Whatever. You're only here for a few months, and I'm too close to retirement to care. Now, roll those up again. I want to see how far those beauties go." With a joking wink, she wags a finger.

Head dropped back, I let out a sigh loud enough to stop a few nearby nurses in their tracks.

"Don't worry about him," Tabitha teases. "I'm breaking him in." The cackle she lets out echoes through the ER. "You know how much I *love* a challenge."

Dear god. I should've chosen a different hospital.

She pulls out the chair next to me and sits. "Have you

found housing yet?" she asks. "Or are you staying with your mom?"

My hackles rise at the idea. I love my mom. I would die for her. But at thirty-four, I cannot move back in with her. Even if it's temporary.

"I found a short-term rental on the edge of town. I move in next week."

Tabitha hums in approval. I've known this woman for less than a week, but damn she's annoyingly easy to talk to.

And she knows it. Before she can respond, though, her phone goes off. With a roll of her eyes, she looks down at it. "Ugh. Hold on, honey. I need to take care of someone's mess. *Again.* I swear, this kind of incompetence will put me into an early grave." She hauls herself up and speed walks to room four as fast as her tiny legs can carry her.

A chuckle escapes me. I do not envy the person about to suffer her wrath.

With another spin, I face the computer again and click on another chart, though without my permission, my mind drifts to my temporary housing situation. My mom does live in town, but I don't think I could handle sleeping on the couch in her one-bedroom condo for three straight months.

I've been there a matter of days, and already, my back is making interesting cracking noises.

On top of that, I've already replaced her car battery, fixed her leaky kitchen sink, patched a handful of holes, listened to ungodly amounts of small-town gossip, and watched countless old-school rom-coms with her. Though in return, I've consumed enough of her homemade baked goods to keep me satiated for days.

Since my dad left when I was a baby, it's been the two of us. Even now, my mom remains my relentless constant. She's been my role model for as long as I can remember. Growing up, I'd get picked on because, while all the other boys wanted to be just like their dads, I admired my mom deeply and wanted to be just like her.

But I still need my own space. While I'm in town, I'm expected at her house every Friday night for dinner, a movie, and a batch of cookies.

Independence as well as free food? It's the best of both worlds.

In college, my goal was to become a travel nurse. With healthcare shortages across the country, I figured it would be a perfect opportunity to expand my knowledge, help people, and satisfy my wanderlust.

But I wasn't prepared for how lonely it could be. I'm fine being *alone*, but I don't enjoy feeling *lonely*. Often, people don't understand the difference. While I enjoy my solitude, I still long for emotional connection.

To connect with a person who understands me on a deeper level.

Who isn't afraid to melt my icy exterior.

Who can be patient with me.

The lasting connections I've formed since college have been few and far between. I've always been a tad aloof. Many see me as standoffish and don't take the time to get to know me, assuming I think I'm better than them. In reality, I'm just a shy, socially anxious guy.

A six-foot-four, socially anxious guy with broad shoulders and tattoos crawling up his arms and down his legs.

Then there's the jet-black motorcycle I restored a few years ago.

I can be intimidating. I get that.

But I'm nowhere near the rough-around-the-edges kind of guy I'm often viewed as.

Unless my cat is threatened. . .then a whole other side of me surfaces.

Like the saying goes—appearances aren't everything. There's always an unexpected depth that lurks beneath the surface, waiting to be discovered.

I'm an avid bread baker—and yes, I've named my sourdough starter—with a rescued orange tabby cat named Barbara. Yet from the outside, no one would believe it. Nor would they believe I pour my emotions into a journal every night because it helps me process my thoughts.

What can I say? I'm a dichotomy of quirks and passions. I can't change the perception of others, and I refuse to waste energy trying.

Maybe it's the endless stream of old-school romance movies I've been watching with my mom, or maybe it's the sluggish pace of the emergency department at this time of night, but I find myself consumed with thoughts of how nice it would be to share my life with someone. To find a person to enjoy the quiet moments with. To explore new places with. To create everlasting memories with. I doubt that's in the cards for me, but a guy can dream, right?

Throughout my travels, I've had fleeting relationships here and there. Like my job, they've all had an expiration date. Would I be willing try long distance? Yeah. But I've yet to find a woman who thought I was worth the trouble. Instead, they're quick to lay out excuses for why they're okay walking away.

You work too much.

I'm passionate about my career.

You're too quiet.

I process my thoughts and feelings more effectively in silence.

You're boring.

I find comfort in living a simple life.

After each failed relationship, I've closed myself off a little more, uneasy being vulnerable around people who don't really try to understand me, who can't look below the surface. Why give a person my heart, knowing they'll break it and then hand the shattered pieces back to me?

Even so, I can't help but hold out the smallest ounce of hope in my heart that, one day, I'll find the right person. That flicker of optimism persists, quietly lingering in the depths of my soul, hidden deep beneath the layers of old wounds and new wishes, waiting to be rediscovered.

I rub my eyes and wince at the sandpaper sensation, then blow out a long breath. If I keep thinking so deeply, I'll exhaust myself before my shift is over.

Later I'll scribble these thoughts onto the pages of my journal.

Right now I need to shut the door to my emotions and concentrate on the patient chart before me—or else Tabitha may strangle me with her stethoscope.

Chapter Three

WITH THE SUN shining and a cool, refreshing breeze touching my skin, I stroll toward my sister's quaint store in downtown Hemlock. It's one of many shops lining Main Street, most of which are decorated with beautiful flowers and vibrant window displays.

Stepping inside my sister's shop is like stepping into a greenhouse. There are leaves trailing down from hanging planters, tables overflowing with various overgrown houseplants, and an overwhelmingly pleasant earthy smell filling the air.

I'd forgotten how much I missed this place.

And it makes me miss my parents. Deeply.

"How long are you in town for this time?" Charlie asks. Her dark brown eyes meet mine between the leaves of the large green plant she's repotting. After our parents died, she moved back home and took over A New Leaf. My brother and

I breathed a sigh of relief when she quit her job and took over my parents' shop. Every time I walk into this store, I can feel their presence.

Maybe it's their ghosts hanging out here. Huh. I'll have to sneak in one night and perform a seance to confirm my suspicions.

With a huff, I slump down onto the old wooden stool at the front counter. "Three months," I reply, fidgeting with a random dead leaf on the plant.

I'm here because, as the senior brand designer at Fernrose Creative Agency, I'm expected to be in the office for a project with my firm's big client. Typically, we work remotely. It's a perk of working for a boutique creative agency. All I need is my laptop, semi-reliable Wi-Fi, and an IV drip of caffeine, and I'm ready for anything.

I spent two months working from Canada a couple of years ago, though when my boss found out, that came to a quick end. Apparently one cannot just work from another country without dealing with lame legal shenanigans.

My sister simply hums, making me wonder if she even heard me. The three of us Thorne siblings are pros at tuning each other out. Hence why Charlie's asked me about how long I plan to stay three times in the last twenty-four hours.

For me, it happens often because my mind has too many tabs open. Though I can't vouch for my siblings.

I survey the prickly green cactus in a cute terracotta pot in front of me.

Let's see if my sister is paying attention.

Slowly, I reach for the spiky devil.

Without looking up from her plant rehabilitation project, she snaps, "Do not touch that. What *is* the matter with you?"

I jerk my hand back quickly, surprised and also impressed by her observation skills.

Under her breath, she mutters, "What is it with everyone wanting to touch cacti? Jesus."

Somewhere nearby, Vera, my sister's comically lazy golden retriever, lets out a long and dramatic groan. Charlie inherited Vera from my parents along with the store.

In unison, we look at the giant furball on the floor, then at each other, both shaking our heads at her grumbly, semi-judgmental noises.

"So you're here for three months," Charlie says. "What's your plan?" Elbow deep in soil, she blows a stray piece of her dark brown hair out of her eyes.

Immediately, it falls back into place, and with a more frustrated huff, she tries again.

Lips twitching at her frustration, I hop up and round the work bench, removing a bobby pin from my hair as I go. Then, carefully, I pin back the unruly strand of hair.

She looks up at me with softened eyes. "Thanks, Joseph."

"Always, Charles."

In our orphan trio, Charlie is the curmudgeonly middle child who's uncomfortable showing affection. We couldn't be more different. She's grouchy and prefers to stay far away from social interactions. Whereas I'm a people-person.

I plop myself back down on the stool, my shoulders slumping. I haven't even been home for a full week and I'm already exhausted. If I'm gonna make it through the day, I need three shots of espresso and at least one pack of gummy bears.

She clears her throat, eyes darting between me and the plant in front of her. "Back to your plans for the next few months. Do you plan to stay with me?"

I bite back a smile. That wasn't so much an offer as a concern. "You know I love any opportunity to disrupt your antisocial nature and annoy you with my mere existence, but I respect you too much to crash in your spare bedroom for more than a couple of nights."

She drops the plant shears onto the counter, breathing a sigh of relief. "I have never loved or respected you more than I do in this moment."

I shake my head, feigning annoyance. "I found a short-term rental. It's not far from the office or your place. I'll be nearby in case you need anything. Like sisterly bonding. Can I paint your toenails?" I tease. "Maybe we can do facemasks and watch a rom-com."

She glares at me. This girl loves hard, but she loves hard from a safe distance. The way to her heart does not include pedicures or movie nights.

"Fine," I say. "I'll pick up ice cream after work, and we can bitch and complain about that overly dramatic rich house-wife show you love."

That gets a genuine smirk out of her. Call it a sixth sense, but I'm pretty good at inferring what people need without being told.

Checkmate, dear sister. You're forced to love me.

The sound of pattering paws fills the store as a brown and black blur makes a beeline for Vera, narrowly missing a table teetering under the weight of large monsteras.

Frank.

Last year, my sister met Finn, a very nice—albeit a tad awkward—guy, and with him came Frank the dog. Frank is blind *and* a kleptomaniac Australian Shepherd. Charlie sends weekly updates to our siblings' group chat about what the dog has stolen most recently.

He barrels toward me and, with impressive precision for a dog who can't see a damn thing, he jumps up and knocks me off my stool. As I tumble to the ground, a few ceramic pots fall with me. I press my hands to the ground to haul myself up, but a sharp pain in my palm makes me yelp.

"Oh my god," my sister cries. "Frank, under the table. *Now.*"

She's at my side a second later, gently cradling my hand. "I'll get a clean towel from the back," she says. "While I'm gone, whatever you do, do not look down. Please." With that, she sprints to the back room.

When I've been told not to do something, I tend to find myself rebelling against that authority. So that's what I do. I look down at my hand to find a deep, angry gash on my palm. Blood seeps from it and drips onto my jeans.

Shit. I've never been good with blood. I don't enjoy seeing a substance that should be safe inside my body, *outside* my body.

The crimson fluid mocks me with every drip, and my traitorous brain can't seem to look away.

Nausea rolls in my stomach, and a second later, a wave of dizziness hits me.

Like it always does, my vision tunnels next, white blurring around its edges.

Don't faint. Don't faint. Don't faint.

I close my eyes and take a few deep, calming breaths. *Don't. Faint.*

Dammit. I'm going to traumatize my sister even more than I already have.

When I open my eyes, the first thing I notice is the blood splattered on the rustic wooden floor beneath me. *Shit.* Not only will Charlie be traumatized, but she'll have an OSHA violation on her hands.

Before I go down, I attempt—and fail—at communicating with my sister telepathically, apologizing for what's about to happen in the middle of her store.

My mouth goes dry, as expected, and I break out in a cold sweat.

The cherry on top? The shallow breathing.

And as the world goes dark, a piercing scream rends the air.

IT'S BEEN a while since I've had a nice, deep sleep. More often than not, my body feels discombobulated due to the changes in time zones, weather, and late-night driving that come with traveling so much.

But at this moment, my brain is devoid of restless thoughts. I feel light, airy, and at peace.

That peace is disrupted, though, by a nudge on my shoulder.

Then another.

Well, this isn't annoying at all. I'm reveling in this perfect slumber and—

A low murmur cuts through my thoughts. It sounds like my sister. The next one comes from a deeper voice, though the words are impossible to make out.

With a groan, I force my heavy eyelids open. Immediately, I'm clouded in a haze of confusion, my mind desperately trying to grasp for clarity amid muddled thoughts.

Where am I? Why does my hand hurt? Why am I lying on

the ground? And why are there so many damn plants in this place?

"Hey there. Welcome back," a deep voice above me rumbles.

A million thoughts swirl in my mind, none sticking, and my tongue feels like sandpaper. There's a dull ache pulsing in my temples, and someone is hovering over me, *watching me.*

I blink a few times, and when my vision clears and I focus on the person still speaking to me, I'm struck speechless.

Holy mother of—

He snaps his mouth shut and peers down at me with searching green eyes. They're bright against the stubbled jaw and tousled dark blond hair. Crouching, and with his lip caught between his teeth like that, he looks concerned, but also *hot.*

As heat creeps into my cheeks, I force myself to look away. His eyes are too damn intense. Instead, I glance over to where he's white-knuckling the counter.

Without my permission, my eyes trace the path of dark tattoos beginning at his wrist and gradually winding up to his muscular bicep. An intricate mix of florals and landscapes, with a few animals tucked between designs.

Color me curious because I want to know more.

How many other tattoos is he hiding? More importantly, where *are they hiding?*

I must be in heaven.

Actually, I don't see my parents.

So I'm most likely in hell. It wouldn't shock me if Satan and his pitchfork were waiting for me. I've pissed off more than my fair share of people in life and I don't plan to stop anytime soon.

Pain radiates through me, and a groan escapes my lips. I feel like I've been hit by a truck, but my head is resting on something soft and vanilla scented. As I inhale, catching another whiff of the pleasant smell, it hits me.

My weak self fainted.

I've never been good with blood. As a kid, I thought I would make an amazing doctor. My bedside manner is, dare I say, impeccable. However, my older brother Jack had one too many bloody, broken noses from football and I became very squeamish. Now, every time I see blood, I pass out.

I'm a phlebotomist's worst nightmare. I'm positive I saw one trembling in their scrubs when she saw me walk into the lab.

Over the man's broad shoulder, a crowd is forming. My eyebrows knit together in annoyance, but underneath the surface, anxiety crawls up my spine, taking hold of me. I'd forgotten how curious the people of Hemlock can be with their whispered gossip and knowing glances. The towns-people think they'll combust if they're not privy to every detail of local nonsense.

I close my eyes and inhale deeply. When I open them, I discover those piercing green eyes still locked on mine, brimming with worry.

Brows pinched, he peers over his shoulder like he's just now noticed the crowd.

Dozens of curious eyes watch on, and phones are out, the curious onlookers recording or taking photos of me lying on the floor. My chest tightens at the attention, and an urge to scream bubbles up inside me. To shout at them to give me a bit of privacy.

Yet I can't find my voice. The words stay lodged in my throat.

The mysterious tattooed man, still hovering over me, now turns to the crowd. What happens next makes me want to propose to him right here, right now.

Chapter Four

Beckett

As I wander down the sidewalk of Main Street in Hemlock, a fresh cup of coffee in hand, a piercing scream slices through the air. Instinct and training taking over, I rush to the plant store, where the pained sound came from, my heart racing.

Inside, a woman is lying on the ground, unconscious and pale-faced.

Immediately, I switch into nurse mode. For me, helping in emergency situations when I'm off the clock has become second nature. More than once, I've been asked to help a fellow traveler with a medical emergency on a plane.

Small towns have their pros and cons. And this is the con. All the passersby have made their way in and are hovering. A whole bunch of nosy Nellies.

Though when I focus on the woman who needs my help, they all disappear from my mind.

Beside her, another woman prods her arm, trying to wake her up.

"Joey. Joey, wake up," the dark-haired woman says, her voice frantic.

I rest my hand on her shoulder, making her aware of presence, then ask, "Mind if I step in and take over?"

She looks at me wide-eyed, as if I've grown three heads.

"S-sorry," I stammer, realizing she doesn't have the full picture. "I'm a nurse at Pacific Care Hospital. I work in the emergency room."

With a shaky breath out, she nods. Then she moves aside, giving me room to assess her friend.

"My boyfriend's dog knocked her off the stool," she blurts out. "She cut her hand on a ceramic pot and fainted. She's never been very good with blood."

"Do you know if she hit her head?"

She shakes her head. "No. She sat up right away, but when she looked at her hand and saw the blood, she passed out."

"Gotcha." I dip my chin. "It was probably just a vasovagal response to seeing the blood. Could you find a glass of water for her, and maybe something with sugar?"

As she scurries off, I check the pulse of the unconscious woman. It's slow, but that's typical after a fainting spell. Reassured that the situation isn't dire, I scan for injuries aside from the nasty cut on her hand. It's not deep enough for stitches, but it'll hurt for a few days.

In one swift motion, I take off my hoodie and ball it up. Then, carefully, I place it behind her head so it's not resting on the hard wooden floor. Stretching to one side, I snag the leg of a low stool and pull it over, then prop the woman's legs up to help restore blood flow to the brain.

When I grasp her shoulder gently, her eyelids twitch, her

dark lashes dancing across the tops of her cheeks, and soon, her eyes are open, her gaze drowsy.

"Hey there," I say, giving her a smile. "Welcome back."

Her large brown eyes lock on me, confusion swimming in them. The smattering of freckles across the bridge of her nose become less noticeable as the color returns to her face.

After a heartbeat, she sucks in a breath, her eyes darting around the shop, brimming with panic.

The crowd of prying onlookers has migrated, closing in on us in this already small space.

With a look over my shoulder, I give them my most stern nurse on duty expression. "Do you mind giving us some space?"

They don't move. Of course they don't. A few are on their phones, cameras pointed at us, probably gossiping already.

Typically, I'm levelheaded. Some may say I'm too calm in tense situations. But at this moment? I'm enraged. Whatever happened to common decency, respect, and privacy?

I take a deep, steadying inhale and add the authoritative voice I've used for years in the ER to the glower I direct at them. "If you aren't helping, stop gawking and get out."

Eyes that were once prying have now gone wide with shock. Yet they're still not moving.

"*Now*," I bellow, my voice echoing off the walls.

There's a collective jolt, then the whole group scurries out of the store without so much as a whisper.

Finally.

The woman on the ground shifts, pressing her trembling hands to the floor like she's going to get up.

Still kneeling beside her, I place my hand on her shoulder once more. "Stay lying down for me. Okay?" The sharp tone is gone, replaced with one I use to put patients at ease.

With a nod, she croaks out a quiet "thank you."

"I'm Beckett, by the way," I say when the shop goes silent. "I heard a scream, and when I ran in, I found you lying on the ground."

Her dark brown eyes grow wide, their rich hue catching the light as shock flickers across her face. She looks like the woman I found at her side when I showed up, their expressions of concern when studying me nearly identical.

"I'm a nurse at Pacific Care Hospital. Not some random dude off the street." I wince as I replay the words in my head. Smooth. "I guess technically I am random, since we haven't met."

This is officially my worst attempt at lightening the mood.

Rather than frown or back away, she gives me a genuine smile.

"*Frank!*" A booming voice breaks through the silence, and a moment later, a tall man with glasses perched on his nose bursts into the store. Face panic-stricken, he scans the store, looking for Frank, whoever that is.

He disappears through a door at the back, and a moment later, he returns, cradling an Australian Shepherd like a fussy baby. I struggle to keep a straight face as the dog's tongue dangles from its mouth, dirt and leaves tangled in its disheveled fur.

The woman I sent for water reappears and makes a beeline for me, while the man and his dog exit through the front door.

"Sorry it took so long. Frank was napping on top of my purse and wouldn't get up, so I couldn't get to the candy. Here." She holds out the bottle of water and a small handful of candy.

"Can you sit up for me?" I ask the woman who's still lying prone on the floor.

With a nod, she places her hands on the floor and pushes up.

I rest one hand on her upper back for stability as I help her into a sitting position. "Have a little water and then eat these." I twist the cap off the water and pass it to her, then open a few of the candies so she doesn't have to struggle with the wrappers. "Looks like you fainted. Probably because of the blood."

She lifts the water bottle to her lips, her hand trembling, and takes small sips. Right away, her shoulders relax and the color returns to her face.

"My sister's name is Josephine, by the way," the other woman says. "We call her Joey. After she faints, she's usually a little out of it."

"Does this happen often?" I question.

"Just around blood. Can't even watch a horror film without passing out cold." She grimaces. "And Halloween is a nightmare for her."

"I'm sitting right here, Charlie," Joey interjects, her words muffled by the candy she's popped into her mouth. *Candies,* by the look of it.

"Uh. It might have been best to eat those one at a time. You look like you're on the brink of a choking hazard."

She stares up at me, her eyes owlish and her cheeks puffed out like a chipmunk. "You said eat these. I thought you meant all of them at once!"

Her sister snorts, then breaks into uncontrollable laughter.

"Charles, stop laughing!" Her mouth is still full, her words barely discernible through all that sugar.

I'm trying to bite back a laugh myself.

Looking away from her, I press my lips together in a thin line, forcing myself to remain composed. When I've collected myself, I turn back. "When you're done with those, let's get your cut cleaned up. Okay?"

She lowers her gaze and gives a small nod.

Standing, I turn to Charlie. "Do you have a first aid kit?"

"Yep. Be right back." Her sister jogs to the back room.

I focus on Joey once again, realizing now that there's an air of familiarity to her. Like I've met her before. I did live in Hemlock for a few years when I was a kid, so it's possible we've crossed paths, but I'm sure I would've remembered her. The delicate smattering of freckles across her cheeks, the lush auburn hair, and the expressive brown eyes would've branded themselves into my memory.

Her sister appears with the first aid kit, her reappearance causing those thoughts to dissipate.

"I'm going to clean your wound," I tell Joey, "but please don't look at it."

"You got it, nurse." She gives me a curt, affirmative nod.

Chuckling at her response, I take her hand and get to work. The ragged cut across her palm is bloody and angry, and when I run the antiseptic wipe over it, she drops her head back, focus fixed on the ceiling, and hisses.

"You're doing well. Stay with me now," I coax.

"I want to stay. I really do. But my autonomic nervous system is thinking about running away." She draws in a sharp breath when I swipe away the dirt embedded in the cut.

A laugh bubbles out of me. This woman is hilarious.

"Man." She sighs. "This gives a whole new meaning to the phrase 'rub some soil on it,' doesn't it?"

I zero in on her face, head tilted, considering whether to correct her. If I did, would that make me look like an asshole?

"What's wrong?" she asks, her brows pinched together with confusion.

"Uh, it's actually 'rub some dirt on it,'" I say, head ducked, focused on the wound again.

She cocks her head to the side. "Interesting. I've been saying that wrong for years, then. You learn something new every day, I guess."

I disguise my laugh by clearing my throat. If she's been saying that for years, how come no one has corrected her?

My eyes catch on a stray leaf stuck in her long, dark hair. The corner of my mouth twitches up.

"What?" She frowns.

I delicately pluck the vibrant green leaf from her hair and hold it between us.

Every cell in my body urges me to weave my fingers through her long, silky hair. Instead, I clear my throat, ridding myself of those thoughts. Then I quickly finish cleaning and bandaging her hand up and help her stand, ensuring she's steady on her feet before I leave. "You should be all set. Keep an eye on that cut so it doesn't get infected, okay?"

"Thank you," both women say, and in unison, they eye one another, brows furrowed.

Yep, they're definitely sisters.

Head lowered, I rub the back of my heated neck. "Glad you're feeling better. I'll see you around. Probably. Or probably not. Hopefully not in the ER, though. Stay out of there." I give them a friendly wink and take a step back.

At the door, I glance back at the pair, noting the blush staining Joey's cheeks. That wasn't there a minute ago, was it?

"Oh. And Joey?" I tease, catching her eye with a smile. "Next time you faint, one piece of candy at a time is perfectly okay."

Today was a long day. Between running errands and helping a fainting woman, I'm exhausted. During my time at the store, Joey didn't say much. Not that I can blame her. Fainting in public is never fun, and I can't imagine she wasn't at least a little embarrassed. Sure, I was probably a bit harsh with the people circling us in the store, but they weren't moving. And by the look in her eyes, Joey was clearly uncomfortable. The nosiness of those people was grating on my last nerve.

As I ride back home from my never-ending errands, I start to overthink, and the need to journal about today's events becomes desperately apparent. I hope I wasn't too robotic. When a medical emergency happens, my mind immediately shifts to the person who needs me. Meaning I forget how to be human because every cell in my body focuses on providing appropriate care.

It's late when I pull up to my mom's condo, so I make my way inside quietly to keep from waking her.

After a quick shower to wash the day off, I shuffle into the dark kitchen for a late dinner, a hand against the wall, searching for the light switch.

When the kitchen is illuminated, I jolt back, my heart lurching.

Barbara, my stealthy orange cat, is perched on the counter, her amber eyes narrowed on me while her sleek tail swishes back and forth.

Looks like she's annoyed with me. Or silently judging me. Most likely a combination of both. Barbara knows how to manipulate me, and she knows how easily I'll fold.

The damn cat is more likely to recruit an army of mice for her cult than hunt them.

I shudder at the thought.

She's smart, cunning, and very cute. The cuteness usually outweighs her negative traits, while her unpredictable demeanor keeps me alert.

"If you could be less judgmental, that would be great," I mutter. "I work hard to provide a nice life for you."

She responds with a disappointed meow.

Barbara is high maintenance, to put things nicely, and she accepts nothing less than the best.

Requirements to take care of my orange tabby include but are not limited to: a special water filter, cage-free chicken cat food, and a piece of banana for dessert each night.

Only the best for her delicate palate.

She's very serious about that damn banana. I once fell asleep without giving her the nightly treat, and she stood on my chest and swatted my face until I woke up.

I rummage through the fridge and pull out sandwich fixings. The faster I can eat, the closer I am to sleeping. But I can't do that until I've written about the day's events in my journal. It's become a ritual, and if I skip this part of my routine, I'll be restless all night. So as I take my first bite, I scribble my thoughts on the page. The dark ink bleeds into the paper, making each memory permanent.

When I get to the part where I ran into the plant shop, I freeze, my pen hovering over the paper. Because what I'm considering writing next may be a bridge too far and too weird. But the urge to get it out is too strong to ignore. The time I spent helping Joey was a bright spot in my rather mundane day. Hours later, I still can't stop thinking about her.

As I close the journal with a quiet snap, I discover that my long-forgotten sandwich has now become Barbara's second dinner.

Another judgmental meow escapes her as we lock eyes. She's trying to assert her dominance in this stare off, and honestly, she'll win this round. Chuckling, I give her a quick scratch on the head. Then I toss out the remnants of the sandwich she almost demolished when I was off in my own world. As I pad to the bunch of bananas on the counter, my hovering, persnickety cat trots over, impatiently waiting for her dessert. I peel the perfectly ripe fruit, break off a small section for her, and hold it out. She gives it a cautious sniff before she takes it from me. Like always, I polish off the rest of the banana in three bites, cringing at the mushy texture and the sickly sweet flavor.

I loathe the damn things. I only buy them because Barbara likes them and she may murder me in my sleep if I don't.

After cleaning up, I flick off the lights and make my way into the living room, my slipper-clad feet scuffing across the wooden floors. When my knees hit the edge of the sectional couch, I fall face first, groaning into the plush cushions. Every muscle in my body sighs with relief.

Barbara curls up near my head, tucking herself between me and the cushion. Her content purrs soothe me, making my eyelids heavy. As I wait for sleep to pull me under, I can't help but think about the auburn-haired beauty with the perfectly freckled cheeks and bashful smile.

Once again, that hint of familiarity returns. I swear we've never met before today, yet a weird, hazy memory floats through my mind like an old, worn photograph, the image nearly impossible to make out.

With a heavy sigh, I pull the soft blanket up to my chin and nestle deeper into the couch. As I drift off, that face returns to mind—the one with kind eyes and a radiant smile that I'm not sure I could ever forget.

Josephine.

Beckett's Journal

April 2

It rained today, again. I forgot how rainy Oregon can get. I'm slowly adjusting to being in Hemlock but still keeping to myself. I don't know how I feel about opening up to anyone here, since I'll be gone again in a couple of months. I think Tabitha could be a retired FBI agent with how accurately she profiles patients. Currently, I'm counting down the hours until I can move into the new rental. A thirty-four-year-old with an achy back should not be sleeping on his mom's couch. It hurts the body and the ego. Ouch.

I was in the right place at the right time today, and I was able to help a woman who needed it. Her name is Josephine. Although I can't explain it, she intrigues me. There's an essence of familiarity that pulls me in. Almost as if we've met before.

Chapter Five

Joey

Today I'm headed to the infamous "big client meeting" at Fernrose.

And unfortunately, I'm feeling a bit withdrawn. I've only been in Hemlock for a few days, and already, I'm completely thrown off. Temporarily living with my sister is bad enough, but to faint in her store? She'll never let me live it down. Then there's the handsome nurse—whose name I cannot remember on account of having almost died of potential blood loss. Needless to say, my brain has shriveled up.

Fine. Maybe I didn't *almost die*, but my brain is definitely not working at full capacity. That could also be because Vera, the snoring golden, enjoys spooning me in the middle of the night, making it difficult to sleep.

My body is failing me one system at a time, and no amount of caffeine could save me today.

Granted, my headspace isn't great most days. I'd say it's

satisfactory on the best of days. Today? It's teetering in the *don't do or say anything that could get me involuntarily hospitalized* category.

I'm trying my damndest not to fall asleep at my desk.

"Everything okay, Jo?" Max questions, as I stretch and let out a long yawn. He and I work closely together since he's the creative director at Fernrose.

I jump, startled by his voice. I didn't know he was here this early. "Yeah. My life has just been a whirlwind since I got here. My mind, body, and soul are crying for help."

"You move into your new place soon, right?" He settles next to me at an empty desk, placing his color-coded folders full of notes in front of him.

So organized. Couldn't be me.

I nod, my eyes gritty from exhaustion. "Yes. I love my sister," I mutter, "but between the late-night horror movie marathons she and her boyfriend are into and my dog niece snoring like a freight train in my bed, I haven't had a decent night's sleep since I've been back."

Max winces. "Looks like you'll have to fake it today. Dig deep and pull up every ounce of energy you have left."

My stomach knots at the edge in his tone. "Oh god. Why?" I'm not sure how much more my nervous system can handle this week.

"I heard the client's project manager is an *interesting* person. Rumor has it her preferred source of fuel is the tears of those who've wronged her."

Shit. I'm going to get eaten alive.

<hr>

Uneasy energy swirls in the air of the conference room. The client company's CEO and project manager are seated already. I recognize them from the internet sleuthing I did on Droplet, a stainless-steel water bottle company looking for a total rebrand.

Droplet's CEO, Bryan, is a fit man in his forties with immaculate posture. While the project manager is a woman in her mid-sixties who projects an air of seasoned experience. Her name is Norma, if I recall.

As I approach the table, she gives me a slow, deliberate look that travels down the length of my outfit. I mirror her actions, glancing down at my denim jacket, vibrant floor-length skirt, and floral-patterned boots. When her eyes finally make their way back up to my face, she's wearing a disapproving frown.

The CEO stands, extending a hand to Max and I and flashing us a smile. "Hey. Bryan. CEO of Droplet."

When I hold my hand out to the project manager, she reluctantly takes it, her grip limp.

"Hi! I'm Joey, senior brand designer. I'm looking forward to working with you all." I keep my voice high and friendly, trying my damndest to turn this situation around.

Almost instantly, she drops my hand, face flat. "Norma. Project manager."

My heart sinks, but I keep my smile in place. Today is not my day.

As Max and I take our seats across from Bryan and Norma, I do my best to ignore the weird energy in the room.

"Thanks for meeting with us," Bryan says. "I don't mind video conferences, but I prefer meeting in person for these types of discussions."

Max smiles. "Couldn't agree more." He's lying. That man

would rather be on the beach with his husband and two kids than sitting across from a CEO who over-whitens his teeth and a perpetually displeased project manager.

Bryan clears his throat and laces his fingers on top of the table. "We're looking for a complete overhaul. The industry is changing and we want to appeal to a younger audience. I'm thinking fun, fresh, and eye-catching. I want people to stop in their tracks when they see our company's products." His eyes are hopeful, his excitement genuine.

Hope sprouts in my chest. CEOs with this kind of energy are usually great to work with. "I love that approach."

"We also need to appeal to our existing older audience," Norma says, her eyes narrowed on me. "They prefer simple and traditional."

Because I'm a professional, I manage to refrain from rolling my eyes. Of course Nefarious Norma likes simplicity.

Bryan steeples his fingertips under his chin. "Yes, we need to appeal to both audiences."

Dammit. Bry-guy and I were so close to hitting it off before she piped in.

"Can *you* do that?" Norma asks.

Max perks up. "Yes, ma'am. We have a very skilled team of—"

"I was talking to your brand designer," she says. "Jocelyn, correct?"

Oh no she fucking didn't. What is her problem? Did I accidentally cut her off while driving this morning?

Could I have crossed her in a past life?

I shake off the thought and plaster on a wide smile. "Yes, Nora. I can most certainly do that."

"It's Norma."

"It's Joey." With a shrug, I cast her a sardonic grin.

"Well, *Joey*. Can you do this for us? Combine both visions?" The devious smirk she's giving me leaves an unsettling sensation in my stomach.

"Oh yes. This is my expertise," I reply, my voice overly cheerful.

Norma homes in on me, scrutinizing every move I make. "Can the final design brief be prepared by next week? Or do you need more time? I *really* want to get this redesign off my plate." Her tone is practically dripping with bitterness, as if this project is an inconvenience to her. As if I've personally offended her.

Don't be a bitch, Joey. Don't. Be. A Bitch.

"Early next week is perfect." I flash her a smile, trying my damndest to not let my expression crack with annoyance.

Perfect might be a stretch, but I'm just spiteful enough to make it happen.

She lets out a sigh, her head shaking, and the tension in the room ratchets up a notch, making it hard to breathe.

Max peers over at me and scratches behind his ear. The signal we use when one of us is swimming in dangerous territory and needs to be reeled in. Unfortunately, that territory for me is matching Norma's energy.

To get through the rest of the meeting, I don my mental armor so the enemy can't smell my fear. Surprisingly, it goes well. Minus the glares from the project manager.

Max blows out a breath as we head back to our desks after saying goodbye to Bryan and Norma. "Wow. What a piece of work."

My shoulders sag. "I thought I was going to turn to stone under her watchful eyes. I was waiting for her hair to turn into snakes."

"We've got our work cut out for us." He stops and turns to me. "You know I adore your personality. . ."

There's a *but* lurking around the corner. I can feel it.

"But you need to be extra careful around this PM."

He's right, and typically, when faced with challenging clients, I have no issue standing up for myself in a respectful and professional manner. But sometimes my emotions can cloud my judgment.

Every so often, we find ourselves working with clients like Norma. It's always the combative and impudent ones who throw me off my game. In practice, I try to come into every meeting with an open and understanding mind. Sadly, some people see this as a weakness and enjoy using me as their punching bag.

I'm not a perfect human by any means. Some days I come off confident and ready to punch back—professionally, of course. Other days, like today, it doesn't take much to wear me down. And the project has only just begun.

Already, Norma is coming on strong and it'll only get worse from here, making for an uphill battle for Fernrose.

"Yeah, I know. I just—" I huff out a breath.

His sympathetic eyes meet mine. "If you ever need backup, I'm here. Scratch the bridge of your nose if you need me to step in, okay?"

That makes me chuckle, lifting some of the anxious weight off my chest. Max and I have so many secret signals that people must wonder why we're always scratching our noses, flicking our earlobes, or tapping our fingers on the table in Morse code.

Of course we know Morse code. Over a holiday break a couple of years ago, we did a deep dive on the subject and have gotten pretty good at it.

"Thanks. I really, really appreciate you." I give him a soft smile.

"Anytime. Now pack up and get home. We both need to dissociate after today."

In the parking lot, I slide into my van and take a deep breath. I refuse to let this woman get to me.

I've worked too hard to become the strong woman I am today, and I'll be damned if I let one unhappy person drag me down into the pits of doubt and despair.

ON MY WAY to Charlie's, I stop at the store for toothpaste. I also want to pick up dog treats to lure Vera off my bed at night.

I scurry into the store, eyeing the gray storm clouds overhead, cursing myself for not leaving an umbrella in my van. The store is eerily quiet, the lights a tad too bright for my liking. Boots squeaking on the tile floor, I stride toward the toothpaste aisle. What should be a quick decision gets a little complicated when I can't decide between the vibrant peppermint or advanced enamel protection.

"Joey?" a man says, startling me out of my toothpaste thoughts.

"Hmm?" I turn, and instantly, my stomach lurches. Great. My high school boyfriend, Kyle. The boy who left me for another girl on prom night. How lovely.

Determined not to show weakness to this man, I plaster on a fake smile. "Oh, hi! Wow, long time no see. How've you been?"

He takes a step closer, then another, and I take one back.

But Kyle clearly doesn't understand the meaning of personal space, because the more I retreat, the more he approaches.

"Wow. You look. . .just wow." He gives me a once-over, his attention making my skin crawl.

I'm a lot more curvy than I was in high school, and usually I'm very confident in my body. Right now, though, I wish I was wearing an oversized floor-length jacket. Kyle is practically undressing me with his eyes.

He takes another step closer, so I take one back. This time, though, I bump into something solid. And a heartbeat later, strong, tattooed hands grip my upper arms to steady me.

"Whoa. There you are, love. I've been looking for you." The voice is deep and gravelly, practically melting my insides.

Holding my breath, I look up, and when I find the hot nurse who bandaged me up a few days ago, I sigh with relief.

His dirty blond hair is messy, his jaw scruffy, and his kind green eyes are fixed on me.

"Next time I'm attaching a balloon to your body so I can find you." He gives me a small smile, then looks at Kyle. "She's always wandering around. I lose her so easily." He shakes his head, laughing to himself. "We should get going, yeah?"

Speechless, I nod.

The hot nurse puts his large arm around my shoulder and guides me to the self-checkout line in silence. His warm vanilla and rich leather scent comforts and overwhelms me simultane-ously, confusing my senses and making my brain foggy.

If I were thinking clearly, I probably wouldn't follow a strange man like this after having just encountered another strange man. But I'm not thinking clearly, and he's a nurse. That has to count for something, right? Either way, I don't sense danger. Quite the opposite, really. Instead, he radiates a quiet sort of protectiveness.

When we're out of sight of the creep, the hot nurse takes a step to the side, releasing me.

Part of me wishes his arm was still wrapped around me. Instantly, I miss the heat of his large body, the way his fingers flexed when he pulled me in closer when someone walked by us.

"Are you okay?" he asks, his concerned eyes bouncing between mine. "Did I read the situation right?"

At five eleven, I don't often find myself looking up at people, but I have to tip my head back a little to meet his eye, and I can't deny that I like it.

"I-I'm fine. Thank you. Your instincts were spot on. I dated him in high school, and it looks like he hasn't changed his slimy ways," I blurt out.

Damn. I can't remember this guy's name. So I do the only logical thing I can think of and introduce myself again. "I'm Joey, by the way." I stick my hand out and plaster on an overly enthused smile.

He lets out a hearty chuckle. The guy obviously knows who I am, or he wouldn't have swooped in like that. But I've been conditioned to never assume.

"I'm Beckett." He wraps his hand around mine, his warmth seeping into me, making my heart beat erratically. He's mesmerizing. And eerily familiar. Like I've seen him before, and I don't mean on the day I fainted at A New Leaf.

"Have we met before?" I ask without thought.

His expression falls. "Uh. Yeah. You fainted at your sister's shop a few days ago, remember? If not, then that could be a problem. Maybe you should—"

My cheeks burn red hot with embarrassment. Wow, Joey. Way to back yourself into an even more awkward situation.

"I remember that," I interrupt, my voice shaking with nerves. "I meant before then. You seem familiar. I thought maybe we'd met before."

"Hey, Joey?"

"Yeah?"

"You can let go of my hand now. Quite the strong grip you got there," Beckett jokes, a blush tinging his cheeks.

"*Oh.*" I drop his hand like a hot potato, mortification coursing through me. "I'm so, so sorry."

I'm going to die alone with six dogs. Maybe that psychic in Reno was right about my future.

"No need to be sorry." He smiles down at me and the corners of his eyes crinkle in the most endearing way.

Before I embarrass myself further, I spin around and scan both boxes of toothpaste at the self-checkout. I forgot to put one down and I refuse to go back and risk seeing Kyle.

"Thanks again for all your help," I say as I snag my receipt. "With Kyle and the whole fainting thing." With a wave of my hand, I dart for the exit.

My face flames as I rush for my van, though the cool spring air brings a little relief.

Until I hear the unmistakable sound of heavy bootsteps behind me. Stomach dropping, I pick up my pace.

"Wait up. Let me walk you to your car. In case that weirdo is lurking around," Beckett insists.

Valid point, hot nurse. Valid point.

With a deep breath in, I stop and wait for him. When he catches up to me, I give him an appreciative smile. "Thanks."

As we beeline for my van, raindrops break through the clouds above us sporadically, a heavy rain shower imminent.

"This is me," I say, stopping by my driver-side door.

Beckett's eyes go wide with amusement. "You're kidding. You drive this?"

I can't help but smile. "Yes. I named her Poppy, actually," I gush like a proud mom.

He tucks his hands into his jeans pockets and circles the retro van, eyes sparkling as he takes her in.

"Incredible," he marvels.

"Thank you. She's pretty great." I run my hands through my hair to calm my skittering nerves, but my rings get tangled. Rain and my wavy hair are mortal enemies.

As I try to free myself, Beckett moves closer, hands open and cautious.

Great. Just what I need. More embarrassment.

"Let me help." His low voice washes over me like a soft wave, calming my nerves, his touch delicate as he carefully untwines my hair.

"You've come to my rescue twice," I tease to hide my humiliation. "I guess two times the charm?"

He huffs a small laugh, his lips twitching. "I think you mean 'third time's the charm'?"

Frowning, I tilt my head. "That's how the phrase goes? Interesting."

He breaks into a full-blown smile, and the expression tangles my insides in nervous, jittery knots that have my body humming with exhilaration.

I need to get out of here while he's still looking at me like I'm not ridiculous. Two embarrassing strikes are enough. If a third occurs, it'll probably take me out.

Clearing my throat, I look up at the sky and then back into his emerald eyes. "We better go before the storm hits. Thanks again for saving me back there." I hitch my thumb over my shoulder.

"Anytime." He dips his chin, his expression sincere. "Drive safe, all right?"

I nod. "You get home safe too, Beckett." Clutching my grocery bag to my chest, I slide into the driver's seat.

As I'm pulling the door shut, I swear he murmurs words I'm not entirely sure I'm meant to hear.

"I'll see you around, Josephine."

Chapter Six

BECKETT

I'VE ALWAYS STRUGGLED with social anxiety. The small talk, large groups of people, and paralyzing fear that the people around me are always judging me makes my mind race with all kinds of uncomfortable thoughts.

Are they staring at me?

Did I say something stupid?

Do I look okay?

Why did I say that?

Will they think differently of me after this?

After, in the safety of my home, I'll replay every social interaction down to the smallest detail.

It's why I rarely go out. When I do, it's almost always out of obligation.

Once in a while, though, I force myself to step outside my comfort zone, like a test to see if I've been magically cured of my socially anxious ways.

That's how I ended up here, in front of Hemlock's animal shelter.

My natural inclination is to go to work and then back home. No dinners out. No bars. But living that way isn't healthy, so I've come up with creative ways to get out of the house without then having to ruminate over my interactions.

One of my favorite solutions is to stop by the shelter and take an adoptable dog out for a day.

Overhead, the bright blue sky hangs with drifting fluffy clouds as the sun warms my body. It's the perfect day to be outside.

I find a parking spot, and the low hum of my bike fades to silence as I twist the key. Swinging my leg over the seat, I pull off my helmet and feel the cool spring breeze tousle my hair. My eyes take in the well-kept animal shelter before me. In the distance, I hear the chaos of what I assume are dozens of dogs playing in the outdoor area. My heavy boots thump on the pavement as I stride to the entrance. The moment I open the door, the three women at the front reception area stop their conversation and give me a slow perusal. I watch as their eyes take me in, from my black leather boots to the dark sunglasses perched on my nose.

This isn't awkward at all.

I give them a friendly smile. "Hi there. I called yesterday about the Doggy Daycation program? I'm Beckett Hart."

One woman clears her throat. "Right! Hello. Erm—" Flustered, she shuffles through the various papers on the desk. "Ah. Here you are. We have you with a lab-corgi mix named Moose today. He's a really sweet dog and could use some extra recognition around town."

I give her a warm smile. I do this not only because I hope to adopt a dog one day, but because I enjoy raising awareness about the shelter and dogs that are available for adoption. They usually wear brightly colored vests that say "Adopt me" that draw attention and earn them a few pets. More than once, I've been told a dog was adopted by a person who saw it out and about like that.

"Can't wait to meet him."

As I'm signing the requisite forms, the distinct sound of nails clacking on linoleum floors catches my attention. Then another volunteer appears with a stocky dog with a sleek black coat. Moose, I assume. His ears instantly endear him to me. One is flopped over, while the other one sticks straight up, like a TV antenna receiving a signal.

A chuckle bubbles out of me as I crouch and scratch the floppy ear. He's equal parts handsome and goofy looking. "Hey, bud. Nice to meet ya."

He replies by giving my face a big, slobbery lick.

"Wow," the woman holding the leash comments. "He's friendly, but it usually takes him a while to warm up to new people. He must really like you."

My heart swells.

One day. One day I'll get a dog like Moose. Barbara will just have to deal with it.

In Hemlock, most everything is within walking distance, so I leave my bike in the parking lot and guide Moose toward town. The sky above is blue and filled with big puffy clouds as Moose trots just ahead of me with a joyful pep in his step.

After several errands around town, I open up my phone so I can check the tasks off my to-do list. As we pause, Moose whimpers and pulls on his leash, making me lurch forward.

Damn. For a short, stocky guy, he's got some muscle to him.

I widen my stance to steady myself and swipe my thumb across the screen, ticking off another—

A solid object strikes me in the chest, knocking the air from my lungs.

"Oof!"

I'm trying to breathe when another mass nearly takes me out at the knees.

With a wild mess of auburn hair in my face, I grasp the shoulders of the woman who's just run into me, steadying her. But despite my efforts, the second part of this party, a dog, I realize now, darts around us. The move only inspires Moose to do the same, and quickly, the two leashes have been woven into a chaotic web entangling me and the stranger. When I get my bearings, I jerk my head back and assess the person I'm unusually and probably inappropriately close to.

Along with the wavy auburn hair, I'm met with a heart-shaped face, sparkling chocolate brown eyes, and pouty pink lips.

Joey.

My chest tightens almost painfully. She's an exquisitely beautiful woman.

Her gaze glimmers and her freckled nose scrunches as she peers up at me.

"You just can't stay away from me, can you, Beckett?" Her rosy lips curve into an infectious smile.

I smile right back, the expression starting slow, then blooming across my face.

Though there are nearly one million words in the English language, I've suddenly forgotten them all. It's as if every word has slipped through my fingers at rapid speed.

The dogs are still doing their dance, checking one another out, causing the leash to tighten around our legs, drawing us even closer. When Joey sways a bit, I slide my hands from her shoulders to the gentle curve of her waist.

Moose spins, and Joey wobbles again, her delicate fingers clutching my biceps for stability. She gives them a quick squeeze. Whether the move was intentional, I'll probably never know. But her face flushes the most beautiful hue of pink once she peers up at me and realizes I'm watching her.

She ducks, looking at the tangled mess. "You know, I think I've seen this happen in a movie once or twice. Never thought it could happen in real life." Her laugh is light, airy, and free. The kind that reminds me of a wind chime on a cool summer's night.

"I'm *very* familiar with this particular kind of movie scene," I mumble.

She startles a little. "I'm sorry, what was that?"

"I. . .uh. . ." I clear my throat. "I just said I was familiar with this kind of movie scene."

She breaks into a beaming smile. "Oh yeah? Do you watch a lot of rom-coms?"

"Every Friday night with my mom." The moment the words are out, I wince. That's probably one of the most embarrassing things a grown man could say to a beautiful woman.

"You regret saying that, don't you?"

Heat creeps up my neck. "Absolutely."

She giggles, and I can't help but join in, despite our current predicament.

Both dogs are now lying on the cool cement beside us, gnawing on a stick. Moose's black coat shines in the sun. The dog beside him is a golden retriever.

"Since you're the expert in these scenarios, how do the

characters untangle themselves?" Joey questions with a hint of mischief in her eyes.

"I never said I was the expert in *this* particular scenario," I say, nerves skittering through me. "But I may have rushed into an airport to prevent someone from leaving once or twice."

"*Oh.*" Her face lights up. "Dramatic. I like that. Are you also familiar with theatrical wedding objections?"

"Just did one last weekend, actually. Groom wasn't too happy," I quip back.

She tilts her head back and bursts into laughter. Her long brown waves gently blow in the breeze, making my fingers ache to push back a loose strand. A surge of pride courses through me, along with a bit of shock, because I don't think banter has ever come to me this easily.

As her laughter fades, I find myself studying her. Our bodies remain closely entwined, with my fingers resting against the silky material at her waist. Her hands are still wrapped around my biceps, the heat of her fingers sinking into my bare skin. Her firm yet tender grip anchors us on this sidewalk.

She traces my features, her brows furrowed thoughtfully, as though she's trying to solve a puzzle. The deep brown of her irises is decorated with flecks of gold and amber, the depth warm, kind, and *entrancing*.

Her glossy lips part, like she's going to speak, but one of the dogs lets out a boisterous bark, making us both jerk in surprise and snapping us out of the moment. A moment that felt fleeting and endless at the same time.

Joey looks away, biting the inside of her lip. "Uh. We should probably get untangled."

"Oh. Right. Yes." I sound like a grunting caveman. One

minute I can speak effortlessly, and the next I'm reduced to monosyllabic words.

Carefully, we unravel the leashes that bind us together, our fingers fumbling awkwardly. We keep our heads down, realizing that we've garnered attention from passersby.

Moments like this are the kind I relive over and over in my head. The kind that keeps me from venturing out in public.

When we're finally free, the dogs have moved to the grass, both watching us, tongues lolling out of their mouths. If I didn't know any better, I'd say they were proud of the situation they put us in.

"Is, uh, that your dog?" I point at the golden retriever.

"Oh god no. She's my parents' dog, Vera." She inhales sharply, eyes darting away, a sudden sadness radiating from her. "*Was* my parents' dog. They passed away a little over a year ago, so my sister inherited her."

My instinct is to step closer, to comfort her, but I retreat out of nervousness. "I'm sorry about your parents. I can't imagine what that must feel like."

As if sensing the shift in her energy, Moose and Vera cozy up to Joey.

Sniffling, she looks up at me. "Thank you," she says, her voice soft but grateful. "It's been a big adjustment, but my siblings and I are doing the best we can. Just taking it day by day, you know?"

I give her a soft smile and nod. Hoping I can offer her a bit of comfort, even though, deep down, I know it can't erase the pain, I say, "It's much easier to take it one day at a time than to conquer grief all at once."

She mirrors my expression, her small smile sending

warmth into this little bubble we've created here on the sidewalk. "Exactly."

For a moment, a comfortable silence hangs between us. A cool breeze sweeps through, carrying distant laughter. When the laughter is joined by the sound of barking dogs from the nearby park, an idea hits me.

I say a silent prayer that I don't make a fool of myself, then I clear my throat. "Hey," I say, my voice quiet and a little unsure, "would you like to grab a coffee—"

A phone rings, then Joey is hastily digging through her bag. "Oh my gosh. Give me one second." A sympathetic look crosses her face as she pulls the device out and slides her thumb over the screen. "Hello?" she says as she brings it to her ear. "Oh no. That bad? Yikes. Yes, I'll be right there." She shoves it back into her purse and peeks up at me. "I'm so sorry. I have to get back to my sister. Hopefully I'll see you around!"

With that, she takes off in an impressive sprint, practically dragging Vera behind her.

When she turns the corner, I crouch beside my date for the day and give the stocky, happy pup a scratch on the neck. "Let's get you a pup cup and see if we can find a family for ya. How does that sound?"

Like he understands every word, he lets out a loud, happy bark.

With Moose trotting along next to me without a care in the world, my thoughts drift to Joey. If I see her again, I *will* ask her out.

Next time, I'm determined to be a little more confident and a little less hesitant.

Beckett's Journal

April 5

I have very few close friends. It's an unfortunate side effect that comes with needing to protect myself from disappointment.

Yet Joey has an undeniable warmth that utterly captivates me. Her shimmering golden brown eyes draw me in, igniting an insatiable curiosity to learn more about her.

So, even though I was petrified, I asked her out for coffee. Or tried to, at least. I need the opportunity to get to know her. Something about her nudges me out of the confines of my comfort zone, and that sensation is beginning to get addicting.

Because when I'm with her, my loneliness fades into the distance.

Chapter Seven

Joey

I NEED caffeine injected into my veins. Like, yesterday. An IV drip would be preferable, but a latte will do. Getting out of bed this morning turned into an all-out battle. When I woke up, Vera was sprawled over me, making it hard to breathe. And nothing says *wake up* like dog breath and a wet nose at six a.m.

On my lunch break, I head to Main Street for a coffee.

My feet pound the pavement as I dodge Hemlock's residents left and right. The sky may be overcast, but the array of spring flowers decorating nearly every storefront make the day brighter.

I've always loved flowers. As a child, my mom would take me with her to the plant nursery, where we'd pick out colorful blooms to adorn our home with. We'd choose the brightest, most vibrant blossoms in every shape, color, and size. When we got home, my dad would be out in the front yard, smiling and ready to plant them for her.

My heart aches at the memory. It's a bittersweet ache, but an ache all the same.

Sighing, I shake the melancholy away and focus on the entrance of Dark Side Brews. The moment I pull open the door, I'm hit with the aroma of freshly ground coffee beans and the sight of. . .Beckett. As I take him in, I can't help but frown. He shifts back and forth on his feet, white-knuckling his coffee cup, looking wildly uncomfortable as Finn, the shop owner and my sister's boyfriend, carries on a one-sided conversation with him.

Looks like it's my turn to rescue Beckett. Finn's a talkative guy. Super nice, means no harm, but the man is a relentless conversationalist.

Casually, I stroll up to the guys and lean on the polished wooden counter where they're standing. "Ah, I see you've met my knight in shining"—I look Beckett up and down, taking in his outfit—"black leather."

The tops of Beckett's ears turn red, and he drops his chin, studying his worn leather boots.

My stomach sinks. Whoops. I think I made the situation worse.

"Oh, *this* is the nurse who helped you?" Finn asks.

"Right time. Right place. Couldn't have asked for better service." I laugh, giving Beckett a gentle pat on his shoulder.

A very firm, muscular shoulder. I don't hate that.

At the contact, he relaxes a little, his shoulders dropping and the grip on his cup loosening.

"Ma'am? What can I get you today?" a voice calls out from behind me.

I turn to the scrawny college-age barista, then peer up at

the menu. "Hmm. I'm feeling like a sugar buzz today. Brown sugar latte, please."

"What milk would you like?" he questions, punching my order in.

I hum again, contemplating. "Two percent is good."

"Oat or almond milk," Finn says, frowning at me. "She's lactose intolerant."

With a huff, I turn to glare at him. "Do you enjoy sucking the joy out of my life's little pleasures?"

He peers down at me from over the rims of his tortoise-shell glasses, one brow cocked. "Your sister won't stop complaining about how *you complain* about how dairy gives you an upset stomach. I'm looking out for myself first and foremost."

"Fair enough. Only the strong survive when it comes to Charlie," I mumble. "Don't tell her I said that. We made a pact." I point at him.

He chuckles. "Don't worry. I remember."

Beckett's eyes dart back and forth between us, his expression one of curiosity and maybe a little skepticism. "A pact?"

I turn and give him a warm smile. "I watch Frank and Vera when Finn and my sister need a date night."

His curious green eyes fill with concern. "Frank? The blind dog that sliced your hand open?"

"He still feels bad about that, by the way," Finn interjects with a wince.

"Frank is a good boy with a lot of big feelings." I stick my bottom lip out, and *finally* the worry lines on Beckett's forehead smooth out. "It's how we bonded initially. We shared a rotisserie chicken and talked about our emotions."

"Next time you two have a bonding moment," Finn says,

checking his watch, "can you not feed him half a chicken? He wouldn't touch his kibble for days after that."

Sighing, I clutch my chest. "How can you fault him for his love of slow-cooked poultry? He's a boy after my own heart."

Finn shakes his head at my theatrics. "I've got to meet with a supplier." He turns to Beckett. "It was nice meeting you. We should grab a beer sometime. It'll be on me, of course, since my dog put you to work on your day off," he jokes.

Beckett clears his throat, a subtle sign of his discomfort, I realize. One I can feel down to my very bones. "Uh. Yeah. Sure," he replies in a noncommittal tone.

I take one big step behind Beckett and shake my head, giving Finn a *don't overwhelm the newcomer with your extrovertness* look.

Thankfully, he takes the hint. With a friendly smile, he spins on his heel and strides down the hall that leads to the back of the shop.

"Oh shoot. I think I forgot my wallet," a woman says behind me. "I'm sorry, just cancel my order."

I turn to the voice, finding a woman with deep purple shadows under eyes and disheveled hair rummaging through her purse as a line of impatient customers waits behind her, only adding to her growing panic.

My heart clenches for her, the empath in me screaming to help. I've been in her spot many, many times. So without hesitation, I step up beside her. "I got this. Here," I say, squinting at the name tag of the barista, "Joe. Put it on my card." I give the woman a soft, reassuring smile. "Are you hungry? Do you want a muffin?"

Her eyes widen in surprise, a flicker of relief passing through them.

She's going to say no, but I understand that look, so before she can respond, I turn back to Joe. "A muffin too, please."

Laughing quietly, the woman presses her palm to her forehead. "Thank you so much. I haven't gotten any sleep the last few days. My sister broke her leg, and I've been caring for her. I'm exhausted. And when I'm exhausted, I tend to be forgetful."

"I have the memory of a goldfish," I chuckle. "So you're in excellent company."

My name twin, Joe the barista, places our orders in front of us, and the woman gives me a smile.

"I have to get back to my sister," she says, "but thank you again."

My heart swells at the gratitude behind her words. "Of course. I hope your sister has a speedy recovery."

As she exits the shop, I take in a deep breath, then let it out with a satisfied sigh. This is one of life's best pleasures. The joy that comes with making another person's day a little brighter. This world can be dark and unforgiving, so I do my best to be a light for those who need it. I'll choose empathy over apathy for as long as I live.

Spinning, I bring my coffee to my lips, and when I lock eyes with Beckett, I freeze. Honestly, I figured he would have snuck out by now. He's clearly not an overly chatty kind of guy.

Yet here he is, looking at me with. . .admiration?

My heart leaps. No. That can't be right.

"What?" I finally take my first sip of overly sweetened coffee and hum as the warm liquid hits my tongue.

"Nothing. That was—" He frowns, brows creased, like he's searching for the right words. "That was really nice. Few people would go out of their way for a stranger like that."

"We live in a society where people enjoy being assholes," I say. "Where being kind and empathetic is seen as a rebellious act. And I am nothing if not a rebel." Grinning, I shoot him a wink.

Beckett looks down at his boots again, rubbing the back of his neck. "And thank you for saving me. Earlier when. . ."

"Ah. Finn," I laugh. "You should see him on *Star Wars* trivia night at the pub down the street." I shudder. "He could talk for hours about how the lightsabers were originally made from camera parts."

Beckett tilts his head, confusion swimming in his expression.

"Not a *Star Wars* guy?" I ask.

"Absolutely not." He chuckles, bringing his coffee to his lips.

"Thank god." I huff a laugh. "One *Star Wars* nerd in this town is plenty." Checking my watch, I ask, "Do you have anywhere to be? I have another thirty minutes until I have to be back at work. Wanna join me? I promise, I won't force small talk or invite you to any crowded places. We can walk in complete silence if you prefer. We can even walk on opposite sides of the street and wave occasionally. I'm cool with that."

My silly comment gets a deep, hearty laugh from him. One that comes with eye sparkling and everything.

The sight fills me with an overwhelming desire to make him laugh like that again. To see if I can get him to transform from the shy, uncomfortable guy he was earlier to this relaxed, easygoing version of himself.

He nods. "I'd like that."

"Wonderful. I'll lead the way."

The coffee shop is busy, crowded with the lunch rush. It's

overwhelming, even for me, so the crisp air and chirping birds outside are refreshing.

"It's easy to feel claustrophobic in there when it gets busy like that," I say, giving him a sidelong look.

Beckett's head is downcast, but there's no hiding the smirk creeping onto his face.

We walk in silence for several minutes, our footsteps falling in sync. The sun is finally breaking through the heavy gray clouds above us, the warmth of it heavenly on my face.

He pushes up the sleeves of his shirt, putting his tattoos on display. My heart thumps a little faster at the sight. I'd forgotten about his tattoos. As we weave through the people on the sidewalk, heads swivel in our direction, passersby staring at us with perplexed expressions, like we're aliens.

I'm tempted to tell them to mind their own business. But something tells me that would make the man beside me want to squirm out of his skin.

So I guide him toward a quiet street lined with colorful historic homes and lush green trees. The only company we'll have are the squeaking squirrels darting up trees and the occasional dog in a back yard.

The quiet between us is natural. Easy. It's like reconnecting with an old friend.

I take in the surrounding neighborhood, the way the early afternoon sun filters through the trees, listening to the chirping birds overhead. Yard after yard is decorated with vibrant flowers of every color, the sight of them making me smile.

Flowers will always remind me of my mom.

I'm lost in thoughts of her when my foot catches on a raised piece of concrete and I lose my balance. Just as I'm certain I'll hit the ground, Beckett wraps his arm around my waist and steadies me, breaking my fall.

"Are you all right?" he asks, his tone laced with worry.

As a kid, I was accident-prone. During the summer, my parents and siblings would bet about how many times I'd fall off my bike.

Embarrassingly, it was an almost weekly occurrence. It was inevitable with the way I'd often drift off into a daydream.

After suffering from so many falls, I'm terrified of them. Of the scraped knees that sting in the shower. Of the possibility of a broken wrist that would throb beneath an itchy cast. Of chipping teeth again.

Willing my pounding heart to settle, I take a deep breath in through my nose and let it out in a trembling exhale.

"Josephine, look at me. Are you okay? Did you hurt yourself?"

When I open my eyes, I'm met with Beckett's distressed expression. "Sorry. Y-yeah," I stammer. "I'm fine. Just shaken up. I'm not good with falling."

"You don't need to apologize." He loosens his hold around my waist, and for a moment, as we begin walking again, his hand lingers softly over my lower back like a gentle guide. It's a barely-there touch, yet it feels like a heavy weight against my body.

I can't help but wonder what his story is, so I dive right in and ask the most pertinent question.

"What brings you to Hemlock?"

He hesitates for a moment, his attention fixed ahead of us, so I take the opportunity to really look at him. He's a very handsome man, probably around six-four, with slightly tousled blond hair. The strong jaw shadowed by stubble gives him an air of rugged charm. The top buttons of his dark gray henley are undone, his jeans are dark, and his brown boots have seen better days.

Warmth blooms low in my belly.

A slutty henley with a peek of warm skin and chest hair is my kryptonite.

The skin around his kind, deep green eyes crinkles when he smiles at me. "I'm a travel nurse in the emergency department. Here on a three-month assignment."

The urge to ask about the wildest things he's seen in the ER bubbles up inside me, but miraculously, I reel in the impulse.

"I'm also here for three months," I tell him. "I'm actually moving into a short-term rental tomorrow."

A sudden gust of wind blows, swirling my hair around my face. Pulling up short, I carefully push the unruly strand behind my ear.

Eyes flashing with amusement, he pushes a rogue lock into place.

When his fingers brush my temple, my breath catches.

His body goes rigid. "S-sorry," he stammers. "I didn't mean to encroach on your personal space. I just saw—"

Placing my hand on his solid bicep, I give his arm a friendly squeeze. "I appreciate it. My hair has a mind of its own. Sometimes it chokes me at night, and it even gets caught in doors. I'll keep you on standby in case it attacks me again," I tease, hoping to tone down his worry.

He smiles at me, his anxiety seemingly assuaged, the charming eye crinkles and smile lines on full display. He opens his mouth and inhales, but before he can speak, his phone goes off. Wincing, he pulls out the device and checks it. Then he drops his head, sighing.

"I'm so sorry. It's the hospital. We're short staffed, so they need me to head in."

"Totally understand." I give him a reassuring smile. "Want me to walk you back?"

His bright eyes flit between mine. "Yeah. I'd like that."

We pick up our pace on the way back to Main Street, and when Beckett walks up to a gleaming vintage black motorcycle, my eyes practically bulge out of my head. Tattoos and a motorcycle? This man intrigues me like no one else has before. He looks intimidating, yet he's quiet and soft-spoken, and he blushes easily. Though both times he came to my rescue, he was confident and commanding.

"Reckless and responsible. Nice." I nod, taking in the shiny chrome details of his bike.

With a hearty chuckle, he swings his leg over the seat. "I'm glad you approve." He pulls a helmet on, and as he buckles the strap under his chin, he assesses me. "I hope we run into each other again, Josephine."

Without waiting for a response, he turns the key and revs the engine. The roar of his motorcycle is thunderous as it echoes through the small downtown area, causing every head on the street to turn toward us.

I can't help the laugh that escapes me. I give him a shy wave, then step back and watch him ride down the road, only turning away when he disappears into the horizon.

Although our walk was brief and quiet, the time together felt profound. Because every time our eyes met, the companionable silence between us spoke volumes.

Chapter Eight

I'M beyond ready to move into my cute little cottage. I've spent too many nights with Vera in my bed and waking up with a cold, wet nose in my ear. How can one dog take up so much damn space?

I blame Charlie. Not once since I've been here has she brought Vera into her room with her. Instead, she shuts the door, leaving me to suffer with the snoring, groaning golden retriever.

I think this is payback for the bear hug I gave her when I got here.

And the ones I've given her every night since.

Sighing, I shake my head. Older siblings can be *so* dramatic.

I'm feeling optimistic as I hum along with the music playing from Poppy's speakers. I don't have much, preferring all my belongings to fit snugly inside this vehicle. Though I have all the essentials, including a few duffel bags full of clothes, my well-loved laptop, and an embarrassing number of travel coffee mugs.

Before I embraced my nomadic life, I tucked a few special belongings into a storage unit near the house where I grew up. Who knows where I'll be in five, ten, even fifteen years? Maybe I'll keep traveling, maybe I'll tire of this life. Either way, I wasn't ready to part with any of it. And for now, I'm content with the open road and the possibilities ahead of me.

Occasionally, my optimistic spirit transforms into a cynical one—for example, anytime I hear from my new nemesis Norma, who thinks my email address is her personal diary. Thankfully, a proper meal typically quells the agitation, and now that I'm not living out of a vehicle, I've been getting more of those. When I'm on the road, I can go a day or two consuming nothing but pretzels and sports drinks. Sometimes a woman's gotta do what she can to survive.

Even if that means demolishing a family size pack of Oreos in a day and washing it down with an unhealthy amount of espresso.

As I navigate the winding road leading to my new place, I take in the towering spruce trees. They're a blur of green and brown as I cruise to the outer edge of Hemlock. The cottage, nestled deep in the forest, was a lucky find. I stumbled upon the listing online and instantly knew I wanted to live there. The home looks like something out of a storybook, with ivy creeping over its log siding and vibrant flowers decorating the open porch.

On the drive to Oregon, I even had a brief daydream about wandering through the dense woods and befriending curious squirrels and rabbits. Not that I would admit that out loud, of course. I'd rather not have the people around me questioning my sanity.

Behind me, my overprotective brother follows a little too close. Every few minutes, I tense up, my body preparing for the jolt.

I swear on my mom and dad's urn if he so much as dents my van with his tailgating, I'll kill him with my bare hands and feminine rage.

Jack, who runs his own construction company, was vehement about accompanying me today so he could ensure the house is up to code. Really, all I want is for him to check for serial killers under my bed.

Unsurprisingly, he grumbled and rolled his eyes when I asked, like he thought I was joking.

So here we are. Jack once again tailgating, and me white-knuckling the wheel, waiting for his obnoxiously large four-by-four to strike my van.

"In half a mile, your destination is on the right," the GPS announces.

Relief washes over me as I force myself to focus on the road ahead. The last few days at work have almost broken me. Norma's attitude makes me want to kick her ass straight into early retirement. Nothing I do makes her happy. She once stopped me in the middle of a presentation because a letter on my slide wasn't properly capitalized.

My pettiness may have gotten the best of me when I respectfully pulled out the editorial style guide to prove her wrong. The satisfaction I got fueled me for a couple of days, though right now, all I want is a nap and a nice, deep cry.

The GPS directs me down a long dirt path canopied by towering trees that ends yards from the adorable cottage.

As I climb out, Jack parks beside me and hops down.

"You really didn't need to come with me," I tell him. "Sometimes I think you forget I'm an adult and can take care of myself."

My brother scoffs, running his hand down his dark beard. "Huh. Feels like just last week, Charlie and I had to play rock, paper, scissors to figure out who would save you when your location quit moving and we knew you'd run out of gas."

I suppose it really was only a week ago. "That tracks," I say. "And I appreciate the way you two stopped to play a game before searching for me. Good use of your time."

"We—" The thunderous roar of a motorcycle drowns out his words, and in unison, we turn to the driveway, where a figure on a jet-black bike approaches.

"Stand behind me, Jo," my brother says, grasping my arm and shoving me behind him.

For once, I'm not a stubborn asshole and I do what he says. Because when a mysterious looming figure on an intimidating piece of steel on wheels is coming directly toward me —while I'm in the woods, no less—it only makes sense to use my lumberjack brother as a human shield.

I'm too pretty and young to die.

The bike comes to a stop beside my van, the man on it dressed in black from head to toe, including the helmet with a tinted face shield that hides his features.

Terrified or not, I can't help but wonder who would win in a battle between a biker bro and a lumberjack.

I love Jack. I do. He's reliable and has an excellent resting bitch face, but at the end of the day, he'd probably lose against the menacing figure now dismounting the bike.

Jack steels his spine, shoulders pulled back, his fists clenched tight at his sides. Tension radiates off him, like he's about to kick this guy's ass and then bury his body in the woods behind us.

Fine. Maybe I didn't give Jack enough credit. Maybe he has a fair shot at kicking biker bro's ass.

Heavy black leather boots crunch against the gravel driveway, filling the ominous silence surrounding us. The man peels off his worn leather gloves as he saunters closer, revealing strong, callused hands. Then he unfastens his helmet and pulls it over his head.

Immediately, moss green eyes meet mine in confusion.

I peek over Jack's shoulder, frowning at the newcomer. "Beckett?"

"Beckett?" Jack glances back at me, then scrutinizes the man decked out in leather and denim.

"Beckett," the hot nurse echoes.

My brother crosses his arms over his chest. "Ah. You used to live in our neighborhood."

I reel back, my breath catching. "He lived in our neighborhood?"

Beckett—devastatingly attractive, as always—stands casually with his helmet under his arm. "I lived in your neighborhood?"

Finally, I step around Jack and tentatively approach him. "W-what are you doing here?"

"Yeah. What are you doing here?" My brother takes a step closer, eyes narrowed.

Beckett clears his throat. "What am I doing—" He waves a hand in front of him. "Actually, I'm going to break the cycle and not repeat everything you say. It's getting to be a little much." A flush slowly creeps up his cheeks, his eyes darting between us.

Head ducked, my brother scrubs his hand down his stubbled jaw and chuckles. "Bashful Beckett. Ms. Hart's son," he says to himself. "My dad and I used to help your mom with yardwork in the summer. She was a nurse, right? She'd leave cookies on our front porch before she'd head to work as a thank you."

How the hell do I not remember this? How does Beckett not remember this? Surely we'd remember each other if we were neighbors as children.

"How do I not remember this?" I blurt out, my mouth working faster than my brain.

"We helped during the summer," Jack says, smirking. "While you were off on mini excursions. You know, trespassing onto other neighbors' property and stealing—I mean *picking*—flowers from their gardens for Mom."

Wincing, I turn to Beckett. "And how do *you* not remember?"

"My nickname was *literally* bashful Beckett. I really was too shy to leave the house back then. Plus," he sighs, "I have seasonal allergies. Guess I assumed my mom hired a yard service. I never knew the neighbors were doing the work." He gives a small shrug, his cheeks going pink, evidence that his nickname was accurate.

"My dad and I were convinced you weren't real," Jack says, his tone full of amusement. "We thought maybe your mom made you up to give us the impression that she didn't live alone."

Beckett nods, his lips twitching. "That wouldn't be too far-fetched for her. She's conjured up wilder stories before."

Jack chuckles. "Especially because I never saw you at school."

"Private school." Beckett grips the back of his neck, squeezing.

"Really? Wow." My brother shakes his head, grinning. "This decades-long mystery is coming together now. You know—"

"I'm glad we're all having this caring, sharing moment," I say, my voice playfully sarcastic, "but if you never saw him at school, how did you know it was him?"

"Ms. Hart calls me from time to time to fix things at her condo." Jack cocks a brow. "You know your mom has a whole wall of photos of you, right? It's hard to miss a shrine of that size."

Beckett lowers his head, kicking at a stray pebble. "Don't remind me. It's hard to sleep when twenty pairs of *my own* eyes are on me." He shudders.

A laugh bubbles out of me. The absurdity of this situation makes my head spin. Still, he hasn't answered my question.

"What are you doing here?" When my tone comes out a little more forceful than I like, I take a step back, cringing.

It happens. Sometimes, when my mind is a tornado of confusion, my questions come out sharp and fast. That personality trait is a bug, not a feature.

Jack puts a hand on my shoulder and jostles me lightly. "Jesus, Jo. Go easy on the guy. He's harmless."

I glower at my idiot brother. "You were the one about to punch him. And you're telling *me* to go easy on him?"

"I'm right here, you know." Beckett's deep voice is quiet, but his words are clear. "Please don't punch me, though. I've already got a deviated septum that makes it tough to breathe at night," he says, tapping the bridge of his nose.

My shoulders sag as I let out an exhausted sigh. I'm having a painfully difficult time trying to tame all the questions in my brain.

Is this a stranger danger situation? Is he following me? Or

is this a weird coincidence? *Please let it be a coincidence. Though maybe I wouldn't be mad if a tattooed biker was following me.*

How was I so oblivious that I didn't know this guy lived on my street growing up? Is this why my parents said my head was always in the clouds?

I take a few deep breaths, centering myself because I'm a tad overwhelmed. When my thoughts stop spinning and my nerves settle, the pieces fall into place.

He's here for a few months. I'm here for a few months.

He needs a temporary place to stay. I need a temporary place to stay.

This was the only short-term rental I could find in Hemlock.

My heart races as the reality of the situation washes over me like cold water.

Are we. . .roommates?

Chapter Nine

Beckett

We're roommates.

Unless she wants me to leave.

I study Joey, then her brother. "I, uh, I think there's been a mix-up. Did the landlord double-book us?"

The landlord, Susan, surely made an error. However, it's a two-bedroom, two-bathroom home, and she was frazzled when I called her about the place.

Jack looks down and digs his phone out of his pocket. "Sorry, I have to take this." He wanders away, putting the device to his ear, leaving just Joey and me. Alone.

"I can—" I begin.

"We don't—" Joey starts.

We exchange a sheepish glance.

I thread my trembling fingers through my hair and make eye contact. "I'm sorry. Please, go ahead." A restless flutter presses against my chest, my anxiety creeping higher by the second.

She shifts on her feet, playing with the hem of her jacket. "I was just going to say we don't have to live together. I can find someplace else."

With my lips pressed together in a firm line, I shake my head. "Absolutely not. I'll find another place to stay. It's not a big deal."

That's a lie, and I'm mildly panicking inside. There's no way my aching body would survive sleeping on my mom's couch for the next three months.

Joey surveys me, then the cottage, then me again, biting the corner of her lower lip. Then she lets out a heavy sigh. "Are you going to kill me?"

I jolt and rear back, my heart thudding. "Wh-what? No. I-I would never. Why would you think that?"

She narrows her eyes on me, the scrutiny in them enough to make me want to hide in a nearby bush. "All right roomie, house rules," she says. "One: You must listen to me vent about work since my sister won't."

I give her a quick nod. "Yes, ma'am. My ears are at your service."

She furrows her brows at that.

Wincing, I duck. "That sounded better in my head, sorry."

"Two," she says, ignoring my comment, "I need my dissociation time. If I'm staring off into oblivion, looking possessed, do not talk to me. Do not look at me. Do not perceive me. Pretend I don't exist."

I swallow thickly. Maybe I should be worried about *her* killing *me.* "Yes, ma'am. I'll tiptoe around you and make my presence scarce."

"Finally, and this is the most important one, okay?"

I furiously nod. At this point, I'm pretty sure my life depends on it.

"Do not touch my snacks. If I see so much as a single cookie or cracker missing, I'll shave your eyebrows off while you're sleeping. Got it?"

Dear god. Maybe I do need to live with my mom. This sunshine girl becomes a raging thunderstorm when snacks are involved.

Except. . .*Why do I kinda like it?*

"Listen. Ignore. Starve. I think that sums up your rules." I give her a sharp nod.

Joey's pink lips curl slightly at the corners, but she quickly presses them together, trying her damndest to suppress a smile. There's no hiding the playful glint in her eyes, though. And it makes my heart rate kick up a little.

I silently beg the universe, desperately wishing for that infectious smile to reappear.

Instead, she settles her hands on her full hips, skirt swaying in the gentle breeze. "All right, Beckett. Your turn."

"My turn for what?"

She cocks a brow. "Your house rules."

I've lived alone for most of my nursing career, so I suppose I don't have house rules.

"I don't have any rules."

She tilts her head, her expression full of disbelief. "You've got to have at least one rule."

I drop my head, studying the ground, racking my brain for a rule that will suffice.

When it hits me, I lift my head, eyes locked on her. "Don't touch Agatha."

"Who the hell is Agatha?"

"My sourdough starter."

As her eyes widen dramatically, I try to keep a straight, serious face. It's difficult. And though I want to laugh at her reaction, I am quite serious about Agatha.

"What in the Martha Stewart do you mean? Is that a joke?"

"Nope," I deadpan.

"You have a sourdough starter. Named Agatha."

I nod. "Yep."

"Why?"

"Why not?"

"I have so many questions." She exhales, her chest deflating.

"I'll be sure not to answer them during your dissociation time." My tone is serious, but my cheek twitches with a smile.

For a moment, we assess one another, feet firmly planted on the ground, eyes locked, and brows pinched.

"Do you accept my rules?" Joey finally asks.

"Absolutely." I dip my chin. "Do you accept my singular rule?"

She lets out an unimpressed exhale. "I suppose," she finally says. "Can you clarify one thing for me, though?"

"Of course."

"How does a guy who looks like he got kicked out of a biker gang have a sourdough starter?"

A deep laugh rumbles in my chest. Feeling brave, I approach her, only stopping when my dirty black boots nearly touch the toes of her well-worn brown shoes. Her breath hitches, and the air between us thickens, charged with an electricity I've never experienced before.

I examine her face, memorizing the pattern of her freckles. "Never judge a book by its cover, Josephine."

The column of her delicate throat moves as she swallows hard. With a furrowed brow, she studies me.

The overthinking part of my brain takes off at a sprint. Most people wouldn't think twice about rooming with a beautiful woman. But I'm not like most people—obviously, since I have a named sourdough starter, enough journals inked with my thoughts to fill a library, and a cat who needs a nightly banana.

Stepping back, I clear my throat. "Are you sure about this? If it makes you uncomfortable, I can find another place to live." I run my trembling hands through my hair. "You probably don't want to live with some random guy. Plus, my work hours are erratic. It can be obnoxious. If I work late, I'll try to be as quiet as possible. Or if you still have concerns about me, I can give you a few character references. I've had a couple roommates in the past. I haven't spoken to them since college, but I'm sure they would—"

"Beckett," she says. "Stop. It's fine. Really. If I'm remembering the layout of the house correctly, it should be easy for us to have our own space. We'll share a couple of common areas and probably won't cross paths much," she rambles. "Like you said, you sometimes work weird hours. And I'm a pro at making myself scarce if I become too much. On top of that, it's only for a few months."

Making myself scarce if I become too much.

That stops me dead in my tracks.

Before I can think better of it, I say, "Wh-what do you mean you're good at *making yourself scarce*? Why would I want you to make yourself scarce?"

Joey opens her mouth, her expression full of confusion, but before she can speak, her brother returns.

"Sorry about that. A client needed me."

As he wanders closer, I take a few steps back, putting a healthy distance between us.

Head down, focused on his phone, he says, "I swear. Everyone in this town is a few cards short of a full deck." He looks up, attention bouncing from Joey to me and back again. "Did we figure out the mix-up? Do I need to call someone to fix it?"

"Susan must have double-booked the house. We figured it out, though. We'll both stay here since the layout makes the space easy to share." Joey shifts back and forth on her feet, her colorful skirt swaying with the motion.

Jack's nod is tentative, his eyes uncertain. "You sure?"

With a frown, Joey studies her brother. "Uh, yeah."

"Good, because that wasn't a client," Jack grits out. "I was running a background check on Beckett."

My stomach lurches. "How the hell were you able to run one so fast?" I'll give it to the guy. He works quickly.

He zeroes in on me, expression hard. "I know a lot of people in high places, Beckett Isaiah Hart. And according to my source, you're a thirty-four-year-old Aquarius who has a credit score of 803. Sound about right?"

"Damn," Joey says.

I twist my head sharply at the comment and find her watching me.

"What?" she asks, head tilted. "That's a superb credit score." She shifts her attention to her brother. "Any criminal record?"

Jack shakes his head. "Not even a speeding ticket. Unlike *someone* I know." He gives his sister a pointed glare.

I can't help but chuckle at the banter, which causes them both to home in on me, eyes narrowed.

I put my hands up in defense. "Sorry, sorry. Not funny.

Speeding isn't a joke. It's a very serious offense that shouldn't be taken lightly." I turn my attention to Jack, and he gives me a sharp, approving nod.

Thank fuck.

"Oh. You're on his side now? Why don't you two live together, then?" Joey crosses her arms, her chin lifted, prepared for battle.

Dammit.

On one hand, I'm worried about which sibling would be the most dangerous when pissed off. On the other hand, I can't help but acknowledge how cute Joey looks right now. Her flushed cheeks, turned-up nose, and pinched brows make my knees go weak.

Not the time, Beckett. Journal about it later.

Jack blows out a deep breath. "While you two figure out whatever it is you're trying to figure out, I'll go inside and double-check that everything works properly. The last thing I want is to be woken up at two a.m. because the furnace isn't pumping out heat and you can't figure out how to switch it over with a simple button."

"That was one fucking time, okay?" Joey groans. "I live in my van 75 percent of the year. I don't know how basic heating and cooling works in a house. Isn't that what people hire you for?" She drops her arms to her sides with a soft thud.

Muttering under his breath, Jack heads inside the cottage with an oversized duffel bag thrown over his shoulder.

My mind once again swirling with confusion, I look from his retreating form to Joey. "Is he also living with us?" I point at the house.

Though her expression is neutral, her tone drips with sarcasm as she says, "Yes. And you two will share bunk beds."

I tilt my head, trying to get a better read on the look on her face. "Are you being facetious right now?"

"Absolutely." The fiery woman spins on her heel, skirt twirling, and strides across the front yard to the cottage.

"This should be interesting," I mumble to myself.

"Heard that!" Joey yells over her shoulder.

I drag my feet, following Jack and Joey into the house. When I step inside, I'm immediately taken aback. On the exterior, the house looks like a quintessential log cabin. On the inside, though, it's warm and welcoming. Cream-colored walls accent the wood paneling in the spacious open-concept living room. An oversized gray couch and a plush chair frame a large, colorful rug in the middle of the space. Tucked off in one corner is a small kitchen with an island that looks perfect for stress baking loaves of bread with Agatha. Floor-to-ceiling windows surround the kitchen, transforming it into a glass observatory enveloped by the dense woods. Dappled sunlight filters through the rustling leaves, casting ever-changing shadows across the countertops.

Joey was right. Two people can live here comfortably without bumping into one another often. There's a bedroom with a connected bathroom to the right of the kitchen. I take the wooden staircase to the second floor and find another bedroom and a full bathroom. The sloped ceilings frame a large skylight, allowing natural light in during the day and glittering stars at night.

It's perfect.

Plus, there's a study area in a small alcove, with a desk sitting in front of a window and overlooking the lush forest.

Simple, old-fashioned contentment fills my chest. I imagine myself sitting at the mahogany desk after work, unwinding and journaling while Barbara lazily paws at my pen. The older I get, the more I appreciate the simple pleasures in life. My favorites being a lazy Sunday with my cat, a long ride on the open road, and baking a successful loaf of bread.

"Earth to Beckett! You okay up there?" Joey's voice pierces through my thoughts, echoing up the stairs.

I shuffle to the landing and find Joey looking up at me with one arched eyebrow. I can't tell whether it's an approving or disapproving arch. To be honest, I'm equal parts scared and intrigued by the look.

"Yeah. Sorry," I say as I slowly descend the stairs. "I zoned out for a bit. Do you mind if I take the upstairs?"

"Sure. I figured you'd want the room closest to the kitchen, though."

I tilt my head. "Why?"

"I heard through the grapevine that you and someone named Agatha enjoy late-night rendezvous involving a good *kneading* after getting *baked,* if you know what I mean."

"Technically, you knead first and then bake. I'll give you an A for effort, though. The pun was clever."

"You're no fun." She makes a mock sad face and then breaks into her classic radiant smile. "All right, I'm going to grab the last of my things from my sister's place. I'll be back a little later."

With that, she and her brother are gone, and I'm left alone with my thoughts amid the quiet, sunlit space. With one more look around the place, I make a plan. I'll do some grocery shopping, pick up Barbara, and unpack my stuff.

I'm cautiously excited about our new living arrangement, though I don't know whether Joey feels the same. What if she absolutely loathes living with me and my cat?

Shit.

I forgot to mention Barbara.

It's fine. . .I think. *I hope.* If she does loathe my cat, my mom would be more than happy to take her for a few months.

As I stand in the empty house, relishing the peacefulness, a small flutter of a crush stirs in my stomach. Thankfully, I'm pretty good at locking down my emotions. It's hard not to be drawn to Josephine. Her laughter is infectious, her smile fills me with light, and she exudes comfort. She intrigues me like no other person ever has, and I want to know more about the kindhearted, caring woman.

Despite the scars left by previous girlfriends, I'm drawn to her.

A small voice in the back of my head urges me to try one more time, screaming, *Maybe this is the one you've been looking for all along.*

But now, as roommates, I worry the dynamic will shift too much. That I've missed my chance. I'm not sure she'll see me as more than a friend.

Eyes closed, I inhale deeply. Then I let out a slow, measured breath to ease my racing thoughts. I need to focus on what I can control in this moment, or else I'll be stuck in a wind tunnel of rumination.

Chapter Ten

Joey

As I navigate the winding roads to my sister's house, my mind whirls, filled with a tangle of thoughts and a slew of unanswered questions.

How did I not know he lived next door for a few years?

Can I really survive living with someone new?

What if he hates living with me and leaves?

Why do I care if he leaves?

Am I freaking out? Yes. Am I being dramatic? Also yes. But living with another person is a big deal.

At least to me. It brings out a whole new set of vulnerabilities and insecurities.

I release a long, weary sigh. There was no mention of living with a man during my last tarot card reading. My tarot girl in Denver was definitely holding back on me.

She explicitly stated my past was the five of cups upright, which signified grief and loss.

Dead parents? Check.

Present was an upright empress, which means creativity.

Brand designer? Double check.

The final card, my future, was the upright ace of cups. She told me it meant emotional awakening and new beginnings. I figured it was fitting, since I experience a new emotion or five every day. Good, bad, and ugly. And new beginnings just seemed so. . .generic. Every day I wake up could be considered a new beginning.

The new beginning I *wasn't* expecting was one that includes a quiet, broad-shouldered man who's more than meets the eye.

Beckett is not my usual type. The strong, silent kind of guy does nothing for me. I enjoy men who look like they're ready to attend a three-day long music festival in the middle of nowhere. The ones who insist we sleep in the woods, under the night sky to feel "grounded by the gravitational force of mother nature" and other nonsense that only makes sense when one has smoked too much of the good shit.

Yes, I tend to go for the guys who look like they haven't had a shower in a day or three.

However, my hormones have done a total one-eighty. Beckett's tousled blond hair, searching green eyes, and indrawn nature have created an undeniable magnetism. Suddenly, there's nothing I'd rather do more than watch that man and his unusually calm demeanor unravel.

My spirit guides have thrown a curve ball, and now they're laughing at me.

When I left the cottage, Jack followed me out. Meaning I somewhat abruptly left Beckett there alone.

Guilt washes over me, settling like a heavy weight on my chest. My parents raised me to be more thoughtful than that.

Looks like I'm well on my way to being a terrible roommate. I've lived solo for the better part of a decade, so cohabitating with another human will be an adjustment.

My sister's front door creaks as I drag myself inside and drop my bag to the ground.

When I force my head up, Charlie is looking at me with enough concern that it makes *me* concerned. It's the most interesting feedback loop I've ever experienced, that's for sure.

"Are you. . .good?" She narrows her eyes like she's trying to decode my facial expression, then gestures for me to follow her into the kitchen.

With slumped shoulders, I trail behind her and settle onto the chair at the wooden dining room table that used to belong to my parents. The familiarity of plant cuttings in water on the surface comforts me a little.

But. . . "No. My tarot girl lied to me. I'm living with a man. My new client is insufferable. And I just want a fucking nap and maybe a snack. Did I mention I'm living with a man?"

Charlie's eyes go wide as she eases into the chair across from me. "You're living with a man?"

"Yep." I sigh. "A rather attractive one, if I'm being honest."

"You've had horrific experiences living with men."

I let out an exasperated sigh and slap the table. "I *know*. I thought those days were over. Remember when Alec left his—"

Charlie puts her hand up to stop me. "Please don't continue. I get it. It's tough living with men." She looks over at her boyfriend, who's on the couch with both dogs, the three of them eating popcorn. "No offense, Finn," she hollers.

Finn waves his hand, brushing off her words. "None taken. Men are gross."

In college, I shared an apartment with a group of friends, two of whom were men. All my memories of that time consist of unwashed, food-crusted dishes, washers filled with musty clothes from football practice, and bathrooms that required a hazmat suit when cleaning.

I shudder. "I know they are. Why do they leave so many little hairs all over the place? And leave the toilet seat up?"

"Because we're disgusting creatures." Finn tosses a piece of popcorn to Vera, who catches it with ease. Then he tosses one to Frank. Since the dog can't see, it smacks his head.

Frowning, I turn back to my sister. "How often does he forget his dog is blind?"

"A lot more than you think." Charlie sighs.

"I heard that. It's been a long day," he mutters. "How about you go back to talking about how my species is gross rather than critiquing my dog parenting skills? Jeez."

The two of us have to stifle giggles as we turn back to one another.

Charlie props her chin on her hand and surveys me. "This man, who is he? Didn't Jack go with you? Why are you living with him?"

"It's the hot nurse," I say without an ounce of emotion.

"The hot nurse?" my sister echoes, raising a singular eyebrow.

"Who's this hot nurse?" Finn yells from the living room.

Annoyed, I spin in my chair and glower at the lanky man on the couch. "Could you not eavesdrop?"

"Sorry! Ignore me," he calls out, a hand in the air.

"The guy who came into your shop when I fainted, Beckett," I tell my sister. "The landlord double-booked the cottage.

Beckett offered to find a different place, but he's only here for a few months. It seemed silly to kick him out. Plus, he said he works weird hours and that we won't see each other much." I sigh. "It can't be *that* bad, right?"

Charlie nods thoughtfully. "And Jack?"

Ducking, I twist a lock of my hair around my finger. "He was there. Ran a background check."

"Sounds about right." She sighs.

"Did you know the hot nurse lived in our neighborhood for a few years when we were kids? Dad and Jack helped his mom with the yardwork."

I fight back a wince. It's sort of embarrassing that it's taken me thirty-one years to truly recognize how oblivious I can be.

"Really?" She sits back in her chair, her brows pinched together, the wheels in her mind turning. "Huh. I had no idea."

It appears being oblivious is a common theme among the Thorne women. No wonder Jack texts us three times a week to confirm we're alive.

Vera wanders into the kitchen and sits next to me, putting half her weight on my foot. I give her fluffy golden fur a couple of strokes and she groans in appreciation.

"It'll be a new experience for me, that's for sure."

Charlie's eyes soften. "If you need a place to escape to, you're always welcome here."

I scoff. "You're only offering that because you pity me."

She winces. "Guilty." Shifting in her chair, she clears her throat. "Can we go back to the tarot card reading part? You glossed over that a little too fast."

By the time I pull into the driveway of the cottage, the sun has dipped below the horizon. The warm, yellow light streaming from the front windows contrasts the deep green of the forest, only adding to the quaintness of the place.

Determined to not make an extra trip back outside to my van, I gather my things from the passenger seat and carefully balance them in my arms, using my chin to anchor the precarious pile.

The house is eerily silent as I use my foot to close the door behind me.

I know better than to yell out "Is anybody here?" when there could be someone hiding in a closet with a ten-inch chef's knife and a penchant for bloodlust.

So I drop all my things by the door and slip off my shoes, readying to investigate without making a lot of sound. My skin prickles with unease, like I'm being watched, as I stealthily move through the house.

My body goes on high alert. Heart racing and adrenaline pumping through my veins, I frantically try to remember how to throw a punch.

Didn't my dad say to keep my thumb untucked when forming a fist? Do I hit up or down to break a nose?

Meow.

I nearly jump out of my skin and let out a high-pitched scream. "What the fuck?"

Stopped in the middle of the living area, I scan the open main floor, looking for the meowing monster.

I can't see it.

I can't smell it.

But I can *most definitely* sense it.

What sounds like a herd of stampeding elephants only

adds to my confusion. A few seconds later, Beckett appears on the stairs.

He rushes to me and places a hand on my shoulder. "Are you okay? What's going on?"

Naturally, as one does, I jolt at his touch, jerking back quickly.

Eyes wide, he snatches his hand away like I've burned him.

Heart racing, I take him in, and. . .*fuck me*.

The man is wearing a black T-shirt that clings perfectly to his muscular frame and shows off the intricate lines of the tattoos that wind down his arms. His gray sweatpants fit him as if they were tailormade for his body, and a pair of black-rimmed glasses sits on his slightly crooked nose.

His black shirt is dusted with a light layer of a white powder.

Squinting, I angle in closer. Is that flour?

Or is it another more controversial type of white powder? Maybe I shouldn't be asking so many questions. . .

Regardless, the man is alarmingly good-looking. Annoyingly so. He's also kind *and* excellent at saving me in unsavory circumstances. It'd be easier to live with him if he was an asshole. I think.

"Did. . .did you forget I lived here too?" he asks, searching my face.

"No," I squeak out.

Yes.

Heat creeps up my neck because not only am I checking out my new roommate, but I'm lying to him. If I'm not careful, I'll break out in hives. Lying always does that to me.

He cocks one eyebrow, his cheek twitching with a hint of a smile. "Okay," he says slowly, "then why are you screaming and looking at me like you've seen a ghost?" As he settles his hands low on his hips, I will myself not to look below his nose. If I so much as glance down at the way his shirt stretches across his toned chest again, I'm in deep trouble.

As his eyes bore into mine, I find myself wanting to stare into them. Wanting to memorize their color and the way the green gets darker closer to his pupils. Maybe it's exhaustion, maybe I'm hungry, or maybe Mercury is in retrograde—but I'm thrown off by him, and I'm not entirely sure what to do about it.

I've dated my fair share of passable men, all very *meh* in their unique way. Truth be told, I've never envisioned settling down.

I figured I would be the forever hot single aunt.

It's not that I'm against long-term relationships. The issue is that I've had more than my fair share of failed relationships and I suffer from more than the average number of insecurities. I guess I've never felt like anyone would *willingly* choose me as the person they're stuck with for eternity.

Sad, but true to how I feel.

I've been told more than once that I'm "girlfriend material, not wife material," which is code for "I'll fuck you, but I won't let you meet my parents."

It all circles back to me being *too much*.

"Are you okay? Have you eaten anything today? Had enough water?" Beckett's deep voice pulls me from my thoughts.

The tightness in my chest eases a little. I like his nursing side. The way he's ready to run through the list of possible causes for my odd behavior fills me with warmth and makes me think that maybe he truly cares about me and my well-being.

This is what usually gets me into trouble. The feeling that maybe I'm not actually too much, that maybe someone genuinely cares about me. Because inevitably, I end up burned. I end up the recipient of mockery, disapproving looks, and general annoyance.

And I refuse to let myself get hurt like that again. So I remind myself that Beckett's just a nice guy. He's a nurse, so of course he's worried about my health and safety. It's ingrained in him. Nothing more. He'd be this caring with anyone.

Brushing the incessant noise in my mind away, I plaster on a smile. "My mind held me hostage for a moment."

He chuckles, a deep rumble emanating from his chest. One that makes a shiver run down my spine. "You have no idea how much I relate to that." He runs his hands through his hair, mussing it up even more.

I blink at him, distracted by the pieces of hair standing straight up before I collect myself again. "I heard a meow and wondered if a stray cat had accidentally slipped in."

Head lowered, he rubs the back of his neck. "I am so fucking sorry. That's Barbara. I should've mentioned her earlier."

I tilt my head and eye the kitchen counters. "Is Barbara another sourdough starter? One that meows? That sounds like a recipe for a lethal food-borne illness."

He barks out a laugh. "No. She's my cat. She can stay with my mom if you're allergic or don't like her." His tone is earnest, comforting.

I can't help but melt a little in response. "Of course she can stay here. I love cats."

The voice in the back of my head is back, screaming at me again. Because in reality, I loathe those miniature lions.

Beckett's face lights up. "Awesome. I'll find her so I can formally introduce you. I want you to be comfortable around one another. And if you change your mind, I'll have her stay with my mom, okay?"

As he takes off, my chest sinks a little. Since we discovered we were roommates, he's focused solely on my well-being, seemingly disregarding his own needs.

It's admirable and rare, but I can't help but feel guilty about it.

If I had to guess, Beckett was tucked away silently upstairs when I got home because he didn't want to be intrusive.

Hell, I didn't even know we were neighbors as kids. Of course he was out of sight upstairs like a shy ghost hiding from the world.

Earlier, he was so willing to find another place to stay, willing to change his whole plan for me.

My heart sinks. Yes, I hate cats. But Beckett lives here too, and he should feel comfortable in his own home. He shouldn't feel like he has to hole himself away upstairs or pawn his cat off on his mom.

He reappears a moment later, wearing an eager smile and holding an orange cat with pale stripes and amber eyes.

Taking a hesitant step forward, I inspect the furry feline. When our eyes connect, I find nothing but irritated judgment.

Then she hisses at me.

The orange furball *hisses* at me like I've scorned her in a past life.

This cat will be my demise.

Chapter Eleven

Beckett

This woman is not a cat person.

It's obvious from the cute furrow between her brows and the uneasiness swimming in her eyes. All I can do is hope she and Barbara will warm up to one another.

"Oh. Wow. She's so. . .*sweet*," Joey says, her pitch a little too high.

It takes all my strength not to laugh. "I promise you, she's very nice."

Barbara uses that moment to hiss at Joey *again*, sending the woman stumbling back a step.

With a grunt, I look down at my cat and then back at Joey. "Um. Maybe I'll just—"

"No! No. It's probably me. Cats are like horses, right? They can sense fear?"

"Are you afraid of cats?"

"No. Yes. Probably. *I don't know*." Joey throws her hands

up, then lets them fall against her thighs with a slap. "My parents adopted a cat when I was a kid, and he was great and all. But—" She lets out a defeated sigh.

"But what?"

"He kept bringing dead birds. My parents swore they were gifts. That it meant he liked me, but it made me so sad," she sputters.

My heart plummets. "Oh, don't worry—"

"No." She puts her hand up. "I'm dramatic and possibly over-emotional. But that doesn't mean I'm weak." She nods once. "I can handle this." She mutters the last part, like she's giving herself a mental pep talk. She studies Barbara again, her lip caught between her teeth, then looks up at me. "You think I'm crazy, don't you?"

I press my lips together, suppressing the smile that's mere seconds from emerging. How is it that she's both so ridiculous and so charming? "I wouldn't specifically use 'crazy.' I think 'eccentric' is more fitting." I keep my tone light and teasing, hoping like hell she doesn't think I'm mocking her.

She crosses her arms and pops one hip out. "Now you're just being nice." Despite the stance and the narrowed eyes, a hint of a smirk plays at her plush lips.

Amusement rolls through me. "If it's any comfort, Barbara has never brought me anything dead. Or alive, for that matter." I set my cat on the ground, and she cautiously pads over to Joey, sniffs her colorful sock-covered feet, and walks away.

"That wasn't so bad, was it?" I ask, unable to hide my amusement.

Joey exhales a relieved breath, her shoulders relaxing. "I thought she was going to bite my toe off."

Head cocked to one side, I grin. "I'm not sure cats do that."

"I once read of a cat who ate its owner," she blurts, her dark eyes wide.

"Yes, because that owner was found dead, and the cat had no other food source." A smirk tugs at my lips. "I think any animal would do that."

"Fine. You're right," she huffs, scuffling into the kitchen.

Feeling daring now that we've fallen into this banter, I follow her. "Have you eaten dinner yet?"

"No," she says over her shoulder. "And if you're asking because you're concerned about my weird behavior, then I'll break it to you now. This isn't about hunger. Unfortunately, this is how I always am."

Unfortunately?

My chest pinches. I happen to like her personality, though I'm not sure how she'd feel if I admitted that.

She hunches over a bag on the counter, riffling through it. "Figured I'd grab a snack and get ready for bed. I have to be up early tomorrow."

I shuffle closer and peer into the bag. It's filled with miscellaneous snack foods, including fruit snacks, pretzels, and crackers.

"You can't just eat snacks." I nod at the bag. "Let me make you something real quick."

She stops her rummaging and peers up at me, lips parted. "You want to make me dinner?"

"You need to eat more than snack foods, Josephine." I pull out a stool from the kitchen island and pat it. "Take a seat and tell me about yourself. Might as well get to know each other, since we'll be roommates for the next ninety days." I give her a playful wink.

With a quiet chuckle, she takes a seat. "That's a very bartender-y thing to say. Let me guess, you tended bar through college?"

I bark out a laugh. "Oh god no. I'm too anxious for that. All those people? All that small talk? Plus alcohol? That's my personal hell."

Surprise flickers across her face. "Seriously? You're a nurse. Don't you have to be good with people and small talk?"

Forearms on the counter, I edge forward and catch her eye. "That's different. I have a purpose. To help the patient. Not entertain them. I may come off as awkward or quiet or even unfriendly, but it's because I have—"

"Social anxiety," Joey finishes for me. "My sister does too, though it's pretty mild. And to be honest, you don't give off unfriendly vibes."

Relief settles over me. I hated to think she'd see me as an aloof, unapproachable guy. In reality, I'm hung up on what she thinks of me. More often than not, my nerves render me speechless and my brain betrays me. Like the day our leashes got tangled on the sidewalk.

But maybe she sees past that. Maybe, for once, I've met a person who can look deeper.

After opening half the cabinets in the kitchen, I find a pan, then I pull the ingredients for grilled cheese from the fridge.

"Food allergies?" I ask. "Intolerances? Do you have an EpiPen?"

She presses her lips together, suppressing a smile. "Nope."

My stomach sinks. Maybe I was wrong. Maybe she'll write me off like everyone else has. "What's so funny?"

"Nothing at all," she replies cooly, fiddling with the sleeves of her soft gray cardigan.

I swallow past the lump in my throat. "I don't believe you."

"That's good, you shouldn't." She winks at me.

Instantly, my fears are erased. She's not judging. She's having a good time. As the tips of my ears heat, I spin away so she doesn't see me blushing.

"Start from the beginning. Who is Joey?" I ask from the stove, glancing at her over my shoulder.

"I was born in 1994 to wonderful parents, Catherine and Jonathan Thorne—"

I turn around, propping a hip on the counter. "Okay, Miss Sarcasm. Not that far back. Fast forward to more recent lore."

She lifts one shoulder. "You said start from the beginning." Her voice drops a touch lower with a hint of seduction. "I was just doing what you told me to do."

As soon as those words leave her lips, they have a clear effect on me. The spatula falls from my hand and clatters to the floor, my whole body heating with embarrassment. Shit.

Joey giggles with a mischievous glint in her eye.

Saying a silent prayer, I pick up the spatula and toss it into the sink.

Universe, please give me the strength to get through the next three months with this fiery woman unscathed and without a broken heart.

"In all seriousness," she says, "I grew up in Hemlock. Moved away for college, got a couple of degrees. Since then, I've been traveling. I love the feeling of not being tied to one place."

I raise my brows. "A couple degrees?"

"Yep. I have my bachelor's and master's, both in the arts —graduated top of the class. I even had those fancy little cord things. My advisor practically begged me to shoot for my PhD, but I needed a break." She shrugs dismissively.

The woman acts like her accolades are no big deal. When in fact, all she's done is incredibly impressive.

"Anywho," she goes on, "I've always loved art. Creating, observing, studying. All aspects of it. I used to sketch constantly."

She goes quiet then, so I peer over my shoulder.

She's slumped against the counter, her lips turned down. "I'm not sure why I stopped," she murmurs.

My chest aches for her, but I don't have the first clue how to respond.

Is this why I'm drawn to her? Because at her core, she's an artist? Because she's my complete opposite? I could see it.

It's refreshing, really.

I turn back to the pan and focus on the sandwich. "What do you do now?"

"I'm a brand designer. Since it's mostly remote, it's the perfect fit, really. I can still travel. But occasionally we're required to come in for major projects. Hence why I'll be here for the next few months."

Swiftly, I grab a plate from the cabinet and slide the sandwich onto it. When I turn around to give it to her, she frowns.

"What?" I ask. "You don't like grilled cheese?"

"It's not that. It's just..." She huffs a breath. "I eat mine with ketchup and I don't think we have any."

I shudder. "That is repulsive."

Jaw dropping, she puts her hands up. "Whoa. Whoa. Whoa. Do you see me shitting on your life choices?"

I put my own hands up, matching her posture. "I'm not shitting on them. I'm only—"

"Judging them?" She lifts a single dark eyebrow.

I shake my head hard enough to make my neck pop. "Not judging. Just processing."

With a chuckle, I make my way over to the fridge. When I pull out a bottle of ketchup and set it next to her plate, she looks up at me with wide eyes.

"I went to the grocery store while you were gone."

"I'm sorry about that." Joey buries her face in her hands, her shoulders rounding. "I shouldn't have left you alone so abruptly. I just wasn't expecting anyone else to be here, and it threw me."

"There's absolutely nothing to be sorry for."

"I was rude." Her hands muffle her voice.

Gently, I grasp her delicate wrists and pull them away from her face. "Don't apologize," I say, keeping my voice low and reassuring. "I would've bolted too if a strange man appeared in my house."

She laughs, the sound like wind chimes on a breezy summer afternoon, and threads her fingers through her hair, making the long strands tumble perfectly over her shoulders. Then she looks down at where I'm still clasping one of her wrists, and her cheeks go pink.

With a sharp breath, I pull my hand away and drop it to my side. I can't help but flex it, still soaking in the warmth of her smooth skin.

She takes a bite of her sandwich, and while she eats, I pull out another stool. As I sit, she gives me a perplexed look.

"What's the matter? Is it bad?" I ask.

"No." She swallows, then clears her throat. "I'm wondering why you aren't eating."

"Oh. I ate earlier."

A flicker of surprise flashes in her large brown eyes. "You didn't have to go to all this effort for me," she says, her words soft. "I'm not worth the hassle, but thank you." Her tone is teasing, self-deprecating, yet, I have a sinking feeling that it goes much deeper than that.

I want nothing more than to wrap her hands in mine and reassure her that it wasn't a hassle. If anything, I wanted to do it. But rather than touch her again, I say, "It was no hassle at all."

She shifts, her teeth sinking into her lip, and eyes me. "Since you know my life story.. . .sort of. Tell me a bit more about you."

She dips the corner of her sandwich in ketchup, and I desperately try not to grimace.

"Tell me about you without judging me for my condiment choice." As she takes a bite, she playfully rolls her eyes.

"I was born on a cold January morning in 1992 to my loving mother, Dana Hart—"

She rears back. "Dude. Come up with your own clever intro." She lets out a playful laugh. "Actually, I have a better idea. Rapid fire questions. Ready?"

My chest pinches. Icebreakers? An introvert's worst nightmare. But. . . "Do I have a choice?"

"Nope."

I sigh and resign myself to the game. I'm not great at talking about myself, but for her, I'll try. "Hit me with them."

"Why travel nursing?"

I rub the back of my neck, soothing the tense muscles there. "My mom was a nurse. And I've always looked up to her. For the travel part, I guess staying in one spot for too long makes my eye twitch. I love seeing new places. So I can be on the coast for a few months, then find myself in the desert. I like a little bit of snow, but I don't want to endure entire winters."

She nods thoughtfully. "Great answer. Favorite national park?"

"Joshua Tree." The answer comes without hesitation.

She stops chewing, her eyes narrowing in on me. "Mine too. Interesting. Zodiac sign?"

"Aquarius."

"Leo," she replies.

"You're wondering if the stars think we'd get along, aren't you?"

She waves me off. "Nah. I wouldn't do that." She hums, her attention drifting. "Not in front of you, at least. So, siblings?"

"Only child."

"Parents?"

"Just my mom."

She tilts her head to the side. "Where's your dad?"

"He left when I was six weeks old." A knot forms in my stomach just like it does every time I talk about my father. "I guess you could say I have daddy issues."

A smirk tugs at the corners of her cheek. "You have daddy issues." She points to me and then points a finger back at her. "And both my parents are dead. Should we attend a therapy session together as a roommate bonding activity?"

I nod, my mood lifting immediately. "Nothing says everlasting friendship like unloading our trauma on each other," I quip.

"Sounds like a solid base for the perfect friendship." She lets out an over-dramatic sigh. "You're exactly my type of guy."

My type of guy.

My heart clenches and those words bounce around in my

brain. She's only making light of the situation, but heat creeps up my cheeks anyway.

If only I really was.

"Enough of the depressing stuff." She takes another bite of ketchup-covered grilled cheese. "Tell me about a movie that makes you cry uncontrollably."

"*That's* less depressing?"

She sits back in her chair. "Huh. Yeah, I guess you're right." With a final bite of her sandwich, she scans the kitchen like she's thinking of another question. "Okay," she finally says. "Tell me something embarrassing that's happened to you."

"Oh. So we're jumping from depressing to mortifying. Got it." I bark out a laugh, and she joins in. "Fine. A few months ago, I asked a patient if they were excited to go home."

She leans in, wearing a confused frown. "What's embarrassing about that?"

I rub my hand down my stubbled jaw, the memory making my chest tight. "The guy had been brought in from the nearby prison."

She winces. "Oh my fucking god."

Head dropped back, I squeeze my eyes shut. "It kept me awake at night for weeks."

"And now I'm suffering from second-hand embarrassment." Her shoulders shake with laughter.

"It rivals that time I told a guy it was nice of his mom to come with him."

"Please don't say it."

I can't help but shudder at the memory, my shoulders hunching. "It was his wife."

Joey breaks into uncontrollable laughter so violent she

nearly falls off her stool. "Jesus, Beckett." Standing, she picks up her plate.

I stand too, reaching for the dish. "Here, I got that." Our fingers brush, and at the sensation, my heart stills.

"No way," she says, her voice quiet. "You've done so much for me already. It's the least I can do."

Shaking my head, I take it from her. "I melted a slice of cheese between two slices of toasted bread."

With a heavy sigh, she sits again. "Fine. Fine. I'm too tired to disagree."

I do a quick sweep of the kitchen, tidying up the mostly spotless space, searching for any excuse to keep this moment between us from ending. "Are you not going to tell me something embarrassing about yourself?"

She scoffs. "Absolutely not. You've seen me passed out and disoriented." Leaning back, she wraps her cardigan tighter around her body. "Now *that's* been keeping me up at night."

My heart thumps against my rib cage. "You have nothing to be embarrassed about."

"Are you going to tell me it 'happens all the time' to make me feel better too?"

"No." I shake my head. "Because a blind dog knocking a person from a chair is not a common occurrence."

"At least you're honest."

When she yawns, I admit defeat. It's late. She's probably exhausted, and now I feel guilty for keeping her up when she should be asleep.

"We should get to bed. You need your rest." I shuffle to the light switch and flip it, shrouding us in darkness except for the faint glow from the light upstairs, casting jagged shadows down the staircase.

She yawns again, sliding off the chair, and pads toward her bedroom. "You're probably right. Good night. I look forward to more embarrassing stories from you."

I let out a sheepish laugh, running my fingers through my hair. "Wait until I tell you about how I accidentally got caught up in a biker gang on my way home from work one day."

Joey rubs her tired eyes, but when my words register, she perks up, her exhaustion dissolving instantly. "Nope. I can't wait for that. Tell me. Now."

"Nope. You've used up all your Daily Beckett Facts. You'll have to wait until tomorrow." I wink.

I don't know what's gotten into me tonight. This boldness is unfamiliar yet welcome.

Joey's peculiar humor and charm aligns perfectly with my own oddities. Already, I feel like I've known her for years—that's how effortless it is with her.

We assess one another in the darkness for a moment too long. Without a single word, we share a knowing smile.

Beckett's Journal

April 9

When I find myself on the same wavelength as another person, the unspoken, comforting connection is indescribable. Even though I can't always put words to it, I can feel it in the depths of my mind and soul.

Like a key clicking into place after I've tried a dozen that didn't fit.

It's how I feel with Joey. It seems strange that it could happen so soon. Can a connection plant and root itself in such a short amount of time? I caught myself wondering that as I watched her across the kitchen island. The way she brushed her silky hair back behind her ears and the shy flush that crept over her when she smiled at me. Taking care of her tonight felt so unbelievably natural and easy. Something so simple gave me so much satisfaction.

I find myself in an internal war with my emotions. Debating whether I should keep these feelings close to my

*heart and see how our relationship unfolds or bury them so
deep they'll be impossible to find.*

Read Receipts

BECKETT

Hey. You forgot your laundry in the dryer. Is it okay if I take it out and put mine in?

JOEY

Go for it!

BECKETT

Thumbs-up emoji

BECKETT

I put the dishes in the dishwasher.

JOEY

Hero. I forgot to load it last night. I'm SO sorry.

BECKETT

Nothing to be sorry for.

JOEY

I heard you crash into something last night
when you came home, so I left the small
lamp on tonight.

I forget how dark it gets in the forest. Sorry
about that.

BECKETT

You don't need to apologize.

JOEY

I think I do. Sounded like you took a tumble
out there.

You're feeling embarrassed, aren't you?

BECKETT

Yep.

JOEY

I'll stop texting now. Enjoy work. Stay
hydrated!

BECKETT

Why is there a squirrel waiting patiently on
the ledge outside the kitchen window?

I've seen it there the last three days.

JOEY

I plead the fifth.

BECKETT

Have you been feeding it?

JOEY

See my previous message.

BECKETT

Joey. . .

JOEY

Her name is Phoebe.

And she likes pretzel sticks.

JOEY

Barbara swats my ankle every time I walk past her.

BECKETT

She wants to play.

JOEY

Are you sure? Because every time I yelp, she looks proud of herself.

BECKETT

Better sleep with your door locked tonight, then.

JOEY

WHAT?!

BECKETT

I made a batch of cookies last night. Feel free to have some.

JOEY

So that's what I smelled at 1am? I thought I was dreaming.

BECKETT

I had a stressful day at work and wanted something sweet.

JOEY

I'm sorry your day was stressful. . .

But I'm really fucking excited for cookies.

BECKETT

:)

JOEY

Proof of life?

It's been 72 hours and I'm tempted to send out a search party.

BECKETT

Thumbs-up selfie

JOEY

Has anyone ever told you that your eyes are hex color #556B2F?

BECKETT

. . .I can't say anyone has.

JOEY

Did I make things weird?

I made things weird. It's been an hour since you last replied.

BECKETT

Sorry. I was removing something from a place it had no business being in to begin with.

JOEY

Yikes.

                                                  BECKETT

                                                    Exactly.

                                              But thank you.

                                        For the compliment.

JOEY

*Photo of Barbara sleeping in a cardboard
box*

I almost recycled your cat.

                                                  BECKETT

                                    Please don't do that.

JOEY

Photo of Barbara's squished face.

This cannot be comfortable.

                                                  BECKETT

                          Of course it isn't. It's an Amazon box.

JOEY

Hold up. Your cat has a preferred type of
cardboard box?

                                                  BECKETT

                          She prefers a nice, cozy banana box.

JOEY

That's oddly specific.

                                                  BECKETT

                          Barbara's a sophisticated cat with
                          sophisticated needs.

JOEY

I'm second-guessing living with you
two now.

BECKETT

Lol.

JOEY

Are you actually laughing or is that because
you don't know what else to say?

BECKETT

Actually laughing.

JOEY

Good. :)

BECKETT

Everything okay?

JOEY

Yes.

No.

Sorry for leaving papers scattered all over
the kitchen island.

BECKETT

No worries. I left them there in case there's
a method to your madness.

JOEY

This client is driving me insane and I was
running late this morning, so I left in a hurry.

BECKETT

Anything I can do to help?

JOEY

Find a cure for asshole behavior?

BECKETT

On it. I'll talk to a few of the docs here.

JOEY

You sure do know how to make a girl swoon.

BECKETT

I left the last cookie for you.

JOEY

I was leaving it for you!

They were excellent, by the way.

BECKETT

When I get home tonight, you better have eaten it.

JOEY

Only if you make more.

BECKETT

Of course I will.

Any flavor requests?

JOEY

Surprise me. :)

BECKETT

Why are there clothes scattered all over the living room?

JOEY

Ugh. Everything looked wrong this morning. Felt wrong too.

And I forgot to do my laundry.

BECKETT

Want me to throw your clothes in the washer?

JOEY

You'd do that?

BECKETT

I'd be happy to.

By the way, whatever you're wearing, I'm sure you look beautiful.

JOEY

Did you organize the pantry?

BECKETT

Yes.

JOEY

By food group AND in alphabetical order?

BECKETT

Yes.

Speaking of the pantry, I found five kinds of gummy bears in there.

JOEY

Variety is the spice of life, Beckett.

BECKETT

I can see that.

JOEY

Who knows, you may like it if I shake up
your routine a little . . .

BECKETT

What if I already do?

JOEY

Are you implying that you ate some of my
gummy bears? Breaking a roommate rule?

BECKETT

Agatha mysteriously moved locations in the
kitchen.

And Barbara doesn't have thumbs.

JOEY

Dammit.

BECKETT

Don't worry, I replaced your gummy bears
with two new bags.

JOEY

And I may have fed Agatha because you
forgot.

She was looking EXTRA bubbly.

BECKETT

:)

BECKETT

You left your sweater on the couch last
night. I hung it on your doorknob.

JOEY

Did you smell it?

BECKETT

Uh. . .no.

That would be weird.

JOEY

Seems like a missed opportunity if you ask
me. ;)

Chapter Twelve

Joey

Living with Beckett hasn't been bad.

At all.

In fact, I'd say he's one of the better roommates I've had.

We've lived together for a couple of weeks, and sometimes I forget he's even there. The man rarely makes himself known. At one point, after three days without proof of life, I texted him asking if he'd moved out. I even asked him if he needed me to feed Barbara or his sourdough starter, Agatha, because I was *that* concerned.

When I do notice signs of his existence, it's usually a light on upstairs or the gentle creaking of the wooden floors above my room while I'm lying in bed, restlessly staring at the ceiling.

I can't help but wonder what he does so late at night. . .

No, I won't allow myself down that rabbit hole of thinking. If I do, I fear I'll never come back out of it.

When I do see him—fleetingly—he's incredibly kind and respectful.

He even offered to do my laundry when I was overwhelmed after working late and had forgotten to wash my clothes.

Another evening, he offered to make dinner for me again. When I hesitated and ultimately declined because I didn't want to be a burden, I swear his forest green eyes dropped with a hint of sadness. That sight alone made me never want to deny him again.

Next time he offers to make me dinner, I'll eagerly accept. Unfortunately, this leads me to my next dilemma. . .

Under absolutely no circumstances am I allowed to fall for my roommate.

But he makes it damn near impossible when he's such a good human.

Then again, he's probably like that with everyone. Like he'd give a stranger the shirt off his back in the middle of a snowstorm, then pretend he's not freezing so that stranger doesn't feel so bad.

Naturally, that makes me like him even more. The cherry on top of his warm and altruistic personality is the lethal combination of his jet-black motorcycle, the swirling ink over his large body, and the love he has for his cat.

Oh. And his biceps. I may or may not have fantasized about sinking my teeth into them on more than one occasion.

Undoubtedly, I'm drawn to him like bees to honey. And I'm certain that beneath the surface, there's another side of him waiting to claw itself out.

That first night in the kitchen, when he made grilled cheese for me, he relaxed a bit more. Especially since it was just the two of us.

Maybe it's the empath in me, but I tend to take socially anxious people under my wing. I know what it feels like to be excluded and it hurts when I notice others being painted as unapproachable when often, they're just nervous.

Not that Beckett is unapproachable. He's kind and soft-hearted. Thoughtful and introspective.

Interestingly enough, I've discovered that we're opposites in an eerily similar way.

We're both travelers, semi-loners, and independent to a fault. But while he's reserved and guarded—I can practically feel the wall he has up—I wear my heart on both sleeves with a neon sign above my head that says *very likely to cry if you look at me wrong*.

Granted, we're only here for a short time, and yes, while the idea of having a bit of fun is tempting, I'm not in the market to get my heart broken. I'm too old and tired to play that game. In my experience, people tend to drift away from me when they meet someone else.

Someone who isn't too much.

Someone who has their life more together.

Someone less *forgettable*.

And I'm not emotionally stable enough to go through all that heartache and self-doubt right now. I've wasted too many nights spiraling down the endless tunnel of my thoughts. Wondering what I could've done to keep some person close to me. Going over and over every single interaction with them, every text message, every conversation. Analyzing and agonizing over every verbal and nonverbal cue. Torturing myself, hoping to find the crack that ultimately led to the shattering of our relationship.

On a lighter note, I'm 99 percent certain that I'm not Beckett's type.

I can be dramatic, scatterbrained, and mildly impulsive. Whereas he's cautious, mindful, and stoic. I wear clothes in every color and pattern imaginable while Beckett seems to be allergic to colors other than black and gray. I can survive off coffee and spite, and I'm pretty sure he needs three solid, protein-packed meals a day.

The very definition of opposites, if you ask me.

An everlasting love story for the ages? Probably not. I'm more likely to get a shark bite at an aquarium.

Yawning, I slink down into the driver's seat and rest my head on the cushion. It's way too early to be at the office. I was so worried I'd miss my first meeting of the day that I'm now sitting in the parking lot twenty minutes early.

Sighing, I take a sip of my coffee and reach for my all-time favorite way to pass time and turn my brain off.

A crossword puzzle.

Sure, I could use my phone or do those fancy ones from prestigious newspapers. But there's something comforting about holding the floppy book in hand and scribbling out letters with a dried-out pen.

I sit up and tuck one leg under the other, then prop my crossword puzzle up on my steering wheel.

Anxiety wraps around me like a suffocating blanket this morning. A knot of dread coils in my stomach at just the thought of meeting with my nemesis, Norma. It's a one-on-one meeting, meaning I'm going in with no backup and no armor. My only resources are myself and my quickly dwindling optimistic spirit.

I chant my daily mantra multiple times in my head: *Don't be a smartass today. You need this job.*

I'm locked in on this puzzle, deep in thought about a

seven-letter word for a commonly used kitchen item that's not a toaster.

Steamer? Nope.

Blender? Doesn't work with the letters already in place.

A hard knock on my van window spooks me, and I jolt, nearly spilling my coffee all over myself.

"Sorry." Max winces. "But I've been standing here like a creep trying to get your attention." His voice is muffled through the thick window, his apologetic expression makes it tough to be mad at him.

Closing my eyes, I suck in a steadying breath. It's not his fault that I'm extra jumpy this morning. I gather my stuff from my passenger seat, loading myself down with three beverages, four notebooks, an extra jacket, and enough snacks to feed a little league team after practice.

Max, on the other hand, only has a sleek laptop case and a single coffee. He gives me a slow once-over, a brow arching as he takes in all my *things*.

Max unsuccessfully tries to hide his amusement. "Looks like you're ready for anything. A food shortage, a power outage, a snowstorm in the middle of spring."

I balk at his comment. "I didn't know it was a crime to be prepared," I say as we cross the parking lot. "Next time there's a flood, we'll see if I allow you to borrow the backup rain boots in my van."

We're laughing as we step across the threshold into our office building. Once inside, we settle into our space, a sprawling open floor plan laid out before us. Each of the long tables lined up in neat rows is topped with three large desktop computers evenly spaced out. The bright morning light streams through the floor-to-ceiling windows at the back of the room, making the polished wood shine and casting the space in an airy glow. It's the perfect atmosphere for a creative agency.

Though pretty soon, Nemesis Norma will be here to dim the warm glow. From our previous meetings and email correspondences, the woman is a walking, talking, hazardous storm, ready to wreak havoc wherever she goes.

"By the way, I'm sorry I can't play defense for you in your meeting with Droplet," Max says, rolling his chair closer to me.

Turning to him, I wave my hand. "No worries at all. I'll be fine."

I am very much worrying and I do not think I'll be fine.

"Good. I'll do my best to be there next time, I promise." He rolls back over to his desk, slips a set of headphones on, and gets to work typing at his desktop.

The office is so quiet I can practically hear my nervous heart hammering in my chest. I have fifteen minutes until she arrives, so I scurry my overprepared self into the conference room to set up. The absolute last thing I need is for technology to fail me in front of an already displeased client.

Once the projector is up and running, I pull up my presentation of ideas for Droplet's branding. Then I go over my notes and hastily run through the presentation one last time, ensuring I didn't miss anything important.

Mood board of ideas and inspiration? Check.

Mock designs even though they gave me zero direction? Check.

Three color palettes because I'm paranoid? Check.

A couple of minutes before our designated meeting time, the ominous sound of heels clacking on the floor starts up and slowly gets louder. Every step makes my heart pound forcefully in my chest. I've always been confident in my abilities, and my past clients have been more than satisfied with the branding I've produced for them. Some have even reached out to me privately, asking me to take on freelance projects for their side hobbies, so I've done my fair share of work for podcasters, photographers, and bloggers as well.

But Norma is in a category of her own. Our emails have been. . .not great. No matter what I say, she's unhappy.

It's like she wants me to fail at this project, which makes zero sense. Why would anyone deliberately undermine their own company's rebranding efforts?

The door squeaks open, and the woman who has haunted my dreams for the last week steps in.

Steeling my spine, I slap on a smile and coolly walk over to her. With any luck, I'm giving off a carefree, breezy vibe. But on the inside, I'm trembling like a Chihuahua without a sweater.

That's how nervous I am.

"Hi, Norma. So nice to see you again." I hold out my hand.

Rather than shake it, she gives me a vacant look and sighs. "Wish I could say the same."

Oh. Okay. Wow. I guess this is how it'll be today.

The receptionist stands in the doorway, eyes locked with mine, sending me a sympathetic look and mouthing *good luck.*

As Norma settles at the table, I take a deep breath, fighting the defeat already creeping into my bones. Then I spin around, head high, and stride to my laptop.

"Let's jump in, shall we?"

Norma gives me a once-over, a sneer on her face.

My stomach sinks. "Uh. Is something wrong?"

She clears her throat. "Shouldn't you be wearing something more professional when meeting with a client? Maybe a pair of slacks? Heels?"

Suddenly feeling insecure, I glance down at my long, flowy dress. It's navy blue with small white flowers on it, and I pulled a thick gray knit cardigan over it this morning. I'm not showing an ounce of cleavage or a peek of shoulder.

Hell, I'm not even showing an ankle because I'm wearing my tall suede boots.

Unease swirls in my stomach. What's this woman's deal? What decade does she think we're living in?

"Thank you for your concern, but we're here to discuss Droplet. Not my clothes," I reply firmly. What I really want to say is *Lady, you and your heels can get fucked.*

Norma gives a displeased hum. "Very well then. Let's proceed."

I give a curt nod. "Based on the approved design brief, I've come up with a couple of options for logos, typography, and color palettes. Taking into consideration your target audience, I kept the design traditional, but still fresh."

She hums, focus fixed on the slide on the screen. "For colors, I was thinking black and white. To keep it simple. I'm not a fan of the green-and-white color scheme."

A huff of air escapes my lungs. Seriously? A black-and-white scheme will make them blend in with their competitors. Almost every insulated water bottle company is using black and white, from websites and print materials, to logos and packaging. I was under the impression they wanted to stand out.

Suddenly, I'm being pulled in two different directions, and I don't like it.

But I give her a hesitant nod. "Sure, I can certainly do that."

The unease in my stomach only grows, making it impossible to ignore. I try to push it aside and not allow it to cloud my judgment, but it's becoming near impossible.

After this presentation, I'm going to need a stiff drink, a hard cry, and copious amounts of sour candy for dinner.

Norma is officially the client from hell.

Chapter Thirteen

Beckett

JOEY
You know what time it is?

Uhh. 10:30pm?

JOEY
Daily Beckett Fact time.

I actually enjoy flossing.

JOEY
You're a dentist's wet dream, aren't you?

I do get a slight high when they mention that I have good oral hygiene.

JOEY
You're an odd one.

I kinda like it.

Joey and I haven't seen each other much in the couple of weeks we've been roommates. My work schedule has been outrageous—we've been short staffed since the flu hit many of the nurses in our unit. Every night, I come home later than the evening before.

My heart quietly yearns to spend more time with her. Some nights, I hang out in the living room, hoping she'll come out of her room. So far, we've mostly just texted back and forth. Each message acts as a tiny window into each other's world, allowing us to gradually reveal bits and pieces of ourselves.

On the rare evenings we do see each other, we'll eat dinner at the kitchen island. The warm glow of the pendant lights creates a cozy atmosphere as we talk about everything from our mundane days to embarrassing childhood stories. So far, nothing has been off limits.

Joey makes me feel like it's okay to be myself.

To be Beckett.

Not nurse Beckett. Not boring Beckett. Not bashful Beckett.

I'm simply *Beckett* to her.

On the drive home from my shift, the low hum of my bike's engine helps me unwind from the day. The trees on either side of the road are a dark green blur. The sky is turning indigo as the sun sets in the distance.

The lights in the cottage are off, but there's a small orange flicker coming from the backyard. My eyes burn from wearing contacts all day, making it hard to make out the light's source, so I head that way and slide open the patio door. In the yard, Joey is sitting in front of a campfire.

Her back is to me, her shoulders trembling, and if I'm not

mistaken, she's sniffling. Heart in my throat, I set off towards her. My heavy boots thud down the patio stairs, and the leaves crunch beneath me as I approach her.

Over her shoulder, a crossword puzzle book comes into view. And from here, my suspicions are confirmed. She's crying, the flames from the fire highlighting the dampness on her cheeks.

"Ensconce," I blurt out.

Shrieking, Joey slaps a hand to her chest. "Holy mother of. . .you scared the shit out of me."

"S-sorry." My stomach sinks. "It looked like you were stuck on twenty-one across." I point at the tattered puzzle book.

She lets out a soft laugh, blotting her face with a tissue.

Heart wrenching at the sadness in her features, I crouch next to her. "Is everything okay?"

She searches my face, her brown eyes sad and her cheeks tearstained. "Yeah. Just had a few bad, *bad* days at work."

"Wanna talk about it?" Without thinking, I wipe at a stray tear rolling down her face with the pad of my thumb.

"Thanks." She sniffles, her voice trembling into a whisper. "But I'm too tired to talk about it. I think I'll head to bed early."

My chest aches, and the urge to take away her pain sweeps over me. "Did you eat?"

She shakes her head. "Too bummed out."

"Yikes. It was that bad, huh? I've been there." I keep my tone light, and I'm rewarded when the corner of her mouth kicks up. I place a reassuring hand on her knee. "Before you go to bed, how about we get a little food in you. I know you aren't hungry, but not eating will make you feel worse. And I'd rather you feel better."

She looks at me, the flickering of fire highlighting the exhaustion on her face. "You don't have to do that. I'm fully capable of feeding myself—"

I squeeze her knee, stopping her mid-sentence. "Josephine," I say, my tone firmer. "Let me feed you. I'm starving after my shift, so I've got to eat anyway. You've had a shitty day, so let me do this for you."

Joey's focus drops to her feet, and she lets out a hushed laugh. "Damn. I lucked out when I moved in with a nurse who can cook, didn't I?"

I let out a warm chuckle and pat her on the knee. She's already in pajamas, the fabric soft under my fingertips. As I rise, I extend my hand, offering a steady grip to help her stand.

Firelight sparkles in her eyes as she inspects it, then drags her focus to my face.

I can't help but drink her in like this. Disheveled auburn hair in a bun, red-rimmed eyes, and flushed cheeks.

All I can think about is how radiant she looks. Even now, when she's sad. The light inside her may be dimmed tonight, but it's not entirely extinguished. Beneath the sadness, I can still see flickers of the self-assured woman I've begun to admire.

With a wistful smile, she places her hand on mine.

I wrap my fingers around hers with a tender touch, relishing the smoothness of her warm skin. Joey isn't fragile —not even close. That's obvious to anyone. Still, something about the way the day has worn on her, the way she sits, makes her seem as breakable as porcelain. The overwhelming urge to take care of her hums under my skin.

I need to make sure she doesn't crack any more than she already has.

When she stands, I release her hand, but rather than doing the same, she tightens her grip, like a plea to not let her go.

So I don't. Instead, I lace my fingers through hers. Our hands become perfectly entwined like two missing puzzle pieces that have finally found their home.

In silence, we walk back to the cottage.

Once we step into the kitchen, she lets go of my hand, and I immediately feel the loss of her touch. Letting my hand fall to my side, I flex my fingers—not once, but twice — as if the sensation of her soft touch has been branded onto my skin. Leaving an indelible imprint not only on my hand, but on my heart.

I usher her to her usual seat at the island, then I gather supplies for dinner.

Our selection is limited tonight, but we have a full carton of eggs and an unopened package of bacon. There's also a loaf of bread on the counter. Fridge door open, I turn to her. "Is breakfast for dinner okay?"

Joey is sitting at the kitchen island, looking down at her lap. She doesn't seem to notice Barbara, sitting across the island, flicking her tail back and forth and conspiring to torment my roommate.

"Yeah, that sounds great. Thank you." She looks up at me with a sad smile. Only then does she acknowledge Barbara. Quickly, the sadness turns to fear. "Not today, cat. I'm not in the mood. Terrorize me tomorrow, when I'm less emotionally weak."

In a shocking turn of events, Barbara listens. She hops off the island and saunters up the stairs to the second floor.

Laughing, I pull out the eggs and bacon. "Ready to talk about what happened today?" I ask, as I set the ingredients near the stove.

"Not really," she mutters.

I spin around and cross my arms, giving her an incredulous look.

She nibbles on the inside of her lip, her attention fixed on me. I hold her gaze but remain silent, waiting.

"The bacon smells good," she finally says.

My lips twitch, but I regain control quickly. "Don't change the subject. You'll feel better if you get it out."

"Ugh. Fine. You win." She twirls a stray lock of hair. "I have a client who is on my ass twenty-four seven. They came to us for a new brand design, but for reasons unknown, she doesn't like me. Today she made a few unkind remarks—first about my clothes, then after the presentation, she mentioned my hair—"

"What's wrong with your hair?" I lay another strip of bacon in the pan, then fill a glass with water and set it in front of her.

"I don't know," she says as I turn back to the bacon. "She said I should fix it. That it doesn't look professional." She huffs out an exhausted breath. "I was so insecure about it all day long that I considered making an appointment to chop it off."

Spatula in hand, I whip around and point it at her. "Do not, under any circumstance, cut your hair."

The corners of her lips kick up. "I won't," she says quietly. "And to top it all off, she wants me to do a ton of edits and she isn't cooperative over email. She even gaslit me into thinking I didn't send her the design questions last week. I had to pull up the emails to confirm I had. And lo and behold, I sent multiple emails that she never responded to."

I rear back in disgust. "Seriously?"

Swallowing a large sip of water, she nods. "Yes. I'm going

to give her the benefit of the doubt," she says, rubbing her eyes, "and keep pushing forward."

I crack a few eggs over a bowl and begin to whisk them. "If it gets too bad, or if she continues to treat you like that, you should talk to someone about it. That's not how you should be treated in the workplace."

A heavy sigh escapes her. "I know. I will." Her shoulders sag. "Is it okay if we don't talk about this anymore? I want to forget today even happened."

My chest pinches in sympathy. "Of course. I'm sorry if talking about it made you uncomfortable. I thought maybe it could help."

"It did help. A lot." She sniffs. "I don't have many friends to talk about this stuff with. So I end up bottling it all in because I don't want to be a burden, and I end up. . ."

"Suffering in silence," I finish for her.

Her head snaps up. "Yeah. How did you know?"

"You're talking to a guy who is a pro at bottling up his feelings. My therapist suggested journaling and I've found it incredibly helpful." I pop two slices of sourdough I made earlier this week into the toaster and pull two plates out of the cabinet.

"Is that why you stay up so late after work sometimes? You're journaling?"

"Mm-hmm. It helps me unwind. And it allows me to process the bad days and remember the good ones." I butter the toasted slices of bread and set them on our plates. "Dinner is served." Smiling, I slide Joey's dinner in front of her. Then I drag the second barstool over, its legs scraping across the tile floor, and position it directly across from her.

I can't help it. I enjoy looking at her.

"Thank you. So much," she says, her eyes swimming with gratitude. "You didn't have to go through all this trouble."

"It was zero trouble at all. I *wanted* to do this for you, Josephine," I tell her, every word genuine. I need her to know that she has someone on her team. Someone who will sit and listen to her. I know what it feels to keep your emotions locked up tight. And I know that, inevitably, they come pouring out.

We're quiet as we eat, and when Joey is finished, she slides off her chair and picks up her plate.

Before she can walk away, I gently grasp her arm. "I got this. Go get some rest."

"What?" She frowns. "You worked all day, then cooked me a meal and acted as my sounding board. The least I can do is put these in the dishwasher. Don't fight me. I'm too stubborn to lose." With a wink, she gathers my fork and plate.

She winks at me.

It's a simple gesture, but it hits me in my chest anyway, leaving me momentarily speechless.

Much to her dismay, I help her clean up the kitchen by tossing discarded eggshells and napkins into the trash and wiping down the counters. I rinse out the dish cloth, and as I turn around, she bumps into my chest. I clutch her upper arms, steadying her.

"Oof! I'm so sorry," she says, her tone apologetic, her smile shy.

She looks a whole lot better than she did an hour ago. Her freckled cheeks are slightly flushed, and there's a sparkle in her eyes.

Words melt on my tongue as I take in every detail of her face. An unruly strand of her wavy hair has escaped from her bun. On instinct, I carefully tuck it behind her ear, letting my fingers linger a bit before I pull them away.

Her breath hitches at the gesture, and the color in her cheeks deepens.

Her lips part, then close. When she opens her mouth again, she stammers, "Th-thank you." She steps back, smoothing down her hair and clearing her throat. "I'm going to head to bed now. Thank you again. For everything." Head down, she slips past me.

I spin, chest tight. "Joey."

She spins around, brow furrowed.

Now I'm the one whose cheeks are heating. "If you ever need someone to talk to—about work, life, anything at all— I'm here, okay?"

Her shoulders sag and her expression brightens a fraction. With a couple of slow breaths, she studies me. There's an unforgettable look of gratitude shimmering in her eyes. "Same goes for you. We lonesome misfit travelers need to stick together."

"That we do." I wink. "Have a good night's sleep."

Once she's gone, I putter around the kitchen for a few minutes, feeding Barbara her daily banana. I've just started the dishwasher when Joey comes back out of her bedroom, her slippered feet scuffing across the hardwood floor.

When the sound stops but she doesn't speak, I peer over my shoulder and find her nibbling on the inside of her lip, her focus fixed on me, words threatening to spill out.

"Everything okay?" I ask, hanging the dish towel up.

"Are you off this weekend?" she asks, her brows slightly furrowed.

"Yeah. Why?" I respond with a dip of my chin.

"Want to do something together?" She wraps her over-sized sweater tighter around her, like she suddenly got a chill.

Her invitation catches me off guard, leaving me momentarily speechless.

"Actually, never mind," she hedges, eyes downcast. "You probably already have plans." With a self-deprecating chuckle, she flicks a small, dismissive wave. Then, abruptly, she spins on her heel and starts heading back down the hallway that leads to her room.

Warmth floods my cheeks and my tongue feels clumsy, making it hard to speak. "I-I'd love to do something. What did you have in mind?"

Stopping dead in her tracks, she whips around, her messy bun bouncing. "Wait. Really?"

"Yeah, really." I laugh, confusion and excitement warring inside me. *Who wouldn't want to spend time with her?*

She rolls her lips and sighs. "It's just. . .never mind. How about Friday? I can cook dinner."

"I have plans Friday evening, but how about Saturday?"

"Oh." Her head dips, but not before I catch the look of disappointment on her face. Though when she looks up again, her expression turns hopeful. "That works."

Before I can find the words to explain that I spend my Friday evenings with my mom watching cheesy romance movies, she's gone again, the door to her room shutting quietly behind her. Part of me wants to follow her and clear the air, but logic wins out. I want to respect her time. She's had a long day and needs her rest before work tomorrow.

Exhaling heavily, I slump into the chair in the living room and stare down the dark hallway at the sliver of light glowing beneath her door. Shadows dance across the hardwood floors as she gets ready for bed, and in a matter of minutes, the lights are off. My cue to head upstairs for the night.

Upstairs, I settle at my small desk overlooking the dark forest. Clear, inky sky stretches before me with only the moonlight illuminating my small writing nook. I turn on the lamp at the desk and begin journaling.

Beckett's Journal

April 23

Something shifted tonight. The connection between Joey and me is slowly strengthening, weaving a thread of kinship that feels unique to us. Tonight, when she asked if I'd like to do something this weekend, I swear my heart pounded relentlessly inside my chest. Is it a date? Or are we just hanging out as friends? Roommates?

Regardless of her reasoning, I'm almost certain I'd follow Joey anywhere just so I could spend more time with her.

Chapter Fourteen

Beckett

JOEY
I'm waiting. . .

For. . .?

JOEY
Being coy isn't very becoming, my dear.

Aren't you tired of these facts yet?

JOEY
Never.

I lay on the floor to decompress. I've been told it reduces stress and anxiety.

Which, as you know, I have no shortage of.

JOEY
Wanna lay on the ground together sometime after work?

Uhh. . .

"You? Going out on a weekend? Willingly?" my mom asks. "This roommate of yours seems like a good guy if he can get you out of your shell." Smiling, she strokes Barbara, who is sound asleep in her lap.

One would think it near impossible for a thirty-four-year-old man to blush, yet here I am. Joey has infiltrated every thought that passes through my mind. I keep my focus fixed on the TV, hoping my mom doesn't notice.

But I can feel her scrutiny, even as I will myself to get lost in yet another Nora Ephron movie. It's clear my mom can see the deep shade of crimson that's painting my cheeks. The first droplets of sweat gather at the back of my neck, threatening to betray me further.

My mom gasps. Realization strikes her that Joey isn't a guy. "Oh. My. God."

Drawing a breath, I look over at her. "Mom. Don't, or I'll put you in a nursing home."

"I didn't say anything." Her lips twitch. "And don't forget you promised you'd put me in one of those fancy assisted living facilities. The kind with a beach-front view."

With an exasperated sigh, I pinch the bridge of my nose. "You didn't have to say it. You're thinking about it. *Stop thinking about it.*"

"Is it so bad for a mother to want to see her son happy? Maybe find someone special?"

I rest my head back on the couch, closing my eyes. "Dana. I am happy. Real life is not like these over-the-top rom-coms,"

I say, nodding at the TV, where two characters are in the midst of professing their love to one another.

"First, don't *Dana* me. Second, you can be such a cynic."

I open my mouth to speak, but she puts her hand up to stop me.

"I know, I know. You've been burned one too many times. People are assholes, that's a given. But not *all* people." My mom gives me a pointed look. "Maybe I'm a hopeless romantic, but you deserve someone kind, understanding, and *patient.*"

A war rages inside me. The socially anxious part of my mind is preparing itself for every possible outcome when Joey and I are together. What if I say something stupid? What if I suddenly forget to speak? What if I need to leave early because I'm uncomfortable and she wants to stay? What if she decides I'm not worth the hassle? *Just like everyone else.*

The other part of me, though, remembers that being with Joey in the cottage is effortless. That I feel safe letting my guard down with her. When it's just us, we exist in our own safe bubble, just two overworked and overtired adults trying to navigate life one day at a time, having late-night chats and doing our best to lift one another up.

I don't know how she does it, but talking to her is as natural as breathing. Maybe it's the way she leans in when I'm telling a story or how she gives me her undivided attention. Or maybe it's the way her eyes sparkle with interest whenever she asks me a question.

She's a special woman, there's no doubt about that.

And that terrifies me. Yet it gives me hope at the same time.

But only until I remember that we're both only here temporarily.

Joey seems to bounce around from city to city often and randomly, whereas my moves are methodical, based on my contracts.

I long to ask her out, but in a few short months, we'll both be off to new places, and I can't see her free spirit having any interest in being confined to one place for months at a time. She said herself that she doesn't like to feel chained to one location. And I wholeheartedly respect that. She's choosing to live her life on her own terms, and she's nothing short of admirable.

My mom clears her throat, the sound pulling me back to the present. "Penny for your pensive thoughts, son?"

"Absolutely not."

She snorts a laugh. "Eh. Worth a shot."

BY THE TIME I get back to the cottage, it's dark out. On my way up the porch stairs, a calm, cool breeze rustles through the trees, causing a chill to run through me. As I step inside, I place Barbara on the floor. She scurries away, quickly disappearing from sight to some hidden alcove she must've found.

I really hope she's not hoarding random objects again. A few years ago, my socks started disappearing one at a time. About 90 percent of them had gone missing before I discovered Barbara buried in a stolen sock pile underneath my bed. When I found her, I jolted back a few feet out of fear because this mound of socks had two moving amber eyes and an orange tail.

I drop my keys into the bowl at the entryway table, then shrug off my leather jacket and hang it on the iron coatrack. It's eerily quiet inside, the only light coming from the small lamp on the entryway table, casting shadows that stretch across the wall.

A glow from the firepit out back catches my attention, and as I pad to the back door, I discover Joey outside, wrapped in a blanket.

On the patio, the cool night air hits my skin, making me wish I'd left my jacket on.

Joey's mostly shrouded in darkness, though the bright orange flames flickering in front of her beckon me closer.

"Liberosis," I say, as I settle down next to her in the second Adirondack chair.

Instead of shrieking like she did a few days ago, she only jerks with surprise. "Dude, you need to find a better way to make your presence known."

"Next time, instead of calling out crossword answers, I'll have Barbara greet you first."

Her eyes dart to mine. "On second thought, please continue sneaking up on me. You can even yell 'boo!' if you like."

I shake my head, chuckling. "You have the weirdest relationship with my cat."

Swiveling, she settles until her whole body faces me. Her eyes are wide with a mixture of surprise and intensity. "Yesterday, the whole time I was folding laundry, she stared at me unblinking and unmoving. Except for the occasional ear twitch. You know cats have thirty-two muscles in each ear, right? Freaky."

Her face is tinged pink from the warmth of the crackling fire. The vibrant orange glow dances across her delicate features, bringing out the kaleidoscope of warm shades in her auburn hair, reminding me of autumn leaves on a sunny day.

Autumn has always been my favorite season.

I give a thoughtful nod. "Unfortunately, she only does that to people whose toes she wants to gnaw on. The ear twitches mean she's ready to pounce."

She scoffs, turning her body back toward the fire. "You're not very funny." Despite her dismissal, she side-eyes me.

I look right back at her, trying my damndest not to break out in laughter.

She shakes her head, shoulders trembling with a giggle. "So," she drawls, her tone suddenly laced with hesitation, "how was your evening?"

Sighing, I settle into the chair and tip my head back to look at the dark sky. "You cannot judge me."

"I'm equal parts intrigued and terrified. Go on," she says, her eyes burning holes in the side of my face.

My mouth kicks up into a grin. "I was watching a silly rom-com movie with my mom."

Silence falls upon us, and when she says nothing, I turn toward her.

She's watching me, eyes round and jaw slack.

"You're judging me." I sigh, turning my attention back to the inky sky.

She hums thoughtfully. "A wise man once told me 'Not judging, just processing.'"

I can't help the laugh that tumbles out of me when she uses my own expression against me. "You're a clever girl, Josephine."

"I aim to please." She winks.

Blood rushes to my cheeks, making me damn thankful we're sitting in front of a raging fire.

Propping my ankle over my knee, I clear my throat. "You built this fire?"

"Nope. The man next door offered to start it for me in

exchange for pictures of my feet." She lets out a deep, wistful sigh. "An offer I couldn't refuse."

Rendered speechless, my head snaps in her direction. "What? Really? Joey, that's not—"

Giggling, she wraps the heavy blanket around her tighter. "Loosen up, buttercup. I was being facetious. Contrary to popular belief, my survival skills really aren't all that bad."

"Says the girl who lives off fruit snacks, espresso, and expired gummy vitamins." I huff, my tone deadpan despite the hint of humor beneath my words.

"I'm still alive, aren't I?"

"When's the last time you got a full panel of bloodwork done?"

She surveys me, mischief flickering in her expression. Then she leans closer, her voice low and sultry. "You know, when you get all nurse-y on me, a tingle runs up my spine."

I swallow thickly. My throat constricts as my focus snags on her full lips—that look a little too enticing right now— before darting up to meet her mesmerizing eyes.

I'm not making it out of this cottage alive. Cause of death: the wild woman sitting beside me.

When I finally snap out of it, Joey's smirking. Of course she is. Because, naturally, my brain forgot how to respond when a woman showed interest in me, especially when I'm already smitten with said woman.

If I'm not careful, Joey *will* become my undoing.

"Cat got your tongue? Or should I say Barbara got your tongue?" she jokes.

The silence returns, words escaping me. Most people would be uncomfortable, yet Joey takes it as a challenge and keeps pushing forward, embracing it.

And I can't help but hope that this means she's taking a chance on me. Daring to see what lies beneath my quiet exterior. Understanding that there are pieces of me that others often overlook because they aren't patient enough to uncover them.

"You could say that," I murmur, a rush of nerves making its way through me.

We fall into silence again, both watching the crackling fire, letting it warm us as the evening temperature continues to drop.

I sink into my chair, my muscles relaxing further. I'm awash in a sense of safety. Being out here, with Joey, feels good. It feels *right*.

"My sister's boyfriend is holding an open mic night at his coffee shop tomorrow," she says. "It'll be two hours of secondhand embarrassment, I'm sure. So I need you to come with me. I don't want to witness it alone."

"Hold on." My heart trips over itself. "You want me to be your emotional support human?"

"I need all the emotional support I can get every day, but the invite isn't about emotional support. It would be nice to have a friend there with me. So I can text my thoughts to you under the table." She tips her head to the side. "Think of it as a twisted bonding experience with the. . .*interesting* residents of Hemlock."

"I see these. . .*unique* residents almost daily at my job." A flashback from earlier this week hits me, a unique scene involving a recent patient. A man came into the emergency department solely for a Viagra prescription. He went into *vivid* detail about why he requires such medication.

"On a complete side note, you really need to share some ER stories. I bet you have some good ones."

I close my eyes, silently chuckling. "That's a HIPAA violation waiting to happen."

"Mrs. Jones already told me that a 'hot tattooed nurse' gave her a 'thorough' exam for her poison ivy rash."

Chin dropped to my chest, I heave a sigh. "That makes me sound wildly inappropriate and unprofessional." The way people love to embellish their medical stories always astound me. "Mrs. Jones had an unfortunate gardening accident which caused a bad rash on her arm."

A silent beat passes before Joey replies. "So. . .like. . .how thorough is 'thorough'? Like are we talking about under her—"

I whip around and narrow my eyes at her. "Josephine."

She holds up both hands, wincing. "Sorry, sorry. Too far. Bad joke."

Right on time, anxiety floods me. Did she only ask to hang out this weekend because she didn't want to be alone at open mic night?

Sweat breaks out on the back of my neck, trepidation steadily coursing through my veins. "Was that your original plan for this weekend? The open mic night?"

She chuckles. "God no. I wanted to kick your ass at mini golf, then go out for ice cream after. Sadly, my sister texted me this morning saying she'd write me out of her will if I didn't attend this small-town cringe fest in solidarity with her." She pulls out her phone, scrolls through her messages and opens up the conversation with her sister.

CHARLIE

You're coming Saturday.

JOEY

I already have plans.

"Oh, whoops! I scrolled too far. Ignore those last two messages." Joey yanks her phone away and fumbles with it, sending it falling to the ground with a soft thud. She snatches it up, and as she straightens, her cheeks are glowing bright red, and not because of the fire.

I can't help but laugh. This flustered side of this usually cool and confident woman may be one of my favorite versions.

"That wasn't embarrassing at all," she deadpans, looking anywhere but at me.

"Slutty. Tattooed. Biteable. Biceps," I punctuate each word, pondering the phrase. "That's a new one."

She lets out a resigned sigh. "Can we please pretend that didn't happen?"

"No." I bark out a laugh. "Absolutely not."

In response, the corners of her mouth curve up into an exquisite smile that renders me wordless.

Before us, the fire is slowly dying, the embers pulsing with a deep red glow amid the ash. A sign that a significant amount of time has passed since I came out here.

It's gone by far quicker than I'd like. That seems to be how time works when I'm in Joey's presence.

My chest tightens at the thought of the night ending. Being outside by the fire with her brings me a sense of peace. The type of comfort that's been unfamiliar to me for far too long.

"I better get inside," she murmurs, pulling her blanket tighter again. "It's been another long day."

"Norma?"

Joey groans. "Fucking Norma indeed."

"Go inside and get some sleep. I'll put out the fire."

Smiling, she stands and squeezes my shoulder with one delicate hand. "Thank you. For sitting out here and talking with me. It was nice."

It really was nice. Joey and I have a connection that I'm sure neither she nor I can comprehend. I place my hand on top of hers on my shoulder. The contrast of her warm hand and my cool fingertips is startling.

Much to my surprise, she doesn't pull away.

"You're great company, Joey."

She lets out a nervous laugh. "I can say with confidence that you're the first person to ever tell me that."

Chest aching for her, I squeeze her hand. "If that's the case, then you're surrounding yourself with the wrong people. They don't see you for who you truly are, and that's a shame."

The delicate column of her throat works as she swallows, and her eyes go misty.

The tears threatening to fall send a shock of panic through me. Shit. "God. I-I'm so sorry. I didn't mean to make you—"

"No. Don't apologize," she whispers, her voice trembling. "I really needed to hear that."

With a sheepish smile, she gives my shoulder another squeeze. Then she quietly makes her way inside the cottage.

The crunching of leaves beneath her feet fades, then disappears completely with the faint click of the door.

I take in a deep, calming breath and focus on the red-orange embers as they slowly die, my mind replaying every interaction we've had so far like my favorite movie.

Every conversation, every innocent touch, and every warm smile we share builds me up further. And they'll only make it more difficult to leave her when my assignment is over.

Beckett's Journal

April 27

Mesmerized is the best word to describe how I feel about Joey. I don't think she even realizes how special she is. She sees the world in bright colors while most of us see it in shades of gray. A true free spirit down to her very soul. Every second I get with her is another memory I want to collect and store for safekeeping. From her effervescent laugh and shimmering eyes to her expertly timed humor and empathetic spirit, she's a rare kind of beautiful.

Impossible to forget and impossible to find twice.

Chapter Fifteen

Joey

I love my bed.

With my eyes closed, I pull my fluffy blanket up under my chin, nestling into the warmth and relishing the comfort of sleeping in on a Saturday after a shit week of work.

I've dozed off again when my chest constricts, making it hard to breathe.

Weird.

It doesn't feel like an oncoming asthma attack and this pressure is. . .warm and. . .rumbly? That can't be right. I crack open one eye, my vision blurry, and find a ball of orange fuzz perched on top of me. It takes my sleep-addled mind a moment to register that the fuzzball is actually Barbara.

Eyes widening, I gasp, and the orange loaf of a cat zeroes in on me, her deep amber eyes piercing into my soul, and meows.

Judging me. Per usual.

"You know how to open doors?" I murmur. "Do you speak human? Perform witchcraft while your dad isn't home?"

Barbara stands and casually pads away in the direction of my bedside table.

I turn over, keeping my focus on her as she strolls across my blanket. "What are you doing?"

The demon looks at me over her shoulder, then at my phone on the nightstand and back again.

Eyes locked on mine, she swats my phone off the table, sending it clattering to the floor.

"Did we know each other in a past life?" I hiss. "Have I wronged you somehow? What is your deal?"

With a parting glance, she gives me a farewell meow and saunters away, slipping through my bedroom's partially open door.

Sunlight breaks through the curtains, streaming into my room. Shadows from the windblown trees dance across the wall, hypnotizing me.

When I hear rustling in the kitchen, I lean over the side of the bed and collect my phone to check the time. Then, groggily, I push the covers off and sit up. The moment my bare feet touch the cold wooden floors, I wince. I hate when my feet are cold. Almost as much as I hate being too hot.

My body wasn't made for extreme temperatures. Dry heat, extreme winters, and torrential rain are not for me. I need a nice not-too-hot-and-not-too-cold temperature. Preferably with low humidity, partly cloudy skies, and maybe a dash of a gentle breeze.

I slip my frigid feet into my slippers, then pull on an over-sized sweater and wander to the kitchen.

Yawning, I rub my eyes as I turn the corner. "You

should've told me Barbara knows how to open—what the hell is happening in here?"

I pull up short, taking in the muscular, tattooed back that belongs to my roommate, who is currently making pancakes.

Beckett looks at me over his shoulder, shyly smiling.

That single adorable look is almost enough to make me faint. My brain is getting a workout, drinking in every detail of this man.

Beckett is shirtless, his gray sweatpants riding low on his hips. The man is all smooth skin, taut muscle, and ink, the tattoos on his arms bleeding into other in places I've never seen.

I wonder where else he has them. . .

And the black-rimmed glasses perched on his nose? They frame his emerald eyes like they're works of art.

Between his shy smirk and the dark lines of intricate tattoos winding around his toned body, the vision before me is borderline pornographic.

For me, at least.

"Hey," he says, flipping a pancake. "Thought I'd make pancakes. Is that okay?"

Correction: The vision *is* pornographic. There's no border-line about it.

Maybe the universe actually listened when I begged for a small break.

And wow, did it deliver.

The aroma of pancakes and maple syrup fills the air, causing my stomach to growl.

I drop my head to my abdomen, and when I look up again, Beckett is looking at me, brows raised. And, mortifyingly, my stomach releases another embarrassing gurgle.

His responding chuckle fills me with ease. "I'll take that as a yes. Sit."

"Should you be cooking without a shirt? Won't things, like, I don't know, splatter? Burn? Potentially injure your erm. . .chest?" My choppy words tumble out of my mouth as I respectfully objectify this man in my head.

"I was reading the newspaper earlier, and Barbara hopped up on the island and dumped my coffee on me. Sorry, does it bother you? I can grab another shirt." The tips of his ears have gone bright red. It's incredibly endearing.

I bite back a smile. Under no circumstance do I want him to put his shirt back on. I'm usually not the biggest fan of receiving gifts, but this is a gift I'll gladly accept without question or hesitation.

I wave a dismissive hand. "I've seen bare-chested men before. Some I wish I could burn from my memory if I'm being honest." I shudder as I recall a rather unfortunate experience at a music festival a few years ago, but I shake off the memory quickly. "They don't faze me one bit."

That's a lie. Because this chest? Consider me fazed. *Especially when he's adding strawberries to the pancakes.*

As I slide onto the chair, I eye his full coffee mug longingly. I used up the last of my coffee a few days ago and keep forgetting to pick more up, meaning I've gone roughly four days without caffeine.

At this point, I would commit unspeakable acts for a cup, but looking at the empty basket next to the coffee machine, it looks like Beckett is out too. And if there's one thing I've learned about nurse Beckett since we moved in together, it's that he needs caffeine in order to make it through his shifts.

Can't blame the guy one bit.

"Coffee?" he asks, catching me still gazing at the mug on the counter.

Sheepishly, I duck, then dart a look at the empty coffee pod basket. "Oh, no, that's okay. I don't want to be a burden and—"

He rounds the island and sets his mug in front of me. "Here. Take mine."

I shake my head forcefully. "No."

He tilts his head to the side, cocking one very handsome brow. "Take it."

I swallow thickly, mesmerized by his determined green eyes and his deep commanding tone. "I'll buy you more," I blurt out as I wrap both hands around the mug.

He wanders away and tends to the pancakes. "Don't worry about it."

"Thank you," I say, my voice barely above a whisper. "I'm so sorry."

Spine snapping straight, he spins around. "Why are you apologizing?"

Why *am I* apologizing?

"I. . ." I inhale, then hold the air in my lungs. "That's a good question. I'm not sure."

He returns to my side and hovers over me. "There's nothing to apologize for, Josephine."

His reassuring voice causes butterflies to take flight in my stomach.

As he goes back to skillfully flipping pancakes and moving around the kitchen like he's spent a million Saturdays doing this, a dull ache hits me in the chest.

The scene unfolding before me is a perfect storm to trigger a flurry of emotions that I'm woefully unprepared for. His comforting laughter and the way he leaned in to reassure me just now makes me wonder if there is hope for someone like me.

The always too much girl.

Suddenly, the air in this kitchen feels thick with unspoken possibilities. My heart thrashes in my chest and my hands tremble as I set the mug on the island again. If he keeps going like this, I'm afraid I'll get too attached and end up disappointed once again.

Despite this fear, this unique kinship we're forming is a breath of fresh air. The dormant parts of my soul are slowly waking in his presence.

He sets a plate with a stack of strawberry pancakes in front of me, then goes back for the second plate.

Rolling my lips to fight off a smile, I look up at him. "How did you know I like strawberries in my pancakes?"

"Easy," he says, the single word rolling off his tongue. "There are two boxes of strawberry waffles in the freezer."

"Wow. Nice to know I'm as easy to read as a coloring book," I remark with a sly smile.

Brows pinched, Beckett studies me. "You can't actually read coloring books."

"Well, uh, yes," I stammer, warmth creeping up my neck and into my cheeks. "That's why they're easy to read. Because you can't, you know, read a coloring book. You need crayons. . .or markers. Really any kind of coloring medium. It's all about preference with coloring books." I suck in a breath, mentally chastising myself for stumbling into this ridiculous monologue. "Actually." I clear my throat. "The joke isn't that funny now that I think about it. Ignore me. Please." Head lowered, I cut into the pancakes and shove a piece into my mouth. Anything to stop myself from talking.

I keep my eyes laser-focused on my plate, chewing the

incredibly delicious pancakes. All the while, I can feel Beckett's attention on me.

Across the room, he exhales slowly, his voice softer than I expect. "I'll never ignore you."

That hits me straight in the chest. His words nearly knock the wind out of me, and I have no clue how to respond to that. So, naturally, I stuff my mouth with another forkful of pancakes, putting my chipmunk cheeks on full display.

Chuckling, he turns around and picks up his own plate.

"When do we have to be at the coffee shop?" he asks as he slides into the seat across the kitchen island from me.

I take a sip of coffee to wash down the unusually large panic bite I took, then straighten myself up in my seat. "It starts at seven, though we should probably get there a little early. My sister may combust and she'll need me there to tell her to keep her eyebrows in check."

Another one of those delicious chuckles. "That bad?"

"Oof. One unimpressed arch of her brow is enough to make a grown man cry. It's why Louis won't set foot into her store." I shiver at the thought of being on the receiving end of one of her looks.

"Good to know." He nods thoughtfully. "Do you. . .want to ride together or separately?"

"Together. It's the first open mic night in the history of Hemlock, so I'm sure parking will be a nightmare."

"Ever been on a motorcycle?"

I freeze, and as I imagine sitting on the back of his bike with my arms wrapped around his muscular torso, clinging to him as the world blurs by, my pulse kicks up.

Part of me wants to play it cool and say yes. But the more logical side reminds me that he'll likely catch me in my lie when I fall flat on my ass while trying to get on the back of his bike. "Can't say I have."

He angles forward, a flicker of what I swear is hope in his eyes. "Are you interested?"

Am I interested? What a silly question. Every cell in my body is screaming at me to say yes. But I don't want to come off too eager. Typically, I'd say something akin to "*Hell yeah. Let's go. Right. Now,*" which may scare a shy guy like him off.

"Of course I'm interested," I say, my tone nonchalant as I pick up my coffee.

His skin warms as he smiles down at his plate. And when he looks up at me, those big green eyes bore into my soul. "Wonderful. Be sure to wear jeans and a pair of boots."

Like this, he's more handsome than ever—smiling, hair mussed from sleep, shoulders loose with ease. Morning stubble shadows his sharp jaw like soft pencil shading. Framed by the morning light spilling through the large window behind him, Beckett could be mistaken for some kind of celestial being.

On the outside, he looks like he could be the president of a motorcycle club. On the inside, though, lives a gentle, thoughtful soul. While many people strive to possess that type of kindness, he doesn't have to *try*. He simply *is*. He holds an air of quiet confidence that speaks louder than his words.

My chest tightens with a quiet glow. Our interactions are always easy like this. It's peaceful yet terrifying at the same time. I've never seen myself settling down, but for the first time, the possibility of a different future unfolds in front of me.

Except this is all temporary, like a gust of wind that stirs the leaves but is gone as quickly as it came. My heart sinks. I only feel this way because it's been so long since I've felt truly understood, since I haven't felt pushed aside like an afterthought. There are likely thousands of men in the world who could ignite these emotions within me. He may be the first, but he surely won't be the last.

Right?

It's reality, yet a shadow of a doubt lingers in the depths of my heart, softly whispering that Beckett may be the only one whose soul is capable of touching mine.

Chapter Sixteen

AFTER BREAKFAST, Beckett ran out to get a few errands taken care of, and I set myself up in the living room to get some work done.

I rarely work on weekends, but the Droplet brand redesign has consumed almost all of my time, so this is the first time this week I've had a moment to focus on a few of my other clients.

While I'm typing away, computer in my lap, Barbara saunters over and drops a small, soft object beside me. Panic immediately washes over me. I swear, if this cat brought a dead mouse to me, I'm leaving this house or kicking her and her owner out.

Swallowing down the nerves, I force myself to look at the. . .pair of fuzzy socks.

Air whooshes from my lungs. *What?*

Hmm. I look down the length of the couch to my slippered feet, which, I'll admit, are still a bit cold.

"Thanks, Babs."

She flicks her orange tail from side to side in a smooth motion, focusing on me, like she's waiting for something. "Ah. I know what you want." I tentatively reach out and scratch her chin.

Immediately, she nuzzles her furry head into my hand and purrs loudly.

Maybe there's hope of a friendship between Barbara and me after all. Even if it's built on a semi-unstable foundation.

As if she could read my mind, she jerks up, her piercing amber eyes locking with mine. Judgmental Barb has returned, I see. Pupils narrowing to slits, she scurries away.

"You are an odd creature, Barbara," I mutter. "But one day you'll love me."

With an exhale, I sink down into the plush couch and check my phone. I have a few hours before I have to get ready for open mic night, meaning I can close my eyes for a little while. I snap my laptop shut, tuck it into the side of the couch, and let my eyelids drift shut.

When I startle awake, my mind reels.

Where am I?

How did I get here?

Hell, *who* am I?

As I take in my surroundings, my mind clears. I'm in the living room, and apparently I've just stumbled out of the kind of sleep that's so deep I wouldn't be shocked if I woke up in a different decade.

Considering how quiet it is, it seems like Beckett still isn't home yet. I check my phone, discovering we have to leave in an hour. I stretch, readying to get up so I can change, and throw the blanket off.

Wait.

A blanket?

I didn't wrap myself up in a blanket.

And when did I put my laptop on the table?

Who the fu—

"I didn't wake you coming in, did I?" Beckett murmurs, the words barely breaking through my sleep-induced haze.

I rub my bleary eyes, then focus on him standing near the end of the couch, holding Barbara to his chest.

Fiddling with the blanket, I ask, "Did you—"

"Cover you in a blanket? Yes." He scratches Barbara's head, and she purrs in absolute bliss.

I eye the coffee table. "And—"

"Put your laptop on the coffee table? Also yes."

"Huh." I nod, confused. "Thanks."

He flashes me a warm smile. "Anytime." Bending at the waist, he sets the cat down. Then he rises to his full height again. "I'm going to head upstairs and take a shower. Meet you down here in an hour?"

Shower. Beckett. Instantly my mind is filled with images. Steam rising from every corner, warm water cascading down his muscular, inked chest. Each droplet glistening as it travels over his defined abs, slowly dripping downward to his. . .

"Are you feeling okay? You're flushed. Have you had enough water today?"

I jolt back to reality. "Hmm? What? Yeah. Showers are great," I squeak. "I like a good shower."

His expression is nothing short of pure confusion, and I can't say I blame the poor guy.

He frowns, but the expression quickly shifts into a devastating smirk as he nods at my nervous rambling.

"All right then. I'll see you in an hour." He turns and heads up the stairs.

I crane my neck, watching him as he goes, shamelessly admiring the way his ass looks in his dark jeans.

After sifting through every piece of clothing in my closet, I finally find my only motorcycle appropriate clothes. I predominantly wear flowy dresses and skirts because they're the most comfortable. As a bonus, I'm prepared for my body's retaliation on the days I decide to add milk to my coffee. Being bloated in jeans? There's nothing more insufferable.

I pull the stiff denim over my legs and jump up and down a few times to shimmy them up over my hips.

Not quite satisfied with the basic straight-leg jeans, black T-shirt, and brown boots, I slip on my favorite jacket. It's hand embroidered with dozens of colorful flowers, each one beautifully unique. I touch up my makeup with a swipe of lip gloss and coat of mascara, then comb my fingers through my hair.

As I open my door and shuffle toward the living room, my pulse picks up and nerves skitter through me. With a thick swallow and a deep breath, I peer around the corner.

Beckett is already out here, sitting on the couch, his handsome face lit up as he scrolls on his phone.

When he notices me, he does a double take, then stands slowly. At his full height, he examines me more closely, starting from my worn leather boots and working his way up my legs. As he takes in the snug denim molded to my body, he draws in a sharp breath, the muscle along his strong jaw popping. I clear my throat, tempted to make a witty comment. But I refrain, not wanting to ruin this moment. With his attention on me like this, I feel powerful. Unstoppable. There's something so satisfying about knowing I can pull this type of reaction from him.

"Ready to go?" I ask sweetly, pretending I didn't notice the way he checked me out.

Beckett swallows hard. "Uh, yes. Yep."

I flatten my lips to hold back a smile. "Lead the way," I say, stepping to the side and motioning to the door.

As he strides past me, I catch a whiff of his scent, and he smells *heavenly*. Like leather and spice, with a hint of vanilla.

I'm convinced that men become a hundred times more alluring when they smell good.

I trail behind him and lock the door swiftly. When I turn around, he's standing by his motorcycle, holding two helmets, the sleek chrome of the machine glinting under the rays of the setting sun.

Feeling bold, I let my hips sway as I saunter toward him. And I'm rewarded as he watches me the whole way.

When we're toe to toe, he sets one helmet on the seat of his bike and twirls a finger, signaling for me to turn around. Then he carefully gathers my hair, the backs of his fingers brushing against the nape of my neck. "Is this okay? Braiding your hair will protect it from the wind."

Breathless, I nod, my pulse quickening beneath his callused hands.

Warmth radiates from him, seeping into me, his leather and vanilla scent clinging to my nostrils, holding me close and rendering me speechless.

With tenderness, he separates my long waves into three sections, and as he brings one section over another, his warm breath fans across my neck. My eyes flutter closed at the sensation and my stomach whooshes. When his cool fingertips brush up my heated skin, goose bumps explode all over my body.

As he braids my hair, he runs through safety measures. "On turns, be sure to lean with the bike. And always keep your feet steady on the footrests."

Once he's finished braiding my hair, he steps around me and picks up a helmet. Now facing me, he places it snugly on my head and when he adjusts the straps beneath my chin, his touch is both tender and deliberate. For a moment, I swear he lets his fingers linger there, as if savoring this intimate moment.

The air around us has grown thicker, warmer, making it harder to breathe. Or maybe that's just me.

With a hum, he takes a step back and puts his own helmet on. Then he straddles the bike with the utmost confidence.

Why is that so hot?

I'm far more hesitant as I swing one leg over the back of his bike, trying—and failing—to balance myself on this seat.

"Use me for leverage," he says over his shoulder.

I can think about ten ways I could use you for leverage right now, Mr. Hart. Don't tempt me with a good time.

With that thought top of mind, I place my hands on his shoulders and get settled.

"Arms around my waist." The sudden quiet dominance in his tone makes my stomach clench.

Yes, sir.

I circle his waist and clasp my hands gently in front of him, fearing I'll clutch him too hard.

"Harder, Josephine. I need you squeezing me harder."

Heat pools in my belly at the command.

Dear. Fucking. God. Does he know what he's saying?

I tighten my hold, but when that still isn't good enough, he grasps my forearms and gently tugs me forward, only stopping when my arms are snug around his torso.

Our bodies are pressed so tightly together, the front of mine melding to the back of his, that we might as well be a single person.

He slides one hand under the sleeve of my jacket, his thumb tracing soothing circles on my skin, leaving a trail of heat in its wake. I'd be lying if I said I wasn't anxious since I've never been on a motorcycle before, though I have no doubt that I'm in excellent hands with Beckett.

"Are you still okay with this? If not, we can take my SUV. I'll just need to unhook the motorcycle trailer." His thumb is still moving in reassuring circles on my forearm, sending waves of comfort through me.

"Absolutely. Let's go before we're late." I give him a playful squeeze.

His chuckle reverberates through me, and I've never felt as safe and secure as I do in this moment.

The next thing I know, the engine roars to life, the kickstand goes up, and the forest blurs around us.

Twenty minutes later, we pull up in front of Finn's coffee shop.

When the engine goes silent, I use Beckett's broad shoulders to support myself and dismount rather ungracefully. Once my boots hit the pavement, I begrudgingly remove my hands from him and undo my helmet.

On the way here, I realized that the end of this night can't come soon enough. I've never been more excited to head home, knowing I'll be pressed up against Beckett's body for another twenty minutes.

Still sitting on the bike, he removes his helmet and rakes his fingers through his blond hair. Somehow, it looks even sexier when it's all mussed and effortless like this.

The thought brings with it another. What about my own hair? Self-consciously, I touch the top of my head.

Beckett's eyes soften. "Your hair looks beautiful, Joey. But if you want to let it loose, I don't mind braiding it again before we leave. It won't be too much."

If it were possible, I'd melt into a puddle on this sidewalk. My limbs are weak, my skin tingles, and my heart pounds hard in my chest.

It won't be too much.

Those words cause a swell of emotion to build in my throat.

Could it be? The *too much* girl suddenly isn't *too much* for someone?

"Damn. This dude's way cooler than me," a man says behind me.

"Would you be quiet?" Charlie whisper-shouts to her boyfriend.

Turning around, I hold my arms out. My sister hates hugs more than anything. Sadly for her, I love giving them. So I pull Charlie into a tight embrace, squeezing her with a little dramatic flair.

She lets out a disapproving, pained groan. "I hate this. Stop it," she says, her words muffled by my jacket.

"One day you'll miss this." I sigh as I release her. Both Beckett and Finn chuckle just as I let her go and take a step back.

Finn holds out a hand to Beckett. "Hey, man, good to see you again."

With a surprisingly easy smile, Beckett accepts the gesture, shaking his hand. "Thanks for having me."

"Let's go inside and get this over with," my sister groans. "The lineup tonight is not great."

Inside Dark Side Brews, twinkle lights adorn wooden beams and tea light candles flicker on the tables, making the place feel cozy. Near the back of the shop, they've set up a small stage for the evening.

"Being a bit dramatic, aren't we?" I joke.

Charlie shoves an open notebook into my hands, the page on top filled with a sample of tonight's participants.

Guitar solo. *Seen it before.*

Poetry. *Not surprising.*

Stand-up comedy. *Obvious.*

Magic trick. *Classic.*

I continue scanning down the long list, though near the end, I have to tamp down the need to gasp.

Erotic short-story reading. *What the actual fuck?*

Eyes practically bulging out of my head, I turn to Finn and wave the notebook in the air between us. "Dude. Really?"

"Now you know why I need you here," Charlie mutters.

"I don't blame you one bit," I murmur back out of the corner of my mouth.

Finn winces. "It's a favor for Aunt Donna."

"Hold on. What's so bad?" Beckett asks.

Without looking at him, I shove the notebook in his direction.

"This isn't that bad—*what?* Erotic short story?" Beckett eyes Charlie, then Finn.

I cover my mouth, trying to hold back my laugh but failing miserably.

"Finn, you know you're sleeping on the couch tonight. Right?" Beckett quips.

Charlie snort laughs while Finn nods, clearly accepting his fate.

Did Beckett just make a joke?

My heart soars. If he can joke like this, then maybe he won't be uncomfortable tonight. Social anxiety can be debilitating, so this feels like a great achievement.

Vera and Frank approach, paws skittering on the wooden floor, the two of them plowing into Beckett's kneecaps.

His eyes light up with insurmountable joy as both dogs wiggle around his legs. Crouching, he scratches the overly friendly dogs who are squeaking with happiness at the attention.

Beckett would be the kind of guy who hangs out with the dogs at a social gathering. The quality is undeniably charming. The dogs clearly sense what I already know. This man has a kind, gentle soul.

Chapter Seventeen

BECKETT

WHILE FINN RUNS around the shop, greeting new arrivals, Joey, Charlie, and I get settled at a high-top at the back of the room.

When Jack walks in and I see all three siblings together for the first time, I realize the resemblance is undeniable. All three share unmistakable large brown eyes and dark hair.

Jack looks around the shop with a scowl. Truthfully, the guy intimidates me. It wouldn't shock me if he knew how to hide bodies without getting caught. When he spots us, though, he breaks into a smile, the expression making him look less menacing.

He strolls over to us and slides into the chair next to Charlie. "How bad is this going to be?"

Joey leans forward to peer over at him. "There's an erotic short-story telling at eight thirty. Charlie hand-picked this person. She's very excited, if you catch my drift."

She winks at her sister, earning a death glare in return. I cover my mouth, stifling a laugh.

Jack runs a hand down his dark beard, brows furrowing as he zeroes in on Charlie. "Really?"

Charlie closes her eyes, inhaling a deep breath. "I hate you. All of you." She huffs, turning to me. "Except you. You're fine."

My anxiety gets the best of me, my throat closing up, so I go with my default—a classic nod and a smile.

The bell above the door chimes, and a moment later a woman covered in tattoos with long, jet-black hair steps inside, carrying a bag of popcorn that's got to be three feet tall. She scans the room and, when she sees us, a look of recognition passes over her face. She heads our way with a pep in her step.

Joey angles close, whispering in my ear. "That's Marnie, Charlie's best friend."

"Sorry I'm late," Marnie says, mildly out of breath. "I had to feed the poor dude handcuffed in my basement." She pulls out a stool and drops the enormous bag of popcorn on the table with a thud. "I brought snacks. They're not the same ones I fed the handcuffed guy, though. Don't worry."

At her admission, my eyes widen and Joey laughs. She leans over again, her lips even closer to my ear this time, her warm breath ghosting over my skin. "Your best bet is to ignore her. The town calls her 'Maniac Marnie' for good reason."

Fighting the urge to shiver, I clear my throat and turn to Joey, smiling. Without words, she mirrors my smile. Warm and understanding. As if we're speaking a silent language that only the two of us understand.

"Who are you?" Marnie asks, barreling right through the moment. "And what are your intentions with our dear Josephine, hmm?" She shoves a handful of popcorn into her mouth, her expression calculating, like she's trying to decipher if I'm a threat.

"Leave the guy alone, Marnie," Jack says, exasperated.

"Joey's roommate," Charlie says.

Marnie stops chewing, and a devious grin slowly spreads across her face.

Part of me is frightened, and the other part of me is. . .who am I kidding? The whole of me is frightened. This Morticia Addams lookalike—who may or may not have a man locked up in her basement—is staring directly at me with a mischievous glint in her eye.

"A roommate, you say? Can I ask how this happened?"

In unison, the Thorne siblings groan and bark out a "no."

Their friend scoffs. "Fine. Just let me know when you set a date. You'll need an officiant, and I'm booked up for the next year. Though I can make room in my calendar, since we're friends and all that. I'll give you the friends and family discount."

"Jesus Christ." Jack covers his face with both his hands.

"Oh my god," Charlie groans, dropping her head on the table.

I pinch my eyebrows together. *Officiant? Is she talking about a* wedding? *Like being roommates means we'll end up married?*

"Yes," Joey whispers in my ear.

Breath catching, I look at her, only then realizing how close our faces are. The air is thick with the aroma of coffee, but Joey's fresh strawberry scent hits me and pulls me in. "I didn't say anything," I murmur, my voice heavy with confusion.

Joey laughs, a beautiful melodic sound that drowns out the overwhelming noise of chattering patrons around us. "Whatever you're thinking about regarding Marnie, the answer is 'yes.'" She laughs. "The answer is almost always 'yes.' Is she a witch? Yes. Is she teetering on the edge of sanity? Yes. Is she unhinged? Yes. Always yes."

I watch as Joey tucks a loose strand of hair behind her ear, but it slips free immediately and falls back into her face. Before she reaches for it again, my hand takes control and does the work for her. When my fingers brush the shell of her ear, her cheeks go pink.

A throat clearing close by startles me. Joey too. And my heart lurches. Her and I both freeze.

How is it possible that I forgot that we were in public?

That move wasn't very roommate-y. If anything, it'll only add fuel to Marnie's wedding fire.

Joey's eyes bore into mine, her lips twitching with a smirk. "Whatever you do, act normal and don't make eye contact with them."

My chest tightens. "They're all staring, aren't they?"

"Oh yeah." Nodding, she rolls her lips like she's suppressing a smile.

I groan. "Lovely."

Shifting uncomfortably in my seat, I act as natural as a person can under the eyes of nosy friends and family members and focus on the stage, waiting for the entertainment to appear.

Thankfully, the lights dim a moment later, casting a cozy glow over the audience. A hush falls over the crowd as Finn casually strolls up onto the stage. His welcoming voice carries throughout the shop as he thanks everyone for coming out tonight.

The first performer steps forward, and it's not bad at all. It's an entrancing acoustic guitar solo that receives a well-earned standing ovation at the end. From there, we're entertained by poetry readings, stand-up comedy sketches, and more musical numbers.

Beside me, Joey holds her phone under the table, the screen illuminating her face, and taps out a message.

A heartbeat later, my phone buzzes in my back pocket. Slowly, I slip it out and position it under the table like hers and unlock the screen.

JOEY

I am so, SO sorry.

A smile tugs at my mouth.

Why?

JOEY

Because it's a lot.

I'm fine.

The dude who did the splits, though? Not sure he's fine.

Beside me, she lets out a quiet chuckle.

JOEY

Guitar girl? Solid 9.2.

The poetry reading from the man dressed up as Edgar Allan Poe? 4.2.

> The Edgar wannabe is definitely on a watch list somewhere.

Joey snorts, the sound making my chest swell with pride.

JOEY

> For sure. He was oddly hyper-fixated on how "hauntingly beautiful" roadkill is.

> I tuned out when he teared up about identifying with the dead opossum he saw on the I-5 last week.

JOEY

> I don't blame you one bit.

> I totally understand if you don't want to hang out with me after this.

> To be fair, even I don't want to hang out with myself.

> If anything, I feel the complete opposite.

JOEY

> Mini golf next weekend?

> I would love nothing more.

We steal fleeting glances, heads still lowered, expressions mischievous, a quiet acknowledgment of our text conversation.

Near the end of the night, Finn steps up to the stage and welcomes the next performer of the evening—the infamous erotic short-story teller.

"And now I'd like to introduce. . ." He tilts his head, his brows lowering in confusion. "Misty Sparkles?"

"I've been waiting all fucking week for this," Marnie says through a mouthful of popcorn.

The performer glides onto the stage, stumbling over her long, glittery dress. Her wig is bright blond and practically luminescent under the intense spotlight.

Next to me, Charlie snorts. "Ah. Misty is actually my old accountant, Betty."

Joey straightens, frowning at her sister. "Betty? The woman who *forgot to file your taxes*, Betty?"

Her sister scoffs. "Oh yeah. Nothing gets the blood pumping like a visit from the IRS, you know?"

Marnie practically growls. "Would you two *shut up*? I need to soak this in."

Betty—I mean *Misty*—settles on the stool and adjusts the microphone. "Hello, my name is Misty Sparkles, and this is my short, erotic story." She clears her throat and holds her head high. "On a chilly December night, I found myself completely bare under a sturdy man. My epidermis was scorching, my phalanges tangled in his long, luscious hair as his wet lips trailed down my thoracic cavity."

Epidermis. Phalanges. Thoracic cavity. What in the entry-level anatomy class is happening here? Flattening my lips, I choke back a laugh.

Joey drifts closer, our arms touching from shoulder to wrist. "Would you say this is the kind of stuff you nurses read to get aroused?"

Closing my eyes, I turn away. Already, I'm moments away from losing my composure.

Misty continues. "His chest hair tickled my aching, peaked, aroused buds as his delectable oral cavity made its way down to my promised land—"

"Holy mother of adjectives," Joey murmurs.

Covering my mouth, I take a few deep breaths through my nose in a weak attempt to pull myself together at Misty's medical grade erotic short story.

"And when his rough phalange grazed over my puckered papilla mammae, I cried out in ecstasy—"

The coffee shop is quiet enough to hear a pin drop when Marnie hoots. "Hell yeah, girl! Make him graze that papilla whatever," she bellows. "Put him to work!"

Despite all my efforts, I lose it, collapsing into a fit of uncontrollable laughter. Beside me Joey does the same, and the two of us fall into each other, our laughs erupting in wheezing gasps. We sound like barking seals. Tears stream from the corners of my eyes as I struggle to catch my breath. Joey grips my forearm tightly, her fingers digging into my jacket as she rests her forehead on my shoulder, shielding herself from the curious eyes of the crowd.

At her touch, the world around me blurs and my heart takes off at a sprint. All I can think about is sinking into the gentle pressure of her body against mine, her warmth seeping through my jacket and into my bones.

Charlie tries to glower at us, but instead, her composure crumbles to dust, and she joins in, her laughter blending seamlessly with ours.

Jack, who is clearly uncomfortable with the performance, has turned a deep shade of crimson and is frozen in his seat like a deer caught in headlights.

Marnie notices Jack's frigid state. "Aw," she teases him. "What's wrong, flannel daddy? I didn't know this kind of story would get you all hot and bothered under that checkered collar. Here, eat some popcorn." She shoves the bag into Jack's chest.

His expression darkens. "Do. Not. Call. Me. That."

The interaction is enough to stop our laughing, and the three of us quickly straighten up and wait to see what will happen next.

Marnie scoffs. "Whatever. Next time you chop lumber, be sure to pull that log out of your ass."

The three of us erupt into laughter all over again, and by the time we pull ourselves together, Misty is already off the stage.

The grand finale is a magic trick. I can't imagine this ending in a success.

When the curtains open, the magician steps out with a dog who looks eerily like Frank.

"For my performance tonight, I will take this dog"—the magician, a man I don't recognize, says, waving his magic wand around the Frank lookalike—"and restore his sight!"

Oh fuck. It *is* Frank.

The audience gasps, the sound making Frank's ears twitch. Whimpering, the poor confused dog lies on the stage. I stand, ready to rescue him, but before I can take a single step, Finn sprints onto the stage.

"Absolutely not. That's it for tonight," he announces. "Thank you for joining. We can't wait to have you back again."

As the curtains close, the audience breaks into applause, whistling, clapping, and hollering for an encore.

The sudden burst of excitement causes my neck to break out in a sweat.

Shit. *Here it comes.*

The rowdy crowd, the small space, and the scrutiny of people nearby who are glancing at Joey and me with curiosity cause my heart rate to soar. The room slowly closes in on me.

The people are way too loud. The space is too cramped.

The air feels too thick. And the invisible force of anxiety presses down heavily on my chest, making it nearly impossible to take a deep breath.

Frustration joins in with the panic. I was fine for the whole duration of the event. Why the hell has my anxiety spiked now? My best guess is that I'm getting too overwhelmed, and my social battery is depleting faster than anticipated.

I take a few steadying breaths, hoping it'll ground me. But it's no use. My chest only tightens further. I need fresh air.

I clasp my hands under the table, twisting them, anxious to get up and dart out of here. I want to leave, but if I do, everyone at the table will look at me funny or ask questions that, frankly, I don't have the answers to.

A soft, warm hand covers mine, sending a flood of calm through my veins.

Joey.

Under the table, she entwines her fingers with mine. Her hand is so delicate, her skin so smooth. She uses her thumb to caress the back of my hand in comforting strokes.

More quickly than I've ever experienced, my panic recedes.

I can breathe again.

Closing my eyes, I suck in a deep breath, filling my lungs with much-needed oxygen. The foreboding that crept over me drifts off into the distance, and reality returns.

In my sea of overwhelming anxiety, Joey is my anchor.

Having her next to me is akin to having a lifeline at the ready. How she knew what was happening inside my mind is a mystery, but she did, and she instinctively knew how to help me through it.

Deep in my chest, that flicker of hopefulness grows into a

small flame. Because with Joey, I become a different version of myself. A version that I like and admire whenever I see my reflection.

As inconvenient as our situation is, I'm falling for this woman. Not only is she beautiful, with an infectious smile, but she's patient and empathetic—especially when my anxiety gets the best of me.

That flame shrinks, though, when I remember that nothing can truly happen between us.

Beckett's Journal

April 29

Tonight, Josephine awakened a feeling inside me I thought I had buried.

Hope.

Hope that there are people in this world who have the patience and the ability to understand someone like me.

This pull toward her is undeniable, tugging at the very threads of my being.

But the stark reality of our temporary situation is something I can't brush aside. I'm trapped in the tumultuous space between the heat of desire and the cold weight of dejection.

For now, I'm going to enjoy these moments with her. Ignore my racing thoughts. Ignore the future. Ignore all the "what ifs."

With her, I'm focusing on living in the present and casting my worries aside.

Chapter Eighteen

I forgot.

I wince. For the last week, Beckett and I have both been engulfed in work, but we've still made time for our firepit chats and grilled cheese dinners. But over the week, my goldfish memory has failed me once again. Panic grips me, because Beckett will be home at any moment. I can't imagine he'll be pleased about spending the evening with two rambunctious dogs. And I don't even know what Barbara will think. Hell, the cat probably hates everyone except Beckett.

Sorry. I meant to send that text to someone else. Can't wait to have the pups over!

CHARLIE

Do you need Benadryl? Or anti-itch cream?

What?

CHARLIE

You get hives when you lie.

And right now, you're lying. You totally forgot your promise.

So do you want cream with aloe or the extra-strength kind?

Fuck right off.

Aloe, please.

Twenty minutes later, Charlie pulls up to the cottage in her SUV, which is bursting with two playful dogs and an over-sized canvas bag filled with supplies.

Shoving my shoulders back, I take a deep breath, mentally preparing myself for the chaotic night ahead. As I stride towards the door, the dogs paw impatiently at the other side, their nails no doubt leaving scratch marks in the solid wood. And adding a fee to my final month's rent to repair the damages, I'm sure.

I brace myself as I open the door, preparing for the chaos. Unsurprisingly, Frank runs headfirst into the couch, unfamiliar with the layout of the place. But that doesn't dampen his excitement. Both dogs wag their tails, their bodies wiggling, their happiness momentarily distracting me from my concern about Beckett and Barbara.

The dogs sniff and explore every inch of the living area.

When they move on and begin padding down the hall to my bedroom, my anxious thoughts return and a heavy pit of worry settles deep in my stomach. I really hope Beckett isn't upset.

Charlie thrusts the hefty supply bag into my arms, then surveys the cottage, taking in the copious number of blankets thrown over the back of the couch or puddled on the cushions, the laptop still open, and my emotional support water bottle on the table.

Nodding, she hums with approval. Then she spins toward me, settles her hands on her hips, and raises a singular dark brow. "Have you slept with him?"

My jaw practically hits the floor. "Charlotte Rose."

"Josephine Iris," she mocks.

"What makes you say that?" I clutch the tote tightly, and what I assume is dog food crunches inside.

One side of her mouth ticks up. "You may think I'm oblivious, but I saw how you two were acting last week."

"You're making shit up." I scoff. "You were totally focused on that weird, medical erotic story."

"I saw you hold his hand under the table." She smirks. It's the classic, sisterly smirk that says *nice try; you can't get anything past me.*

"Since when does holding hands equate to sex?"

She cocks her head to the side, giving me a skeptical look. "He tucked a lock of your hair behind your ear. You blushed a color I didn't think was humanly possible. *Come on.*"

The air whooshes out of my lungs. "When did you suddenly become Sherlock Holmes?" I tighten my grip on the bag even more, wishing I could use it as a shield against my sister and her inquisitiveness

Before she can answer, the door creaks open and Beckett

steps into the house, wearing his wrinkled blue scrubs and a tired expression.

I hate that he's so damn attractive even when he's exhausted and disheveled.

It's not fair.

He stops in his tracks and looks from my sister and her smug smile to me, still clutching this bag for dear life.

My heart sinks. Dammit. At the very least, I hoped I could catch him before he walked in so I could warn him about the animal slumber party.

"Is everything okay here?" he questions.

Charlie's smile turns warm again. "Everything's great. Thanks again for having the dogs over." With that, she passes by him and steps out the front door. When it shuts behind her, I swear I can hear her laughing.

Beckett stands in the middle of the living room, leather jacket draped over his arm, perplexed.

With this fucking bag *still* in my arms, I hug it even tighter. First it was a shield, but now I need it for emotional support while I break the news to my roommate.

"I broke a roommate rule," I hedge.

His eyes go wide. "You touched Agatha again?"

I rear back, my heart jumping into my throat. "What? No." Finally, I set down the bag at my feet and Beckett peers over to see what's inside. "I forgot to tell you that I agreed to watch Vera and Frank for the night. I'm so sorry. I don't know if Barbara even likes dogs, but I wanted to give you guys the chance to leave for the night in case you didn't want them here." I suck in a breath, then barrel on, my words coming out in a trembling rush. "Again, I'm so sorry. It wasn't intentional. My mind has been consumed with work stuff, which leaves little room for anything else.

Because of the stress, I haven't been sleeping well." I huff. "I also should drink more water, though that's beside the point. And my sister. . .god she is so happy with Finn. I wanted her to have a nice date night and these dogs are a handful. And—"

Beckett drops his jacket, then strides across the room and grabs my shoulders, his green eyes brimming with concern.

I'm not sure if he's concerned about tonight's circumstances or my impressive ramble, or if he's simply concerned about me.

"Breathe for me, Joey. I need you to take a slow, deep breath."

Silently, I nod. He's probably worried about how tonight will go, but secretly, I hope he's concerned about me.

Beckett assesses me, his attention dropping to my lips, which I realize now I'm worrying with my teeth.

He eases one hand from my shoulder and traces the edge of my bottom lip with his thumb, coaxing it free from my nervous bite. That simple touch causes a soothing calm to spread through my body.

God, what I'd do to sink into this feeling, hold on tight, and never let go.

The pressure in my chest gradually loosens, and my breathing evens out.

"So," he says in a low voice. "Where are the little monsters?" There's a glint of intrigue in his eyes. He's still touching me, both hands on my biceps again, both thumbs moving in calming circles.

My heart surges. "I don't know, and I'm honestly terrified." I snap my head to one side, then the other. Shit. There's no telling what they've gotten into by now.

Beckett releases my shoulders and lets out a loud, high-pitched whistle. Within milliseconds, the dogs are skittering and sliding across the floor like two newborn deer.

Quickly dropping to his knees, my roommate greets the eager dogs.

They wag their tails and whine, even more excited than when they arrived. Like they've reunited with a long-lost friend. Every couple of seconds, one of them body-checks Beckett, vying for his attention.

My panic drifts away as he breaks into a bright smile.

Fifteen minutes later, the dogs have finally calmed down. Both are splayed out on the floor, blissfully content as we rub their bellies.

I turn to Beckett to apologize again and find that he's watching me. In the dim light of the living room, his eyes crinkle softly at the corners and his lips curve into a warm smile that lights up his entire face.

Confused, I frown. "What?"

He looks away, the tips of his ears turning red, but forces his attention back quickly. "Nothing. It's just. . .n-nothing," he stammers.

Meow.

I jolt. Beckett does too. Vera and Frank both flip over, on high alert, their ears and noses twitching.

Oh fuck.

Barbara saunters down the stairs without a single care in the world, but when she sees the four of us, she arches her back, the fur along her spine standing straight up.

Then she bolts for the kitchen, a blur of orange, and without missing a beat, the dogs take off after her.

Damn. Never in my life have I seen animals move that fast.

I'm actually quite impressed.

Beckett and I scramble to our feet and sprint into the kitchen. But there's no sign of the animals. Panting, I spin in a circle. Beside me, Beckett zeroes in on the door with a magnetized flap I swear wasn't there an hour ago.

Where the hell did that come from?

It's a perfect escape for a persnickety feline and her two canine groupies.

He yanks the door open and bounds out into the dark, calling after the animals.

Just as I'm crossing the threshold, Barbara speeds back inside, running over my feet.

I blow out a breath. All right, one down, two to go.

As I close the door behind me, Beckett emerges from the dark, herding the dogs like cattle.

I can't help but want to laugh at the absurdity of the last ninety seconds.

Vera prances inside first, with Frank trailing close behind. So close that I can't even see his face.

Strange. Then again, Frank is a strange dog.

Beckett's out of breath, his chest heaving as he shuts the door. I'm still processing the chaos, my mind whirling.

"We need to nail this door down," he pants. "They're fast. Especially the blind one. He moves like he can see just fine."

I scurry to the junk drawer and yank it open. "I think I saw duct tape in here. Think we can use it as a temporary hold?"

Beckett nods. "Good idea."

We work quickly, pressing the sticky strips across the flap and sealing it shut as best as we can.

When we're finished, I sag against the counter, my head dropped forward, once again laughing. "What goes down must come up, right? It can only go up from here."

Brows pulled low, Beckett scratches the back of his neck.

"Um. That's not how the saying goes. Or how gravity works. It's what goes up must come down."

Head cocked, I put my hands on my hips. "Really? I've been saying that wrong all my life?"

Lips pressed together like he's trying not to laugh, he nods.

"Huh. Then—" A faint squeak from the living room makes me snap my mouth shut. "Did you hear that?"

"No." He takes one step toward the living room, listening. And again, there's a squeak. "Now I do."

I push off the counter and tiptoe into the living room, finding it empty. "Where did the animals go?"

"Uh," Beckett says, coming up behind me. "I don't know. And I don't like how quiet it is all of a sudden."

I turn to him, finding his eyes wide with panic.

My heart thumps in response, fear washing over me.

"Shit!" we say in unison.

Beckett lets out another whistle.

Half a second later, Barbara sprints down the stairs.

Followed by Vera.

Then Frank.

Frank, who has a brown squirrel in his mouth.

I gasp. "Frank, *drop it!*"

The dog miraculously obeys, and the squirrel makes a run for it. I'm not sure where the little guy is running to, but he better find a good hiding spot fast.

Both dogs scramble across the hardwood floor again, and Barbara skitters across the coffee table before leaping onto a chair. Vera gallops after her, tongue hanging out of her mouth. Meanwhile Frank the kleptomaniac, with his mischievous track record, is playing a game of hide and seek with his new friend.

A lamp clatters to the floor, a picture frame falls off the wall, and a pile of old magazines scatter everywhere.

The chaos intensifies as the squirrel pops out from under the couch and makes a break for the kitchen, with Barbara, Vera, and Frank hot on its heels.

Apparently Barbara and the dogs have formed an alliance in order to evict the intruder.

The trio barrels toward us as the squirrel skitters by, and just as I'm certain they'll take me out, an arm wraps around my waist and I'm yanked out of the way. I slam my eyes closed, and when I open them again, I'm submerged in darkness.

"Where are—"

Beckett places a gentle finger over my lips. Then his mouth is at the shell of my ear, whispering low. "We're in the closet."

This close to him, I can feel every ridge and valley of his muscled chest and his heat is seeping into me like the gentle rays of the sun on a lazy summer afternoon. His arm remains wrapped around my waist, with no signs of letting me go anytime soon.

"Barbara is resilient," he continues. "She'll be fine. Vera will surely get tired soon. She was already slowing down when I brought her in. And Frank." He sighs. "I think he wants to make friends with the squirrel, not kill it. Either way, we need five minutes away from the commotion behind this door."

His warm breath ghosts over my ear, causing my skin to pebble. Even after a full shift at the hospital, he smells incredible—minty and clean—and it makes it very difficult for me not to bury my face in his chest.

The door rattles, and there's a thud, making me jolt. On

instinct, I press my hands to Beckett's firm chest to steady myself.

He inhales sharply, but I swear his hold on me tightens. From the tips of our toes to our chests, our bodies are pressed intimately together. The sensation makes my blood run hot and my skin tingle.

Under my hands, his chest rises and falls rapidly, his heart racing beneath his scrub top.

The air in this cramped closet crackles with electricity, and my mind hazes over with desire. With a trembling hand, I cup his cheek, rubbing my thumb along his stubbled jaw.

Now that my eyes have adjusted to the darkness, I note the way his eyes flutter shut as he leans into my touch. A content groan rumbles from his chest, rich with longing and vulnerability.

The sound tempts me to pull his lips down to mine and kiss him without restraint.

Time stands still, and it's just the two of us alone with racing pulses and heaving chests.

He dips his head, forehead resting against mine, and with his other arm around my waist, he pulls me closer—if that's even possible. Our lips linger mere inches apart, so close our breaths mingle.

His arousal is obvious, pressing low and firm on my stomach. The sensation makes the ache between my thighs intensify, and my knees almost give out on me.

He shifts closer, his lips nearly whispering against—

Two pitiful whimpers sound on the other side of the door, shattering the moment, followed by an impatient meow and a curious squeak.

Beckett reels back and clears his throat.

Hands shaking, I find the knob and push the door open. A

rush of cool air hits my overheated skin, dousing the desire in my veins.

Just outside the door, we find the furry creatures behaving in an oddly respectful manner.

Including the squirrel.

Thrown off by the moment we just shared, I focus on the dogs, willing my heart rate to slow. "Do you. . .uh. . .want to see if you can get the squirrel back outside while I hold these two back?"

"Yep."

One word. A single syllable. It cuts through my chest like a sharp knife.

I feel like I messed up somehow. Like I crossed some line that I didn't even know existed.

CHARLIE AND FINN pick up their dogs just after midnight. Beckett and I smile and swear they behaved perfectly, which causes Finn to narrow his eyes and call us out for lying.

We fold quickly, telling them the whole sordid tale.

When they're gone, I plop onto the couch, resting my head in my hands.

Since our moment in the closet, Beckett has been quiet. More so than usual, shuffling around the house with slumped shoulders and his brows pinched like he's deep in thought.

Maybe he is.

Me? I've been doing what I do best: assuming the worst. He's probably ready to look for another place to live after all of the chaos we just survived. And it's my fault. We were caught in a turbulent whirlwind of dogs, cats, and squirrels, and by the time we got them settled, the cottage was in complete disarray. I can only imagine that stressed him out further, knowing he likes a tidy house. Finally, to top it all off, that charged, intimate moment we shared. A moment that has now morphed into an unspoken tension that lingers between us.

Beckett pads across the floor and eases into the chair in the corner.

Head still in my hands, elbows resting on my knees, I'm weighed down by guilt. In a shocking turn of events, Barbara decides to curl up next to me. Even she senses that I pissed her dad off.

Heart in my throat, I drop my hands and stare at the ground. "I'm so sorry, Beck—"

"Would you stop that?" he says, his tone firm.

I snap up, breath held in surprise.

Hunched forward in the chair with his elbows resting on his knees, he levels me with an intense look. One that's nearly impossible to decipher.

Oh fuck. He's probably irritated, and I don't blame him.

"S-sorry. I know—"

He stands abruptly, cutting me off, and strides across the room. He settles next to me, and rather than pull away when his knee brushes mine, he leaves it there.

Nerves skitter through me, making me fidgety. I pick at my cuticles, tempted to bolt into my room and forget this night happened.

Beckett covers my hands with one of his, stilling my restless fingers.

"Stop apologizing when you have nothing to be sorry for," he says quietly.

Shoulders sagging, I force myself to look at him. His

empathetic green eyes are locked on mine, tempting me to lose myself in them.

I swallow the lump of emotion in my throat. All my life, I've been an apologizer. My dad used to swear I had to be part Canadian because I would apologize for even the most minor inconvenience.

Beckett tucks my hair behind my ear, his lips kicking up at the corners. "Tonight was wild." He licks his lips, assessing me, the scrutiny making my skin itch. "But it was really fucking fun. I can't remember a time when I experienced every single human emotion in the span of a few hours."

Shaking my head, I chuckle. "Sure, it was fun while it lasted. But you're a cat person. I don't know how you managed to keep it together during all the destructive mayhem the dogs bring with them." I shudder, recalling the memory of the squirrel finding a home in Frank's mouth.

He laughs. The sound goes straight to my heart, lightening my mood instantly. "Yes, I'm a cat person. But on my days off, I volunteer at the shelter and take dogs out. I love them. I've always wanted one. Or more, really. But my job makes it difficult."

My heart aches at the longing in his voice, though the sensation is quickly squashed when a memory hits me. "That day we got tangled in the leashes, you were volunteering?" I snap up straight. "I thought you were doing someone a favor."

He shakes his head. "Nope. Every city I go to, I volunteer as often as I can. It's one of my favorite things to do, actually."

Sighing, I bow my head. "Of course you do volunteer work. You, sir, are a walking, talking green flag." I mumble the last few words.

"What was that? I didn't catch the last part," he teases. "Something about a green flag?"

What should've stayed firmly inside my mind has escaped.

I vehemently shake my head, fighting a smile. "Nothing. Ignore me."

In response, he scoots closer, crowding my space, and drapes an arm over the back of the couch. "I don't want to ignore you. Ever."

My stomach flips, like I'm at the top of a roller coaster.

Goddammit. This man.

This can't happen. Our friendship, roommate-ship, whatever this is, has an expiration date. Yet his compassionate smile, kind eyes, and soft touch slowly tug at my seams, unraveling my control. A chaotic storm of emotions swirls in my mind, each one fighting for my undivided attention, while I, on the other hand, shove them down, hoping they go away.

Unfortunately, it's getting more and more difficult to tame these turbulent feelings.

Chapter Nineteen

BECKETT

JOEY

I'm heading to bed early. . .

Is this your way of asking for your Daily Beckett Fact?

JOEY

Obviously.

How weird do you want it?

JOEY

The weirder the better, baby.

If I have time, I like to air dry after I shower.

Ten minutes go by with no reply.

Did I make things weird?

ALL WEEK, memories of Joey's lush curves pressed against me in that closet have haunted me. Along with the sensation of my fingers sinking into her warm skin, her strawberry scent, and the way her plush pink lips parted when I almost kissed her.

Every night, I replay that moment as I fuck my fist in the shower. If I don't, every thread of restraint I have around her will snap. It's the only way to ease the tension.

After the moment in the closet, my nervous system glitched and I started shutting down.

It was clear she was worried about the shift in my demeanor, and as much as I wanted to tell her what was going on in my head, I couldn't because I didn't understand it myself.

I spent hours journaling that night. Decoding my feelings like a cryptogram, only beginning to make sense of things as I scratched the details into the pages of my journal.

Even now, I can't get a handle on it all. All I know is that it'll hurt to leave her when my assignment is up. What I'm feeling isn't just some generic crush—

"*Hello*. Earth to Beckett." Tabitha snaps her fingers in front of me. "What is going on in that beautiful blond head of yours?"

I jolt back and drag a hand down my face. "I wish I could tell you."

"Your week's been that bad, huh? I feel that. One of the night shift residents and I almost got into it," she mutters. "I've been thinking about replacing the sugar packets he uses for his coffee with salt."

I huff a quiet laugh through my nose. "Replace half of his pens with ones that have run out of ink. It's the gift that keeps on giving."

She slaps my shoulder, her expression brightening. "This is why you're my favorite. Quiet and unassuming but with a devious side. The tattoos also help." As she stands from her chair, she winks, patting me on the shoulder. "Whatever you're going through, hang in there, big guy."

***

AFTER SUCH AN EXHAUSTING NIGHT, my body is drained, yet my mind is still wired from my shift.

So I drag myself upstairs and into the shower to wash the day away. The ER was an absolute nightmare today. From initiating appropriate treatment plans and performing procedures to patient advocacy and working with social workers. I'm tapped out.

With steam billowing around me, I rest my forehead against the cool shower tile and will myself to relax. The hot water cascades down my back, loosening the knots in my muscles.

When I'm feeling a little better, I open my eyes, ready to scrub away the day, and as I reach for the soap, a bright pink object catches my attention. In the corner of the stall is a pink rubber duck with a mohawk. I pick it up and examine it, holding it close to my face since I've already removed my contacts, and I try not to shudder when the beady eyes bore into my soul.

How the hell did this get in here? More importantly, *why* is it in here?

Shaking my head, I put it back where I found it and finish my shower. As I step out of the shower, a chill hits me. Rather than air dry tonight, I grab my towel and pat my body down quickly to stave off the cold.

I tug on my favorite pair of gray sweatpants and a faded black T-shirt, then fumble around, looking for my glasses.

In the kitchen, I stop in front of the large window and quickly spot Joey. As usual, she's hunched over her crossword puzzle by the glow of the fire. Smiling to myself, I take a moment to admire the view. Wrapped in another colorful blanket, this one with shades of purple and blue, she looks content. Peaceful. Her expression is one of concentration as she fills in the letters of her puzzle, yet there's ease there too.

As I pad across the yard, I take in the navy night sky and countless twinkling stars. The air is chilly, nipping at my skin as the rich scent of burning firewood envelops me.

"Fortuitous," I say, lowering myself into the chair beside her.

She jerks upright, her brown eyes widening. "Every. Damn. Time," she mumbles under her breath.

I can't help but chuckle. "You had a long day too?"

She lets out a deep, annoyed sigh. "Norma."

"Fucking Norma," I grouse. "Need me to talk to her? I'm still in contact with a few of the bikers in that gang I accidentally got caught up with."

She rears back, her mouth hanging open. "What?"

"Super nice dudes," I tell her. "They host a flea market most weekends and donate the money to charity."

"You're just full of surprises, aren't you?"

"I gotta keep you on your toes, Josephine." I wink. "Are you doing anything tonight?"

She tilts her head. "Why?"

I run my hands through my damp hair. "I need to work out some nervous energy."

She pulls her lip between her teeth. "Uh. Okay?"

"I was wondering if you could help me." I don't know how else to put it, so I go with the straightforward approach.

Joey blinks at me like an owl. The deep orange flames reflecting in her eyes make them sparkle. "I don't know where this is going and I'm scared to find out. Yet I'm weirdly intrigued."

Feeling a bit bold, I grin and lower my voice, angling in closer. "How good are you with your hands?"

She gives me a dead stare, and I swear she isn't breathing.

After a moment, she heaves out a breath. "Beckett. This isn't funny." She surveys the fire for a moment, then turns back to me. With a resigned sigh, she says, "Okay, it's a little funny."

"All joking aside," I say, "I wanted to make a loaf of bread and thought you might like to join me."

She rolls her lips, holding back a smile. "Wow. I didn't know we'd reached the point in our relationship where you'd be willing to share Agatha with me. You can be a bit *kneady*."

I huff a breath out of my nose. This woman. I swear she's

the reincarnation of a suburban father figure trying to be cool. Her jokes are more likely to make a person groan than laugh.

Yet I find it unquestionably charming.

Her eyes widen. "Did I make things weird? I made things weird. Let's head inside before I make more of an ass out of myself." She heaves herself up, and with slumped shoulders, she shuffles her way to the cottage.

Despite my best efforts to hold it in, a burst of laughter escapes me.

She whips around and stomps her foot. "You're supposed to be nice and laugh, even if my joke isn't funny. I'm off my game this evening. *Ugh.*" With that, she trudges inside.

Joey's little quips, whether poorly timed jokes or funny comments under her breath, never fail to amuse me. It's part of what makes her so extraordinary in my eyes. She has a unique charm that's impossible to replicate.

After putting the fire out, I head in. Stepping into the kitchen feels like entering a little bubble created for just the two of us. The outside worries drift away and the stresses from the week disappear.

I reach for my phone, cuing up a playlist of gentle melodies. Then I get to work wiping down the countertops in preparation.

"Can you get the flour out?" I ask as I'm gathering the rest of the things I need.

Joey pads over to the cabinet to the left of the fridge and pulls it open. A scream rends the air, piercing through the stillness of the kitchen and sending my heart racing.

On high alert, I dart across the room and put myself between her and the danger.

Only then do I discover the issue.

Barbara.

Tucked away deep in the dark cabinet, my cat has burrowed herself between my baking supplies. Only her glowing amber eyes are visible like this. It's enough to even creep me out.

I wince. "Sorry about my stalker cat. I'll get her out of there."

"How does she get in here? And how does she get in my room? She comes in while I'm sleeping and knocks my phone off the bedside table."

"Huh." I peer at my cat. "So that's where she's going at night."

"*That's where she's going at night?*" she mocks. "Maybe you should put a tracker on her. Your stalker cat's new hobby is watching me sleep, and it's unnerving."

Crossing my arms, I prop myself up against the cabinets. "Do you think she stays there all night?"

Glaring, Joey runs her hands through her wavy hair. "Beckett. She's. *Your.* Cat."

I try my best to keep a straight face, but she's so adorable when she's angry, and the laughter spills out of me.

"You should know," she grouses. "Get control over your daughter."

I lift one shoulder lazily. "I can't keep track of her if I'm asleep."

"Well, try harder." She props her hands on her hips, her chin lifted. "I wake up every morning nearly suffocating because she's curled up on my chest."

Lucky cat.

Skirting around Joey, I snag the flour from the cabinet, followed by Barbara. I set her on the floor, and she quickly skitters up the stairs, leaving Joey and me alone in the kitchen.

Silently, I pour most of Agatha's contents into a bowl,

then add water, salt, and flour. All the while, Joey watches me intently. I make sourdough so often I could probably do it in my sleep, so the dough comes together in no time. I turn it out onto the floured countertop and divide the dough into two equal portions, then dust my hands with flour. "All right," I say, nodding to one half of the dough. "Get some flour on your hands like this. Then you want to push the dough away from you with the heel of your hand like this." I demonstrate, then pull the dough back and repeat the process. "When you're ready to shape it, cup the sides and tuck while dragging it toward your body."

She eyes her hands and then the dough. "I don't have much confidence in myself." Then, with flour-dusted hands, she clumsily kneads it, pushing and pulling it back to her.

With one hand, she scoops flour straight out of the bag and sprinkles it onto the counter.

Inwardly, I cringe, making a mental note to purchase a new bag of flour this week.

"Hey, Beck?" she says.

Still kneading my own dough, I lift my eyes to her. "Yeah?"

"When two loaves of bread go on a date, do you think one of them brings the other *flours*?" Her face is stoic as she delivers the line.

How many puns does this woman have lined up?

Sighing, I tilt my head to the side. "That's a solid five out of ten joke."

She rears back, causing a few pieces of hair to gracefully fall into her face, and points a dough-covered finger at me. "Oh, come on! You know you secretly love them."

I do love them. A lot. I also love riling her up and watching the way her cheeks turn pink.

I wonder what else could make her blush like that.

Clearing my throat, I look at her over the rims of my glasses. "I think love is a strong word. More like tolerate?"

She rolls her eyes, a devilish smirk playing on her lips, and I wonder what mischief is going through her mind. Seconds later, she closes the distance between us in a few confident strides, then playfully slaps my chest, leaving a bright white handprint on my black shirt.

Without pause and without a word, she steps back to her spot at the counter and continues working on her dough.

For a moment, all I can do is gape at the handprint.

In more ways than one, Joey is leaving her mark on me. With each passing day, she's branding herself on my soul.

Taking a deep breath, I turn my attention back to the countertop and focus on kneading.

Before long, she is wiggling her nose like she has an itch she can't scratch and eventually gives in and uses the back of her wrist, leaving a smudge of flour on the tip.

This small, innocent moment makes my heart skip. She's completely unaware of how charming she is.

It's impossible to focus on my sourdough because I'm so intensely wrapped up in watching her.

Tonight, she's wearing an oversized pink cardigan with white flowers on it. It drapes loosely over her body while her light blue sweatpants fit snugly, accentuating her curves. Her long auburn hair tumbles down her back in soft waves, though she's got it pulled up in the front, leaving a few strands framing her face.

Her stunningly beautiful face.

I can't take my eyes off her.

The way her eyebrows crease with confusion.

How she bites the inside of her lip with uncertainty.

The way her cheeks flush when she gets frustrated.

Right now, she looks so soft and at ease. My arms ache to wrap her up. To hold her snug against my chest and shield her from the cruel world and people like Norma.

Blowing a piece of hair out of her face, she peers up at me. "What's the matter? Am I doing something wrong?"

My cheeks heat a little. Looks like I've been caught staring. "No."

"Then why are you looking at me like that?"

I inhale a deep breath and steal my nerves. Then I say it. "I just. . .I like looking at you. That's all." When the warmth in my cheeks turns into an inferno, I dip my head, keeping my focus on my dough, wishing I could take the words back and knowing that for the next week, I'll be worrying that I made her uncomfortable.

"Could you show me how to knead again? I think I got lost along the way. My hand-eye coordination has never been the best." Her laugh is light and airy, the sound easing my anxiety.

"Yeah. It's like this." I slow down my moves and show her again.

She hums. "I still don't understand. Can you guide my hands with yours? So I can feel the motion?" She looks over at me, her eyes big and innocent, her smile sweet.

I swallow hard, my heart hammering, and it's a battle to keep my voice steady. "Absolutely."

On shaky legs, I shuffle up behind her but avoid touching her. Though if she wants me to guide her hands, I have to get closer.

I clear my throat. "Do you mind if I touch you? I don't want to make you uncomfortable or—"

"Please," she interrupts, her voice barely above a whisper.

I take half a step closer, and at the first brush of contact, barely more than the fabric of my T-shirt shifting against her sweater, my breath stalls out. Joey angles back a little, closing the distance between us.

Her soft curves are now firmly pressed against me, causing heat to rush through my veins. Noticing some of her hair has slipped in front of her face, I push a few loose strands behind her shoulder, and when my fingertips graze the sensitive skin of her neck, her skin pebbles.

Hands trembling, I twine my fingers with hers. Then I dip my head, my jaw brushing against her smooth hair. "You move it like this." I move her hands, rolling the dough away and then back to us once, then again. As we work through the motion over and over, I swear sparks of electricity arc between us.

The contrast between the dark swirls of my tattoos and her pale hands should not be this arousing, yet it makes my pulse pound in my ears.

With another push of the dough, my cheek brushes hers, the rasp of my stubble against her smooth skin audible over the music.

Her breath hitches, and she leans in closer.

With each passing the second, the atmosphere charges further.

I can only see the side of her face, but I'm enraptured as she darts her tongue out, wetting her bottom lip. In response, my hands tighten around hers, and she shudders, melting deeper into my embrace.

Fuck, do I want to taste those lips. Feel them pressed against mine. Discover what kind of noises she would make as I thread my fingers through her hair and tip her head back so I can deepen the kiss.

Anticipation coils in my stomach, my body a live wire ready to explode.

Closing my eyes, I breathe her in, letting the aroma of strawberries and campfire invade my senses.

It would be so easy to kiss her breathless right here, right now.

If I don't step away now, there will be no turning back. I don't think I could stop myself from hauling her up onto this counter and guiding those long legs around my waist.

With one more inhale, I try to pull myself together before I do something I'll regret in the morning.

Joey peers up at me, her hands stilling, her lips parted and her pupils dilated, making her brown eyes look almost black.

My heart thuds loudly, an invisible force pulling me closer—

Meow.

We jump apart like we just got caught by our parents, the bubble around us shattering.

Being caught by Barbara might be worse than being caught by parents. With the way she's shooting daggers at us, I worry for our safety tonight.

It's then that I notice the time above the stove. Shit, it's almost midnight and Joey has work in the morning.

I stagger back farther. "I'm so sorry. I didn't realize how late it was."

Joey wraps her sweater tighter around her, a habit that signals that she's nervous or feeling shy, I've noticed.

Looking everywhere but at me, she nods. "Yeah. I should get some sleep. Do you want me to help you clean up before I turn in for the night?"

"Absolutely not." The knots in my muscles return. "I'll clean up out here. Have a good night."

Running her hands through her hair, she nods. Then with a murmured *good night*, she shuffles down the hall.

When her door snicks shut behind her, I slump to the floor, resting my head in my hands.

What am I doing?

Beckett's Journal

May 13

I feel pulled to her. Like we're two wandering souls.

Maybe it's because we're in our own little bubble in this cottage. But my mind drifts back to the open mic night. How she was aware of me and how I was feeling when panic set in. She grounded me in that moment without even knowing it. Holding my hand to show me I wasn't alone. That she was right there with me.

Piece by piece, my resolve is breaking.

Chapter Twenty

JOEY

OUTSIDE THE OFFICE WINDOW, bleak gray clouds blanket the sky, promising rain and distracting me from work. Okay, maybe the clouds aren't to blame. I'm distracted because I can't stop thinking about all of my interactions with Beckett over the last seven-ish weeks.

When we're together, he never makes me feel like I'm an inconvenience. When I make a mess in the kitchen, he simply chuckles. If I forget to buy coffee for myself, he insists I use his. Last week, when I left my clothes in the washer and got sidetracked, he quietly moved them to the dryer for me.

Each time I apologized profusely.

Each time he told me there's nothing to be sorry for.

He hasn't once scoffed at me in a demeaning way. If anything, his deep green eyes flash with amusement when my brain buffers and stalls in a moment of forgetfulness.

With him, I feel accepted for who I am. Like my value and

worth aren't based on my outward traits but on my innermost self.

The only part that truly matters.

"Ready?" Max's voice invades my introspection.

I let out a heavy sigh, my heart sinking. "I suppose."

We have another meeting with the Droplet team today, and quite frankly, I'm in no mood for Norma's bullshit.

I'm exhausted, and on top of that, my bra is digging into my side and my new shoes are pinching my feet. And I would commit murder for some chocolate chip ice cream.

That's how I'm feeling this afternoon.

The moment I step into the conference room, Norma gives me another once-over and shakes her head. Being the immature person I am, I roll my eyes and hope she notices.

I sit at the long conference table, open my laptop, and share it to the wide screen in front of us. This is my second round of designs for the team to review, so with any luck, one of them will be acceptable.

With a steadying breath, I start my presentation. "Here are the concepts with the requested changes. My thought process behind these—"

"I don't like them," Normal blurts out, interrupting me.

Well, I don't like you, Norma.

Even Bryan reels back a little at her outburst.

I suck in a sharp breath. "The last time we spoke, you said you wanted—"

"The black and white is boring. We asked for color." She scoffs.

Anxiety grips my throat. "That's not what—"

"We approved a color palette during the design brief. Why didn't you follow that?"

My shoulders cave in on themselves, and suddenly, I wish

the floor would open up and swallow me. "I did. You told me you didn't want—"

"I told you no such thing."

My stomach lurches. Oh my fucking god. I can't even get a single thought out of my mouth. And on top of that, the woman is gaslighting me.

She tsks, her nose in the air. "I expected more from Fernrose."

Anger swells in my chest, and when I discover all eyes on me, unease joins it. Norma is making me look like an unqualified brand designer who doesn't listen to her client. And that makes the whole company look bad.

I sit back, speechless. How does one even defend themselves when another person comes at them this hard and fast?

Bryan clears his throat and adjusts the cuffs of his sleeves. "How about we move forward with the rest of the presentation? Sure, the colors aren't what we were hoping for, but I love the choice in typography."

Heart pounding, I nod and move to the next slide.

It's funny how a person can so easily yank another's confidence away. And the worst part is I don't understand why.

RAINDROPS SPLATTER on my windshield as I drive along the dark, winding forest road back to the cottage. Even though it's not even five p.m., the trees shadowing the road block out what little light is left in the day.

All I want is to wash my makeup off, get into a pair of oversized sweatpants, faceplant into my bed, and forget this day ever happened.

By the time I pull in the driveway, the rain is falling in slanted sheets. Lit up the way it is, the cottage looks warm and inviting. A safe haven from my shit day. With my bag over my head, I sprint to the front door. Inside, I slam it behind me and drop my head against its surface heavily.

"Everything okay over there?" a deep voice says, startling me.

Without opening my eyes, I say, "Are you asking if I'm okay mentally, physically, or emotionally? Actually, it doesn't matter. The answer is a firm no to all of the above."

Beckett lets out a deep, rumbly chuckle that turns my insides to liquid. Every time this man laughs, my knees almost give out.

Quickly, I kick off my wet boots. Then I drop my bags from aching shoulders, letting them hit the floor with a resounding thud.

My roommate is sprawled out on the couch with Barbara sleeping peacefully on his chest and a well-worn paperback in his hand. He's wearing a black cardigan over a thin gray T-shirt and loose black sweatpants that sit low enough on his hips to expose the thick band of his boxer briefs. When he shifts on the couch, the hem of his shirt rides up, offering me a glimpse of his defined lower stomach.

My mouth goes dry as I stare at his strikingly hand-some. . .well, *everything*. Everything about this man is attrac-tive and it's more than skin deep. His personality. His heart. Hell, even his hobbies are hot.

He peers at me over the rims of the glasses positioned low on his nose. Wide-eyed and clearly confused about why I've gone frozen.

It annoys me how good he looks right now, all effortlessly sexy, with a sleeping cat on his chest. In contrast, I'm sure I look like a rat that's emerged from the depths of a sewer. My hair is wet, and I imagine mascara is running down my face. Don't even get me started on how puffy my eyes must look.

Grumbling, I stalk toward my room. "I would like to opt out of today," I say flatly. "Is there a form for that?"

Beckett huffs a laugh. "I don't think so."

"Figures," I mutter. "Women haven't been allowed to opt out of emotional suffering for centuries."

His face twists into a look of horror.

I sigh. "Seriously! There was a time when women received lobotomies for having emotions. Which is completely absurd. Meanwhile, the big, strong, manly men were out there starting wars and calling it leadership."

Beckett's face pales. He opens his mouth, but I keep going. "And before that? They treated 'hysteria' with a *pelvic massage*." I waggle my eyebrows. "Which is just a Victorian way of saying vibrator therapy. Who needs to talk when you can have an orgasm or five? It's probably the only time in medical history women left an appointment satisfied."

His ears turn crimson and it fills me with joy.

I lift an eyebrow, smiling. "So if I start showing signs of *hysteria*, just hand me my vibrator and call it preventative care. Anyway, I'll be right back."

After a quick shower to wash away this horrible day, I slip on a set of pastel blue pajamas with strawberries on them, then wander back out to the living room.

As I approach, Beckett smirks, taking me in from head to toe.

"Why are you smirking at me? I'm not sure I like that smirk."

He flattens his lips, though his eyes dance. "No reason."

I stomp over to the couch, hands on my hips. "No, there's a reason and I want to know what it is."

"Strawberry waffles, strawberry pancakes, strawberry-patterned pajamas." His eyes flick back to his book, but the flush on his cheeks deepens. "And you even smell like strawberries." With a breath out, he licks his lips as he turns the page. "I like it." He whispers the last part, but the words come through to me loud and clear.

Blood roars loud in my ears, drowning out the rain pounding on the roof of the cottage.

All the while, he flips through his book, unaware of the effect that his comment had on me.

Mind boggled, I head into the kitchen to grab a drink of water. Outside the window over the sink, the shaking of tree branches shows me the wind has really picked up. The tall trees bend with each howling gust and rain pelts the window. Above me, the kitchen lights flicker.

I look up, ready to call out to Beckett and warn him the lights may go out, but before I can, darkness blankets the cottage. Setting my glass on the counter with a thud, I let out a tired sigh. This day truly can't get any worse.

Or maybe it can and I jinxed myself. The night is still young, after all.

Beckett's slippers scuff on the floor as he makes his way into the kitchen. "Do you know where the flashlights are?" He opens a drawer and rummages through it.

"The drawer second from the bottom," I reply flatly, still staring out the window. "Candles and a lighter in a drawer above that one. Maybe we should light a few of them."

He sidles up beside me, placing his large hand on my shoulder. The touch should light me up inside, but I'm too drained to do anything but stare out at the rain.

"You've had a terrible day," he says softly. The back of my neck prickles with awareness as I sense his penetrating stare, the way he studies me. *Worries about me.*

He glides his hand to my upper back, his heat soaking into me, and moves it in soothing circles.

Relishing the sensation, I drop my chin to my chest and close my eyes. Under his touch, my tense muscles finally loosen.

With each hypnotic stroke, another of the day's terrible events melts away.

"Go lay on the couch and relax, Josephine. I'll handle this."

While some of the tension has drained from me, I'm still all out of fight, so I nod and shuffle my way to the living room.

In the corner, Barbara has made herself at home on the chair. When she sees me, her ears perk up and she flicks her tail from side to side. Dare I say, she looks happy to see me.

Even I can admit she looks pretty cute right now.

I collapse onto the soft cushions with a groan and curl into a ball, watching Beckett set two candles on the coffee table, along with a glass of water, a bowl of pretzels, and a cross-word puzzle book.

When he notices my curious expression, his voice suddenly turns shy. "In case you get thirsty, hungry, or bored."

Appreciation blooms deep inside my chest, causing tears to prick at the backs of my eyes. Sniffling, I bury my face in a pillow to keep them at bay.

For so long, I've taken care of myself.

Over the years, I've wished I had someone to help lift me up when I've hit my lowest.

Now, after being by myself for many years, this quiet, thoughtful man has proven to me again and again that despite all the darkness in the world, there are still selfless people out there who will bring the light.

The living room that was once shrouded in shadows is now cast in a deep orange glow. The rain hammers relentlessly on the roof and the haunting howls of the wind fill the quiet living room.

It's the perfect night to curl up in bed, wrapped in my favorite blanket, and fall asleep to the sounds of the storm.

Yet I can't stomach the idea of not being in his presence. We don't even have to speak.

I just want to exist with him.

He pads to the chair, but when Barbara sprawls out, belly up, he thinks better of it and settles on the opposite end of the couch. From the coffee table, he picks up his paperback. Then he shifts to get comfortable.

"You're different, you know," I say, my voice muffled by the cushion.

A breathy laugh escapes him. "How so?" He opens his book and sets his bookmark on the arm of the couch. "You can stretch your legs out. I don't mind if you put them in my lap."

If he keeps this whole caretaking act up, I wouldn't mind putting my entire body in his lap.

"When I fainted, you came in like a knight in shining armor, swooping in to save me. Then creepy Kyle found me in the grocery store, and again, you swooped in."

"I get that a lot actually."

"Really?" I shift on the couch, stretching out my legs so they rest on his thighs.

"Mm-hmm. It's one of the reasons I got into nursing. When I see someone who needs help, the shy, worried parts of me shut down and I turn into a different person entirely. A guy who is sure of himself, who knows exactly how to navigate the situation."

"Have you always been like that?"

"Growing up, I was an observant kid, I guess. Quiet and watchful, according to my mom." He rests his hands on my shins. "I got very good at reading expressions, and at an early age, I could tell when someone was in distress."

I let out a sound that's half laugh, half snort. "Guess that explains how you always know when to bring me my emotional support crossword puzzle."

Looking down at his hands, he smiles. "When I was a kid, a girl a few years younger than me, fell off her bike in front of our house. She didn't cry, but I could see the panic in her eyes and in the way she kept searching around her, like she was looking for a sibling or a parent to help. But there was no one."

I stare up at the ceiling and close my eyes. For some reason this story sounds eerily familiar. Maybe it's a coincidence, but I swear I've heard it before.

"I raced over to her," he continues, "and took my jacket off, then used it to put pressure on her bloody knees until I saw an adult and shouted to them that I needed help. When the girl saw the man, her eyes filled with relief. It was her dad."

My body stills.

No, I haven't heard this story before.

I've lived it.

I'm the girl. The one who fell off the bike.

Memories rush back like a wave crashing into shore.

I swallow back tears, silently praying he'll finish the story.

"I remember it like it happened yesterday. That man looked at me with so much relief and gratitude that I was there to help his daughter. Even commended me for my calm demeanor." He chuckles. "He even told me he was happy I made it in time to cover up her bloody knees with my jacket—"

"Because she fainted at the sight of blood," I say, my voice cracking and hot tears sliding down my cheeks.

The couch shifts under Beckett's weight as he turns toward me. "Yeah. How did you know?"

Sniffing, I sit up, removing my legs from Beckett and tucking them under myself. "Because *I* was that girl who fell."

Head bowed, he laughs quietly. "That's why you're so familiar to me."

It's so weird how the universe works. We've spent our adult lives on the move, chasing dreams, yet here we are, drawn together by an invisible string. It didn't matter how many miles were between us or how much time had passed—somehow, we were always connected.

I swallow down the thick lump of emotion in my throat. My dad felt terrible for not being there to help me sooner, and after he bandaged my knees, he took me for ice cream, even though my mom had already started making dinner.

Another round of tears falls as I think about that day. As I think about my dad.

Still, I smile at the memory. Smile when I realize that Beckett met my dad all those years ago, and that moment made such a profound impact on his life. I glance up at him and I'm certain he's ready to wrap me up in his arms. "That moment really stuck with you. The relief a person feels when you're there to help them. You carried that all the way into adulthood."

"Exactly. Being a steady presence for another person fills me with purpose. Though it doesn't take away who I am at my very core, which is—"

"A quiet, introspective, deeply caring individual," I finish for him.

He chuckles. "I was going to say shy and socially awkward, but you made it sound much more poetic. Thank you for that."

Silence blankets the room as I replay this conversation, as I consider the past and the present and maybe even parts of the future. During my tarot reading before I moved back to Hemlock, Willow told me I'd have an emotional awakening and a new beginning. Now, I can't help but wonder what my life could be like with someone like Beckett by my side. Could this be fate or destiny or whatever spooky shit Willow brings up during my readings?

I force my treacherous, overthinking brain to halt those thoughts from progressing any further. Because outside of Hemlock, our lives are completely different. It was a complete and total coincidence that we ended up back here at the same time.

One of the candles on the coffee table dies, making the room a little darker. The timing couldn't be more perfect. I need some breathing room so I can clear my mind. This room and my mind are feeling too small for my comfort.

I slip my feet from his lap, but as I haul myself up, one leg goes tingly and gives out, causing me to tumble directly on top of Beckett.

Mortified, I blink up at him. He's watching me with a look

that's equal parts amusement and tenderness, his arms around me.

Heart in my throat, I say, "I'm so so—"

With a gentle, knowing smile, he presses his index finger to my lips to keep me from apologizing.

And my chest expands. I fear I may be in too deep with this man.

Chapter Twenty-One

"I CAN'T HELP but think there's a reason we've been pushed together. Maybe it's all a coincidence," he says, tucking a strand of my hair behind my ear, his fingers lingering there, "but it sure doesn't feel like one. At least not to me." His eyes flicker between mine. Even in the dim light, the hesitation there is obvious. So is the longing.

Still lying on top of him, I take him in, getting caught up on his strong throat, watching it flex as he swallows.

Beckett's voice drops to a rough whisper. "Josephine." His hand finds my face, and I flush at his touch. My skin prickles as his fingers slide into my hair, coming to rest at the nape of my neck. His thumb traces the curve of my cheekbone, and I forget to breathe. While his touch is featherlight, the intensity in his eyes is overwhelming.

He holds my face in his palm tenderly, like I'm his most prized possession.

He closes his eyes for a moment and when he opens them again, he draws in a deep breath and studies me, like he's memorizing every detail of my face, his chest rising and falling rapidly.

A muscle along his sharp jaw twitches. "If I don't kiss you right now—even if it's only once—I'm going to spend every day of my life regretting it."

His words slice through my chest, cracking it wide open. To feel this wanted, this cherished, sends a tsunami of emotion through me. My heart pounds so violently I worry it'll work its way right out of my chest.

With another stroke of my cheek, he leans in closer. "I'm going to kiss you now, Josephine. Is that okay?"

Wordlessly, I nod. Every part of me is aware of him. The weight of his emerald gaze, the warmth of his breath ghosting over my sensitive lips. Right now, there's nothing else.

Just him.

Just me.

Only us.

With one hand buried in my hair, he closes the distance between us, and when he makes contact, it's just a hesitant brush of his lips against mine at first. Tentative and tender, just like he is.

Though beneath the surface, there's an undercurrent of restraint he can't hide.

He pulls back and releases me, but I catch his wrist and bring his hand back to my hair. "You can do better than that."

With a twitch of his lips, he dips his head, his mouth colliding with mine. This kiss isn't tentative or tender. No, it's filled with a charged intensity. With the longing that came with every accidental touch and lingering look.

A moan vibrates deep in his chest, and I whimper in

response, my body giving me no other choice. I cradle his face, relishing the solid press of his stubbled cheek, needing more of him.

I need him to take *more*. He has it in him—he just needs a little push. I thread my fingers through his hair and pull him in closer, as if we aren't already sharing the same breath.

As if he can read my mind, he tilts his head, sweeping his tongue into my mouth and deepening our kiss.

It's passionate. It's consuming.

It's everything I didn't know I needed.

I'm weightless. Suspended in a reality that only exists for the two of us, here in this small cottage on a dark, stormy evening, my body burning up with building arousal.

The light flickers on overhead, and the appliances in the kitchen all beep, dragging us back to reality.

He pulls away, breathing heavily, wearing a pained expression, like this is the last thing he wants to do. Eyes glassy, he rubs his thumb along my sensitive bottom lip. The corners of his mouth lift into a smile that doesn't quite reach his eyes.

It's as if we've been doused in cold water and forced back to real life.

I close my eyes, disappointment washing over me. Dammit. Why the hell did the power have to come back on?

In the dark, anything was possible. In the light, we're hit with a stark reminder of the glaring difference between fantasy and reality. One we can escape *to* and the other we can't escape *from*.

We're both wordless, my head bowed, his attention bouncing around the room. We both know we got caught up in the moment. Maybe it's because we're lonely and starved for connection. We got carried away because it felt a little too good to finally be desired.

With a shaky exhale, I scramble off his lap. He grasps my hips and helps me to my feet, and when he releases me, I try my damndest to ignore the way my heart drops. He doesn't make eye contact with me when he stands or when he collects the candles and returns them to the kitchen or when he whistles for Barbara to follow him.

To be fair, I can't bear to look at him either. My heart is too fragile.

At the staircase, he hesitates, and I finally look up. His back is turned to me, his muscles tensing under his thin shirt. "I'm, uh, going to head to bed. Good night, Joey." His words come out strangled, like he's battling with himself. With one foot on the bottom step and his hand white-knuckling the banister, he shakes his head. Then he ascends the stairs.

The sound of his door closing reverberates through the house, hitting me with a symbolic sense of finality. Encapsulating unspoken feelings and emotions that are now forever locked away.

I rub my tired eyes and sigh. I should get some sleep. Tomorrow I can be easy, breezy, *nothing bothers her* Joey. But tonight, I'm giving myself permission to wallow and ruminate.

I turn off the lights and make sure the doors are locked for the night. Then I slip into my room and close the door, the latch clicking into place. Leaning my back against the cool wood, I let out a long breath and pinch the bridge of my nose, trying to ease the tension and regret building inside me. That kiss dragged me so deep beneath the surface that I couldn't see the light. Truthfully, I was more than okay with that. If anything, I would have stayed much, much longer if I could.

A soft creaking noise outside my door breaks through my thoughts, and I straighten, listening.

Maybe it's Barbara

"All right, Babs," I say, pulling the door open, "you can come—" My breath catches and my heart stutters. On the opposite side of the threshold, Beckett stands with his hand poised to knock. "What're you doing here?"

He steps in close, leaving us toe to toe in the doorway. "Something we hopefully won't regret."

With his index finger, he hooks the waistband of my pajama pants and drags me against him. Then he threads his fingers through my hair and grasps my nape.

His hold on me is strong yet careful. A blissful balance that makes me feel deeply cherished.

Irreplaceable.

Unforgettable.

No one has made me feel the way he does—it's addicting and euphoric.

As a storm of emotions overwhelms me, my heart hammers behind my ribcage. My legs tremble, and as my knees buckle, Beckett wraps a firm arm around my waist. His rough hand slips under my shirt, fingers sinking into the heated flesh of my lower back.

Through my thin cotton pajama pants, his thick erection presses into me and I stifle a moan. A deep, needy ache unfurls in my core. The urge to press my body against his, to seek friction and relief, consumes every one of my thoughts.

His eyes burn into mine. "Are you okay with this?"

Breathless, I nod. "Yes."

Jaw tight, he searches my face. "Do you want this?"

I tip my head back so he can see the truth in my expression. "Desperately."

I need this man's body on my body. I'm not picky about how he does it, just as long as he does it soon.

"If at any point you want to stop, we'll stop." His stern voice sends a chill through me and makes my stomach twist in anticipation.

I clutch his T-shirt and slam my mouth to his.

Groaning, he backs me over to the bed, and when I hit the mattress, I fall backward, bringing him with me. Instinctively, I wrap my legs around his firm waist, pulling him closer to me. For a moment, he pulls away, pausing just long enough to remove his glasses and place them on the nightstand before his lips find mine again.

His warm, firm mouth works against mine with confidence. The stubble on his jaw grazes my cheek as he tilts his head to deepen the kiss. I feel his heartbeat against my palm, racing to match my own. Our breathing becomes erratic, gasping for air between kisses—desperately needing more of one another.

He grinds against me, his hard length pressing against my clit through my pajamas. When I whimper, he swallows the sound and rolls his hips. In seconds, my pajama pants are soaked and I'm meeting his thrusts with fervor.

I drag my nails lightly down his back, then grasp the hem of his shirt. He pulls back so I can tug it over his head. Then, breathing heavily, he drinks me in. His tattooed forearms are resting on either side of my head, his dark, lust-filled eyes scanning my face like he's cataloging every detail, like he's counting every freckle.

Expression softening a fraction, he balances on one arm and cradles my face. "You captivate me." The sincerity in his tone makes my heart want to explode. Once again, he leans down and brushes his firm lips against mine, letting them linger for a few seconds.

He trails his fingers down my neck to the first button on my pajama shirt, then with his eyes on mine, he waits for permission.

Frantically, I nod, and he quickly undoes the top button, then places an open-mouthed kiss on the freshly exposed skin. My body hums with every press of his lips. With each button he unfastens, he drops a kiss to my skin, each more intense than the last.

The sides of my pajama shirt fall open, leaving my bare breasts exposed. Bending down, he finds my neck and licks and kisses his way down my chest, then draws my hardened nipple into his mouth. A groan reverberates from his chest, and I bite my lip with a whimper. Before he pulls away, he gently nibbles the sensitive flesh followed by soothing the bite with his tongue.

Hands buried in his hair, I cry out, lost to the sensation.

He dips his fingers into the waistband of my pajama pants and drags the fabric down, but only an inch or two. Impatient, I clutch the elastic, but before I can yank them down, he grasps both of my wrists with one hand.

"Patience, Josephine," he says, eyes on mine.

My full name drips from his tongue like smooth honey, nearly turning me into a puddle.

This man could break me in two, and I'd probably thank him for it. Then I would ask him to do it again.

Releasing me, he hauls himself up to his feet. Towering over me in the warm glow of the bedroom like this, he's a true work of art. Intricate lines of ink trail down his arms and chest. The hardened planes of muscle on his stomach contract with each heavy breath. The dusting of hair on his lower abdomen narrows, trailing down to the large bulge in his pants.

He grips my calves and yanks me to the edge of the bed, pulling a squeal from me.

Beckett taking control is the most erotic thing I've ever experienced.

Head bowed, he pulls down my pajama pants at an agonizingly slow pace. And when I'm completely bare, he drops to his knees and smooths his large hands down the expanse of my legs, parting them. He presses a firm kiss to the inside of one thigh, then the other, then moves higher.

When he gets to the juncture of my thigh and pussy, panic rushes through me. "Wait."

Immediately, he pulls back. "Too far? I'll stop—"

"No," I cry. This is so embarrassing. I'm going to ruin the moment, but I feel comfortable enough with him to tell him this. Pushing up onto my elbows, face heating, I say, "I've never come from oral before."

He rubs soothing circles over my thighs, but he doesn't speak.

"Sometimes it takes a while for me to finish. . .in general. I end up getting too in my head and my mind wanders off. I stress about taking too long, which, ironically, makes it more difficult to come." My voice is shaky and apologetic. "So, for me, it's more about the journey than the destination, you know?"

I drop back, eyes squeezed shut, hoping he isn't one of those guys who'll take that confession as a challenge. Who'll tell me it's just that I haven't experienced the right tongue or hands or whatever and he can change that for me.

"That's totally normal, you know," he says, still caressing my legs. "You're not broken or defective. We don't have to do anything you don't want to do." When I get brave enough to look at him, he's wearing an understanding smile. "But I can assure you, I'll stay down here for as long as you'll let me. I just want to make you feel good, so please don't worry about me or my feelings."

Swallowing, I decide it's not worth the debate, so I nod once. "Then make me feel good."

He pushes my thighs farther apart, then trails his lips over the delicate skin, the roughness of his stubble sending a thrill through me.

With a hungry glint in his eyes, he covers my pussy with his mouth and sucks.

Head dropped back, I gasp, and as he drags his tongue over every bit of me, I can't help but moan.

When he draws my clit into his mouth and sucks, my vision goes spotty and I cry out.

I pull on his hair, urging his mouth closer, writhing under his touch. I'm rewarded when he slips two fingers inside me and curls them, hitting a spot that no man has ever found. Frantic, I roll my hips, eager for more, chasing my orgasm.

It's right there and I'm terrified I'll get lost in my head and lose it.

As if he can read my mind, he pulls away, though he doesn't stop stroking me. "Josephine," he commands. "Look at me."

I do as he says, lifting onto my elbows.

"I told you I'd stay here for as long as you'll let me. Do you want me to stop?"

With jerky movements, I shake my head. No, that's the last thing I want.

"Thank god," he murmurs. Then he dives back in, latching on to my clit again.

Head dropped back, I revel in every flick and swirl of his tongue, the vibrations from his groans, and the way his fingers slide inside me. He's exceptional at this, and the way he's taking pleasure in my pleasure only heightens the intensity of the moment.

Smiling against me, he grips my hips and pulls me closer, like he's a man starved.

Warmth pools low in my stomach as I grind my pussy against his hungry mouth. Every flick of his tongue pulses through me, winding me tighter. I'm on the brink of snapping when he lets out a satisfied groan.

At the sound, a surge of pleasure overtakes me. From my fingertips down to my toes, my orgasm consumes me. My back arches off the bed as I surrender to it completely. Beckett stays with me through it all. His fingers remain curved inside me and his mouth slows to a reverent kiss, waiting for the last aftershocks to subside beneath his lips.

Chest rising and falling, I struggle for air as I sink into the tangled sheets. I'm weightless. Every tense muscle in my body—from my clenched jaw to my shaky thighs—sighs with relief as I float in the afterglow.

I'm not sure if I want to laugh or cry or high-five the man nestled between my legs.

Between my knees, Beckett stands to his full height and smiles down at me, his lips swollen and glistening, his hair disheveled. Casually, he wipes his mouth with the back of his hand and winks.

This shy, quiet man fucking *winks* at me.

And I melt.

Chapter Twenty-Two

THE WINK MAY HAVE BEEN a touch too cocky, but after the way she trusted me and opened up, I was fucking soaring.

All I wanted was to make her feel good, and I accomplished that.

The sated, dazed look on her face awakens something inside me. I want to be her safe spot for as long as I can be. I want to chase away every insecurity and break down every stubborn barrier she's built over the years.

Her flushed, freckled cheeks, kiss-bitten lips, disheveled hair, and bare body spread out over the bed are the most beautiful things I've ever seen. I want to do nothing more than explore every curve, line, and edge of her softness.

This is the beginning of the end for me. Josephine will ruin me for everyone else.

And I'm okay with that.

Her dark lashes lie fanned against her flushed cheeks

while her eyes, wide and soft, find mine and remain like that, wholly consuming me, as I take the foil packet from my pocket and push down my sweatpants. Once I've rolled the latex over my length, I kneel on the bed, my knees sinking into the mattress, then rest my forearms on either side of her head, framing her face like a priceless, living portrait.

Her dark hair spills over the pillow, her chest rising and falling rhythmically. The lamp's glow highlights the gentle lines of her collarbone, the dip between her breasts, and the soft curve of her waist.

She's perfect in every way.

Propped up on one arm, I fist my cock and run it over her slick core.

She writhes at the sensation, back arching and seeking more friction.

A breath shudders out of me. "Are you ready for me?"

"I've been ready," she pants, hooking a leg around my lower back and pulling me to her.

Slowly, I push inside her, welcomed by her warmth.

She gasps, gripping my shoulders as I gently work myself deeper.

The way her nails dig into my shoulders, biting into my skin, unlocks something raw inside me—an unbearable longing to belong to her and only her. To give her every piece of me. The pieces I've been too scared to give to anyone else.

"It's too much," she pants.

"Look at me," I command, brushing a stray lock of hair away from her forehead. "Breathe, Josephine." With two fingers, I circle her swollen clit. Her eyes flutter shut, dark lashes sweeping across her pink cheeks.

A soft, breathy moan escapes from her parted lips, and her muscles relax, allowing me to fully sink into her.

"Look at you," I groan. "You're taking me so well."

With both legs wrapped around my waist, she presses her heels into the small of my back, inviting me to take her deeper. With every thrust, she clenches around me. It's an intoxicating combination of pressure and heat. As I quicken my pace, rolling my hips and stroking her clit, her breathy gasps grow louder, filling the room. When her legs quiver around me, I focus on keeping my rhythm, my focus set on getting her to come a second time, cataloging every flicker of pleasure that paints her beautiful features. To pull pleasure like this from her has until now only been a fantasy during sleepless nights.

Tonight I'm determined to make it a reality.

Eyes shut and panting, she drags her nails down my back in erratic strokes, and then she tightens around me, letting out a cry. Seconds later, she surrenders to her orgasm as it consumes her quivering body. "*Beckett,*" she cries out, voice breaking with raw emotion as she arches off the bed.

At the sound of my name on her lips like this, pride and satisfaction overflow inside me.

After she comes down, she places her hand over my beating heart, then trails her fingers up to my cheek. Attention fixed on my face, she pulls me down and takes me in a breath-taking, bruising kiss.

That soul-stealing kiss is my undoing. *She* is my undoing.

My own climax crashes into me with a relentless force, stealing the breath from my lungs, my cock pulsing inside her, the sensation consuming me. Leaving me trembling, panting, and wanting more.

With my mouth still firmly on hers, my thoughts narrow until all I focus on is *her.*

The warmth of her skin.

The sound of her voice.

The way her heart beats against my own.

Pulling my lips away, I drop my forehead to hers and suck in a breath.

The way she clings to me speaks volumes. Legs and arms both wrapped around me in a possessive embrace, as if she's worried I'll drift away. Our warm, damp bodies meld into one like two desolate roads converging after a long, lonely journey.

I don't want to lose this. This moment with her.

I don't want her to let me go. Eyes closed, I focus on the way her arms feel around me, the way her heart steadily beats against my chest, and the way her breath trails across my skin.

Eventually, she loosens her grip, her fingers sliding down my back in a tender caress before falling onto the bed.

It takes all my restraint not to pull her back

"I think I forgot my name for a moment." She giggles, covering her eyes with the back of her hand. The lightness of her tone makes me want to kiss her again.

So I do.

It's slow and languid, igniting another flame inside me. "That's because you were too busy screaming mine," I murmur against her lips.

She playfully shoves me off her. "You cocky son of a bitch." Then she's on top of me, straddling me, looking picture perfect. She's all smooth skin and smiles as she drags her fingertips down my chest and abs, studying the ink covering my body.

I can't help but let out a deep groan, appreciating the view of her magnificent tits.

Fuck. Me. Her soft, curvy body is an absolute fantasy.

Smirking, she waves her hand in front of my face. "Hey. Hello. Eyes are up here. Did you not get your fill of me yet?"

Chuckling, I shake my head. "No. No, I didn't."

She tips her head back, a heartfelt laugh bubbling out of her. "Okay. Well, before we go for round two, I need something to eat."

Round two? There's going to be a round two?

I decide not to question her.

She slides off me, then pads over to the bathroom and shuts the door behind her. I take a moment to discard the condom and gather our scattered clothes off the floor.

A few minutes later, she walks out in a plush bathrobe.

The corners of my mouth kick up into a smile. "I'll make something to eat. Go wait for me in the kitchen while I get cleaned up."

She breaks into a shy smile, those full freckled cheeks I love so much taking on a light pink hue.

As I pass her, I press a kiss to her temple.

When I emerge from her room, I find her actually *playing* with Barbara, dangling the cat's favorite fish toy, wearing a bright smile.

When she senses me, she takes me in from head to toe, lingering mostly on my bare chest beneath my cardigan.

"Heads up, if you continue walking around looking like that" —she waves her finger at me—"we may not leave this cottage."

Shrugging, I wander into the kitchen. "Not sure I see an issue with that."

When I pull a box of macaroni and cheese from the cabinet, she tilts her head, her eyes narrowing. "You're just full of surprises tonight. Mr. *you need a decent meal and can't survive off snacks* likes boxed mac and cheese?"

At the sink, I fill a pot with water. "Do you not?"

"Oh, I do. A lot. But—"

"Let me guess. Only with ketchup?" I peer back at her as I set the pot on the stove. "What is it with you and that condiment?"

In classic Joey fashion, she rears back with a dramatic flair. "Don't shame me for enjoying such a versatile condiment. One, I may add, with a complex flavor profile. It enhances the flavor of everything."

I spin around, settling my hands on the island. "Tell me you don't dip your steak in ketchup."

She clutches her chest. "Jesus, no. I'm actually offended you'd think so poorly of me."

With a shake of my head, I whisper, "So dramatic."

Eyes twinkling, she angles in. "Mm-hmm. But I think you like it."

She's absolutely not wrong. I like her more than she probably realizes.

"You know," she says, scratching Barbara's chin, "the faster you cook for me, the faster I'll get on my knees for you."

Heart lurching, I straighten. "Y-yes, ma'am. I'll get right to work."

Her playful chuckle fills the dimly lit kitchen as I turn up the heat of the burner, wondering how I can get these damn noodles to boil faster.

"Sorry. Sorry. I shouldn't have said that," she blurts out. "I was trying to be funny."

Turning around, I level her with a concerned look. "Joey, I have a serious question for you. But you don't have to answer it if you're not comfortable."

She catches her bottom lip with her teeth, suddenly looking anxious. "Okay."

Slowly, I press my thumb to her lip, pulling it free. "Why do you apologize for things that don't deserve an apology?"

Swallowing audibly, she ducks her head, focusing on her hands in her lap. "I've always thought that I'm too much," she finally says, her voice on the verge of breaking. "Too loud. Too persistent. Too talkative. Too caring. Too sensitive. Just too much of *everything*." She lets out a bitter laugh. "In the seventh grade, this kid yelled at me from across the hall saying that I was so annoying and that I annoyed everyone around me. I guess it kind of stuck with me."

I cover her hands with mine to get her to stop wringing them. "Want me to find them and kick their ass?"

That gets a genuine laugh out of her.

"Listen, I've seen some shit in ER," I go on. "I think I could pull it off without getting caught."

She shakes her head, her lips curling in a sad smile. "I try to push it aside and act like I don't care. But I do, and I think I always will. It doesn't help when certain people only reinforce those insecurities." She sniffles.

The sound of sizzling water splashing onto the burner interrupts us. Quickly, I bring her hands to my lips and kiss her knuckles. "I want you to tell me more. I want to hear everything. But I also don't want to burn down the cottage. Or the forest behind us."

Chuckling, she covers her face. "Ugh. I'm so sor—"

I tug her hands away and duck so she's forced to look at me. "Josephine."

Her head snaps up, and with half a smirk, she pretends to zip her lips.

When the macaroni and cheese is done, I set a bowl in

front of her. And when I snag the ketchup from the fridge, her face lights up.

As we eat in silence, the sound of clinking forks on plates surrounding us, I peer over at her, hoping she'll open back up.

But knowing her, she probably thinks she's a burden to me.

If I had to guess, she thinks her feeling any type of emotion is a burden to others.

For me, that couldn't be farther from the truth. She thinks she's too much? Frankly, I can't get enough. If anything, I want more of her.

Clearing my throat, I wipe my mouth with a napkin. "Now that you're fed and watered, we should continue our conversation." I push my plate away and rest my elbows on the counter.

With a huff, she rolls her eyes. "Do we have to?"

"Yes."

"Why?"

"Because I said so."

"You know, this bossiness is making me feel some type of way." She smirks, opening up her bathrobe, giving me a peek at what she's hiding underneath.

Which is nothing but bare, silky skin waiting to be touched.

Don't look down. Don't fall for it. She's baiting you.

I narrow my eyes at her. "Josephine. Don't deflect."

Tipping her head back, she lets out a long sigh and tightens her robe. "Okay, okay, fine. I worry about being me. Authentically. Because. . ." She presses her lips together, looking away from me. "Because all my life, I've never been chosen. In sports, friendships, relationships—you name it, I'm picked fourth or fifth. I don't even make it in the top three. It seems like I'm always picked last, and I wonder if I'm the problem. I like who I am, but if others don't, then maybe I need to change. Take Norma." She sighs. "She didn't like me from the start, and I've been nothing but nice and professional."

My heart plummets to the floor. The mere thought that she's been made to believe she's anything less than extraordinary is upsetting on so many levels.

The way her voice breaks and her shoulders curl unravels a protectiveness inside me.

"First of all, Norma has her own issues to work through. It sounds like she may need to talk to a professional about her. . .encyclopedia of issues."

Joey gives me a sad smile.

"Second, you're in good company," I say. "I was never anyone's first choice, either."

Understanding and relief wash over her face. "Really?"

"Mm-hmm." I nod. "Senior year in high school, a girl asked me to prom as a dare."

Joey leans in closer. "Isn't that from a movie?"

I scrub a palm down my face, chuckling. "Unfortunately. They thought it was funny, though. Joke's on them, because when I took my glasses off, I didn't get hotter like the protagonist usually does."

With a small smile, she reaches over the counter and grabs my hand. "I would've asked you to prom. Glasses or no glasses, it wouldn't have mattered to me."

Of course it wouldn't have. Because she has this remarkable ability to see a person for who they are beneath the surface. She can identify the layers of complexity hiding there. Complexities that never deter her from showing people grace and kindness, no matter how cruel the world is to her.

I give her hand a squeeze, wanting nothing more than to wrap her in my arms and never let go. "You'd be my first choice if I were to go to prom."

Joey playfully rolls her eyes. "That's just the OxiClean talking because we had sex."

Confusion swirls in my brain, and I need a solid thirty seconds to decode her statement before it dawns on me. "Do you mean oxytocin?"

She frowns, puzzled. "Is that the thing that gets released during sex? If so, then yes."

God, she's fucking adorable.

I bite back a laugh. "Yes, that's the hormone that gets released. Along with serotonin, dopamine, and endorphins."

"You're in luck," she chirps. "I happen to be lacking all of those, so I guess we should get back to it. You've got your work cut out for you."

Heart thudding against my ribcage, I slide off my chair and cup her face. Kissing her deeply, I savor her soft lips and her warm skin.

"What was that for?" she asks when I pull back.

"I really like this." I tap gently on her temple. "And this." This time I tap her chest, over her heart. "Never change. Promise me that." Because Joey's heart and mind are to be cherished.

Eyes shimmering with unshed tears, she nods. "I promise."

Beckett's Journal

May 20

There's no denying we have a connection—one built on a deep sense of understanding. Joey's uncovering a side of me no one has ever seen. A side no one has ever deemed worthy enough to take the time to expose.

She's patient with me, giving me time to show her my innermost self. Even on those evenings when she looked utterly spent from work. She was tired, but never tired enough to skip a meal together.

She's igniting a part of me I thought had been extinguished permanently.

At the same time, I worry. What happens next? Are we meant to have more than this? I don't think I can stay away and by the way she looks at me, I don't think she can stay away either.

Chapter Twenty-Three

JOEY

"I SLEPT WITH HIM." I cover my face with my hands and groan.

"I knew it!" my sister shouts, startling a sleeping Vera.

"You dirty little harlot," Marnie says. "I'm proud of you, Jojo."

Charlie gives her best friend a devious look. "You know what to do."

With a curt nod, Marnie jumps out of her seat and sprints toward the front of A New Leaf, flipping the *open* sign to *closed*.

I sigh. They want uninterrupted gossip time.

In a matter of seconds, Marnie is back, plopping herself down onto the stool and settling her chin in her hands like someone impatiently waiting for presents.

Shrugging, I pick up a stray leaf from the countertop and

spin it between my fingers. "We had sex. That's all. No big deal."

Me and the phrase *It's no big deal* rarely go together. With me, it's always a big deal. In fact, despite having just said otherwise, I'm thinking this is a *ginormous* deal.

My sister sits back, arms crossed and one eyebrow raised. "Joey, you're on the verge of breaking out in hives."

I tuck my chin, and sure enough, there are already pink splotches forming on my chest.

God dammit. Whose bright idea was it to give me a nervous system that exposes my lies? It's impossible to keep secrets with a built-in lie detector like this.

I tip my head back and groan. "Fine. I'm afraid that I'm going to catch feelings. Or maybe I already have. I don't know."

Eyes wide, Marnie shakes her head. "Wow. Now that you're back in Hemlock, you really came, saw, and conquered. . .and then came again. Didn't you?"

"*Marnie*," Charlie and I yell.

Wincing, she gives me an apologetic look. "Sorry. Okay, in all seriousness—"

My sister scoffs at that.

Marnie shoots daggers in her direction. "As I was saying, I didn't think you'd fall in love so fast after getting your donut glazed."

I slap my hand over my mouth to stifle a laugh.

"I'm firing you," Charlie deadpans.

"Have you two thought about attending couples counseling?" I tease.

"No," Charlie huffs.

"I keep asking her to go," Marnie nearly shouts.

Chuckling, I rest my arms on the wooden counter. "It's not

love. It's just affection. He's so nice and thoughtful. And he doesn't ever get annoyed with me."

"Even when you failed to mention watching the dogs? I was sure he'd be looking for a new place to live after that," Charlie says.

"Even when I failed to mention the dogs." I nod. "He also volunteers at the animal shelter and watches movies with his mom on Friday nights. The man bakes bread, for crying out loud. And it's really fucking good bread."

Marnie giggles, though she covers her mouth like she's trying to rein herself in.

Inhaling deeply, I look at her. "Go on."

"What?" Her mouth turns down at the corners.

"Come on. Get it out of your system. It's bubbling out of you."

Lips pressed together, she eyes me, then Charlie. "Is he going to knead your buns tonight?"

My sister and I groan in unison at her ridiculous humor.

"May I?" I ask Charlie

She sweeps an arm out in front of her. "Be my guest."

I lock eyes with Marnie. "You're fired."

Accepting her fate, she bobs her head. "I deserve that." Her lips twitch as she straightens. "Bread baking is a definite green flag."

My sister hums. "Yeah, that would do me in. I love a good carb."

"Yeah," Marnie says, "I do love a steamy dough daddy, that's for sure."

"So," my sister drawls. "What are you going to do?"

My stomach sinks. "Pretend everything is fine and ignore my feelings, hoping they'll go away."

"Ah, yes. Because that always works out so well in the end," Marnie jokes.

I let out a resigned sigh. "There's an expiration date. One that could easily take us to opposite sides of the country. We lead totally different lives. I can't see us having a successful relationship outside of Hemlock. We're too different."

Eyes narrowed, Charlie scrutinizes me. "Maybe you two aren't as different as you think."

———

THROUGHOUT THE DRIVE back to the cottage, Charlie's words replay in my mind. On the outside, we couldn't be more different. Yet, on the inside, there are undeniable commonalities. In a short amount of time, we've discovered that we feel safe enough around each other to be ourselves. I don't judge him for his social anxiety; he doesn't judge me for. . .well, anything. All my apologizing and forgetfulness don't faze him one bit.

At his core, Beckett's a *good* guy. The type of guy a girl could bring home to her family. The kind said family would fall head over heels for. The type of guy who makes all the old ladies swoon because he holds the door open for them with a smile and a blush.

The type of guy who makes *me* smile and blush.

When I pull up to the cottage, the only light on is the one over the front door. Beckett must be working late tonight. It's been a few days since we've seen each other. And I kinda miss him.

Maybe it's because I've been alone on the road for so long, but it's refreshing to have someone to come home to at night. There's a sense of comfort in having a person I can joke around and share a meal with after a long day.

Inside, I turn on the lamp on the entryway table, then lock the door behind me with a sigh. The place is silent, so tonight it's just me, myself, and. . .

Meow.

And Barbara.

The persnickety cat saunters down the stairs, her tail flicking back and forth.

To be fair, we have been getting along better. So she is growing on me.

Once I've dropped my bags at the front door, I make my way to my room to slip on my pajamas and a bathrobe. I made the grave mistake of wearing jeans today, and I lost circulation in my lower extremities about three hours ago.

In the kitchen, there's a sketchpad and an assortment of sketching mediums on the island. Graphite pencils, charcoal, colored pencils and even a few ink pens. Confused, I step closer, and that's when I see the note.

I know you use crossword puzzles to decompress, but I read an article a couple of days ago that mentioned drawing can reduce stress hormones. You mentioned that you used to sketch and weren't sure why you stopped, so I thought this might help. (Although, I'm not sure I was supposed to hear that because you mumbled it.) Regardless of my accidental eavesdropping, I saw these today and thought of you.

I hope you like them and don't think I'm overstepping.

PS Barbara told me she wants a portrait of her.

PPS Barbara also said she wants you to draw Norma. She said something about clawing it up once you're finished? Not sure. You'll have to take it up with her.

PPPS There's also a new crossword puzzle book on the coffee table as an apology in case I overstepped with all of this.

-B

Heart in my throat, I read it again.

And again.

I take in each word carefully, at a complete loss. Appreciation swells up inside me at the thought of Beckett going out of his way for me. That he remembered such a simple detail I mentioned offhand weeks ago speaks volumes. This is a true reflection of his character. Always watching. Always listening. Always observing.

With a trembling hand, I pull my phone from my bathrobe pocket and send him a quick text.

You didn't overstep.

I know you've been worrying.

BECKETT

Thank fuck. I've been checking my phone every thirty minutes. The charge nurse was about to take it away.

Wow. You've been a bad boy at work, haven't you?

BECKETT

Josephine. . .

Not the time nor the place.

And why is that?

BECKETT

Scrub fabric isn't very forgiving.

Fair enough.

257

In all seriousness, thank you for the sketchbook and wide assortment of drawing materials. It's so thoughtful.

BECKETT

You're very welcome.

I know work has been tough lately, and I wanted to put a smile on your face.

*Hopefully put a smile on your face.

You know, because I was worried about overstepping and all that.

Lucky for you, you succeeded.

Grinning like a fool, I peer over at Barbara, who's laser-focused on me.

I wander over to her and scratch her head. "If I feed you, do you promise not to bite my fingers off?"

Barbara purrs into my palm in response.

I'm taking that as a good sign.

After I get her settled with her dinner, I flop onto the couch with my crossword puzzle, only to discover that the little black-and-white squares don't hold their usual appeal tonight. Attention drifting to the kitchen island, I bite the inside of my lip. Then, with a long breath in, I walk over and grab the sketchbook and graphite pencils.

It's been years since I've drawn anything more than a silly doodle on scrap paper. When I was younger, I would draw so much that my parents ran out of room on their fridge to display my work.

Jack was always annoyed that my art got prime real estate on that fridge while his below-average spelling quizzes got tucked behind my drawings.

Charlie, on the other hand, couldn't have cared less. If anything, she would snatch one of my drawings and use it as a bookmark. In fact, that sentimental curmudgeon of a woman still has a few in her favorite books.

Settled on the couch again, I tuck my legs beneath me and flip open the sketch pad. For several minutes, I stare at the empty page, not knowing where to begin. At first, as the tip of my pencil hovers hesitantly over the page, I'm convinced I've forgotten how to sketch altogether.

Gripping my pencil firmly, I press it to the paper and, with deliberate strokes, sketch the thing I love the most.

Wildflowers.

Petals and leaves unfurl before me, creating bountiful blooms that fill every inch of the paper. I've always loved the untamed beauty of wildflowers. How no two blossoms are alike—each imperfectly perfect but beautiful all the same. It's captivating, the way their vibrant colors paint rolling green hills and decorate rugged seaside cliffs. Or how they sway in the breeze, steady and confident.

They're all special in their own alluring ways.

Kind of like Beckett is to me.

Hours pass as I shade and highlight to create texture and depth, making sure the flowers burst off the page.

Barbara leaps up onto the couch beside me, then drops her fish toy onto my pad of paper. It lands with a soft plop. The poor thing has seen better days. There's a hole in the body, and the fabric is pulling apart, the stuffing spilling out onto my sketchpad.

I survey the orange cat who's wearing a pitiful look. Her large, amber eyes bore into mine, pleading with me to fix her toy. So I pick up the wounded fish and turn it around in my fingers a few times, assessing the damage.

I sigh, my shoulders sinking. "Because I'm not a monster, I'll patch your little buddy up. Okay?"

Her ears perk up, then she jumps off the couch.

In the kitchen, I rummage through the drawers, looking for a sewing kit. It doesn't take long, of course, because like any good kitchen, this one has a junk drawer. A drawer in which all miscellaneous objects go to live. . .and die. This one is overflowing with old rubber bands, loose change, and takeout menus dating back to the early nineties. As well as a small sewing kit.

I flick on the overhead light in the kitchen, readying myself to perform surgery. Barbara, who is now my assistant, jumps onto the counter next to me. My home economics class in school didn't make a lasting impression on me, so I can't say that I'm any good at sewing. Still, I thread the needle anyway, pick up the fish, and start stitching. I have to hold the damn fish so close to my face to make such tiny stitches that I'm starting to get a headache.

When the front door opens and closes, I lower my patient. My eyes take a moment to adjust, but when they do, I discover Beckett standing in the doorway of the kitchen.

Tall. Scruffy. And edible.

Naturally, I'm so distracted that I prick myself with the needle.

"Shit." I bring my finger to my mouth without looking at it. I'm not in the mood to faint again.

Beckett drops his stuff at the door, and in a few quick strides, he's next to me, pulling my finger from my mouth and holding it with care as he inspects it.

A tingle shoots up my arm at his soft touch.

Blood or no blood, with the way he's holding my hand and how his warmth seeps into me, I may actually faint.

He looks tired, with purple circles beneath his eyes and extra disheveled hair, as if he's been running his hands through it. Even like this, he's undeniably handsome.

Noticing my staring, he smiles lightly, his eyes crinkling at the corners. "What's the matter?"

I return his smile, leaning into his touch. "Has anyone ever told you that you have an aesthetically pleasing face?"

With a shake of his head, he barks out a laugh. "I can say for certain no one has used those exact words. 'Aesthetically pleasing'? Did you read the dictionary as a kid?" In one smooth move, he slips his fingers between mine, and instantly, the sting from the needle prick gives way to the relentless thumping of my heart in my chest. Each heartbeat echoes in tandem with the rhythmic swipes of his callused thumb gliding over the back of my hand.

I want to kiss him. Bad.

Would that be weird? We haven't really spoken much about our night together, but we also haven't seen one another.

As I consider, his eyes dart from our hands to my mouth, like maybe he wants to kiss me too—

Meow.

Jolting, I glare at the cat.

Beckett releases me and picks up the now repaired toy. "I see you performed surgery tonight." His grin lights up his entire face. "I can't tell you how many times I've stitched this thing up. I'm shocked it's lasted this long." He tosses the fish to Barbara, who just glares at him.

"Uh. Why does she look like she wants to murder you?"

With a sigh, he checks his watch. "It's past her banana time."

"Her what?"

"Every night she gets a piece of banana. If not, she'll throw a tantrum." He makes his way over to the fruit bowl and plucks out a ripe banana. Then he breaks a small piece off and holds it out to her.

With my brows pinched together and gaze firmly on Barbara, I ask, "What do you do with the rest of the banana?"

He lets out a weary breath. "I hate bananas with a passion. So I usually compost them. If I can't compost them, then I eat them. I just try not to gag."

A laugh bubbles out of me.

He crosses his arms, his shirt stretching over his thick biceps. "What's so funny?"

This is such a ridiculous fact. And oddly fitting for our whole relationship. . .or friendship. . .or *whatever* it is we have.

"Bananas are my favorite fruit," I say, not bothering to temper my smile. "Did you know humans share like 50 percent of their DNA with bananas?"

"Uh. No?"

"Does this mean that you hate 50 percent of yourself? Wow, we need to work on your self-esteem, buddy." I grimace teasingly.

He rolls his eyes, clearly over my antics. "Just for that, you're in charge of giving Barb her nightly banana," he says, pointing the fruit at me.

"Are you trying to offload your parenting duties on me because you don't like a fruit that shares half of your DNA? I expected more from you, Hart." I tsk.

"Easy there, Thorne." He shuffles closer and sets the banana in front of me. "Here. Get your potassium in for the day."

I wince. "I can't eat that in front of you."

"Why?" He tilts his head.

Brows raised, I look from him to the phallic-shaped fruit and back again.

"Oh. *Oh*. Totally fair. I respect that."

The poor guy's cheeks turn so red that I almost feel bad. It's incredibly endearing. This tough-looking guy, with chiseled features and a body covered in ink, blushes so easily.

The clock behind him catches my eye, and I sigh. "I should probably head to bed. I need to be up early tomorrow." I slide out of the chair, but before I can go far, Beckett stops me with a hand at my elbow.

My chest flutters at the contact, and suddenly, I don't feel so tired. And when he speaks five simple words, every cell in my body is reawakened.

"Eat dinner with me, please."

Chapter Twenty-Four

BECKETT

UNKNOWN NUMBER 1

9am at Timber Trail next weekend. Don't be late. The starter got pissed at us last time.

UNKNOWN NUMBER 2

Who's bringing the beer?

UNKNOWN NUMBER 3

It's 9am, boys. No one should be drinking.

UNKNOWN NUMBER 2

After the week I've had, I need it.

UNKNOWN NUMBER 3

It's not good for your liver, son.

UNKNOWN NUMBER 1

I think the ibuprofen has already taken my liver out.

Hi. Wrong number.

UNKNOWN NUMBER 1

Is this Beckett?

Uh. Yeah.

UNKNOWN NUMBER 2

Then it's the right number.

UNKNOWN NUMBER 1

Welcome to the Fore Horsemen, bud!

UNKNOWN NUMBER 3

I still hate that fucking name.

I'm going to block these numbers.

UNKNOWN NUMBER 2

No you're not. Talk to my sister. I think she forgot to tell you something.

"I AM *SO* SORRY." Joey paces in the grocery store parking lot, her face riddled with guilt.

Being roommates and all, it's much easier for the two of us to tackle grocery shopping together than separately. As a bonus, it means we get to spend more time together, and she looks too damn tempting to resist tonight.

I grip her shoulders, stopping her, and look deep into her worried brown eyes. "Josephine. Stop. It's fine."

"Stop saying it's fine. I keep forgetting to tell you stuff because my memory is similar to that of a hamster who's spun around her wheel one too many times."

I tilt my head, arching a singular brow. "The dog babysitting and golf. Just those two things."

"And the time I forgot to replace your coffee when you really needed the caffeine." She winces, her nose crinkling in the most adorable way.

"So? I picked one up on the way to work."

"And I forgot to tell you that I borrowed your phone charger, and you spent half an hour looking for it."

"Again, so?"

"And when I already fed Barbara dinner two nights ago."

"She got a second dinner. I'm sure she likes you better than me now."

"And that I borrowed your sweatshirt."

I fall silent, my mind swirling. "Wait. The navy blue one?"

Eyes diverted, she nods.

"Huh. That's where it went?"

Her body deflates. "It got mixed up with my laundry and then I realized how warm it is. And I'm always cold. So I've been sleeping in it."

The mere thought of her slipping my sweatshirt on before bed causes my blood to simmer. I envision the soft fabric gliding against her smooth, bare skin as it caresses every curve that I long to taste again.

Mistaking my silence for anger, she says, "Are you. . .are you upset?"

I force my brain to focus on anything other than her naked body, because my jeans are already tightening at the memory of our night together. My body is far more honest than my resolve.

"Nope." The word comes out low and gruff.

She frowns. "Then what's wrong?"

"Just need a moment," I croak out as vivid images of Joey, her bare skin glowing in the dim light as she writhes beneath me, play in my mind like a movie.

Eyes narrowing, she examines me, starting with my heated face. She stops abruptly though, when she gets just below my belt and snaps her head up. "I-I didn't think. . .Oh. Yeah. It makes sense now. Me wearing it to bed made you think of me naked, which made you think of—"

"Joey?"

"Yeah?"

"Stop talking."

"Yes, sir."

"Joey?"

"Yeah?"

"That's not helping either."

She winces. "Fuck. Sorry."

The woman doesn't have a single idea how captivating she is.

Inside and out. Everything about her is alluring. And I can't get enough. I constantly want more.

Releasing her, I step back. I take a few steadying breaths, willing my body to cool down. "Let's get the shopping done. Then you can prepare me for what I'm about to get myself into with the"—I pull out my phone and check my messages—"the *Fore Horsemen*."

She throws her head back, laughing, then curls her fingers around my bicep and leads me toward the store's sliding glass doors. "The name could use some work, that's for sure."

"You think?" I huff out a laugh as I grab a cart.

As we stroll up and down the aisles, we pick out random items, including extra coffee.

While Joey peruses the bananas, inspecting the bunches, she mumbles something about Barbara only deserving the best. "We should prepare you before the big game," she says a little louder. "Mini golf seems like a solid idea. I'm in the mood to kick your ass."

Chuckling, I round the cart and step into her space, then lift her chin with my knuckle.

Like this, our lips are millimeters apart, our breath mingling. Anticipation hangs thick in the air between us.

Her pupils dilate, her breath catching.

"I'd like to see you try." With that, I place a gentle kiss on the tip of her nose and release her.

She lets out a deep, quivering exhale. "Such a fucking tease."

In the aisle, I ask, "Who's in this group?"

Humming, she holds up two boxes of granola bars and assesses them. "Jack, Finn, and Marnie's dad." She tosses one of the boxes into the cart from an impressive distance.

"Nice throw," I commend her. "Did you say Marnie's *dad*?"

"Yep. Victor. If you think Marnie is scary. . ." She shudders playfully. "Actually, I've never met or seen the guy before. Just heard the horror stories."

"And I got roped into this, how?"

"It had something to do about the fourth person in their group not being able to come. I tuned Jack out pretty quickly. When Finn mentioned you, I told him I'd ask you first." She stops in the middle of the aisle, staring off into the distance. "That little asshole."

"Huh?"

"Charlie," she says, threading her fingers through her hair. "I've been worrying that I gave them your number without your permission. I knew I couldn't have." She shakes her head. "Charlie, or Marnie, must've taken my phone and gotten it."

I hum. "So technically you didn't forget to ask me anything. You were the victim of polite theft."

She groans. "No device is safe around them. Again, I'm so sor—"

"Josephine," I warn playfully.

With a giggle, she dips her head, her face disappearing behind her hands and long hair.

I drape my arm around her shoulder, pull her closer to me, and press my lips to the top of her head, inhaling the scent of her strawberry shampoo.

This feels right. All of it. Her in my arms, talking about our upcoming plans, laughing in the middle of the grocery store without a care in the world. I can envision a life like this. A boring, mundane weeknight made special because I'm with a woman who makes me feel at ease.

As she laughs, my chest tightens with a mixture of bitter-sweet emotions. Happiness, because being with her brings out the truest version of myself. Sadness, because despite our connection, I worry this is temporary. And that the expiration date looms around the corner like a dark, haunting shadow. Waiting. Lurking.

For now, I push those thoughts aside and live in the moment, determined to enjoy the time we have together to the fullest. Spending any amount of time with Joey is a gift. Because, to me, she'll always be the girl who was brave enough to pull me out of my shell with quiet acceptance.

As I release her, I tuck a loose strand of hair behind her ear. "Come on, let's get out of here."

***

JOEY YAWNED every couple of minutes through dinner, the circles beneath her eyes a darkened purple. So when the meal was finished, I sent her to bed, then cleaned up the kitchen. As much as I wanted her to stay and talk to me, to hear her soft laugh echo through the kitchen, she needs the rest.

After Queen Barbara side-eyed me for a full ten minutes, I sliced a perfectly ripe banana for her, then headed upstairs, where I sat at the desk overlooking the large oaks and pines out back, barely visible against the navy sky, and filled a few pages of my journal.

When my mind has finally slowed, I wander back down to the dark kitchen for a glass of water. I'm filling the glass at the sink when Barbara slinks out from the hall leading to Joey's room.

Certain she closed her door, I pad that way. But sure enough, it's ajar. In the inky darkness of her room, a faint glow across Joey's face catches my eye. She's scrolling on her phone and tossing in her bed.

"Hey, is everything okay?" I whisper.

She shoots upright. "Huh? Oh yeah. I just can't sleep. Sorry if I woke you up."

We haven't talked about our night together. If anything, we keep pretending nothing has changed. Like it's no big deal when roommates sleep together.

But I haven't stopped thinking about it. Not for a second. I haven't stopped thinking about how much I want her in my bed every night. And I ache to feel her bare skin on mine again.

I should know better. I should turn around now and head back upstairs.

"Can I come in?" I ask instead.

"Of course."

Lit by the faint slivers of moonlight peeking through her sheer curtains, she shuffles to one side of the bed and pulls back the covers for me to slip under.

I ease onto the mattress, slipping my legs beneath the blankets, and situate myself so that I'm on my side facing her.

"What's on your mind?" I ask.

She lets out a heavy sigh. "I'm too anxious to sleep."

The pale moonlight highlights her weary features, giving her an ethereal glow.

I run the back of my knuckles along the curve of her smooth cheek, savoring the sensation as I commit every line of her exquisite face to my memory. "I know something that can help with that."

"Oh yeah?" Her breath hitches, drawing my attention to her mouth, then the delicate column of her neck. Beneath my touch, her pulse flutters like the wings of a bird. Fingers trembling, I continue the journey. Her skin pebbles as I inch closer to her breasts.

When I come to the first button of her pajama top, I peer up at her face.

With a small nod, she encourages me to continue.

This moment is the epitome of silent intimacy. No words need to be spoken.

Slowly, I undo each button, then let the sides of her top drape over her curves. With one hand, I cup her breast, the skin impossibly soft. I trace my thumb around her nipple, feeling it harden beneath my touch. Then I pinch it lightly between my fingers, and she gasps—a sharp intake of breath that's a mixture of surprise and pleasure.

She eases to her back, her shirt falling completely open, leaving her pale skin bathed in moonlight.

My mouth dries up at the sight of her. Her long auburn hair spills across the pillow like a waterfall, and her full breasts rise and fall gently with each breath she takes.

I've never seen a more beautiful woman.

As I work my way to the elastic waist of her pants, she takes the initiative, her fingers stretching over my hand and slipping it beneath the fabric to her pussy.

Like this, she guides my fingers over her slick heat, her body trembling and breath quivering as I caress her clit lightly. When I move in slow circles, gliding rhythmically across the tender skin, she removes her hand and her eyes flutter closed, her hips rising involuntarily, begging for more.

I slip two fingers inside her and work slow circles over her clit with my thumb. Unable to control myself, I run my tongue along her peaked nipple, then draw it into my mouth and suck softly, then drag my teeth over the sensitive flesh.

Gasping, she arches off the bed and clutches my hair.

The bite of her nails against my scalp causes a groan to escape me. It takes every ounce of strength I possess to pull away from her tits, but I want to watch her unravel under my touch.

See her cheeks flush.

Watch the way her mouth parts on a soft gasp.

Relish her euphoric expression as her orgasm consumes her.

No, I don't want it. *I need it.*

She sinks her teeth into her plump bottom lip, moving her hips frantically, chasing her release. Her muscles clench around my fingers as her thighs quiver against my wrist. Tugging harder on my hair, she turns her head and buries her face in her pillow as she screams out a muffled moan.

With my eyes locked on Joey, I withdraw my fingers slowly and bring them to my lips, savoring the taste of her. When she faces me again, her eyelids are heavy, her gaze veiled in desire, and her breaths come quick and shallow.

With my mouth at her ear, I murmur, "Next time, I want to watch you come. No more hiding from me."

Skin pebbling, she grips me by the collar and pulls me in with surprising strength. We collide in a frantic, fervent kiss that sucks the air from my lungs.

She breaks away, catching my lower lip with her teeth, and slips a hand under the hem of my shirt. As she releases her hold on my lip, she drags her nails over the ridges of my abs, then lower, palming my erection through the fabric of my sweatpants. Dropping my head, I close my eyes and exhale sharply. Any other night, I'd already be inside her, but tonight is about her and her only.

Tenderly, I grasp her wrist and lace our fingers between us. "Tonight was just as much for you as it was for me. I enjoy making you feel good. Sleep well, Josephine." I trail a knuckle over her cheek and place a chaste kiss to her lips before leaving her room.

Beckett's Journal

May 27

It pained me to leave her room tonight.

All I wanted was to lie there with her tangled in my arms. I just wanted to hold her until she fell asleep. Every piece of her, even the pieces she thinks are flawed, captivates me.

She's weaving herself into the fibers of my soul, making it impossible to untangle myself from her.

Chapter Twenty-Five

JOEY

THE BLARING screech of my alarms jolts me awake.

Turning off the incessant shriek, I flop back in bed and stare at the ceiling, my mind still clouded in a sleepy fog. It takes a few moments for the memories of last night to surface. It felt like a dream, but as my mind clears, a near perfect picture of Beckett and myself forms.

We need to talk about what's happening between us. It's silly how difficult it is to string together a few honest words. *I'm truly the perfect example of emotional intelligence.*

We've found ourselves tangled up in each other's lives both metaphorically and physically, so yes, we should talk about it, but that's easier said than done. Sometimes I get so scared of the unknown that I'm better off not knowing. It hurts less.

Fear of the unknown can be paralyzing, and right now, I'm

enjoying this little world we've created. Our unexpected connection is what's thrown me into a spiral. It's as if the universe dumped a bucket of ice water on me, screaming, *"Wake up! Not everyone is an asshole! There are decent humans out there!"* And here I am, living with said decent human.

Beckett's more than decent, though.

He fascinates me. Sometimes, when he's not looking, I watch him, examining him like he's an expert-level crossword puzzle. When he catches me looking, the corner of his mouth kicks up into a devastating smirk. Then he goes back to whatever he was doing.

Completely unfazed by my oddities.

His acceptance of who I am makes my stomach flutter and causes energy to flow through me.

He doesn't get agitated by my forgetfulness. If anything, he thinks it's charming. When I fall asleep on the couch, he covers me up with a blanket, then places a note next to me because he knows I'll wake up discombobulated. Then there's the sketchpad. Maybe the most thoughtful gift I've ever received.

Groaning, I roll over, burying my face in the pillow. The one Beckett was lying on. His intoxicating scent lingers. Vanilla and leather. A scent that, now that I know more about him, is so fitting.

So perfectly Beckett.

When I've found the motivation to pull myself out of bed, I slip into my slippers and robe, then make my way out to the kitchen.

The morning sun paints bright yellow streaks along the cabinets, enveloping the kitchen in an airy glow and highlighting Beckett where he's sitting at the island.

I swore he was working today. Or maybe I forgot, and he works tomorrow?

Either way, faced with him now, my cheeks heat. The man with the skillful fingers is casually sipping his coffee and reading the newspaper with his glasses perched on his nose.

Usually, I would focus on how effortlessly handsome he looks. But all I can think about is that folded newspaper in his hand.

A *newspaper*.

Nowadays we mostly read the news on our phone or tablet. But actually, this doesn't surprise me. Beckett is an old soul.

"A newspaper? Where'd you find one of those?" I joke, shuffling my way to the cabinet. Once again, instead of addressing the elephant in the room, I ignore it. Because that's what I do best.

He glances up at me over the rims of his glasses. Between his speculative stare, snug black T-shirt, and overgrown scruff along his sharp jaw, I'm a goner. The newspaper in his hand only adds to his sex appeal.

I do love a man who supports the local dailies.

Don't think impure thoughts. Don't think impure thoughts.

"I thought you were working today," I say.

"I called off."

"Uh. Why?" I lean against the kitchen sink, facing him as I sip my coffee.

"You don't remember what you said last night, do you?"

The heat is back, creeping up to my cheeks as I flip through the possibilities. Granted, I may have *thought* a lot of things, but I didn't think I actually said them out loud.

Now's the time I need to play the cool, calm, and collected

Joey. Even though on the inside I'm leaning more toward hot, chaotic, and perturbed.

Swallowing a too-big sip of coffee, I use the moment to come up with a reply. "I say a lot of things. You'll have to refresh my memory." As I bring the mug up to my lips, his attention snags on my mouth, though he quickly meets my eye.

He lets out a deep chuckle. He slips off his glasses and rubs his hand down his face before sitting back in the chair with his arms crossed. He fixes me with an inquisitive expression, the lines of his face creased deeply. "Mini golf? You said you're 'in the mood' to kick my ass."

Oh, right.

Wait a second. I set my half-empty mug on the counter a little too roughly and level him with a confused look. "You called off work today for *mini golf?*"

"Yep." He slips his glasses on again and picks up the newspaper, flipping the page and then folding it in half.

"Why?"

He doesn't so much as look up from the article he's reading. "Why not?"

"Don't you need to be there to handle the kids who swallow tiny objects or deal with people not knowing how to hold a knife properly or sticking something somewhere or—"

"Helping a woman who fainted because of a rambunctious blind dog with no sense of awareness?" he teases, finally looking at me.

I shoot him an unimpressed glare. "Ha ha. You're cheeky this morning, aren't you? Bold Beckett is coming in hot today."

Biting back a smirk, he turns back to his newspaper and takes a small sip of coffee. "Funny. I didn't hear you complaining about my boldness last night." One side of his mouth quirks up. "Anyway, I won't go hard on you during our mini match this evening."

Hit with a bout of bravery myself, I saunter over to him and pluck the newspaper out of his hand. Then, with my mouth at his ear, I say, "But what if I like it hard?"

His skin pebbles and I swear he stops breathing.

So with a quick peck on his cheek, I spin on my heel and saunter back to my room. At the doorway, I peek over my shoulder, and sure enough, his cheeks have turned my favorite shade of red.

"What are you looking at?"

Beckett jolts, fumbling my sketchbook, wearing a guilty expression.

We spent the day cleaning up the cottage—unloading the dishwasher, folding laundry, and all the other fun stuff that rarely gets done during the work week. Now, the sun is moments from setting and we're about to leave for our date.

Is this a date?

Ugh. I'm in no mood to answer my overthinking brain's questions right now, so I shove those thoughts behind a locked door and inhale a cleansing breath.

His eyes dart from me to the sketchbook, and a deep red flush creeps up his neck. "I-I didn't mean. . .s-sorry, I—" he stammers.

I'm not upset with him in the slightest. But it's cute how flustered he gets around me sometimes. There's nothing in that book that I wouldn't be willing to share, though I am curious as to why the camera app on his phone is open.

I zero in on the device, then him. "And the camera app? Planning to steal my work and sell it as your own? Could you at least cut me a bit of the profit? I did work *very* hard on those." I tsk, crossing my arms and leaning my hip on the counter.

I didn't work hard at all. An hour tops because I was absentmindedly sketching my worries away and dissociating from my life.

He opens his mouth, then snaps it closed again, like he's searching for a response.

Feeling guilty for stressing him out, I wander closer and pretend to pick lint off his henley. The shirt is snug in all the right places, pulling taut over his shoulders and chest. "Relax. I'm just joking." I rest my hand just above his heart. "But if you do sell them, just send some of the profit my way, okay? Ready to go?"

<hr>

THIRTY MINUTES LATER, I'm scrolling on my phone while waiting in line to pay for our round of mini golf—Beckett's treat, he insists—and surrounded by neon signs, creaky windmills, and lit-up cartoonish obstacles.

He shoved his credit card into my hand, muttered something about making sure the car was locked, then disappeared.

"How long have you two been married?"

I look up from my device and find an older woman standing next to me, her brows raised in anticipation.

"Oh, me?" I stammer.

She nods, then her gaze focuses behind me.

I peer over my shoulder, and sure enough, Beckett has returned. He's leaning casually against the wall several feet away, hands deep in his pockets. Sensing my attention, his eyes lift to mine, and he breaks into an adoring smile.

"*That*. That is what I'm talking about," says the woman. "He's been standing there looking at you just like *that*."

What is this woman talking about? Confused, I turn back to her, nervously tucking a strand of hair behind my ear. "I. . .uh. . .we're just friends. Roommates, actually."

"Honey, friends don't look at each other like that. Neither do roommates."

My heart stumbles over itself as I process her words. "Like what, exactly?"

"He looks at you like nothing else in the world matters. Like you're his purpose in life. That's why I thought you two were married." Smiling, she leans in closer. "The women over there were trying to get his attention, but he kept his sights locked on you and only you. *Especially* when you weren't looking."

My stomach clenches with anxiety as my heart pounds behind my ribcage. A flurry of emotions overwhelms me.

Am I leading him on?

Did we take things too far?

He can't be looking at me like that. . .can he?

That last question is the one that replays in my mind. Because no one ever looks at me like that. If anything, people look through me, as if I'm a ghost who's a terrible inconvenience in their lives.

Not like I'm their purpose.

"If I were you, I'd keep that one." The lady's eyes crinkle with kindness as she gives me a reassuring pat on the shoulder.

"Next," the teenager at the register yells, startling me.

"Sorry, sorry." As I stumble to the counter, my cheeks heat

with embarrassment. Once again, my head is in the clouds ruminating over everything.

The irritation in this kid's expression speaks louder than words, though that doesn't stop him from verbalizing it. "Sorry my ass," he mumbles.

My breath catches, and before I can find my voice to respond, a large body appears next to me.

Beckett.

"You wanna try that again?" he scolds.

The teen's eyes widen, and he takes a step back.

The muscle in Beckett's jaw pulses. He cocks one eyebrow at the kid, waiting for him to reply.

"Um. I-I'm. . .I'm the one who should be sorry, ma'am," he stammers. "It's been a long day, and I didn't mean to—"

Beckett lifts his hand, interrupting the teen. "Here's some advice—don't be an asshole. The world is shitty enough as it is."

Shoulders sinking, the boy nods. "Your game is on me tonight. Sorry for upsetting you." He holds out our putters and a pair of golf balls.

For a miniature golf course, this place is actually romantic. Shimmering twinkle lights wrap around nearby trees, illuminating the course as the sun dips below the horizon. The air is filled with laughter and the occasional cheer.

"What was that back there?" I tease, giving Beckett a sidelong look.

"I didn't appreciate the way he spoke to you. That's all." He shrugs.

I huff a breath. "I could've handled the twerp myself."

He lets out a deep sigh. "Yeah, but you shouldn't have to. You don't always need to fight your battles alone and you deserve to have someone in your corner."

I pull up short, a wave of emotion washing over me, making my chest flutter.

And this man *wants* to be in my corner. Not out of obligation, but because he genuinely cares.

He turns around, brows pulled low, and backtracks.

"Is everything okay?" he asks.

"Yep! Just a rock got stuck in my shoe," I blurt out a little too fast, buying time to compose myself.

He narrows his eyes like he doesn't believe me.

Dammit. He's too attentive to fall for little white lies. Especially mine, since I'm a terrible liar.

I may or may not have gotten written up at my first job out of college because of my *nonverbal communication skills*. My face can be even more expressive than my words. In order to rectify my behavior, HR required me to take a class about body and facial language. Imagine how difficult it was for me to keep a neutral face through the course. My muscles were practically twitching with the need to make a *what the fuck am I doing here?* expression.

Standing at the first hole, Beckett rolls up the sleeves of his black henley. And just like Pavlov's dog, I practically drool. All around us, people stare. For a man so shy, he sure knows how to command the attention of an audience.

I may or may not be objectifying him.

Who am I kidding? Of course I'm objectifying him.

When he bends to set his ball on the green, the way his jeans hug his ass is a treat to anyone who looks his way. The fabric molds to every curve and contour of his lean form, causing my pulse to quicken. The denim brand should really hire him for their advertisements.

He clears his throat, and I snap my head up. "Whatcha looking at over here?"

Once again flushed with embarrassment, I ramble, the words falling out of my mouth at an impressive speed. "Wow. Beautiful weather we're having, huh? Not too hot. Or too cold. A slight breeze. Perfect. Very comfortable. I hope the stars come out tonight. Then again, there's a lot of light pollution here. Did you know that more than one-third of the world's population can't see the Milky Way due to—"

"Joey?" He takes a step closer.

"Yeah?" I say, finally looking him in the eye.

"You're okay." His lips curl into an amused smile, soothing my nerves.

And it might be my imagination, but that sparkle in his eye is one of affection. Or maybe adoration?

I could spend all night trying to decipher what that little glint means. Regardless, it sends a fluttery wave through my body.

"But I can't have you distracted when you're so hell-bent on winning," he jokes.

I wave him off. "I wasn't distracted. I was just—"

"Being opportunistic?"

Yep.

With a sheepish grin, I say, "Guilty."

Chuckling, he turns back to his ball.

We probably look hilarious together. He's in head-to-toe black, all tattooed and scruffy, with perfectly disheveled hair, while I'm in a long, colorful floral dress that hits at my ankles and an oversized denim jacket with decorative embroidery. All I need is a flower tucked in my hair and a bit of devil's lettuce coursing through my veins, and I'm all set for a peace and love music festival.

The way his muscles and tendons flex as he lines up his shot has no business being this erotic. I would love golf much more if all the men looked like him while holding a club.

With a steady, smooth swing, he hits the ball and. . .that sly son of a bitch.

It stops no more than three inches from the hole.

Mouth hanging open, I look at him and then his ball and then back at him. "Dude. What the hell?"

He sways a little, embarrassment rolling off him. "I played in college." Shrugging, he steps aside so I can set my ball down.

"That information would've been nice to know beforehand. Then I wouldn't have been so cocky," I mumble.

Tipping his head back, he belts out a laugh. Tonight, he's carefree and relaxed. Holding a putter in one hand, his arms hang loose at his sides, a soft smile on his lips that hasn't once disappeared since we arrived.

This is the Beckett the world should get to know.

And I'm honored to have the privilege of seeing this side of him.

Chapter Twenty-Six

Beckett

I'm anxious.

Several times this morning, Joey reminded me that if I didn't want to golf with the guys, she'd take my place.

No offense, but if she plays golf the way she plays putt-putt, the group won't be home until after dark.

I didn't mind our lengthy game. It gave me more time to spend with her. If anything, I kept encouraging her to take her time lining up the ball so I could get *even more time* with her.

I told her I was fine to go golfing. Mostly because she already felt guilty and I didn't want to make things worse.

Every time she apologizes for a trivial slip-up or perceived misstep, my heart breaks. The urge to scoop her up in my arms is so strong sometimes that my limbs ache. I want to take away every unnecessary apology and every ounce of misplaced guilt she's ever felt.

Instead, when she thinks she's upset me and she shrinks

back, I reassure her with my words. Gentle, soothing, and uplifting. Hoping that one day, with time, she stops feeling the need to apologize.

I get the sense she's always apologized for taking up space. And she shouldn't have to shrink to feel like she fits in—she deserves to take up as much space as she wants.

She deserves to own her fire.

To stop apologizing.

To remain passionate and vibrant.

Joey deserves *to be Joey*. And no one else.

Ten minutes before the time we're scheduled to meet, I pull into the course parking lot. I was nervous about parking and wanted to leave early. Once my car is in park, I lean back in my seat and use a breathing technique my therapist suggested I try when I'm anxious about a social gathering. On my third deep breath, my phone pings with a notification.

When I unlock it, I find a selfie of Joey and Barbara.

JOEY

I'm getting the vibe you're anxious and not excited.

So here's a photo of me holding a very grumpy Barbara.

Photo of Joey and a very grumpy Barbara

Laughing to myself, I open the photo and zoom in. Sure enough, Barbara's eyes are narrowed to slits as Joey presses their faces together.

But Joey? She's undoubtedly radiant.

Her hair is wild like it always is in the morning, with pieces sticking out in every direction. Her smile, my favorite feature, is bright, and her freckled cheeks are slightly pink.

I click save because this is most definitely a photo I want to keep forever.

> Barbara looks displeased, as usual.

My thumbs hover over the keyboard as I push my doubts aside. Then, with a breath in, I type out exactly what I'm thinking.

> And you look beautiful, as usual.

JOEY

I think you may need new glasses.

Don't you get an eye exam every year? Our eyesight does get worse the older we get. . .

> Joey?

JOEY

Yeah?

> Take the damn compliment.

JOEY

You got it.

Thank you. :)

A knock on my window startles me, making me fumble my phone. I catch it before it can clatter to the floor, then turn and find Finn standing just outside my car, waving and smiling.

Lifting my hand, I give an awkward wave.

"Sorry! I didn't mean to startle you." His voice is muffled behind the window. "Joey said you're a coffee guy. I didn't know what kind you like, so I brought a variety." He holds up a full drink carrier.

I appreciate that Finn went out of his way for me, yet it can be so awkward when people go above and beyond to make someone comfortable. *Especially* for the new guy in the group. Or for the anxious guy. Or in my case, both.

Still, I acknowledge and appreciate the gesture.

I climb out and give him a semi-awkward smile as he holds out the coffee carrier for me.

"Uh. Just black coffee is fine. Thanks."

Smiling, he hands me a cup, then sets the carrier on top of his car and pulls his clubs out.

Unease unfurls in my chest, making me second-guess my decision to come.

Before long, Jack arrives, followed by a man in his early sixties.

The older gentleman may be close to twice my age, but the dude looks like he could murder a person with a single glare. He's about my height, with salt-and-pepper hair and a goatee. And his biceps look big enough to crush a watermelon. Like me, he's covered in tattoos. Except his are colorful rather than all black.

"That's Marnie's dad." Finn slides up next to me.

"Him? The guy who looks like he got kicked out of the military and is banned from at least fifteen countries?" I gape.

"Yep. Now you understand why Marnie is the way she is. Pretty sure the guy has mafia ties, though it's impossible to tell whether Marnie is lying."

Eyes wide, I dart a look at him. "Jesus."

As he chuckles lightly beside me, my muscles relax a fraction and my chest loosens.

Okay, maybe this won't be so bad. We can bond over our

shared fear of Marnie's dad and hope we aren't tied to the mafia by association now.

Jack strolls over to us, peering over his shoulder at Marnie's dad more than once. "I don't know who's more terrifying. Him or his daughter," he says, grabbing a coffee from Finn's drink carrier.

"If one of us doesn't make it home tonight, we know who to point the detectives to," I say, bringing my cup to my lips.

Both guys laugh lightly, the sound putting me even more at ease. Though the nerves are back when Marnie's dad approaches.

We fall silent, all straightening in his intimidating presence.

Our posture has never been better.

"Gentlemen," he says with a curt nod.

"Marnie's dad." Finn returns the gesture.

Blinking, I eye him, then Marnie's dad. Does this guy have a death wish or what?

"What?" Finn says, frowning.

Marnie's dad clears his throat, cocking a single dark eyebrow. "Names? My kid likes to leave out details."

"Jack," the lumberjack to my left says, not making direct eye contact.

When Marnie's dad looks at me, I startle. "Uh. B-Beckett."

"Finn," my friend with a death wish blurts out.

With a slow nod, the old guy gives the three of us another once-over. "Victor."

Definitely has mafia ties.

Victor plucks the final coffee from Finn's carrier without a word, then heads for the clubhouse.

Finn, Jack, and I look at each other like we're three kids who've just pissed off their dad.

"All right, boys." Jack peers over his shoulder. "If we want to make it out alive, we need to be on our best behavior."

As we approach the pro shop, my anxiety spikes again and I pull up short.

Jack and Finn pause and turn, both giving me questioning looks.

I blow out a breath. "We need to play rock, paper, scissors."

"Huh? Why?" Jack asks.

"Because." I swallow past the lump in my throat. "One of us has to share a cart with him." I nod at Victor, who's standing outside the building, watching us from behind dark sunglasses, his lips pressed into a thin line.

"Fuck," Jack and Finn say in unison.

FINN CHOSE SCISSORS AND LOST.

Naturally, we've been giving him shit about it all morning. The contrast between the muscled man in his sixties and the lanky nerd is comical.

Jack and I sit in our cart, sipping our coffees while Finn and Victor line up their fairway shots, squinting against the early afternoon sun that glints off the damp grass.

"How's living with Jo been?" Jack asks quietly. "Does she still leave her socks everywhere? And random coffee mugs on the counter?"

I chuckle, adjusting my sunglasses. "She's a great room-mate. Aside from the whole sock thing."

He shakes his head, his lips twitching. "Gotta love that kid. She's always been like that. A little forgetful here and there. Our parents used to say her head was permanently in the clouds because she liked the view from up there so much better." His voice drips with nostalgia and affection as he looks out at the open fairway.

Yep. That description's apt, though she does seem to enjoy coming down from her dreamy clouds to be with me on the ground, where our worlds collide. She brings vibrancy into my rather mundane life. Every day with her is an adventure, and I find myself wanting nothing more than to just exist in her space.

"Fore!" Victor yells. "That damn lanky kid," he mumbles with annoyance.

Jack and I stifle our laughs as Finn stalks our way. Looming over the cart, he glowers. "I don't want to be your friend anymore."

"I didn't know we were friends," Jack teases. "I just considered you the dude fearless enough to date my sister." Smirking, he lifts his coffee to his lips.

Finn narrows his eyes on me next.

"What? I'm not in one place long enough to have friends." I put my hands up in surrender.

"Fuck off. All of you." He stalks away, though halfway to his cart, he glances over his shoulder, laughing.

We lift our coffee cups in solidarity. "Good luck, brother," Jack shouts.

Facing forward again, Finn raises his hand and gives us a well-deserved middle finger.

When we finish the front nine and stop for a quick break, I pull my phone from my back pocket and discover a message from Joey waiting for me.

JOEY

I'm dying over here with no updates. How's it going? Do you need me to rescue you?

The corners of my mouth turn up, probably making me look like a love-struck fool.

I think you should worry more about Finn. Marnie's dad is having a little too much fun with him.

JOEY

Oh my god. I can't wait to hear more later.

How are YOU, though? Where's your social battery at? I can make up an excuse and tap you out. . .

I appreciate that. But shockingly, I'm doing okay.

Better than okay.

JOEY

Good! Do you think you'll be up for the barbecue with everyone at Jack's place after? If not, I'll make up an excuse.

Will you be there?

JOEY

Yes!

Then I'll be there too.

Chapter Twenty-Seven

By the eighteenth hole, my whole body ached, and exhaustion is now creeping in, not just from the physical activity, but from the socializing.

I text Joey when I pull up to the curb to let her know I'm here. She insisted on meeting me at the car so I wouldn't walk into the gathering alone.

Because the last thing I want is multiple sets of eyes on me.

A moment later, she rounds the house, coming from the backyard. I straighten up in the seat of my car, already feeling lighter. Her rosy cheeks and beaming smile have already renewed my energy.

She looks as gorgeous as ever in a long, flowy red dress in a floral pattern with buttons trailing down the front. The neckline dips into a V, exposing a hint of her cleavage.

Desire curls inside me. There's nothing but a few buttons between me and her immaculate tits.

Could I convince her to unbutton one or two of them? Just for me?

I shake the thought away as I climb out of my SUV. This is a family gathering.

A breeze tosses her wavy hair across her face as she approaches. Out of habit, I tuck the silky strands behind her ear.

She threads her fingers in mine, scanning my face. "It's a lot back there. So if you need a break or you want to leave early, our secret phrase is 'Barb's Banana.' Got it?"

Damn. When she looks at me like this, I wonder if she can see how hard I'm falling for her. How much I appreciate her thoughtfulness.

No one has ever taken the time to check in on my well-being like this. Ever.

I've never known of a person so eager to push their own feelings aside to make another person more comfortable.

Struck by her kindness, words fail me.

In response to my silence, she blurts out, "Sorry. I know I'm being a lot. I'm just worried about you. You can tell if I'm being too—"

I cup her face in my hands and kiss her. The moment our lips touch, she melts into me. She tastes sugary sweet, like she's been sipping on cola all afternoon.

She tastes like *mine.*

"Get a room. We're having hotdogs for dinner, not *horndogs.*"

I stumble back. Fucking Marnie.

"Jesus Christ, Marnie. Watch it. My daughter is right next

to you," Jack scolds. "Sorry guys. Continue on with. . .whatever you were doing. Not my business."

Laughing, I eye Joey, finding her face as red as I know mine must be.

"I came out here because I didn't want you to feel awkward, but now. . .yikes."

"Worth it. Let's get this over with." I grab her hand and lead the way to the backyard.

Just as I suspected, the moment we turn the corner, six sets of eyes home in on us. When a set of brows joins in, waggling, it makes the situation even more uncomfortable.

"Victor, can you get your child under control?" Charlie pleads.

"You think I haven't been trying to do that for the last thirty-six years? Give me some credit," he scoffs, bringing his Diet Pepsi to his lips.

Charlie's face twists. "It's absolutely repulsive that you drink Diet Pepsi and not Diet Coke."

Victor smirks. "It's caffeine free too."

"You disgust me with your soda choices," Charlie scoffs.

Finn watches the two of them banter, fear swimming in his eyes. "Don't poke the bear, Charlotte."

"He's all bark and no bite. I can handle him," she grouses.

"She terrifies me." Victor points at Charlie. "You? Not so much. Sorry, kid."

Laughter bubbles up out of Marnie. "Papa V's not wrong. I gotta agree with the old man. Sorry, Finn."

Finn adjusts his glasses. "Is today pick on Finn day? Did I miss the memo?"

"Nah, we only do it because you're a good sport about it, Gumby." Charlie pecks his cheek.

"Whatever," he grumbles.

Just past the two of them, a little girl sits at the table eating a popsicle. She can't be more than nine or ten.

"That's my daughter, Lucy," Jack says, handing me a beer.

Eyes widening, I look from him to her again. "Daughter?"

Joey groans next to me. "Oh, my god. I didn't tell you about Lucy. I'm literally the worst human. The worst aunt."

"Sometimes she even forgets to mention she has siblings. We know not to take it personally." Charlie shrugs.

"I wondered whether you had a kid after you spoke so passionately about the problems in the education system," I tell Jack. Immediately, unease seeps into my veins. Shit. Was that offensive? In case it was, I tack on, "You made excellent points, by the way. Teachers deserve to be paid more and the system could benefit from implementing more mental health services."

With a laugh, he pats me on the back. "Thank you. Lucy's a bit shy, so don't take offense if she doesn't say anything to you."

Joey sits next to Marnie, leaving me the spot between her and Lucy.

As I settle, I let out a breath. I'd much rather sit next to the quiet child than the unpredictable woman.

I sit silently as I take in the guests around the table, who are all chatting.

"Aunt Jo said you're also shy." Lucy looks up at me, her eyes wide. She has dark hair like her dad, but where all the Thorne siblings have brown eyes, hers are blue.

I give her a warm smile. "*Very* shy."

She leans in closer, like she's got a secret for me, so I dip my head. "I'm so sorry. This family can be *a lot*. Be thankful it's not Christmas. If you're ever here for a holiday, I know of a few good hiding spots."

Closing my eyes, I press my lips together to stifle a laugh. I like this kid. She's wise for her age.

"That's good to know. Thanks for the tip," I say.

"In this family, the introverts need to stick together." Sitting back, she continues to eat her popsicle.

My family has always consisted of my mom and me. Now, as I watch these people interact, a palpable sense of family wraps around me in a comforting embrace.

Each and every one of them has a past that has molded them into who they are today. And it's clear they accept and celebrate each other without judgment.

At the end of the day, we're all imperfect humans bound together by an unspoken mutual respect.

The thought makes my chest tighten. And the emotion only grows when it hits me that instead of closing myself off, I should've been surrounding myself with these kinds of people all along.

THE SUN HAS OFFICIALLY DIPPED below the horizon, casting the sky in strokes of deep purples and blues. The late spring air has a slight chill to it, though the fire in the firepit cuts through the cold. Jack and I are the only ones outside, both needing a reprieve from socializing.

He reminds me a bit of myself. Though he's a bit more uptight, he shares an appreciation for peace and quiet.

When my phone buzzes in my back pocket, I dig it out, and when I find Joey's name on the screen, warmth blooms in my chest.

JOEY

I didn't know dorky polos could look so hot.

Yeah? Is it working for you?

JOEY

It's more than working for me.

Now's a good time to tell you that the dress
you have on is working for me.

JOEY

I saw you trying to peek down my neckline
a few times.

Guilty.

And I won't apologize.

JOEY

Wanna get out of here? I can show you
what's underneath at home.

It's not much since I forgot to do laundry.

I reread that last message about ten times, my heart thumping at the mental image of her naked body beneath me. I've been wanting to tear the buttons off that tempting dress with my teeth since the second I saw her.

JOEY

Or we can stay longer if you'd like.

I'll be inside in 30 seconds.

I launch out of my chair, making it wobble before settling on all four legs again, and rush for the house, ignoring Jack's confused stare.

Inside, I stop short and take a breath, careful not to appear too eager. Then I make my way to Joey's side. As she talks to her sister and Marnie, I can't help but notice that one of the buttons on her dress has come undone. The delicate lace of her bra peeks out, framing her full breasts in a way that makes my pulse quicken. Desire spreads through me, and every muscle in my body tightens at the sight of her before me.

Joey's face lights up. "Hey. Ready to get out of here? I got exhausted all of a sudden. The week must be catching up with me."

Marnie tilts her head, her eyes flickering between us. I swear to god this woman better not be a mind reader. . .

I clear my throat and rest a hand on the small of Joey's back. "Absolutely."

The smile she gives me is enough to stop my heart.

Jack strides in and gathers supplies for s'mores. "You sure you guys don't want to stay a little longer?" he asks, holding up a bag of marshmallows.

Marnie clicks her tongue. "Yeah. . .I don't think that's what either of them is hungry for right now, Jackson."

Joey, face red, claps once. "Right. Okay," she says. "It was so nice seeing everyone. Have a good night. Thanks again for the ride, Char."

Too embarrassed to speak, I raise my hand and leave it at that. I can ruminate about my informal goodbye later.

Right now, I need to get Joey back to the cottage and get her naked.

On the drive home, the air between us is thick with desire and anticipation. It's only a thirty-minute drive, but each minute seems to last an hour.

I need to touch this woman, so I place my hand on her thigh, giving it a light squeeze. When she only smirks down at it, I slide it a little higher, then higher again, keeping my focus on the road ahead. The tension and excitement escalate with each subtle movement, and Joey joins in, shifting and causing the side of my hand to graze against the heat radiating from her core.

"You forgot to do laundry?" I croak.

"Yep. Wanna feel for yourself?" The teasing lilt in her voice is almost enough to make me come undone.

I swallow thickly, my heart pounding. When the pads of my fingertips sink into her plush thigh, her breath hitches.

"Yes," I grit out, facing straight ahead.

I reluctantly ease my hand away from her perfect body. Joey stirs beside me, dragging the hem of her dress up her legs.

The sound of the fabric gliding up her smooth skin has my cock aching.

She's being such a fucking tease, and she knows it's killing me inside.

Finally, I steal a glance over at her. If she pulls the flimsy red material any higher, she'll be completely exposed to me.

Jaw clenched, I fight the urge to pull off the road and fuck her in the back seat.

With her hand on mine, she guides me higher and higher up her bare thigh. When her warmth registers, I let out a groan and explore the expanse of smooth as silk skin until I reach the place where her breath catches.

She's soaked for me.

As I brush against her pussy, she releases a breathy moan and her hips lift, her body seeking the relief she desperately craves.

"Beckett. Please," she breathes out, her tone laced with desperation. She spreads her legs to give me better access.

In the mood to tease her, I trace the soft contours of her sex gently but avoid the place where she needs me the most.

Every time she shifts her hips in a wordless plea, I withdraw slightly.

Eventually, she groans and drops her head back. "I swear if you don't—"

"If I don't what?" I ask, chancing a quick look at her flushed face. "I like it when you get this needy."

Enjoying this game, I continue teasing around her clit, still avoiding the contact she craves.

Head resting back, she turns my way, her eyes glassy. "What do you want? What will it take?"

I brush over her clit once with my middle finger, pulling a gasp from her.

"Unbutton your dress and beg for it."

Chapter Twenty-Eight

JOEY

I KNEW EXACTLY what I was doing.

The second I saw him in that polo shirt—indecently snug across his chest and tight around his tattooed biceps—I wanted that man inside me.

Unbutton your dress and beg for it.

Beckett gets bold when he's turned on. And when he's like this? I'd let him break my back and then thank him for it. . .and then ask him to *break it again.*

My hands tremble with anticipation as I undo my buttons, revealing my bra. My breaths come out hot and uneven with need. My nipples graze the intricate lace, straining against the fabric and begging to be touched. Pair that sensation with Beckett's hand between my thighs, and my body is already wound tight.

Every sensation is amplified, my senses soaring to new heights.

The faint scent of his spicy cologne wraps around me.

The sounds of our heavy breaths, needing one another.

The warmth of his rough fingers between my thighs.

The look of hunger on his face.

Now I'm dying for a taste of him.

"Fuck," he growls, quickly homing in on my breasts, taking in every curve with an intensity that makes my skin tingle.

I'm burning up with need for him while he still has his eyes on the road. Though the muscle along his jaw pulses once, then again. A clear sign that I'm pulling on the final thread of his restraint.

His throat works as he swallows, a storm brewing beneath his composed exterior.

Pulse pounding, head resting against the headrest, my tits exposed, and thighs parted, I beg. "Please. *Please* touch me."

His sharp intake of breath only arouses me more.

"Here's how the rest of the drive will play out," he begins, eyes still fixed on the road. "You're going to play with your nipples and I'm going to play with your pussy. That way, by the time we get home, you'll be ready for me."

Oh. My. Fucking. God.

A whirlwind of emotions surges through me—a mix of pride at his newfound confidence and the overwhelming need for him to pull over so I can crawl onto his lap and close the distance between us.

Swallowing thickly, I glide my hands up my body, tracing a path over the lace of my bra and to the swell of my breast. My skin awakens under my touch, heat unfurling with every subtle caress. I cup and knead the soft flesh, reveling in the sensation before tugging down the cups of my bra. As the fabric slips away, exposing my hardened nipples, I drag my fingertip lazily around one, teasing Beckett, then twist it gently. Pleasure surges through my veins and my back arches off the seat.

Every few seconds, he looks away from the road, drinking me in, his hand tight on the wheel, his knuckles turning white from the pressure. "Fuck, Josephine. So beautiful," he murmurs, his voice a deep, gravelly whisper.

The burning desire in his tone makes me squirm in my seat. The sheer intensity causes my skin to pebble and a quiet whimper to escape my lips.

Every nerve ending in my body is screaming to be touched. My core clenches, begging to be filled by him. "If you don't touch me, then I'll have to take matters into my own—"

He sinks two fingers inside my pussy, cutting off my threat.

I cry out, hips bucking, greedy for more. Greedy for whatever he'll give me.

I need more.

Curling his fingers, he strokes me in a way that's making me delirious.

My hands fall to my side as my body relaxes into the feeling.

"I didn't say you could stop touching yourself, Josephine." His rough voice breaks through my euphoria.

"S-sorry," I stammer. With trembling hands, I return to work, my fingertips grazing against my sensitive nipples. Heat flares across my cheeks. I press my lips together to suppress the needy whimper that almost escapes me.

"Just like that. Thank you, baby." The rasp of his approval coils around me like a vise. Each syllable hits me like a reward I didn't know I wanted. Or needed.

The corner of his mouth tilts up into a satisfied smirk that has my stomach tightening with pleasure.

He withdraws his fingers at an agonizingly slow place, then he's teasing my clit. With expert precision, he works my body in a way that sends every atom spiraling with an intense desire.

Each motion fires off shockwaves of pleasure, the tension building inside me. As he works my clit and I focus on my nipples, I barrel dangerously close to the edge.

"I'm so close."

"Don't come yet. Not until I'm inside you."

He removes his hand, the loss of him heart-wrenching. I'm completely devoid of any thoughts aside from his tone, his touch, and his presence. My body's burning up, the blood roaring in my ears.

The rest of the drive is silent—and short, thank god—which is fine by me because I don't think I could form a coherent sentence like this.

I'm too dazed to do anything but wait for Beckett to haul me out of the passenger side and throw me over his shoulder.

I'm a woman with hips and height. No man has ever casually thrown me over his shoulder. Plus, I thought that was only reserved for the movies.

"*Beckett*," I screech, snapping out of the fog. "Put me down. I'm too heavy for you to be manhandling like this."

With long, determined strides, he heads for the door. "Josephine?" he says as he unlocks it easily.

"Yeah?"

"You're not heavy. Let me manhandle you just this once."

A laugh escapes me. "Sir, yes, sir."

Once he's kicked the door shut, he makes his way to the

kitchen. It's dark aside from the streaks of silvery moonlight dancing across the floor.

He sets me on the island, his hands smoothing up and down my thighs. With each caress, my dress inches up my body, the fabric flowing onto the countertop. The top of my dress, still unbuttoned, slips down my shoulders, leaving me more exposed. I'm completely at his mercy. Exhilarated by the intensity of this moment.

He grips my flesh, his touch one of pure possession. "I've been dreaming about these thighs all fucking week."

I lean back on my hands and shift my legs, making room for him. "Then do something about it."

His eyes snap to mine, molten, like he's ready to devour me. He pulls me to the edge of the counter, and without any more teasing, he drops his head and drags his tongue up my center slowly, savoring me.

Head dropped back, I gasp, my thighs clenching involuntarily. The way his stubble scrapes against my skin only heightens the sensations.

He groans against me, the sound one of relief, continuing to worship my clit.

I let myself sink into the pleasure. My hips roll, my body wanting more as I rock against his face. Heavy pressure builds deep in my core. I'm on the edge when he pulls away, lifting me off the island and spinning me around. My hands land on the counter as he looms behind me.

His hot, hard body wraps around me. "I told you," he whispers against the shell of my ear. "I want to feel you coming around my cock."

He flips my skirt up over my hips and smooths a hand over my ass with a groan.

"So ready for me," he says, slipping a finger inside me, causing me to whimper.

His belt clinks, then the sound is followed by the slow rasp of his zipper descending. The subtle crinkle of foil as he tears open a condom wrapper kicks my heart rate up. My breath catches as he positions himself, the blunt pressure of his cock teasing my entrance. With a hand on one hip, his fingertips digging into my skin, he pushes in slowly, allowing me to feel every inch of him. And when he's seated to the hilt, a guttural groan rips from his chest.

My back arches as he rocks into me, his movements merciless. Caught up in his own pleasure, he bites the juncture of my neck. The sting of his teeth sinking into my skin leaves me wanting more.

With one hand abandoning my hip, he trails a slow path down between my legs. Without slowing his pace, he circles my clit in a way that makes my thighs tremble.

"Don't stop. Please don't stop," I plead.

"I won't, baby. I promise I won't," he grits out against my neck.

In seconds, I'm coming undone.

I shatter in his arms. My body trembles as he continues to fuck me through my orgasm, overwhelmed with pleasure. My legs are dangerously close to giving out, but he tightens his grip to keep me steady.

Then he's pulsing inside me, my name falling from his lips like a prayer.

Josephine.

It sounds melodic like this, dripping with lust, accompanied by staccato breaths. Rather than pull out of me right away, he rests his forehead in the crook of my neck, his warm lips pressing soft kisses onto my flushed skin.

After we've cleaned up, we crawl into my bed, the sheets cool against our heated bodies. Nestled against Beckett's chest, I trace the intricate lines of his tattoos with my fingertips. He strokes my upper arm in slow circles, his face buried in my freshly washed hair. A comfortable silence stretches between us as we each become lost in our own thoughts.

Eventually, he inhales, his chest rising against my cheek. "This. . .is starting to feel like something between us, isn't it?"

I close my eyes, inhaling the scent of his skin. "It is."

He pulls me closer. "I'm not sure if this is the right time or place. . .or how to even approach this topic—"

Please say the words I want to hear. Please say them with your whole chest and mean them with your whole heart.

He swallows audibly. Then, "I-I don't want this to be over with you. Just because we leave at the end of the month doesn't mean we have to stop whatever *this* is."

As relief floods me, I'm tempted to crawl on top of him entirely. Hell, I'd crawl inside him if I could.

"I think we accidentally became a couple. Or just really bad friends with benefits. Either way, I feel like we did a lot of this backward."

"Accidental coupling sounds more like us."

"If this stands the test of time, then we won't have to worry about the adjustment period of living together."

"You already know my work schedule."

I hum. "And you already know I leave my socks in random places."

"I still don't understand why you can't put them in the hamper," he murmurs into my hair.

I pat his chest. "Don't worry. I don't even understand why I do half the things I do. I'm sure you love it, though."

"Yeah. I really do," he breathes.

I'm not sure if he wanted me to hear it, but I did. Loud and clear. With each passing moment, I'm falling harder for this man. Daily, I wonder what a future with him would look like.

Beckett's Journal

June 1

A future with Joey would look like everything I could ever dream of and more.

A future that looks like peace and belonging. Steady and certain. For so much of my life, I've been unsure of where I fit in. Traveling from city to city, silently hoping I'd find my place. With Joey, there's no more wondering. No more hoping.

From the beginning, she's looked at me like I belonged in her world.

Every time she places her hand in mine, it feels like a secret promise between us.

A promise where neither one of us will let go of the other.

Chapter Twenty-Nine

JOEY

I'VE HAD this day marked on my calendar since the project began.

It's time for the final presentation.

The conference room feels more like a war zone, though, with the way Norma is glaring at me.

It's possible that today could go really well, though it's just as likely I'll spend my lunch hour crying in my van.

Time will tell.

Max gives me a sympathetic look. He's been looking at me like this for weeks. He asked multiple times if he could take over the project, but I kept telling him no. I wanted to do this. I wanted this challenge.

I may be overly sensitive and apologize too much, but I am damn good at my job.

I'm practically vibrating with nerves. I even took a puff of my inhaler because I was worried I'd have an anxiety-induced asthma attack.

"Thank you all for being here. Let's walk through the deliverables, shall we?" As I click to the appropriate slide, I pretend my hands aren't shaking.

The first slide reveals Droplet's new logo—both in color *and* black and white.

Bryan studies the image wearing a pleased smile, while Norma tilts her head to the side.

Moving my cursor over the logo, I explain my thought process. "I made a few minor revisions to the original design. I've included both the black and white and the full-color option *to appease all audiences.*"

A small, snide remark never hurt anyone, right?

I click through to their brand and style guideline next. "I've added your main colors with optional tints and shades to the guide, as well as additional branding colors so everything is cohesive and visually appealing to the audience. Bryan, you mentioned liking a sans serif typeface, so I used one and added several weight options. You can use the different styles as you see fit, such as headings and subheadings on your website."

Slide after slide, I explain my thought process. Including visual elements, design assets, usage, and more.

I even made a few mockups of the logo under different lighting conditions because Norma asked in one of her many emails whether the logo would "speak" to the consumer under both fluorescent and natural lighting. Did I know logos could do that? Nope. But I made it my mission to find out.

When done with my presentation, I turn my attention to both Bryan and Norma. "I really enjoyed working on this project, and I hope you're happy with the final deliverables.

I'm prepared to send all the design files over in the appropriate versions for each application and platform. I'll include specific details like which ones are best for your website, social media, print, and more."

For a moment, the conference room is dead silent. Max is holding his breath, I'm drenched in sweat, Bryan is still staring at the screen, and Norma's eyes are narrowed on Bryan.

"Incredible," Bryan says, his eyes lighting up.

"Nice," Norma says coolly. "I like the options."

I let out a breath of relief, and it looks like Max is breathing again too. I'm fairly certain this is the closest to a compliment I'll ever hear from her.

The rest of the meeting passes by in a blur of logistics and small talk.

Afterward, while Max, Bryan, and Norma file out of the conference room and chat with the CEO of Fernrose, I make my way back to my desk, needing a minute to breathe.

It feels like I've lived a hundred lives today and I'm exhausted.

As I answer a few emails, minding my own business, Norma saunters over and looms over me.

How symbolic.

With a hip propped against the desk next to me, she clears her throat.

I glance at her from the corner of my eye but don't stop typing. What does she want now?

"Joey," she says, "let me ask you something."

I huff, my hackles rising. "Sure."

"Bryan was telling me about your *alternative* lifestyle."

I don't know where she's going with this. Bryan and I chatted once about national parks, and I mentioned that I traveled while I worked and that I could give him a list of my favorites.

"I work remotely and travel across the country. It's not like I'm living on a commune." I pause, my fingers hovering over the keyboard. "Then again, that doesn't sound too bad right now," I mumble.

She sucks her teeth in disapproval. The sound makes me want to crawl out of my skin.

"What I'm gathering is that you're not tied down. No husband, no kids, no. . .*family*?"

That last part stings more than I would have thought it could, but I don't let her see that. Because *I do* have a family. My circle is small, but they're still family. "What are you trying to get at, Norma?"

"Don't you think it's time to settle down? It's cute when you're in your twenties and traveling the world, but you've got to be in your thirties by now. Doesn't that seem a bit juvenile? Don't you want to feel more. . .complete? Fulfilled? And don't you want a loving husband and a house in the 'burbs kind of life? Maybe a couple of children?" She clicks her tongue. "Maybe it's time to be an adult now, dear. All this traveling and wearing colorful clothes and bouncing from place to place without a care in the world isn't setting you up for future stability. Just something to think about." With that, she spins on her heel and strides toward the door.

I silently hope that she slips on her way out.

Unfortunately, I'm not that lucky.

Sitting back in my chair, I stare at my computer screen, completely dazed.

Even after the successful meeting, that single interaction is enough to take me back to the days when my insecurities ran rampant and controlled my life.

And suddenly, I'm second-guessing a lifestyle that I was once so confident in.

It's funny how all it takes is one shitty person to make someone doubt themselves.

"You're rid of her, right?" my sister asks.

I flop back on my bed, fluffing the pillows behind me with one hand while holding my phone up so I can see her. "Yeah, I am. The last couple of months have been hell."

"I was about to grab the pruning shears and show that bitch who's boss," Marnie yells in the background.

Stomach sinking, I lower my voice and say, "Are we sure she hasn't killed someone?"

"No. No, we aren't," Charlie whispers back. "Wait, what's wrong?"

"Huh? What do you mean?"

"You're biting the inside of your lip like it's your last meal. Is everything okay?"

Nope. Everything is not okay. Norma's parting words have been replaying in my mind for hours.

"It's nothing." I sigh, trying not to let my shoulders slump. "Just something Norma said before she left."

Charlie's eyes fill with concern. "What was it?"

"It's nothing. I don't want to be a—"

"If you say the word burden, I'll send Marnie over there with the pruning shears."

My heart lurches. "Heard that loud and clear."

I take a deep breath and collect my tangled thoughts. They're twisted and tied together in a knot that's nearly impossible to undo, but eventually I clear my throat and dive in. "She said my lifestyle was juvenile. The traveling, the lack of a spouse, and even my choice in clothes." Angry tears burn behind my eyes. I promised I wouldn't cry over this, yet the sting of her words is still sharp. "Maybe she's right. Maybe I need to change my ways. Settle down, find someone who will complete me, and live my little picket-fence life in the suburbs. Maybe how I'm living is *wrong*."

Charlie sighs loudly. "First of all, you don't need to change *anything*. And there's nothing *wrong* with your life-style." Head tilted, she hums. "Ok, you should add more fruits to your diet, but I digress. Second, you can't let someone as insecure as Norma cause you to doubt yourself. Don't give her that kind of power."

Groaning, I thread my fingers through my hair. "I know. I know."

"Just remember, while you're busy doubting yourself, other people are looking at you with envy. They're intimidated by your ability to remain true to yourself. So many people slip on a disguise every day, wanting to hide who they really are. You? You've never been like that. And Norma? It's envy. She's unhappy, and she thinks it'll make her feel better to bring others down with her."

I huff. "I hate when you get insightful with me."

"Why? Because I'm usually right?"

"Unfortunately, yes. Don't let it get to your head."

"Too late!" Marnie calls out.

I shake my head, smiling for the first time in hours. After the day I've had, my chest finally feels lighter, freer. Like I can finally take a deep breath again.

"Thank you for this. Seriously. I'm sorry for being a—"

Charlie lets out an annoyed sigh. "Oh, my god, *shut up*. You're not a burden. Stop apologizing."

"So. . .you *do* love me?"

She rolls her eyes. "Don't make a big deal out of it."

Frantically, I shake my head. "No. Never. I can't believe you just admitted to having feelings."

For a while after the call, I lie in bed, ruminating. It's not the quantity of people one surrounds themselves with that matters. At the end of the day, it's the quality. I may not have a huge group of friends, but the small team of people who stand behind me would go to battle for me, even on my darkest days. They accept and love me, through and through—even though I apologize too much.

They stand by my side when the world walks out on me.

They support all my rights *and* my wrongs.

They see inside my heart and soul. And they look past the facade I show the world.

The banging of pots and pans disrupts my thoughts. Curious, I make my way down the short hallway.

In the kitchen, Beckett has pulled out his baking supplies. His hair is damp from the shower, and the faint clean scent of his shampoo wraps around me. He's dressed in a pair of black sweatpants that hang low on his hips, and as he pulls a bowl from the top shelf, the hem of his gray T-shirt lifts, giving me a glimpse of his inked, toned skin.

Steamy dough daddy, indeed.

Fucking Marnie. Granted, she's not wrong. The man before me is most definitely living up to his nickname.

"Hey, Beck," I slide onto a stool at the island, setting my chin in my palm.

With the mixing bowl in his hand, he spins around and a smile breaks free on his face. When he smiles at me, his entire face lights up like one of his long-forgotten wishes has come true.

"Hey, stranger," he jokes. "I haven't heard from you all day. Is everything okay?"

Unable to look him in the eye and lie, I play with a loose thread on my sweater. "Yep."

Nope.

My sister's tough-love pep talk only did so much to untangle the web of intrusive thoughts in my mind.

He sets the bowl down and crosses his arms. "You couldn't be less convincing if you tried." He rounds the island and sits next to me. "I can always tell when you're lying because you break out in hives." He parts one side of my cardigan, unveiling a hint of my skin, and traces a lingering path from my collarbone to the base of my throat, leaving a trail of goose bumps in his wake. "Right here."

I let out a humorless laugh. "I hate that my body betrays me."

He glides his fingers up to my chin and tilts my head, forcing me to meet his worried eyes. "Talk to me. What happened today?"

"It's fine. I don't want to be a—"

"If that next word is *burden* or *burden adjacent,* I'm not accepting it. You'll need a better reason."

Powerless against the intensity in his voice, I break down and tell him everything. Once again, he has an impressive way of creating a safe space for me to crack open my heart and bare my soul.

Because with Beckett, I never have to worry about being *too much.*

Chapter Thirty

BECKETT

NORMA SAID I have nothing tying me down, no family or a spouse or kids. That my lifestyle is juvenile.

She said I should want to feel more complete. More fulfilled. Am I not complete as I am? Maybe I do need someone to complete me.

What does "future stability" even mean?

Maybe she's right. Maybe I need to grow up. My clothes. My hair.

Am I living my life all wrong? Is there even a right way to live?

The words *maybe I need to change* bounce around in my head until I see red.

I hold Joey's hands as she fills me in on her conversation with Norma, and when she's done, she looks exhausted.

"Do you want that?" I ask a little too forcefully.

She sniffles. "Want what?"

"That life. *The 2.5 kids, picket fence in the suburbs with a dog* kind of life."

With a scoff, she wipes at her eyes. "No. I don't. Except for maybe the dog. That would be kind of nice."

I angle in, trying to look her in the eye. "Do you want to change your style, your hair, your personality?"

A dry laugh escapes her. "Absolutely not. It's just. . ."

"It's just what?"

Finally, she meets my gaze and sighs. "I feel like she validated all my fears in a single conversation. That if I want to be accepted, if I want to be chosen, then something *or everything* about me needs to change. That I have to shove myself into a box that fits the supposed norm. No matter how uncomfortable it feels."

I give her hands a reassuring squeeze. "Joey, your authenticity is something I envy and admire. You aren't defined by anyone else's standards, and you know what? People light up when they're around you. They laugh when you tell a joke, their shoulders sink with relief when you show them kindness, and they smile brightly when you give them a compliment."

Frustration courses through me. I'm not mad at her, but at how shitty people can be.

"And if someone doesn't like that, then fuck 'em. You can't see it because you only see your flaws right now, but you have this energy that captivates people."

Tears roll down her cheeks. "Do you mean all of that?" There's a deep ache in her voice that spears me in the heart.

I cup her face and wipe at the tears, waiting to ensure she's really listening before I say this next part. "I mean every word." I let out a slow breath. "Never let anyone dictate how you feel about yourself or how you should live. How other people feel about you and what their perception is of you is *not* your burden to bear. Got it?"

"Got it." Arms looped around my neck, she pulls me in for a hug. I hold her tight, ensuring there's no space left between us, and bury my nose in her silky hair.

Her breath fans across my ear. "Thank you."

"Always." I place a kiss on her temple, letting my lips linger there for a bit before she pulls away.

In this moment, I know that no matter where our lives take us, I'll always be on her team.

Standing, she wipes her face with the sleeve of her sweater. "Can I ask what we're stress baking tonight?"

"Cookies." I get up from my chair and make my way over to the fridge.

She brings the back of her wrist to her forehead, swooning playfully. "A man after my own heart. Put me to work, chef."

I gather the eggs and butter and add them to the other ingredients I've already pulled out. "Technically, I'm a baker. Not a chef."

"Eh. Semantics." She comes up beside me, watching as I measure out ingredients. "What kind are we making?"

"Sugar cookies. Basic, but gets the job done."

Joey rests her head against my shoulder as I carefully measure the ingredients. "Do we have sprinkles? The rainbow kind? I swear the artificial dyes add the best flavor. Maybe we could sprinkle the cookies with those."

This close, when I tilt my head, I can easily count the freckles on her pink cheeks. I could get used to this. Used to us. Standing side by side, baking cookies in a tiny kitchen late at night.

The sparkle of appreciation in her eyes right now is enough to make my chest overflow with emotion.

Without a second thought, I cradle the side of her face and trace my thumb over the smooth curve of her cheek, savoring the warmth of her skin and searching her eyes for a hint that she feels the magnetic pull between us like I do.

I press my mouth to hers in a tender kiss that will forever linger in the back of my mind. Her lips are smooth and plush, molding perfectly to mine as if they were made for kissing me and only me. Pulling back slightly, I rest my forehead against hers, wanting to bottle this quiet, intimate moment up so I can enjoy it again later.

Her stomach grumbles, breaking the moment, and amusement floods me.

"Sorry, sorry." She winces. "I haven't eaten much today, and as soon as you said cookies, my stomach woke up."

I nod to her usual seat at the island. "You sit. I'll bake."

"Can I make a request?" she asks once she's in place, elbows on the counter and chin propped in her hands.

There's a devious look in her eyes. A look that I don't know whether to trust.

I plug the hand mixer in and set it on the counter. "I'm scared."

"You should be. . .I mean *shouldn't* be."

"What's the request?" I sigh.

"Could you bake like this in nothing but an apron?"

I fumble the sugar, tipping the bag over so the granules spill all over the quartz. I could have made a million guesses about what she'd ask, and I still wouldn't have come close.

Dishrag in hand, I clean up my mess, trying to ignore the way my face heats. "I don't have an apron."

She breaks into a maniacal laugh. "I wouldn't object to that."

"Josephine," I playfully warn, a smile twitching at my lips.

"Beckett," she retorts, mimicking my tone. "I had a bad day. *And* I cried. Come on. I need a win."

The rag falls to the counter as I survey her, getting lost in her eyes like I always do. I'm powerless against her. Time and again, she so effortlessly pulls me out of my shell. She makes me feel safe and free to be my true self.

A resigned sigh leaves my chest. "Fine. Just this once." Grabbing the hem of my shirt, I pull it over my head.

She hums, her lips curling into a satisfied grin as she takes in the contours and ridges of my body. "Eh. We'll see about that."

I toss the shirt aside and reach for the button on my jeans, head shaking in amusement, knowing full well I'd give her anything she asked for.

ALL MORNING, I've been baking loaves of bread for my mom's competitive gardening club. I'm not sure what makes it competitive, and frankly, I'm too afraid to ask.

Joey is helping, packaging up the last of the loaves now.

"Wanna come with me to drop these off?" I stack the boxes of sourdough. "I was going to stop by the shelter first and pick up a dog for the day. I figured it would be a good opportunity to get eyes on the pup and a good excuse to escape early."

Joey rears back. "Uh. No way. I'm an absolute mess. Look at me!"

Several strands of hair have fallen out of her ponytail,

lying limply against her navy blue sweatshirt—well, my navy blue sweatshirt—and she's covered in flour.

"But you're my mess." I push a wild lock of her copper brown hair behind her ear, my fingertips lingering against the delicate curve of her cheek.

She rolls her eyes, but the corners of her mouth turn up. "Very cute. Very charming."

"Is that a yes?"

"Would this be the equivalent of meeting the parents?"

"Since you'll be meeting my mom along with a few dozen other veggie enthusiasts in her overgrown backyard, I'd say yes."

Sighing, she swipes at a streak of flour on my chest. "I could take you to meet mine if they hadn't already washed away from shore. They're somewhere out in the middle of the Pacific by now. Maybe we can take a boat ride someday."

"I'm not. . ." I swallow past the lump that's suddenly lodged itself in my throat. "I'm not sure if you're joking or if I should be concerned or—"

"Dark humor, Beckett. You'll get used to it." Eyes flashing with levity, she strolls to her room. "Give me fifteen minutes."

Chapter Thirty-One

BECKETT

As I'm signing in at the shelter, an employee appears from the back room, her eyes lighting up. "You took Moose out last time you were here, right? A couple of months ago?"

I glance back at Joey, who's exploring the lobby. "Uh. Yes."

Relief washes over her face. "Would you like to take him out again? He'll be so happy to see you."

A shot of confusion rushes through me. "I got an email a few weeks ago saying that he'd been adopted."

She sighs, her shoulders slumping. "He had, but last week, the family brought him back, saying he was 'too needy.'"

Scoffing, Joey steps up beside me. "What kind of soulless bastard returns a dog for being too affectionate?" When we both turn to her, she holds up her hands in defense. "Sorry. That came off a bit brash. But I still stand by what I said."

Chuckling, I turn my attention back to the employee.

"We'll be happy to take him out again. We should have plenty of opportunities to introduce him to people today, so hopefully we'll find him a permanent home."

"Also," Joey says, tapping her fingers on the counter, "if you could give me the name and number of the person who returned—"

"Joey," I interject, trying not to laugh.

"What? I just want to have a little talk. No harm. No foul."

Moments later, Moose skitters through the kennel doors, then weaves between our legs in wiggly circles.

I crouch, arms wide. "Hey, bud! It's been a while."

Joey giggles, clipping on his leash. "What a happy guy. Those ears could pick up radio signals."

Rising to my feet, I hold out a hand to take the leash. "That's part of his charm. Stumpy legs and floppy ears."

The warm sun and clear skies make for a beautiful day as we wander to my SUV and get Moose loaded up. "Let's find you a home, buddy."

Music blaring and windows down, I pull out onto the street.

"All right," Joey says. "What should I know about your mom before I meet her? I can't believe we're at this stage of our relationship," she teases. "What a backward romance we have."

Grinning, I tap the steering wheel to the beat of the music. "So dramatic."

She shrugs, eyes sparkling. "Eh. At least it keeps things interesting."

"Things you should know about Dana." I sigh, pondering how much of my mom's eccentricities are acceptable to share. "She collects salt and pepper shakers, gets overly emotional at TV commercials, and names all her plants."

"Houseplants? I feel like that's normal."

"No." I shake my head. "Her entire garden. She hosts a small funeral after she's cleared out her garden at the end of every summer. She follows it up with a large dinner, where she serves all the veggies she's picked, plucked, or pulled."

Joey turns in her seat to fully face me. "You're fucking with me."

I scoff. "I wish."

A mischievous grin takes over her face. "Should I ask her thoughts on cross pollination? Do veggies get kinky?"

"Now you're the one fucking with me."

"Unfortunately, I'm very serious about cross pollination. Who wouldn't want a melon-squash-cucumber-corn hybrid?" She sinks into her seat and watches the scenery. "I wonder if she's caught any of her plants cheating. Like what happens when the beans pollinate with peas? Is that taboo?"

"Generally speaking, beans can't pollinate with peas. Or other legumes, for that matter." I check the rearview mirror again. Moose's ears are flapping in the breeze and I swear he's smiling. "And a melon-squash-cucumber-corn hybrid isn't possible either."

She whips around, eyes wide with wonder. "Do I want to know how you know that?"

I let out an exasperated sigh. "One too many of these competitive gardening functions."

"What do these events entail?"

"There are usually ribbons for the largest grown crop. That kind of stuff."

"Think anyone will show me their eggplant? I'll take a cucumber or a squash too." She tosses her head back, cackling. "I'm not picky. I enjoy all phallic shapes and sizes."

With a roll of my eyes, I sit a little straighter. "I'm ignoring this ramble."

"I think that's for the best." Her laugh is light and airy and it fills me with warmth.

Thirty-minutes later, with Moose on a leash and fresh loaves of bread in tow, we wander into my mom's backyard. Between Moose's happy trot and Joey's radiant smile, I can't decide who's enjoying this day more.

At the sight of the crowd gathered around my mom, my chest tightens.

As if she can sense the change, Joey gently grasps my arm and pulls me to a stop. Eyes boring into me as if she's speaking directly to my soul, she says, "Hey. We got this, okay? If you need a break, tap me in. If you need to leave, send me a text. If you need a distraction, I'll let Moose run wild in the garden. Sound good?"

I give her hand a silent *thank you for being you* squeeze. "Sounds good."

My mom does a double take, a wide grin spreading across her face. "Beck!" She strides our way, looking from me to Joey to Moose, who's panting with excitement. "And company!"

Joey shifts the large paper bag of sourdough bread to her other hip. "Hi! We haven't met. I'm Joey."

My mom's green eyes widen and she waggles her brows at me.

Unsurprisingly, heat rises to my cheeks.

Joey, bless her, takes a step forward and distracts my mom. "You have a beautiful garden, Ms. Hart."

"Please," my mom says, waving her off, "call me Dana. And thank you. My veggie babies are enjoying this beautiful stretch of weather we're having." She peers down at Moose, who's looking up, tongue lolling from the side of his mouth. "And who do we have here?" She crouches, giving his floppy ears a scratch.

"This is Moose. We're taking him out for the day, hoping to find him a forever home," I say.

"He's such a handsome boy," she coos, her voice hitting that ridiculously high note that's reserved for puppies and babies. "I'm sure he'll love all the attention he gets here." Standing, she settles her hands on her hips. "You look like responsible parents. Just keep him away from the bell peppers. He's been eyeballing them."

Moose wags his tail in response, though I don't know whether it's a happy wag or an admission of guilt.

"We brought lots of bread," Joey chimes in.

"Let me take that bag from you." Mom holds her arms out. "Beckett, Nancy has been dying to talk to you."

Groaning, I drop my head. "Not about the mole."

She winces. "About the mole."

"Mom, couldn't you—"

She puts a hand up. "Beck, I tried. You know how she gets. If you do this for me, I'll let you sneak out the front in twenty minutes. Deal?"

"Deal," I reply.

Joey snorts. "Seems like we're all on team 'get Beckett out of here unscathed.' I had a plan in place too."

My mom's green eyes sparkle. It's a look reserved for moments when someone understands and accepts me. An expression that says *Finally, someone else sees the part of my child that I always knew was there.*

"You talk to Nancy," Mom says to me. "Joey and I will take the sourdough inside." With a swish of her floral dress, she heads for the back door.

Joey trails behind her, glancing at me over her shoulder, her wavy hair bouncing with each step. She mouths "good luck" and gives me a thumbs-up.

A laugh bubbles up inside me, though the sound catches in my throat at the rush of gratitude flowing through me. I've never felt worthy of being understood and accepted by another person. But Joey doesn't see my anxieties as flaws. Rather, she sees them as just a small piece of who I am.

To her, my anxiety is a single brushstroke on an expansive canvas—noticeable up close yet never defining the picture she holds of me.

TWENTY PAINFULLY LONG MINUTES LATER, after I've answered all of Nancy's mole-related questions, I push through the back door. At my side, Moose is panting like he's just ran a marathon, when in reality, he's been lounging in the backyard, getting belly rubs from strangers.

As I set a bowl of water on the floor in front of him, laughter drifts in from the living room, the airy sound drawing me in. I round the corner to find Joey and my mom looking at the wall I aptly call "The Beckett Shrine." It's filled from top to bottom, end to end, with photos of me at every awkward stage of life. From the infamous nineties bowl cut to a mouth full of braces, she's got it framed and nailed to the wall.

The laughter turns into chatter, and my mom asks, "Has Beckett shown you his prize-winning eggplant yet?"

My stomach drops to the floor and all the air leaves my lungs. Oh my fucking god.

Joey, who was taking a sip of lemonade, slaps a hand over her mouth, sputtering. "Uh, nope. Can't say I've seen any prize-winning anything of his"—she smirks at me—"yet. I'm sure he's packing something gold-star worthy, though."

My mom follows her gaze to me. "Oh. I was showing her your eggplant."

"Mom, you cannot say stuff like—"

She slaps my shoulder. "Don't get your boxers in a twist. I meant this photo over here." She points to a dusty old frame. The photo inside is of scrawny, eighteen-year-old me holding an impressively large eggplant.

"Wow. That big boy has some girth to it," Joey jokes. "I like the little curve it does at the tip."

Lips pressed in a firm line, I narrow my eyes at her. She's only adding fuel to the innuendo fire.

"And just look at how proud he is holding that girthy thing!" My mom beams, completely oblivious.

Or maybe she knows exactly what she's doing.

With Dana, it can be difficult to tell whether or not she's intentionally stirring the pot.

"Yeah. So proud," I mutter. "I spoke with Nancy. All seems well."

"Thank you, thank you." She claps once. "Now that you've done your good deed, you're free to go."

"Deeds," I correct her. "Plural."

My mom rolls her eyes. "Bread baking is hardly any trouble for you. You have enough pent-up anxiety to open a bakery."

That gets a chuckle out of me. She's not wrong.

"It's true," Joey chimes in. "Now I know why his forearms are so defined. It's all that kneading."

With a groan, I tip my head back to the ceiling. "You two can't be trusted together."

Both women laugh, the light sound filling the room.

My mom turns to Joey, taking her hands, her green eyes filled with appreciation. "It was so lovely to meet you. Please come back and visit," she says, her gentle voice full of sincerity.

We exchange our goodbyes, lingering a bit longer than necessary. Mom and Joey have bonded quickly, it seems, and with every step toward the door, one of them blurts out another thought they want to share. Eventually, my mom crouches to give Moose one last ear scratch. His tail thumps against the wall with glee and it makes us all laugh.

Outside, the sunlight streams through the lush trees. I take a deep breath, relishing how good I feel right now. Moose pads alongside us as I lace my fingers with Joey's. She glances up at me, brown eyes sparkling, and for a moment, I get lost in her radiant features.

This woman is truly special in a way that's difficult to explain. She makes the world brighter, turning ordinary moments into memorable ones.

Moose snores in the back seat the whole way back to the shelter while Joey hums to the music and I sneak glances at her as often as I dare.

Dropping Moose off at the shelter was gut-wrenching, his soft whines piercing through our hearts. Before we left, we loved on him, promising to see him again before leaving Hemlock.

A couple of my mom's friends showed interest in him, falling in love with his floppy ears and soulful eyes, and promised to visit him tomorrow. Part of me hopes one of them adopts him so I can ask for updates on his life. Maybe even visit him occasionally when I'm back in town.

As we drive along the winding road, dappled with late

afternoon shadows, I rest my palm on Joey's warm thigh. The simple touch grounds me to the present moment.

Today was a good day.

It was as easy and natural as breathing. Every day, this woman finds ways to make me feel safe while still making me laugh. She pulls me into the light when I'm used to staying in the dark corners. Being with her feels safe and *right*.

I want more days like this with her. More light, steady days. More days where I don't have to second-guess myself. More of this quiet sense of belonging that shrouds me when I'm with her.

And more of the kind of peace I thought I'd never find.

Chapter Thirty-Two

THE RAIN HAMMERS on the rooftop in a ruthless fury as I huddle under a blanket on the couch, doing a crossword puzzle. Beckett should be home at any moment, meaning Barbara is curled up next to me as I consider twenty-seven across.

Good or bad vacuum review. What does that mean?

A lightbulb in my head goes off. *Sucks!*

This could be my future. Sitting inside on a rainy night, doing a crossword puzzle while I wait for my partner to come home. I'd probably have some subpar meal cooked for him when he strolls in after a bad day at work. We'd complain and laugh, wondering how people can be such idiots. Afterwards, we'd cuddle on the couch and watch reruns of our favorite TV shows. Maybe I'd make popcorn, and he'd jokingly complain that eating the entire bag will make me sick and that I should've eaten more at dinner. But I didn't eat more at dinner because I was too busy staring into his kind eyes as he talked about his day. Too busy picking out each shade of green in his irises. Maybe I was thinking about our upcoming weekend plans, which likely involved baking bread.

A sudden ache hits me deep in the chest.

Maybe I *do* want that life, but more than anything, I want a life with *him*.

My phone buzzes on the coffee table, the low vibrations ripping me from my daydream. The number is unfamiliar, and though I'd normally let it go to voicemail, my gut is telling me to answer it.

I slide my thumb over the screen and bring the device to my ear. "Hello?"

"Hi! Joey?"

Unease curls in my stomach. "Uh. Yes. May I ask who's calling?"

"It's Bryan from Droplet. Sorry for calling so late. Listen, my whole team in Seattle is impressed with your work. We've got an open creative director position, and I would love for you to consider it." His voice, upbeat and happy-go-lucky, grates on my nerves a little.

"Uh, I'm not sure what to say."

Except, my overachiever actions are now formally meeting my impostor syndrome consequences.

"Take a few days to think it over and then give me a call. If you're interested, I'll take care of accommodations. All you have to do is bring yourself and your amazing creativity."

I do appreciate the stroke to my ego, even though it doesn't erase the uneasy feeling in my stomach.

"Sure. I can do that."

"Great. Talk soon."

Bryan's off the phone before I can even say goodbye.

I slump back on the couch with my phone clutched in my hand. The room is quiet aside from the patter of rain on the roof and the circus music playing in my mind. The universe must be playing an elaborate joke. Nothing, and I mean *nothing*, about this makes sense.

Norma has surely blacklisted me, yet the very company she works for wants to bring me on?

I'm so. . .confused.

The front door swings open, and I jolt, my heart lurching.

Beckett removes his soaked jacket and shoes, then wanders into the living room. The bright smile on his face falls when he sees me.

"You okay? You look like you've seen a ghost." He strides over and kneels down in front of me.

Right about now, I could use a ghost—specifically, the ghost of my dad. That man had a solution to every problem I encountered during the first twenty-nine years of my life.

He splays his hands over my legs, his warmth seeping into me.

"Hey, baby, what's wrong?"

I snap up straight.

Baby. That nickname.

There's another topic I'll be ruminating over tonight. Great.

"I—uh—I got a call," I say, my voice trembling.

His brow furrows in concern. "Is everyone okay? Charlie? Jack? Lucy? Finn? Marnie? Frank? Vera? The tarot card lady?"

A smile tugs at my lips as he lists all the important people *and animals* in my life. I cup his face and stroke his stubbled cheek. "Yes. Everyone is fine. I got a call from the CEO of

Droplet. They want to interview me for a creative director position."

His eyes go wide. "That's amazing. Wait. I didn't realize you were thinking about changing jobs."

I drop my hand to my lap and shake my head. "I wasn't. He called me out of the blue. Said his team was really impressed with my work and they wanted to interview me for an open position."

"That's incredible." He squeezes my knees. "When's the interview?"

"I was so shocked that I didn't know what to say. So he told me to think about it and call him back. But it sounded *really* promising."

Head tilted, he studies my face. "Where's the hesitation coming from, then?"

"I-I honestly have no idea. Maybe it seems too good to be true. Makes me wonder if Norma is playing an elaborate prank on me."

"Joey." He ducks, catching my eye, stopping me from letting my overactive imagination take over.

I let out a heavy sigh. "Okay, fine. That's a bit melodramatic. I'm sure Norma's off turning some poor, innocent employees to stone with her glare."

He lets out a deep chuckle, patting my thighs. "How about we talk more about it over pancakes? I just need to shower first."

"Are you trying to make me fall in love with you?" I ask. The moment the words leave my mouth, my stomach lurches. Shit. "I meant that as a joke. You know, because I love breakfast for dinner. Actually, I love all dinner. The food you make is superb. And not just your food—anyone who cooks for me is a Michelin star chef in my mind. I'm not actually, or actively, falling in love with you. Oh my god. That came out rude. It's a figure of speech—"

"Joey?"

"Yeah?"

He beams up at me, his eyes full of kindness and deep understanding. "I know what you meant," he says gently. "You don't need to over-explain."

"Then why did you let me go on for so long?"

A warm chuckle escapes him. "I wanted to stop you at the chef comment, but I was curious about what else you would say."

"Jerk," I tease.

"You love it. . .or maybe you don't?" He hits me with a heart-stopping wink.

I wrinkle my nose in feigned disgust. "Go shower. You smell like latex and bleach."

With a shake of his head, he cups my face. Then he leans in and places the most tender kiss on my lips.

A kiss that says *Don't worry, I have you. I know you. I understand you.*

It's a kiss that lingers long after he pulls away and disappears up the stairs.

When his bathroom door closes, I slump back into the couch with a heavy sigh. For a moment, I was free of my spiraling thoughts, but now that Beckett is gone, they're back and in full force.

Is this the universe testing me? What the hell is happening? Is this a sign from above?

More and more, I've been thinking about what a future with Beckett would look like. But if I take this job, what would that mean? Would he want to stay in one city for the rest of his life? Could he imagine staying with *me*? Would it be fair to him if I expected that? Though he did seem genuinely excited for me.

But of course he did. He's a beautiful anomaly and unlike anyone I've ever met. Of course he cared. That's who he is. He's the kind of man who shows up when I need him the most, always murmuring soft reassurances, soothing my self-doubts with kisses, and picking up on the smallest details.

Am I getting ahead of myself? Am I caught up in the ideas of potential, half-formed dreams?

I don't have the faintest clue.

Maybe this relationship we've fallen into is temporary. A scenic stop on a long road trip. One that deserves to be fully explored but isn't the end goal.

A cherished memory. The kind that leaves a lasting impression, lingering in a person's mind for decades to come.

But not the destination.

No. He's so much more than a stop along the way. He deserves the love of someone who knows what she wants, knows where she's going. And right now I am *not* that person. My direction is akin to using a broken compass—lost and uncertain.

Maybe I need to take this next step.

Me? A creative director?

The mere thought is thrilling and daunting.

Do I even have what it takes for this type of role?

I guess the only way to know is to take the plunge into the unknown.

While Beckett and I briefly discussed not wanting this to end when our time in Hemlock is up, this new development adds complications.

It made sense to date long distance while we both traveled. We share an insatiable sense of wanderlust, both reveling in the adventure of exploring a new city and creating new memories with each road we travel.

Now, with the prospect of an on-site job on the horizon, it all feels a bit too complicated for my liking.

And at what point does this become too much for him?

<hr>

"I CAN FEEL your mind overworking again," Beckett murmurs into my hair. "What's going on in there?"

Rather than talk over pancakes, we ate mostly in silence. Now, like this, tucked into his side on the couch while Barbara is sleeping peacefully on the top of the cushion behind us, I know I should be completely honest with him, but I'm petrified.

Burying my face in his shirt, I murmur, "I really like you. I like *this*. I like *us*."

His muscles tighten a fraction. "I'm afraid of where this is going."

"Don't be. I'm being dramatic. *Again.* I'm wondering what the plan is after, you know, all of this." I wave a hand, face still buried because this topic is making my eye twitch.

The vibration of his soft laugh reverberates through my cheeks. "After our time here is up, I assumed we'd follow each other around. I'd discuss my assignment locations, you'd give me your thoughts, and we'd choose any destination. . .without snow, of course."

I huff out a laugh. "I know I'm putting the cart before the horse, but I like to prepare for disasters. So what happens if I get the job? That's a disaster I need to prepare for."

"First of all, stop burrowing yourself into my side. I can

barely hear you," he teases, "and you're digging into my ribs."

With a huff, I sit up. My hair falls into my face and Beckett, like he always does, smooths the strands back.

"Second," he says, cradling my cheek, "say the words and I'll follow you."

A surge of emotions knocks all the air out of me. Happiness blooms while fear lurks in the shadows.

"We barely know each other," I say. "I'm not worth the hassle. You can't give up what you want in life for someone you barely know."

He angles in, expression intense. "Not acceptable."

Confused, I frown. "Huh? What?"

He cups my face in both of his hands now, holding me as if he's afraid he'll shatter me. "Do *not* talk about yourself like that. I never want to hear the phrase 'I'm not worth the hassle' come out of your mouth again. You're not and *will never be* a hassle."

"Following me is a big commitment," I argue, "and we've only known each other for a couple of months."

"Josephine, let me make something clear to you." His palms still rest against my cheeks—grounding, soft. "I am *very* certain about how I feel about you. I stand by what I said. Say the words, and I'll follow you."

More words. More words to ruminate over.

Beckett's Journal

June 17

As she fell asleep in my arms on the couch, I couldn't look away. The soft rhythm of her breath on my chest, the subtle way her fingers curled into my side—holding me as if she were afraid I would drift away.

I want a life with her. A life where we start the day holding each other and end it passionately tangled between the sheets.

Sometimes, if you want things to flourish, you need to give them space to grow. I'm willing to give her space to grow, but I need her to know that she can always count on me, no matter how many miles apart we are.

Because between her compassion and empathy, her mesmerizing eyes, and a smile that could thaw the iciest exteriors, I'm unquestionably spellbound by her.

Chapter Thirty-Three

The moment I set foot in the lobby of the skyscraper, I feel out of place. The marble floors gleam under the artificial lights while the scents of cleaning products and forgotten dreams swirl around me.

I spent maybe a little too much money on a more "professional" outfit. Black dress pants, a crisp white shirt, and a black blazer.

An overpriced penguin costume, essentially.

My plane landed in Seattle yesterday afternoon, and Bryan put me up in a pretty nice hotel with an incredible view of the city. If only I had more time to explore while I'm here.

My low heels click against the floor as I approach the front desk, where I apparently have to check in before being granted access to the elevators. It's rather obnoxious.

I smile at the security guard. "Hi. Joey Thorne. I have an eight a.m. meeting with Droplet."

He scrutinizes me, his brows knit together like he has no idea who I'm talking about.

Letting out a heavy sigh, I say, "Josephine Thorne."

"Ah. That makes sense. They've got you down as Joey, so we were expecting a man." He laughs like he's told the most hysterical joke.

"Of course you were, because we live in a dumb patriarchal society," I mumble under my breath.

He rounds the desk, head tilted. "Sorry, what was that?"

I snap my spine straight and plaster on a fake smile. "Oh, nothing. Just rehearsing for the meeting."

With a hum, he heads for the elevators. "Follow me." He uses a key card to open the stainless-steel doors, and once I'm inside, he presses the button for the thirteenth floor. My heart lurches. I thought many high-rise buildings omitted the thirteenth floor. Then again, I've always been superstitious. I don't step on cracks, I always throw spilled salt over my shoulder, and I've never killed a ladybug.

After a painfully awkward ride up, the shiny elevator doors open up straight into Droplet's lobby.

It's not anything like what I expected.

It's cold and sterile, the fluorescent lighting harsh.

All the employees are dressed in impeccably pressed suits and perfectly tailored dresses. Despite the sharp clothing, their expressions and demeanor lack warmth or personality.

I made a good call with the outfit today. I can only imagine the looks I'd get if I'd shown up in my colorfully embroidered denim jacket. For a company focused on insulated water bottles, one would think that their employees wouldn't be so serious.

On the outside, I blend in seamlessly with everyone else, but on the inside. . .I have my doubts.

Every person milling around nearby has hunched shoulders, like they're weighed down with invisible burdens, and dark circles beneath their eyes.

As I shuffle toward the receptionist, who also seems less than thrilled to be here, Bryan swoops into my personal space.

Eyes wide, I take a step back to put some distance between us.

"Joey, good to see you again," he says, extending his hand.

His handshake is so corporate. Whereas mine is closer to shaking hands with a wet noodle.

"Hi," I squeak out, suddenly unsure of my decision to interview for this position. I feel like a tiny fish swimming in an expansive ocean, worrying I'll find myself suddenly surrounded by the sharks.

"Before we head to my office to discuss the position, let me give you a tour." He beams, his smile unnaturally white, then leads me around the office space.

Eventually, because the universe is out to get me, we run into the last person I want to see.

Norma.

She looks me up and down. Surveying my slicked-back hair, the tight bun that's giving me a headache, and my sensible and professional suit. Then a calculating smile stretches across her face.

"Hello, Joey." She reminds me of a ventriloquist's dummy, lifeless and disturbing. It makes my stomach twist with disgust.

"Hi, Norma," I say, my voice falling flat as I stare at her forehead, brows furrowed, hoping she thinks she's got something on her face. I read somewhere once that periodically glancing at someone's forehead while talking to them can cause them to feel insecure and uneasy.

When she wipes her forehead with the back of her hand, I cheer internally.

Nothing turns me on more than a little psychological torture. It's a balm for my soul.

We quickly say farewell to Norma, continuing the tour, and accepting enough handshakes for me to warrant draining an entire bottle of hand sanitizer. Eventually, we end up in Bryan's office, and he gestures for me to sit in the chair in front of his desk.

I ease into it, biting back a wince. This is why I never wear heels. My feet are killing me. I'm pretty sure a few blisters have made a nice, bloody home on the backs of my heels.

There's a bit of awkward silence as taps his keyboard, all but ignoring me.

When I can't stand the quiet anymore, I blurt out, "Is this when you ask me to tell you about myself? Maybe why you should hire me? I can also list off a few weaknesses which are actually disguised as strengths."

Unamused by my humor, he only blinks at me. "Oh." He clears his throat. "This isn't an interview. The job is practically yours."

"Uh. I was just making a joke because—you know what? Never mind. Tell me more about the position." I cross my legs, settling my hands in my lap.

He shifts in his chair, facing me now, hands clasped on top of his desk. "I'm so glad you asked. As the creative director, you'll be in charge of overseeing the creative process for our various campaigns, projects, and more. You'll oversee a team of copywriters, graphic designers, photographers, and web developers."

Pausing, he raises his brows, like he's waiting for me to ask for more information. I don't want to be an asshole, but I already know what a creative director does. I want to know the good stuff. Tell me how many weeks of vacation I have and how many mental health days are acceptable to take before I'm at risk of getting fired.

I nod. "This all sounds wonderful so far." I don't even recognize my own voice. It's so steady and calm.

"Great. The benefits are exceptional. We have top-tier health and wellness benefits and an executive bonus structure on top of your salary." He passes me a sheet of paper, where a six-figure number has been typed out. My eyes practically bulge as he goes on. "You'll have six weeks of vacation days and an equity grant, vesting quarterly over three years. And we'll pay for the cost of relocation, and we'll set you up in a hotel for sixty days while you look for a place to live."

Holy fuck.

This is an incredible offer. Life-changing, even.

"Our employees love working here," he says, pulling out one more sales pitch. "Some even willingly stay late and work on the weekends. It's not expected, though."

His tone changes at the end, like he's lying. Like this company most definitely expects their employees to put in more than forty hours a week.

"The last thing I'll mention is the mandatory employee etiquette training," he says casually. "You'll complete that before stepping into your role."

For maybe the first time in my life, I'm overwhelmed by a gut instinct. This job offer is too good to be true, and that last little bit is all I need to know to confirm it.

Bryan's words linger in the air, a reminder that in this

world, it doesn't matter how competent I am. Skill alone will never be enough.

"It's very basic," he goes on. "A run-through of things like global business and networking etiquette."

Head tilted, I search his face. He's holding back what he really wants to say.

Bryan clears his throat. "Along with professional attire and body language etiquette since we do have an image to uphold here."

I stay silent

"All employees are required to take this training," he tacks on, shifting in his seat.

Sure, Bryan. If it makes you feel better, keep telling yourself that.

"This will enhance your confidence and help you build strong relationships with stakeholders. It may even open doors for new opportunities. Including some *very exciting* promotions." His words come out in a long, barely coherent string.

Fingers laced in my lap, I lick my lips, considering how to respond.

"Did I mention the salary? Also, I can talk to our HR Director about giving you two extra weeks of time off. Plus a holiday bonus. What do you say?"

My head spins. The position is a good one. But at what expense?

And does this mean I have to choose between a life on my own terms and the life I'm told I should want?

IS A PERSON'S STORY PREWRITTEN? A path they must get lost

along in order to find their way again? Because I feel utterly lost and alone right now.

I told Bryan I need time to think about the offer.

Financially, I'm doing just fine at my current job. I planned, saved, and invested just like my dad taught me. Sure, the healthy salary increase that Droplet is offering is attractive, but the money isn't my top concern. It's the gnawing anxiety of having a life-changing career move knocking on my front door. The shadow of bigger and better opportunities looming over me, all while I'm plagued by doubts.

The relentless pressure of feeling like I need to do more with my life.

The persistent thoughts continue to scream at me, trying to convince myself that I have to settle down and create a home in one place in order to be fulfilled.

The unsettling worry that I'll never find where I belong.

The first thing Droplet wants from me is that I completely change who I am. They want me to be someone I'm not, and it struck a painful chord.

They like my work. But they don't like *me*. And that fuels my worry that I'll never be enough.

Fucking Norma and her insidious whispers. Planting seeds of doubt that if I don't do *this*, I will never achieve *that*. Seeds that eventually grow into menacing fears that threaten to undo all the confidence I've worked to build.

I'm angry with myself for letting a single person burrow under my skin. But sometimes, that's all it takes—one person to pummel everything I've meticulously constructed over the years.

Bruising the delicate flesh of my self-esteem.

Cracking the mirror of my self-acceptance.

Unraveling the threads of positive affirmations woven into my self-worth.

All of it can disappear without notice.

Still, I mull over the what-ifs. I'm a firm believer that everything happens for a reason, even if that reason remains elusive until much, much later.

I'm being torn apart at the seams. I'm at my breaking point, being pulled in different directions, each tug more painful than the last.

On the flight home, exhaustion takes over and I fall asleep.

"Hey, thanks for picking me up," I say to Jack, as I hoist myself up into his truck.

My brother, who's wearing his classic blue flannel and baseball hat, sneers.

My heart sinks. "What?"

He rips off his sunglasses. "What the hell are you wearing? Why is your hair like that?"

"Ugh." I drop my head back against my seat. "I didn't have time to change, and now I'm stuck in this polyester penguin uniform."

"I don't like it. It's not you."

I scoff. "You're telling me, brother."

He pulls away from the curb and heads toward Hemlock.

Shifting, I survey him. "Can we stop at the store for a family meeting?"

He freezes, his hands tightening on the steering wheel. "Did that roommate of yours get you—"

I put my hand up. "If you utter one more word, I'll never take my shoes off in your pristine house again."

He shoots me a glare. "Fine."

Thirty minutes later, as the evening sun hangs low on the horizon, painting the storefront in shades of amber and gold, we step into A New Leaf.

"Charlie." I shoulder my way in roughly, nearly knocking the bell above the door loose. "Family meeting."

Jack follows behind me, his dusty work boots scuffing across the wooden floors.

"For the love of god, what do you want?" My sister appears in the doorway to the store's back room, wiping her hands on her apron, but when her eyes land on me, she goes rigid. "What the hell are you wearing? And why are you both here? Don't tell me that roommate of yours got you—"

"For the love of all that is holy, would you two shut up? Leave Beckett out of this." I yank out a stool and lower myself onto it.

"Why is your hair slicked back and why are you wearing *black*?" Charlie screws up her face in disgust. "And why are *you* here?" She sends a pointed glare to Jack.

He pulls out another stool. "She wanted to have a family meeting and I was too scared to ask questions."

My siblings look at me with matching, concerned expressions. So I spill everything, my voice trembling as I explain every worry, fear, and concern that has been bouncing around in my head.

The fear that I should be doing more with my life. The poisonous thoughts that Norma put in my head, my concerns about never being enough while also being too much. My suspicion that the employment etiquette courses are their thinly veiled attempt at reconstructing my identity.

The words spill from my lips in a breathless rush, and when I've gotten them all out, I slump against the counter. "Shouldn't I want this, though? Shouldn't I want a fancy job title and more responsibility?"

With his arms crossed over his chest, Jack studies me. "No. Not at all," he finally says. "Jo, just because an opportunity falls into your lap doesn't mean you're obligated to take it. You get to choose what's right for you."

"But I would be leveling up, getting a salary increase." I sigh. "I'd be growing up—"

He angles forward, elbows on the counter. "If you took that job right now and moved to Seattle, would you look back in twenty years and be happy with your decision? Or would you regret giving up this life you truly love for a nice paycheck that you can't do much with because you're working too much?"

I scrub my hands down my face, anxiety rolling through me. "I wish Dad was here to tell me what to do," I whisper.

My brother and sister share loaded looks, silence hanging between us for too long.

Finally, Charlie takes a deep breath and shocks me by leaning over and holding my hands in hers. This must be serious because she hates physical contact of any kind.

"All my life I've admired you for not remaining in the boxes people put you in," she says. "You've always done things on your own terms and in your own special way. And no matter how shitty people are to you or what kinds of obstacles life throws your way, you maintain a light that brightens up the darkest of rooms." She licks her lips and glances at Jack, who nods, before looking back at me. "Don't let that light of yours dim because you feel like you *have* to take this job. You don't have to do anything you don't want to do—no matter how good it may seem on the outside. Don't force yourself into something that feels wrong. Got it?"

"Yeah. All of that." Jack nods, his expression sincere.

The two of us stare at him.

"What?" he asks, his eyes going wide. "I agreed with her."

I let out a light chuckle. "You're a man of many words, Jackson."

Charlie, without missing a beat, quips, "Let's get him a dictionary for Christmas."

"Don't be sarcastic," he grumbles.

"Never," Charlie and I tease in perfect unison.

As my sister's words resonate through me, I know what I need to do.

"Jack," I say. "Can you drop me off at the cottage?" I need to get Poppy and get to my storage unit before the place closes for the night.

Beckett's Journal

June 22

She twirls her hair when she's nervous.

Her cheeks flush the perfect shade of pink when she's angry.

When she gets out of the shower, she smells like sun-ripened strawberries.

Sour gummy bears (not worms) are her kryptonite.

Her favorite color is purple because her middle name is Iris.

She cries during nature documentaries yet believes she can be a homicide detective when she watches true crime shows.

If she strays from her morning routine, her whole day gets thrown off.

Every day her laughter drifts through my mind, the soundtrack of my waking thoughts and peaceful dreams.

She's unaware that her vibrant spark has ignited a flame inside me. One that'll burn for her for eternity.

She's taught me that love doesn't always have to be loud and in-your-face.

It doesn't have to be loud in order to be strong.

It could be subtle and understated. Quiet and peaceful. Because more often than not, quiet love is given from the loudest hearts.

Joey may possess a big personality, but the small gestures are what mean the most to me. Holding my hand under the table to quiet anxious thoughts, creating code words to signal when I'm overwhelmed at social gatherings, and swooping in to save me from awkward conversations.

I'd say I've shown her what she means to me in simple ways too. Cooking for her when she hasn't had a decent meal in days, encouraging her to sketch more, and reassuring her with gentle words.

All are acts of quiet love.

Because her heart has been looking for a safe place to land. And I've been looking for a heart to cherish, wanting nothing more than to be that safe space for her tender heart.

Chapter Thirty-Four

JOEY

WHILE I WAS IN SEATTLE, Beckett was busy helping his mom around the house, so we only texted here and there. When the message I sent before boarding the plane still shows that it hasn't been read, my stomach sinks.

I'm still mulling over the job offer, and I need him. He's always a great sounding board and the voice of reason. But this isn't a conversation that can be had over a text, and I don't want to intrude on his time with his mom.

Regardless of what he said about me never being a hassle, I can't ignore the insidious voices that creep in from time to time.

Gravel crunches under my tires as I pull into the storage unit complex, and once I've punched in the code, the creaky gates open slowly.

In high school, I took a sociology class, and one of our projects was to create a time capsule. The idea was to open it after ten years. Ten years turned into fifteen, and honestly, I'd forgotten about it until my nap on the plane.

I dreamed that my mom and dad were sitting in a field of wildflowers, smiling at me. My mom's curly brown hair exactly how I remember it and my dad's eyes filled with kindness. . .and *pride*.

He looked proud of me and I couldn't understand why.

"Find the shoebox," they told me.

Before I could ask them what they meant, the pilot announced we were landing shortly and I was jolted awake.

As I open the door to the storage unit, where my siblings and I store so many keepsakes from our childhoods, my hands tremble. With a deep breath in, I start my search. Each box brims with history and memories. There are old family photographs, dusty antiques that my dad promised we wouldn't sell for profit, and old sweaters that still smell faintly of my mom's perfume.

On my tiptoes, I reach for another dusty box on a top shelf. When I pull it forward, a smaller weathered cardboard box comes tumbling down, hitting the concrete floor with a hollow thud and a large puff of dust.

It's a shoebox.

It's wrapped in duct tape, so I find the small pocketknife I keep in my purse, and carefully slice open the seams of the box. Inside, I find embarrassing photographs of my high school self and a few little trinkets that mean nothing now. But beneath them, I discover a letter addressed to me from my dad.

My heart leaps into my throat as I hold the worn yellow paper between my fingertips. Closing my eyes, I take a calming breath. Then I carefully unfold the letter.

Grief rolls over me at the sight of his barely legible handwriting. Each word is pressed into the paper with force, the way Dad always wrote. I trace my fingertips over the indentations, sniffling back tears. The picture in my mind is as clear as day as I imagine him sitting at his desk with his reading glasses on, writing this letter to sixteen-year-old me.

Dear Joey,

I'm writing this letter for your time capsule project. If you read this before you're twenty-six, I'm hiding your car keys.

Ever since the day I first held you in my arms, you've reminded me of wildflowers. The ones your mom and I would see when we traveled up and down the Pacific Coast Highway during the springtime.

Like a wildflower, you've always been resilient. You thrive where you're planted and grow on your own terms.

In the last couple of years, I've overheard your conversations with Mom (no, I wasn't eavesdropping—the walls are thin and your voice carries). You often mention how you've never felt that anyone has chosen you. That you feel different. Like you don't belong.

So I want to remind you of one of my favorite days that I've spent with you.

Remember that day we spent in that flower field off the coast when you were ten? You never once looked at those wildflowers and thought they were unworthy because they were different. You admired them because of their uniqueness. You chose to pick them for your mom because no two flowers were the same. You saw them for what they were—beautiful, strong, and free.

And that, my daughter, is exactly what you are. Beautiful, strong, and free.

*Never forget, it's okay to be different. In fact, I encourage you
to continue being different (normal people are overrated
anyway).
Remember, if you feel like you don't fit in, you're on the right
path. So long as you stay true to yourself, you'll bloom where
you're planted.
Because, just like a wildflower, your individuality and
authenticity make you one of a kind.
Love always,
Dad*

I PRESS the letter to my chest as hot tears stream down my face.

Then I cry so hard I can't breathe. My chest burns, and I have to sit with my head between my knees for several minutes. Eventually, my lungs fill and the tears dry. This is what I needed to see. This was the sign I was looking for.

And as I clutch the letter in my hands, sniffling, I've never felt more sure of myself.

BY THE TIME I pull into the driveway, night has fallen. The sky is a deep navy, the stars glittering above me.

I need to speak to Beckett. I need to tell him everything.

I sprint inside, drop my bags, and call out for him.

The house is dark aside from the small entry table lamp.

"Beckett?" I call again, stepping farther into the living space.

Nothing.

When I'm met with silence, my stomach drops. I can't get ahead of myself and think the worst. It's not fair to me or him.

So I head to my bedroom to change into comfortable clothes, dead set on donating this penguin suit as soon as possible.

Meow.

Before I get there, Barbara calls for me from the top of the steps.

"Hey, Babs," I coo. "You hungry?"

She flicks her tail back and forth, then darts away like something has frightened her.

That's weird.

She meows again, the sound more insistent, and when she does it a third time, I shuffle to the stairway. I hesitate at the bottom, gripping the wooden banister as I consider my options. I've never actually been upstairs, and the idea of crossing that barrier into Beckett's territory makes me uncomfortable. It's his space and I have no business entering it. Yet Barbara is still meowing, the noise now echoing down the hall, and I'm getting worried that something is wrong.

At the top of the stairs, I find a small vintage desk under a window.

Barbara sits on it regally, her head held high. Her wide amber eyes focus on me, then shift to the side.

I follow her line of sight and find a weathered journal with a note on the front that says *please read.*

Confused, I reach for it, my fingertips grazing the texture of well-worn leather. I flip through it, finding nothing but blank pages. But as I get to the front and catch a glimpse of Beckett's handwriting, anticipation floods me.

Josephine,

I know you're torn about what to do. I wasn't sure how to articulate this, so I wrote it down. Writing is always easier for me.

Nothing you do will make you feel complete because <u>you were never incomplete to begin with</u>.

You've been whole all this time, and in the last few months, I've fallen in love with you. All of you.

I didn't mean for it to happen, but I don't regret it.

I fell deeply in love with all the beautiful, imperfectly perfect facets of you. Whether you leave your socks all over the house or make a complete mess when making dinner—I love all your pieces.

And yes, even the ones I still don't understand.

But knowing you and your beautiful mind, the words above aren't enough.

So, Josephine, I'm writing this to tell you that I choose you. I'd choose you in every lifetime, every version of reality, and in infinite universes. I'd find you and I'd choose you over and over again.

As I put my pen to the paper, I long to fill this journal with our story.

And I know what you're thinking. "What happens when this journal ends?"

Lucky for you, I have a whole stockpile. I'll never run out.

There will always be a journal waiting to be filled with the memories we make together. Ready to be flipped through during shared sunny mornings and rainy nights.

Because, Josephine, I love you in ways you can't even begin to imagine.

I'll supply the journal, and together, we'll capture moments and put them on this paper. Just you and me. . .and Barbara.

MY HANDS TREMBLE as I close the journal. His writing is messy and impatient, like he couldn't get his thoughts out fast enough because he feared he'd forget them.

He understands the language of my heart, and he has shown me over and over that I'm deserving of the same kind of love I give.

When a person's heart is understood in the way that he understands mine, it's like coming home after a bad day and being wrapped up tight in a pair of comforting arms.

Beckett doesn't just talk safe, he *feels safe.*

I press the journal against my chest, my heart fluttering behind my ribs, and look out the window at the shadowy forest.

I need to talk to Beckett. To hear his voice. To tell him I feel the same way.

The weight of his words washes over me, like the warmth of the sun kissing my skin after a cold winter.

With a deep inhale, I turn, ready to find my phone and call him. Ask him to come home.

Instead, I find him standing on the landing at the top of the stairs. The soft orange glow from downstairs barely silhouettes his body in this tiny alcove. His blond hair is mussed, like he's been raking his fingers through it, his dark-rimmed glasses are askew, his emerald eyes tender and earnest.

My breath hitches. "I-I didn't hear you."

"I'm stealthy." He takes a step closer to me, hands in his pockets.

"Y-you love me?" I question, my voice unsteady.

"I do." He takes another step forward.

My eyes blur with tears, my chest aching. "Are you sure?"

He lets out a quiet chuckle that wraps around my soul, healing all my broken pieces, and with one more step, he cradles my cheek and brushes his thumb over my skin.

As he takes me in, his eyes are filled with sincerity and love. So much so that I can't look away. "Yes, Josephine. I'm sure."

I blink back my tears. "Hey, Beckett?"

"Yeah?"

"Follow me."

"Anywhere."

Maybe I've never been chosen until now because the universe wanted me to wait for him. For the man who's also never anyone's first choice. Now here we are, choosing each other.

Chapter Thirty-Five

BECKETT

"FOLLOW ME."

"Anywhere."

The sight of her dressed in drab colors makes my chest ache with longing to bring her back to herself.

I start with the bun, releasing it and letting her auburn waves tumble down her back.

"There she is," I whisper, threading my fingers through her tresses.

Then I unbutton the stiff blazer and the starched white, dress shirt. I press a soft kiss to one shoulder as I drag the fabric over it, then do the same to the other. I blaze a trail across her delicate collarbone and up the smooth column of her neck. Her eyes flutter closed and she lets out a sigh of relief.

With every layer I remove, her eyes soften further and her

shoulders sag more. I undress her slowly, bringing back the woman I love, adore, and cherish.

On my knees in front of her, I unbutton her pants and coax them down her legs until they pool on the floor. Once she's stepped out of them, using my shoulders to steady herself, she looks like my Joey again. The beautifully clumsy woman with colorful clothes, untamed hair, and a laugh that goes straight to my soul.

I adore every inch of her.

Rising, I cup her face again, relishing the softness of her skin and her strawberry scent as I press a soft kiss to her lips.

She sighs against my mouth, wrapping her arms around my neck and drawing me closer.

I pull away a fraction, murmuring, "I hated that fucking outfit."

Her laugh is light, free. "Me too. It's going straight into the donation pile."

"That's what I like to hear." I crush my mouth to hers and slip my hands to the clasp of her bra.

"Wait. I need to shower. It's been a long day and I feel gross."

I press a kiss to her nose. "Let's shower together, then." With my thumbs, I caress her warming cheeks. I lower my voice. "Let me take care of you tonight."

"Okay," she whispers.

While we wait for the water to warm, Joey leans against the sink, hugging herself. Still in her head. Still worried.

As steam billows around us, fogging up the mirror, I grasp her chin between my thumb and forefinger and tilt her head up. "You can let go now, Josephine. I'm not going anywhere. You're here. With me. For however long you'll have me."

Eyes wide, she simply nods. She's the first to step into the shower, tilting her head back, letting the water stream over her hair and face. I step behind her and squirt a healthy amount of shampoo into my hand.

Joey hums, eyes closed, and sinks into my fingertips as I massage her scalp, caressing away the day's burdens. Her body slackens, leaning against mine as I glide my fingers down to the base of her neck and loosen the tight, tense muscles there. With a washcloth in hand, I scrub her body, tracing a sudsy trail down the curve of her spine.

When I've washed every part of her, I massage her scalp one more time, then coax her to lean her head back so I can rinse the shampoo out.

Under the hot water and wrapped in steam, she places her hands on my face, stroking my jaw.

"What's the matter?" I ask as tiny droplets collect on her eyelashes.

"I love you. So much," she whispers. Her voice is barely audible over the water tapping against the shower tiles.

I crush my mouth to hers, basking in the soft warmth of her lips, and pull her soft curves against the hard planes of my chest.

This is what heaven must feel like.

I'm not sure how long we stay in the shower, holding one another under the spray, but the water has gone tepid before we step out and I wrap her in a plush towel.

"Stay with me tonight, please," I plead as I tuck my own towel around my waist.

I want nothing more than to hold her and soak in her warmth.

I want to wake up with her in my arms, knowing this wasn't a dream.

She exhales softly. "I was hoping you would say that."

Her eyes are filled with soft certainty, unshakable trust, and the quiet acceptance we both deserve in our lives.

Desperate, I cover her mouth with mine, urgent and hungry, stealing the air from her lungs.

And when I slip my tongue between her lips, she moans, her delicate fingertips tracing the edge of my jaw, leaving trails of heat in their wake.

I press closer to her, our damp skin melding as I tangle my fingers in her hair and tug gently, deepening the kiss. Against my bare chest, her wild heart beats in rhythm with mine.

Joey pulls away, though she stays close enough that her nose brushes mine. "I need this off." She tugs at my towel and lets it fall to the ground. "And I need you inside me." She nips my bottom lip, one hand wrapping around my erection. As she strokes, I close my eyes, surrendering to her touch.

When her movements stop abruptly, I snap my eyes open.

The look on her face is one of pure mischief as she takes a step back and allows her towel to fall to the floor.

My heart trips over itself as I take her in. Long legs, plush thighs, full breasts. All on display before me. I want to spend the rest of my life mapping out every curve with my tongue.

I take a step forward, aching to touch her, but she stops me by putting her hand on my chest.

"You took care of me. Now let me take care of you." Eyes filled with lust lock on mine, and then she drops to her knees.

She drags her hands up my thighs to my clenched abs and back down again. A wave of euphoria hits me as she explores every ridge of my body, making my pulse race violently.

She grips the base of my cock, then licks up my shaft slowly, torturously. With her eyes still locked on mine, she swirls her tongue around the head and pulls me into her mouth. The heat of her mouth surrounds me, stealing the breath from my lungs. Holding back takes everything I have.

"Fuck, Joey." Her name leaves my lips in a half prayer, half plea as I thread my hand into her hair.

Eyes fluttering closed, she moans, sending vibrations of pleasure through me. Then she's slipping her free hand between her legs and stroking her clit.

The sight of her touching herself as she takes me deeper is enough to take me out. Swaying, I grip the countertop on either side of me hard enough to make my knuckles ache.

When dark spots dance in my vision, I gently tug her head back. She releases me with a wet, obscene pop and blinks up at me, breathless, her swollen lips curling into a satisfied smirk.

Cock twitching, I haul her to her feet. "Grip the sink for me, baby."

I can't take my eyes off our reflection. Her dark hair falls over her pale skin and soft curves. Behind her, I'm all sharp angles and dark ink. The stark contrast between us is devastatingly erotic.

We're so different, but so perfectly matched in all the ways that matter.

I smooth over the dip in her waist down to the flare of her hips, then slip one hand between her thighs, gliding over her slick heat, stroking her until she's writhing against my fingers. "Don't move. I'll get a condom."

As I pull back, she grasps my wrist. "No."

I still, blood roaring in my ears. "No?"

"No condom. I have an IUD." Panting, she peers over her shoulder. "Also I was recently tested. Nothing to report."

All the air leaves my lungs and my grip on her hip tightens. "That makes two of us. Nothing to report, either." I kiss her slowly, reverently. "God," I say when we come up for air. "The thought of being inside you, feeling all of you—"

Eyes closed, she shudders. "I know, Beckett. I know," she breathes, arching into me. "I'm yours."

Once I've notched myself at her entrance, I slide into her slowly, savoring every inch of her softness.

With a gasp, she pushes back into me, greedy for more. Slick and tight, her body melds to mine like we're made for each other.

Because we are.

"Fuck," I groan, clutching her hips tighter. "You feel incredible."

Every gasp and breathy moan escaping her pink lips pulls at the threads of my resolve. I hold back, tensing my muscles to keep from tipping over the edge, but her sweet sounds are making it difficult to keep this up.

"Yes," she gasps, face flushed. "More."

Because I can't say no to her, I pound into her harder, every movement urgent and desperate.

Head tilted back, she exposes the column of her throat in the dim light. I fist her long auburn waves and tug, tilting her head to side, then nuzzle the hollow where her neck meets her shoulder, inhaling the warm scent of her skin.

We're a tangle of ragged breaths, pleasured moans, and pounding hearts as I rock my hips into her.

The image reflected in the mirror is obscene. It only turns me on more.

"Look at us, Josephine," I command. "Look how perfect we are. Look how perfect *you* are."

She turns her head, and as she takes us in, her brown eyes widen. She's lost in the way we look, overtaken by sensation, her pussy clenching around me, pulling me deeper as if her body is desperate to keep me inside.

I lock eyes with her in the mirror. "All of me." My voice is ragged and desperate. "My soul, my body, my heart is yours. Forever."

I release the silken strands of her hair, then slide my hand over her soft stomach and down to the apex of her thighs. With two fingers, I find her slick, swollen clit and rub small circles over it. Against me, she trembles and her breaths grow short and frantic.

"I'm so close," she pants, her knuckles turning white as she grips the counter on either side of her. "Please don't stop."

"Never, baby," I promise against the shell of her ear.

She cries out my name—a breathless sound that breaks into a whimper—and her body shudders against mine as her orgasm consumes her. With a final deep, satisfying thrust, I let go, give in to the pleasure shooting through my veins, and bury my face in the crook of her neck.

As we come down, we're both panting, sweat-slicked, and trembling.

"We need another shower, don't we?" she jokes. Her chocolate brown eyes shimmer as she smiles, and a tender warmth blooms deep in my chest.

I brush away the damp strand of hair clinging to her forehead and press my lips to her freckled nose. "I'll get the water going."

God, I love this woman.

Chapter Thirty-Six

BECKETT

I'VE DREAMED of mornings like this for so long, always believing I'd never actually have them.

Quiet. Slow. Simple mornings. *Spent with the woman I love.*

Call me old-fashioned, but simplicity is highly underrated. In such a fast-paced society, we need to take a moment to slow down and appreciate the wildflowers every now and then.

Hazy mid-morning light peeks through the windows, highlighting the mahogany streaks in Joey's hair as she digs into her strawberry pancakes, absentmindedly chewing while working on her crossword puzzle.

A deep yearning for this woman clings to my soul, my heart breathing a sigh of relief. After years of idly searching, I found *her.* The woman who can look past my exterior, social anxiety and all, and is willing to stand by my side.

I want this life and all the ones after *with her*.

I want endless years of late-night stress baking and making a mess in the kitchen.

I want to babysit dogs who have a penchant for terror and stealing small animals.

I want honest conversations around the bonfire, across the kitchen counter, and on the couch.

My social anxiety is tolerable at best, but with Joey by my side, I will no longer let it control me. Sure, I'll still get uncomfortable, but Joey is like my security blanket. I never have to measure my words when I'm with her.

It's indescribable, the comfort I experience with her. For the first time in my life, I feel safe. With Joey, I can finally take a deep breath. I can show her all the parts of myself that I've hidden from the world and know she won't try to change me. She'll meet me where I am, and that feels like home. With her, I don't have to face anything alone. I don't have to carry the weight of the world by myself.

From the day I met her, I've been hers. Enraptured is the best way to describe the sensation that hit me the moment I was near her.

"Come for a ride with me today," I blurt out.

"Hmm?" She snaps her head up, fork halfway to her mouth.

I lean forward, resting my forearms on the counter. "Come for a ride with me. I found something the other day I want to show you."

With a playful smile, she tips her head back and laughs. "I thought you said 'come ride me.' I was about to tell you to let me finish my pancakes first."

Head tilted, I consider the thought. "Tempting. But we can do that later. And I'll feed you a snack first."

With Joey's arms wrapped snug around me, I roll down a winding dirt road, only slowing when I get to a small clearing. Once we've removed our helmets, I pull a blanket and an assortment of her favorite snacks and drinks from my saddle bags. Then I clasp her hand and lead her to our spot.

Just off the dirt road is an enormous field of wildflowers. Bursts of purples, pinks, blues, yellows, and oranges surround us, with lush green hills in the distance.

"Beckett," she whispers, taking in the beauty of the place.

"I thought you'd like this."

"I love it. And I love wildflowers. How did you know?"

Head bowed, I rub the back of my neck. "That time you caught me snooping through your sketchpad."

Clutching my leather jacket, she pulls me into her and crushes her lips to mine. "You weren't snooping. You were just. . .admiring in secret."

A breeze blows a lock of her hair over her face, and as always, I tuck it behind her ear. "Only you could make an invasion of privacy sound charming."

Pulling away, she takes a step back. "It's one of my finer qualities." She takes off and twirls, wildflowers all around her, but her foot gets tangled and she tumbles to the ground.

"I'm okay! I'm fine," she says as I dart for her. "My foot got caught on something."

As I kneel at her side, just like I did all those years ago, I take off my jacket and cover her scraped knee, shielding her from the sight of blood.

"Luckily I brought a first aid kit," I say softly.

"Yeah, I need to come with a warning label." She lies flat on her back and sighs. "And maybe some bubble wrap."

Once I've retrieved the kit, I clean the wound carefully.

"You planned such a romantic day. I don't know if this fall is a bad omen or not."

"It's not a bad omen," I tell her, securing a bandage over the scrape. "History decided to repeat itself today and I take that as a sign that you and I are meant to be."

Side by side, we lie in the field, watching the fluffy white clouds drift over us. I stretch my arms above my head and close my eyes, relishing the warm sun on my face.

When she tugs at my sleeve, pulling it higher, I smirk.

I'm shocked it took her this long to notice my newest piece of ink.

"Uh. Were you not going to show me this?"

A couple of weeks ago, I added a miniature version of her flower drawing to my inner bicep. It complements the sleeve of vines, ferns, and towering trees. There was a small area of skin that happened to be untouched by ink. I took it as a sign to scale down her drawing and mark myself with it forever.

"It was there when we showered together," I say, eyes still closed. "So I haven't been hiding it. You just didn't notice until now."

"If I'm ever going to survive this world, I need to get better at being aware of my surroundings," she mumbles.

I turn on my side, facing her. "I love that your head's in the clouds while my feet are on the ground. We balance each other."

"Why did you get something so permanent? How can you be so sure about us?"

"Writing down all my memories of you in my journal wasn't enough for me. I couldn't fight the need to brand myself with a small part of you." I swallow down a lump of emotion. "I want you with me wherever I go. I needed that constant reminder that there's a person in this world who understands me, accepts me. Who happily swam below the surface of my anxieties. Who reached far into my depths, then pulled me up to reveal the worthiness I thought I'd lost long ago."

Joey draws me into her and kisses me, slow and deliberate. A kiss filled with so many promises and the gentle assurance of a lifetime still waiting for us.

We stay there for hours, talking, soaking in these last moments before we venture off to our next destination. Our next stop? Wyoming. When I received the email with the options for my next assignment, I chose Jackson Hole. Joey had mentioned how she always wanted to see the herds of bison at dusk. Back then, we were still dipping our toes in the water of this relationship, but I chose it with the hopes that maybe she'd visit me. Or that we'd run into each other by happenstance. It was a lofty dream. One I'd think about as I fell asleep each night.

Now, the once lofty dream has transformed into a reality. Because in a few short days, we'll head east to the mountains.

Joey talks about plans and goals she wants to achieve. Starting her own business. Creating brand strategies and designs for nonprofits across the country. But while she maps out the course to get there, she'll continue working at Fernrose to pay the bills.

I can't wait to support her and her dreams. She's so animated as she describes them. Her mind jumps from one idea to the next in a single breath. Her eyes sparkle with optimism and her fingers tap furiously on her phone as she types out her visions.

Joey is radiance personified.

As she goes on, I can't help but smile.

"Why are you looking at me like that?" she asks, tucking a strand of her dark hair behind her ear.

"I love hearing you talk," I say, eyes locked with hers.

She breathes a sigh of relief. "Oh. I thought I was talking too much."

"I can't get enough."

"Are you sure you want this? You want me? Because honestly, sometimes I get annoyed with myself." She lowers her head, fidgeting with the stem of a purple iris.

I tip her chin with my thumb and forefinger, forcing her to meet my gaze. "I'm sure, Josephine."

A shadow crosses her features, the memories of old wounds resurfacing. "You know, I've been told I can be too much."

I release her chin and lace my fingers with hers, loving how perfectly our hands fit together. "And I've been told I'm not enough. We'll level each other out."

"Okay. Well, I overthink."

My lips twitch. "And I over-explain."

"I only eat the red and green gummy bears."

"Perfect. The clear ones are my favorite anyway." I give her hand a reassuring squeeze.

"You're an absolute menace." She laughs, the melodic sound floating over the field.

I lean in close, breathing in the scent of her strawberry shampoo. "Stop trying to find excuses for me not to love you. You're stuck with me."

Her lips turn down a little. "You're sure you love me?"

"Endlessly and beyond words. I'd use up all the paper and ink in the world trying to describe how much I love and adore you."

A breeze sends flower petals of every color—vibrant

purples, bright yellows, and vivid pinks—swirling around us, their sweet, earthy scent accompanying them. Joey's hair catches in the wind, strands glittering in the afternoon sun.

I've never seen anything more breathtakingly beautiful than her.

And as I drink her in, a vow settles deep within my soul.

Joey will never again have to worry about whether she's too much. Or not enough, for that matter. She'll never fall asleep thinking she's unloved or uncherished.

Because to me, she's everything—my wildflower, my forever.

The rare bloom I never expected to find—one who took a chance and grew her way straight into my heart.

Epilogue

TWO YEARS LATER

APRIL 2

I'VE LEARNED *the best parts of life are the ones that are unplanned and unexpected.*

Every morning I wake up with Joey's warm body pressed against mine, her gentle breathing a reminder that I've found my home in the arms of a free-spirited woman who took a chance on me.

For the last two years, Joey, Barbara, Moose, and I have been all over the country. From the forests in Maine to the beaches of San Diego—we're slowly checking off destinations on our bucket list.

It's not just a list though, it's the memories that come with it. Like Joey's laugh echoing when Moose took a nosedive in

Lake Michigan trying to catch a fish. Or the way her wavy hair shined bright copper in the blood orange Sedona sunset as she cuddled Barbara. Or the rainy nights we spent in a cramped, one room rental in Maine sharing a pint of half-melted ice cream with one bent spoon.

Those moments are snapshots of why I'm so deeply in love with Joey.

I love all sides of her. But my favorite is the wild, uninhibited version of Joey. All untamed hair and no filter, laughing without a care in the world.

It's the side of her I admire the most because it's in stark contrast to myself.

I'm the calm to her chaos.

On paper, we're incompatible. In reality, we're a perfect match.

She drags me out of my shell with warm hands, and I whisper that it's okay to retreat into hers instead.

When she needs calmness, I share some of mine. When I need chaos, she lends me some of hers—a flawless fit.

Because our meeting was no accident.

I needed someone to show me what it felt like to be accepted.

She needed someone to show her what true love felt like.

Together, our love continues to grow like a wildflower.

Untamed, beautiful, and resilient.

Joey has changed everything for me in the best way possible. The way she sees the world in vibrant colors—finding beauty in gas station sunsets and roadside wildflowers—opened my eyes to a life I never knew was possible for me. Sometimes I catch myself watching her when she doesn't notice. The way she talks to Moose and Barbara like they understand every word.

Our little family—me, Joey, a judgmental cat, and an overeager dog—have created something beautiful out of nothing. A life where morning coffee tastes better shared and wrong turns lead to the right places—"

"Beckett! We have exactly twenty-eight minutes until the courthouse closes," Joey calls out to me, her voice carrying through the ocean breeze.

My head snaps up from my daze to see Joey's freckled nose and flushed cheeks hanging outside the passenger window of Poppy. Moose squeezes next to her, tongue lolling and floppy ears on full display.

I smile back at them, noticing Barbara sleeping peacefully on the dashboard, catching the last bit of sun before it melts into the ocean.

"Give me thirty more seconds," I tell her. "Oh. And can you get Barbara off the dash before we start moving?"

"I don't want to die before I get married, Beckett."

Chuckling, I shake my head. "Let me finish my thought before I forget it."

She flashes me a wink. "You got it, lover boy." The tips of my ears burn hot.

Even after two years of being together, I still blush whenever she flirts with me.

Turning back to my journal, I press my pen to the paper and write my final words for the day.

"—Now, our story will continue to flourish in our next chapter of life together. Because today, Josephine Iris Thorne —with her tender heart and breathtaking smile—will become Josephine Iris Thorne-Hart."

Acknowledgments

This book wouldn't exist if it weren't for the most supportive group of people standing behind me every step of the way.

Mr. Wilde, the MVP, the OG plant daddy, you are my biggest supporter and number one fan. Thank you for always believing in me, and thank you for tearing apart my final draft and making it better. (Yes, you do have some really great ideas.)

My pups, Kira and Lucy, thank you for providing zero help but maximum emotional support. Your ears make great places to dry tears.

To my friends and family. (I know this is broad, but I also don't have many friends, and my family is very small, so you all should know who you are. C'mon now.) Thank you for the late-night brainstorm sessions, group text rambles, voice notes that double as podcasts, and crying FaceTime's.

Emma, thank you for reading the earliest, roughest, ugliest draft of this book and seeing its potential. Also, thank you for dealing with my constant questions, random ideas, and "Am I doing this right?" texts. You are truly such a special person.

To my amazing beta readers, Kat, Maria, and Sarah— thank you for enduring all the embarrassing typos and confusing plot holes. This book is infinitely better because of all of you.

Laura, thank you for proofreading. Seriously, you were a

lifesaver catching those little errors that I would've missed. And missing words. . .I always miss words. You know this, I know this. It's a character flaw, but you're stuck with me.

This book may be fiction, but my gratitude is very real. From the bottom of my heart to the very top of it—thank you. Thank you to everyone who has read my words, bought my books, or supported me in any way, shape, or form. You have no idea how much it means to me and how it fuels me to keep writing.

Also by Samm Wilde

A New Leaf

About the Author

Samm Wilde is a romance author who weaves words into worlds filled with humor and heart.

When she isn't obsessing over word count, second-guessing plot points, or anxiously deciding between synonyms—you can find her lying on the ground with her dog or eating emotional support cake.

Samm writes to remind us all that love, even with all its imperfect quirks, is a feeling worth embracing.

Find her on Instagram @AuthorSammWilde

Sign up for her newsletter at sammwilde.substack.com